SADDLE
3   P9-DDI-622

Advance

Lovelier

"*Lovelier than Daylight* showcases a fascinating episode of American history, interweaving romance, suspense, and historical detail with unusual depth and realism. Skillfully and sensitively told, the story is a beautiful portrayal of God's redeeming work and of love triumphing over all. Another moving, memorable novel by author Rosslyn Elliott!"

— Laura Frantz, author of *Love's Reckoning* and *The Colonel's Lady*

"With a page-turning plot, endearing characters, captivating prose, and a theme that transcends time and genre, *Lovelier than Daylight* had moments of such raw honesty I had to stop to fully absorb them. Not only does Elliott know how to tell a compelling story, she knows how to explore a sensitive topic from all angles, which will surely elicit lively conversation among reading groups. An incredibly satisfying ending to a beautiful series."

— Katie Ganshert, author of *Wildflowers from Winter*

"In *Lovelier Than Daylight,* Rosslyn Elliott takes her reader by the hand and leads them through the portal of time, back to 1875 in small-town Ohio, where things are about to get rather explosive. Beautiful prose, stunning scenes, dramatic dialogue, and a touch of mystery are carefully woven throughout the story. Elliott tackles the difficult subject of temperance with grace and prowess, careful not to choose sides, but delivers the very clear message that in all things, even where there are no easy answers, God is sovereign. Another delightful read from this wonderful author!"

— Catherine West, award-winning author of *Yesterday's Tomorrow*

Acclaim for Rosslyn Elliott's previous novels

"Elliott gives the reader the gift of high quality historical fiction in the first Saddler's Legacy book."

— *Romantic Times* review of *Fairer than Morning*

JEFFERSON COUNTY PUBLIC LIBRARY

"*Fairer than Morning* is a fabulous debut! Rosslyn Elliott has not so much written a story, but crafted a tale with a dedication to depth and detail equal to that of the artisan she brings to life . . . Rosslyn Elliott is a welcome new voice, almost luxurious. Readers deserve this indulgence."

— Allison Pittman, award-winning author of *Stealing Home* and *Lilies in Moonlight*

"*Fairer than Morning* is a book to savor. As you read this exquisitely written story, the present fades and you are drawn into a tale of cruelty, honor, love and deliverance. When you reach the last page you close the book wishing for more. However Rosslyn Elliott's characters will go with you, forever embedded in your heart."

— Bonnie Leon, author of *Touching the Clouds* and the Sydney Cove series

"Rosslyn Elliott weaves a gripping story full of fascinating historical details. She creates realistic and poignant characters who touch your heart with a message of true grace and forgiveness. *Fairer than Morning* is the kind of book you'll think about long after you read the last page."

— Jody Hedlund, best-selling author of *The Preacher's Bride*

"A novelist to watch! Elliott excels at bringing a by-gone era to life with all of its charm and its flaws. An unhesitating indictment of cruelty and a celebration of the freedom of spirit which can only be found in God."

— Siri Mitchell, award-winning author of *She Walks in Beauty*, regarding *Fairer than Morning*

"Elliott follows up her acclaimed debut, *Fairer than Morning*, with another enchanting, inspirational tale."

— *Library Journal* review of *Sweeter than Birdsong*

LOVELIER
THAN
Daylight

Also by Rosslyn Elliott

Fairer than Morning

Sweeter than Birdsong

LOVELIER
THAN
Daylight

Book Three

THE SADDLER'S LEGACY

ROSSLYN ELLIOTT

THOMAS NELSON
Since 1798

NASHVILLE DALLAS MEXICO CITY RIO DE JANEIRO

JEFFERSON COUNTY PUBLIC LIBRARY

© 2012 by Rosslyn Elliott

All rights reserved. No portion of this book may be reproduced, stored in a retrieval system, or transmitted in any form or by any means—electronic, mechanical, photocopy, recording, scanning, or other—except for brief quotations in critical reviews or articles, without the prior written permission of the publisher.

Published in Nashville, Tennessee, by Thomas Nelson. Thomas Nelson is a registered trademark of Thomas Nelson, Inc.

Thomas Nelson, Inc., titles may be purchased in bulk for educational, business, fundraising, or sales promotional use. For information, please e-mail SpecialMarkets@ ThomasNelson.com.

Published in association with the literary agency of WordServe Literary Group, Ltd., 10152 S. Knoll Circle, Highlands Ranch, CO 80130. www.wordserveliterary.com.

Publisher's Note: This novel is a work of fiction. Names, characters, places, and incidents are either products of the author's imagination or used fictitiously. All characters are fictional, and any similarity to people living or dead is purely coincidental.

Library of Congress Cataloging-in-Publication Data

Elliott, Rosslyn.
  Lovelier than daylight : a novel / by Rosslyn Elliott.
    p. cm. — (The saddler's legacy ; bk. 3)
  Summary: "When her nieces and nephews fall victim to their alcoholic father's mistakes, Susanna Hanby vows to rescue them. In 1875, Susanna Hanby travels to her sister's Ohio farm—but no one is there. Her sister's alcoholic husband claims that she has run off and dumped their six children at the county orphanage, and he doesn't care. Desperate to keep the family together, Susanna seeks help from her uncle Will in Westerville. Johann Giere is heir to a thriving German-American brewery in Columbus. When he helps a saloon owner take beer to Westerville, Johann expects a fight between the new saloon and the driest town in America. He doesn't expect to meet Susanna, a pretty temperance crusader who wins his sympathy. The small town erupts in gunpowder and fire, but Johann vows to help Susanna rescue her nieces and nephews. Susanna grows to admire him even as she detests his business. He finds her lovelier with every passing day, until they both face an impossible choice between passion and principle. Lovelier than Daylight is a novel of faith and grace inspired by the real Hanby family of Ohio and their role in the Westerville Whiskey Wars"— Provided by publisher.
  ISBN 978-1-59554-787-3 (pbk.)
  1. Sisters—Fiction. 2. Temperance—Fiction. 3. Ohio—History—1865—Fiction. 4. Domestic fiction. I. Title.
  PS3605.L4498L68 2012
  813'.6—dc23   2012026507

Printed in the United States of America

12 13 14 15 16 17 QG 6 5 4 3 2 1

For my husband and daughter, with much love

One

TALL GRASS AND WILDFLOWERS BLOCKED HER VIEW and stranded her in the middle of the meadow. Susanna's arms prickled as if someone watched her—but surely no one else was out here in the country on this June morning already hot and breathless.

Scores of fleabane daisies studded the wall of grass like flat yellow eyes, unblinking. The heavy air pressed from all sides, its stillness broken only by the hum of a wasp that circled above her head.

Her sister needed her. She must get to the farmhouse as soon as she could. She gripped the handle of her heavy valise with both hands and pushed through the grass, peering for marks of passage to keep her on the overgrown path. Her back grew warm under her bustled polonaise and corset, and her petticoat dampened beneath her skirt. She wanted to lift her curls away from her neck and fan herself, but she trudged on. At least her straw hat kept the sun out of her eyes.

This summer refused to relent, with its constant liquid heat, harsh as the burn of whiskey on the tongue. Susanna had tasted a sip of whiskey once, at her father's request. He wanted her to know its flavor so curiosity could never tempt her, even though she promised him drink held no allure for her. Whiskey had done more than enough harm already.

She would not think of that. She was here to bring companionship and merriment to her sister and her children before she headed off to college in Westerville.

In her valise she had a surprise that would entertain them for hours—layers and layers of thin paper in seven colors. With it she would show her nieces and nephews how to make something wondrous, exact replicas of the flowers in her botany book. She could not wait to see the joy of creation ease their cares, at least for the few days she was with them. A smile pulled at the corners of her mouth. The children would crowd around and ask with bright eyes what was in her valise—they knew there would always be a surprise. She only wished she could give them more.

A brick chimney poked above the grass, which finally opened to a clearing. Her sister's house squatted ahead with its familiar, peeling white planks. Rusted farm tools lay by its walls, and the fields beyond bore only a sparse cover of wilting corn. But any neglect was not Rachel's fault. With a lazy husband and six little ones to feed, Rachel could not go out in the fields and do everything herself.

Susanna hurried forward, her shoulders aching from the pull of the valise.

Why hadn't the children come out to greet her? Clara or Wesley should be out doing their chores, even if the little ones stayed inside.

She stopped. Something had happened to the flowerbeds. The blooms lay crushed and browned along the foundation of the house. Her throat knotted—Rachel must be so sad. The only color and luxury at the home had come from the flowers she had so patiently watered and weeded. All dead now.

She set her luggage at the bottom of the stoop, climbed up, and knocked. No answer. She laid a tentative hand on the knob and pushed the door open a crack. "Rachel?" Her call sank into eerie silence. Her stomach hollowed and she gripped the knob tighter. She eased the door open. The small parlor with its threadbare furniture was empty.

A few steps took her into the dim hallway and back to the bedroom. No one was there. The sheets were rumpled, the quilt hung on the floor, and the baby's cradle was empty. Something was wrong—her breathing quickened.

No, she must not panic. Perhaps her nieces and nephews were upstairs, caring for Rachel there. In her most recent letter, she'd mentioned having a mild fever. If she were still feverish, Clara and Wesley would be caring for her, as their father would be of little help.

The motionless, musty heat of the house gave her a queasy feeling, but she climbed the narrow stairs in the hall anyway. There were two bedrooms upstairs, one for the two older boys and one for the three girls.

"Clara?" she said into the stillness. Both bedroom doors were open, and an unpleasant odor seeped out. A cold flutter started in her chest. She pulled her handkerchief from her skirt pocket and steeled herself to step up to the doorway. It was too quiet. Clutching the handkerchief to her nose, she edged forward.

The room was in shambles, and vacant. The odor came from a few soiled diapers strewn across the floor with flies creeping over them. An old quilt lay in a heap on the bed, as if the children had been playing with it. This was not like Rachel at all. Difficult as her circumstances might be, she had always kept her home clean and orderly. Susanna tried to swallow but her mouth was paper dry.

The boys' room was deserted, and the bedclothes in equal disarray. A drawer had been pulled out of the shabby dresser and lay upended on the floor.

She hurried down the stairs, her heels thumping on the wood. She must return to town and ask if anyone knew the whereabouts of Rachel Leeds, George Leeds, or their children. She would not lose her head, she would stay calm. But she gripped the banister with white knuckles.

She should leave a note for them, in case someone returned while she was gone. A simple desk stood against the parlor wall. She rummaged through its first drawer. There was only a scrap of paper, but it would do. But no ink—perhaps there was a pencil. She opened the second drawer to find it empty.

"What are you doing here?"

The breath froze in her lungs and she whirled around.

George stood inside the door, rank with the stench of stale liquor. He wore no tie, and his shirt and vest were stained and wrinkled. His oily mustache ran down into his beard, which was unhealthy and sparse. It was hard to believe he had ever been a handsome, hardworking farmer who had courted and won her merry sister. But Rachel was not merry anymore, thanks to him.

"Where are Rachel and the children?" Her voice was taut as a frayed rope.

"She's gone."

Her vision narrowed to his slack, tilted face. Had Rachel left him? Where would she go, with all her children?

He blinked at her. "She left. Went off with some other man."

"That's not true. She was ill—she wrote to me."

"Maybe she had brain fever, maybe that was her excuse." His mouth twisted in a bitter grimace. "Guess she wasn't too sick to ride the train."

Rachel. Susanna's heart contracted. "Where are the children?"

"She gave 'em to the county."

"The county?" She could only repeat it, dazed.

"To the orphan home."

"But why would she do that?"

"Maybe she didn't want 'em in the way of her and her new man. And I sure as heck can't manage 'em. They're motherless now."

"But they're not fatherless. You let your children go to an orphanage?" She felt her hands shaking and hid them behind her skirt.

"She didn't ask me. She left a note. But now it's done, I'm not going to fight it. And don't get smart with me, Susanna Hanby. You Hanby women let your looks puff you up, think you're more important than you are. I could pick you up in one hand, just like your sister. Well, you see how she turned out—nothing but a loose woman."

He was full of lies. Rachel had never been vain, even though she was pretty. Her nails bit into her palms. She'd like to dig them into his uncaring face instead. "What orphanage?"

"I dunno. In Columbus. What, do you think I could take care of all of them, plus a baby? That needs a woman."

"No, just a sober, decent man!" She flung herself past him and out the door, stumbling down the front steps. All six children, gone. And what could she do if Rachel had signed them over as wards of the county and George did not want them?

She seized her valise and hurried away. It could not be true. Rachel would not do such an awful thing. Perhaps he himself had given the children away to the county.

But George would have no reason to lie.

Unless he had harmed Rachel.

No, she must not think of that or she would not make it back to the railway station. Her sister would write to her and all would be made clear.

She could not bear the whiskey-sodden inhumanity of George. Anger glowed like a pillar of fire to lead her—she closed her eyes, took a deep breath, and let it blaze. She would find the children. They must not be separated and given to strange families, perhaps unloved and subjected to callous treatment.

She had told Rachel about George, and so had her parents. If only Rachel had listened and refused to marry a man who drank, none of this would have happened. Of course, when they met, George didn't drink day and night. He was just a happy-go-lucky, merry farmer who stopped into the saloon at week's end. But they had warned Rachel, nonetheless, about what the future might hold, and she had not listened.

Susanna could not think ill of her sister, not after all she had suffered. Certainly not now, when she didn't even know where Rachel had gone.

She sloughed off the trembles from her arms and legs and kept walking. Should she go back to Milford Centre and tell her parents so they could get the children back?

How they would do it, she did not know. Their last savings had gone for the tuition money she needed to go to college in Westerville—money now folded in a tight bundle of bills in her handbag. Her parents were growing old and barely eked out a living from their small plot of land, one cow, and chickens. They would not be able to give any further help—they had already given her all they had. She was a Hanby, and they were sending her to Otterbein, where all Hanbys attended college.

No, she could not go back—she must go on with her journey as planned. Westerville was only a little way farther down the railroad. Her Uncle Will and Aunt Ann had more worldly means than her parents, didn't they? Perhaps they could even rally the Hanby cousins to help, though they were spread far and wide now across the country and even on foreign missions.

She staggered in a pit of dried mud and yanked at her valise to keep her balance. George Leeds had been a good man, once, before the whiskey had ruined him. The whiskey! She would like to put all the barrels and bottles in a pile and burn them.

The heat made her dizzier. *I will not faint. I will not.* Her bodice was soaked and moisture ran from her hairline down her face, as if her whole body wept the tears she could not afford to shed.

Uncle Will would never let his great nieces and nephews be lost. If he had a spare dime to his name, he would use it on their behalf.

Light glinted from a tin roof ahead. She was almost to the station.

Her nieces were so little, Della and Annabeth. And baby Jesse would not remember his mother or his family at all if they gave him away.

Where was her sister? She dropped her bag with a *thump* in the dusty track and pressed the heels of her hands hard to her eyes.

Nothing could be done until she made it back to civilization, which she must do on her own. She hoisted the bag and went on, fixing her gaze on the pitched roof of the tiny railroad station. She would not fail Rachel or the children.

Two

"THE *NEW YORKER STAATS-ZEITUNG* IS LOOKING FOR A good newsman." Mr. Reinhardt flourished a folded newspaper in Johann's direction and gave him a keen look over the top of his wire spectacles.

Johann pretended nonchalance and cranked the great iron wheel of the printing press. The tray slid forward, hesitated, and slid back, imprinting its rows of German letters on first one sheet, then its reverse side. The machine's regular *clack* echoed off the walls of the large room.

"You hear me, Johann?" Mr. Reinhardt raised his voice. The noise of the press was no match for his ripe baritone, heavy with the Bavarian accent of his native land.

"Yes, sir." Johann did not look up but continued to run the press. A redheaded boy stood beside the cylinder, peeling each sheet and taking it to the drying rack.

"And you are not interested?"

"For what position?"

"Reporter. Crime."

Johann's head snapped up and he met the older man's knowing gaze.

The editor opened the paper and pointed at the back inside page, as if Johann could read it from five feet away. *"Ja.* They want someone with experience, it says right here. Someone who has written a number of crime articles for a German paper."

New York, where presses could take ten sheets at once and print eight thousand sheets an hour. Where men skulked through oyster cellars and opium dens by gaslight, and stories lay so numerous and thick a reporter could wade knee-deep through them every time he walked out of his brownstone. The Mecca of every newspaperman's dreams.

Johann brushed it away. "I can't do that, Mr. Reinhardt." He concentrated on the hypnotic swing of the press tray below him.

"Why not?"

Some explanations were best swallowed. He kept silent.

Mr. Reinhardt looked down at the paper through his spectacles and read aloud, "'Candidates must present a clipping of one self-authored crime article of national significance, a story to rouse the interest of even the most jaded city dweller.'"

"That's quite a challenge." Johann's interest flared. "Especially for us yokels out in Columbus." He did love a good contest.

Mr. Reinhardt chuckled. "I think you should go get a story to win you the position. Take it as a challenge. You can always turn it down." He folded the paper up again. "I've seen your face when we talk about New York. Admit it, you want to go."

Johann turned the wheel a few more times. "Very well, I'll find a story." He could write something worthy of the prize, if he put his mind to it. The alluring gaslight and shadow of the metropolis stuck in his imagination. Even bustling Columbus was like a small village by comparison.

The door from the street smacked open and another of the

printer's boys ran in. "*Danke*, Herr Giere," the blond boy said to Johann. "Sorry I was so long at lunch." He rushed over and took the wheel as Johann stepped back to give him room.

"You're welcome. I don't mind taking over for a while. You know I like the press." Johann turned to Mr. Reinhardt. "I must be going, sir, my father's waiting." He grabbed his hat from the peg and headed for the door.

"Show them what we are made of in the West, Johann!" The subdued roar of Reinhardt's voice chased him out into the open air.

"Front Street," the driver called out, pulling at the reins of his team of horses. The mighty omnibus rumbled to a stop—twenty passengers crowded in the seats, looking surly in the blistering summer heat.

Johann stepped down to the rutted road and nimbly evaded the swish of a passing carriage. A hundred more paces brought him to the brewery yard, which was lined with wagons yoked to huge horses. His father had invested in the new Norman imports. The dappled grays with round, muscled shoulders and haunches were more than capable of pulling the heavy lager wagons. Still, Father often wished aloud for the cream-colored German draft horses of his youth.

Johann walked past them, raising his hand to Heinrich, their brewmeister, who stood beside the first team.

The red-cheeked man waved back with his one arm. "*Guten Abend.*" Confederate bullets had left Heinrich with an empty left sleeve. But like the other men from German Village who had returned missing arms or even legs, Heinrich worked twice as hard to make up for it. And Johann's father would never dismiss a workman who had sacrificed his own body for the Union. Not after what the Giere family had lost in the War.

Johann headed for the thick smell of hops that rolled out the barn-like doors.

"Johann." His father stood in the door frame, his blond head ashy with middle age. He pointed upward so his brown linen coat stretched over his muscular shoulders. "You see the new sign?" Up on a ladder, one of the brewery men had whitewashed out the words "Giere Brothers." On the new white surface, he was painting in the letters "Giere and Son."

"You like it?" his father asked, smiling, but with a hint of melancholy. He walked over to Johann, his hat held to his chest. "It can't stay forever the old way. It is ten years now—we must go on. Fritz would want it."

Johann hoped the sharp stab of guilt didn't show on his face. "It's good. It's what Uncle Fritz would've wanted." He patted his father's shoulder and searched in vain for words, the glamour of New York searing his conscience.

His father cleared his throat. "A customer needs our assistance." He gestured back beyond Johann.

Johann pivoted. Over in the corner by the loading dock, the third team of Norman horses stood at their wagon with several barrels already on board. The floor workers were loading another barrel as a tall, thin man watched.

"Let me introduce you to him." His father took Johann's elbow with affection and swept him across to the visitor.

"Mr. Henry Corbin, this is my son, Johann, who will be glad to assist you."

"Glad to meet you, young man." The thin man pumped Johann's fingers in a strong grasp. "A new enterprise, and we'll take all the help we can get." His accent was rough, uncultured.

"A new business, Mr. Corbin?" Johann asked. He was tired, but he must be polite. The Hoster Brewery down the road was a formidable rival, and the Gieres had to keep every customer for their brewery to survive.

"We're going to open a saloon in Westerville." Corbin put his hands on his belt and surveyed the next barrel going on the wagon with a smug expression.

"We, sir?" Johann asked. "You have a partner?"

"My wife and I. She and the children will come to live in town later, after I'm settled in."

Johann said nothing but raised an eyebrow at his father while Corbin wasn't looking. Westerville was the most stubborn temperance town in Ohio. Everyone knew it. Even the Hosters hadn't succeeded in opening the market for lager there.

His father gave him a slight nod. "Yes, a courageous move. Mr. Corbin will not be unopposed, we all know. But the people of Westerville should have their choice of whether to have beer and *gemuetlichkeit*. Which means, Mr. Corbin, good fellowship and feeling, to us Germans."

"Indeed." Mr. Corbin did not seem interested in a mouthful of foreign syllables. "I see we're loaded for the train."

Heinrich walked over to the wagon and pulled himself up to the narrow driver's seat with his single arm. He could not carry barrels easily, so in addition to supervising the brew, he drove every day for deliveries. Mr. Corbin stared at the empty sleeve dangling before him. Heinrich did not look at his passenger, his hearty face reddening.

"Mr. Corbin, I'm afraid you'll have to ride with your cargo," Johann's father said. "It's a wagon, not a Pullman car."

They both laughed.

"Pshaw, Mr. Giere. The better to watch over my goods." Henry Corbin leapt into the back, light as a bird taking wing. A very tall, skinny bird.

"And, Johann, you will go with them."

"To Westerville?" Johann veiled his surprise, adjusting his summer coat over his shoulders in the sticky heat.

"*Ja*. Only an hour at most, each way on the train. You can help unload. Mr. Corbin has qualms about the safety of his cargo."

Westerville townspeople would not be pleased. There would be no welcome for a saloonkeeper in that small town dominated by the United Brethren Church and the Methodists. This could get very interesting. Johann gripped Corbin's proffered hand and climbed over the side to sit between the barrels.

The new sign above the brewery jumped out at him like an accusation: no more Giere Brothers, only Giere and Son. He whistled a few notes of a waltz to chase away the specter of his dead uncle as the wagon pulled away and onto the bumpy street. How could he deprive his father of his partnership, when his father had already lost his only brother in the War? If only his father had other sons.

But even if he won the New York job, he did not have to go. He would worry about that later.

Westerville versus the saloon. It might make a good story.

Three

A TRAIN'S WATER CLOSET WAS NOT THE BEST PLACE for a lady's toilette, but it would have to do. Susanna wet her handkerchief with the water in the tin pitcher and scrubbed at her blanched cheeks to bring back some color. Nothing would disguise her exhaustion, but she must wait to break the bad news until she had at least greeted her aunt and uncle with some semblance of normalcy. She refused to arrive at Uncle Will's as a hysterical banshee—her sister's husband would not reduce her to that. She would be calm and precise when she told them, sticking to the essentials. A resolute focus on Rachel's innocence and George's lies would allow her to speak without giving way to tears.

Her uncle and aunt had spent their lives protecting the innocent and weak from the violent and strong—she had every confidence that they would know what to do. She had grown up listening to her father's stories of their courage and righteousness. If any two people could help, she would choose Will and Ann Hanby.

The train slowed, and she clutched the edge of the vanity to regain her balance. She stowed the handkerchief in her handbag, slipped through the heavy door, and walked back to her seat just as the train stopped. The ornate wood carving and upholstery were so luxurious she almost hated to leave the train. It would be easier to ride on, as if in a dream, and let everything outside fade. But somewhere her nieces and nephews waited, and they would be scattered to the winds unless she acted soon.

Thank goodness it was still two months until the start of the college term. Perhaps she could straighten out this catastrophe, find some explanation and reunite Rachel with her children, and then go on to begin college as her parents had intended. She did not want to disappoint them—they thought so highly of her academic abilities. But though study had always come easy for her, she did not really have a passion for most of the classical studies—only botany, and ladies were not often welcomed in science. But she had trusted that her future would become clear to her once she enrolled. Now, with Rachel missing, how could she care about college at all?

The door clanked and the porter entered, natty in his brass-buttoned uniform. The train was not crowded, and no one else seemed to be disembarking from this car.

The porter retrieved her bag from overhead. "May I take this to the platform for you, miss?" He might pity her pale appearance—or perhaps the porters were always so polite.

"Yes, please."

Outside, he helped her down to the platform.

"Thank you."

A voice called from yards away, "Susanna!"

Aunt Ann walked toward her, slowed by age but with a glow on her face that wiped away the creases. It was still a shock to see her hair completely white, but her pretty, delicate bone structure was unchanged, even in her sixties. Behind her was Uncle Will, using a cane to make his way down the platform, his hair still thick but also snow white. Susanna's father was sixty-five, so Uncle Will must be sixty-seven. As the youngest of all the Hanby cousins, Susanna would easily pass for their grandchild instead of their niece.

The sight of their dear faces made her pulse quicken. She did not want to tell them. She waved and mustered a weak smile.

Aunt Ann reached her and laid her gloved hands on Susanna's shoulders, looking at her from arm's length like her own cherished child. "You're so lovely. How you've grown up in the last few years! Welcome."

"Thank you." Susanna's smile broke and fell away.

"What is the matter?" The concern on her aunt's face might melt Susanna's self-control. Uncle Will caught up and rested his cane on the ground, silent, taking in her distress.

"I stopped by to see Rachel on the way." She took a breath, stopped, and swallowed. *Lord, help me.* If she did not want to break down, she must hold tight to the fierce burn of anger that had sustained her at the farmhouse with George.

"What is it?" Aunt Ann's eyes, usually soft and rich as loam, had marbled into a searching look.

"Rachel wasn't there." She launched herself onward, rushing through it. "George said she went away with another man. And he said she took the children to the county and gave them away."

Her aunt's face drained of color. "Gave them away?"

"He said the children went to an orphanage. All of them. We must get them back." Her voice broke and she cleared her throat. *Hold fast to the truth, tell them.* "And I don't believe what he says about Rachel. She would never do such a thing!"

"Of course not," her aunt said.

Susanna steadied herself with Uncle Will's solid presence at her right elbow. "George said the children have been taken to Columbus."

"Most likely the Hannah Neil Mission," her uncle said. His usual mellow tone had tightened, and he eyed the train as if to jump on it like a man half his age. "We'll inquire there first."

Aunt Ann laid a hand on his arm. "Wait," she said gently. "The children won't be sent anywhere for at least a few days, and probably a few weeks. Let's get Susanna to the house and give her something to eat and some tea."

The tension went out of his stance, though the lines around his mouth deepened as he nodded to Susanna. "Your aunt is quite right—you need to rest."

The last thing she could do was rest. She didn't even want to eat, with her stomach clamped, her mouth filled with a taste like rusted nails. "Rachel would never leave her children, and especially not for a . . . for a sinful reason." She bit her lip—she must not worry them further, but the echo of George's past threats whispered in her memory.

"My dear, we'll believe only the best of her. I'm so sorry you had to carry this burden alone on your journey." Aunt Ann took her hand again and did not let go. Uncle Will waved to the porter, who carried Susanna's bag after them through the station and set it down beside the road. The train whistled its imminent departure. The clouds had rolled in during her journey—the overcast sky trapped Westerville in airless heat that made even the dust too leaden to rise into the air.

"Need a ride, Bishop Hanby?" A young man with a mule

cart called from across the road. "My father told me to take you at no charge, whenever you needed it."

"Why, thank you, Jim," her uncle said. "A ride would be very welcome. But you needn't call me Bishop—Mr. Hanby is just fine."

The young man reined his mule and cart over to where they stood. Uncle Will handed his cane to her aunt, leaned down, and lifted the valise into the back of the cart.

"And we will sit on the buckboard," he said to Susanna. "Not elegant, but better than a walk with a heavy load."

She nodded as Aunt Ann squeezed her hand in silent reassurance.

Her aunt was always so kind. Susanna and Rachel had loved their occasional visits to the Hanby home in Westerville. Rachel had a crooked smile that made her pretty face impish, charmed her cousins, and made them strive to amuse her.

How would she find her sister? She covered her fear with the first comment that came to mind. "Is the new house close?"

"Just down State Street." Her uncle's response was quiet. They had lost their former family home after Uncle Will had guaranteed loans for Otterbein College. When the college almost failed, the Hanby home was taken and sold by Otterbein's creditors. But her uncle had never shown bitterness—only dedication that a college would survive in Westerville. And survive it had.

The cart rattled down the road until it stopped in front of a whitewashed frame home, nondescript, with a small barn in back.

The boy unloaded the valise and brought it to the porch. With a touch of his cap in farewell, he ran to his cart, slapped the reins, and sent the mule trotting back toward the station.

Uncle Will held the front door open and Susanna went in behind her aunt.

As she untied her hat ribbon, she took in the changes. Gone were the large, thick rugs she remembered from the other home. Instead, a simple rag rug lay on the scuffed floor. Two old rockers stood by a small wood stove, and two other slat-back chairs were the only other furnishings except for a shelf of books over the mantel. It was a shock indeed. They were hardly better off than her own parents.

"You will sleep in the upstairs room," Uncle Will said. "We'll show you later."

"First I'll make something to eat," her aunt said. She moved to the kitchen table, her blue gown rustling behind her. Even after bearing eight children, she was still small and graceful.

"I'm going out to the barn," Uncle Will said. "If we plan to go to Columbus tomorrow, I should finish the bridle tonight and get it to the store." The door clapped against the frame behind him.

Her aunt mixed flour and water, then rolled dough into dumplings the size of grapes. Susanna paced around the kitchen in search of some task, past a rack of utensils and a neat row of tin canisters. Even in this orderly room, everything seemed wrong to her, out of kilter. For months she had looked forward to the serenity she would find in her studies here at college as she explored the miraculous, perfect design of botany. Instead, all was violently uprooted, her family torn apart and scattered without reason or answers. But she could not simply cease to function. "May I help you with something?" Her own voice sounded strange to her, uncertain.

Her aunt wiped her hands. "Why don't you go to the barn

and talk to Will while I make supper? He would be glad of the company. He works out there alone so often."

"Yes, ma'am." In a way, it would be easier to talk to her uncle than to her sympathetic aunt, whose kindness might draw out more pain from the depths where she could feel it lurking.

Outside, the whitewashed door of the barn stood open. The muted gray of the afternoon light fell on Uncle Will's bowed white head as he sat on his saddling bench. But there was nothing in his hands. They were clasped together and his eyes were closed. She stood and let the peace of his prayer wash over her in the quiet.

He looked up. "Come in." He indicated a stool for her not far from his own seat. "After supper we'll walk over to the telegraph office and see if we can wire the Hannah Neil Mission."

She took a deep breath. "Thank you."

"We'll find the children. Don't worry." He placed a piece of cream-colored leather on the bench in front of him and turned to select a tool from the table. "You and Rachel have always been fond of flowers."

What prompted that? Her chest constricted at the memory of the ruined blossoms in her sister's garden. She did not trust herself to speak.

Uncle Will began to tap a hammer against his chisel, carving up tiny curls of leather around its blade.

His knuckles were swollen with rheumatism, though his hands still looked strong. Working the leather for hours must make him sore. But he did not seem to mind.

After a few minutes of tapping, he set down his tools and pulled one leg over the bench to stand up. He crossed to her and laid a circle of leather in her palm. Embossed in the creamy surface, a bell-shaped blossom hung from a stem as if suspended in the air.

She traced its delicate lines. "A snowdrop?"

"My father-in-law's design, passed down to me and then my sons." Uncle Will's brown eyes were deep under his whitened brows. "A symbol of hope, Mr. Miller always said."

She tucked the leather circle into the hidden pocket of her skirt but kept her fingers closed around it, feeling its smooth lines.

The mention of her cousins jogged her memory. "Where's Cousin Samuel?" Her uncle's youngest son usually resided in town. "I know he's traveling, but Mother didn't say where."

"He's investigating business in Alabama. He'll return in a few months."

Her uncle had other sons too: Willie had become a doctor and moved away, and Ben and Cyrus—well, she wouldn't open that old wound.

"And we'll go to the telegraph office after supper?" she asked. A plan brought clarity, gave her something solid to grasp.

"To be sure. Shall we go in and eat?" He offered her his arm and they walked toward the house.

"I should also write a letter to my parents and mail it," she added.

How would she tell her parents what George had said? She would not defame Rachel with his lies. And she certainly couldn't tell them about their grandchildren yet—it would break their hearts. On second thought, she'd better delay that letter to her parents until she had some better news to mix in with the bad.

And she prayed that would be very soon.

Four

"WESTERVILLE! FIFTEEN MINUTES HERE!" THE CON-
ductor cried.

Johann jumped down to the platform. That should be plenty
of time to unload the barrels, especially if the porters and
Corbin helped.

Corbin stuck two fingers in his mouth and let out a piercing
whistle that drew every gaze on the platform. A driver with a
heavy wagon noticed Corbin's wave, sat up straight, and clucked
to his mules. They plodded up within a few yards of the train,
placid, accustomed to the strange steel monster huffing beside
them. "You looking to haul freight?"

"Just to State Street." Corbin agreed to the fare and he
and Johann transferred the beer barrels, boxes, and luggage
onto the wagon. When they were seated amidst the load, the
driver looked back at Corbin. "You said the Widow Clymer's
building?"

"That's right." Corbin sounded smug.

The driver slapped the reins, and the mules heaved against
the yoke. The wagon lurched and Johann grabbed a leaning
bottle in a crate as they rolled down the road.

The driver twisted to look over his shoulder at the cargo. "And what brings you to Westerville, mister?" he asked Corbin.

"I'll be opening a drinking establishment."

The driver's gaze snapped up to meet Corbin's. "In town?"

"That's the plan."

The driver pursed his lips and sent an exaggerated breath through them. "That's why you have the barrels?"

"Exactly." Corbin stared ahead as if daring any man to stand in his way.

"And will it be a beer hall, like the Germans do in Columbus? Lager and ale?"

"It'll be an American saloon. Sure we'll have lager, but we'll offer fine whiskey and gin too."

The driver's eyes widened and he turned back to his mules. The silence lengthened as they drove to the genteel shops on State Street. The wagon halted.

The driver pointed at the oak door and glass windows beside them. "That's Widow Clymer's place. Guess you're renting it." He sounded none too pleased and jumped off the wagon to secure the mules. "Well, get your goods and go. I'm going to get an earful from my neighbors for bringing you in with that load." He folded his arms across his chest and stood next to the hitching post.

Shoppers moved in and out of the stores, crossing the street in the afternoon's gray haze. The door of the apothecary's shop opened and an elderly lady emerged, attired neatly in a cream dress and hat, her back straight. Only the fading of her coloring and the caution in her step gave away her advanced years.

Poised to cross the street, she stopped, her gaze riveted on the beer barrels. A young woman rushed out of the store and almost collided with her.

"I'm sorry, Auntie. Are you all right?" Receiving no response, she edged around the older woman and eyed the wagon. "Is something the matter?" She was pretty, her brown hair curling long in the back beneath her straw hat.

"What is it, Ann?" A man with an abundance of pure white hair used a cane to step up beside the elderly lady, then followed her gaze. "Ah." His face was still strong, under the marks of age, and he regarded the beer barrels with careful deliberation. He crossed a few steps toward their driver and shook his hand. "Noah, I haven't seen you this week. What's this?"

"I ain't responsible. I didn't know what they had planned until we'd already pulled out of the station." The driver took out a plug of tobacco, shoved it in his mouth, and chomped it with disgusted verve. "I may be from Blendon, but I know this'll be trouble. Don't tell anyone it was me that brought him."

Johann had moved to the back of the wagon and lowered the tailgate. "Corbin. Let's unload."

"Is that beer?" the older lady asked.

"Yes, ma'am," said the driver.

Corbin and Johann levered the first barrel off the wagon and hauled it to the door.

"Wait," Corbin said, and lowered his end to the ground as Johann stood it upright. Corbin reached up over the door frame and retrieved a key. Widow Clymer must have told him where to find it. The lock turned with a click and Corbin shoved the door open. "Roll that on in, Mr. Giere."

"Giere." The old man with the cane said under his breath, looking curious. "A German name, and that of a Columbus brewer, if I don't mistake myself?"

A flush burned up Johann's ears and to his cheeks. Too

often such questions were followed by insults about godless foreigners who drank on Sundays. He heaved the barrel just inside the door and started for the wagon again. Corbin could get it to the cellar himself.

"They're opening a saloon, Mr. Hanby." The driver's tobacco bulged in his cheek when he spoke. "Right here in the Widow's building."

Johann and Corbin wrestled another barrel to the ground. The white-haired gentleman pondered in silence, offering his wife his free arm, while she in turn held the arm of the young lady. All three looked as if they could be from the pages of a magazine—the perfect elderly couple and their beautiful companion. And the young lady was arresting indeed, with her large green eyes and delicate features. She had the ethereal look of a creature not quite of this world, as if she might float away like dandelion fluff in a summer breeze.

Corbin set his jaw and shouldered forward into the new saloon. Johann followed with a crate, uncomfortable as he passed the three bystanders.

When he deposited the crate and headed back for more, the wagon driver spat his tobacco juice again. It spattered on Johann's shoe. He should take that driver by the scarf around his neck and teach him some manners. But his father's wishes came first, and that meant gentlemanly behavior no matter what.

"They've got whiskey and gin as well as lager," the wagon driver said.

Johann was only a foot from the young lady and saw horror splash across her face at the mention of strong drink. He kept his steady pace. He did not enjoy disturbing young ladies, even if they were a little too fussy in their sentiments. No need for such outrage over a man's glass of lager on a Sunday afternoon.

"I wish you would not, sir." The young lady spoke straight to Johann.

Why was she so vehement, with her small fists knotting into her skirt? It looked as if he should fear an attack from this willowy creature. He ducked his head to hide a smile.

"It is not a subject for mirth." She took a step forward, her jaw clenched.

"Indeed not, miss." Now it was not so amusing. What kind of hornet's nest would Henry Corbin stir up, in a town where women became pugilists at the sight of a beer barrel? "I'm afraid I'm not responsible for Mr. Corbin's decision to locate his establishment here," he told her. "I simply fulfill his order, as my father wishes."

"Then, if you are a gentleman, I hope you will consider a lady's appeal. Supply other towns with the devil's brew if you must, but not our town." Her voice rose, and the elderly woman laid a hand on her arm.

"There, Susanna, let's be about our own business." The white-haired lady tried to lead her charge away, but neither the girl nor the old man moved from where they stood.

"I think you should consider what my niece says, both of you." The old man scrutinized both Johann and Corbin as they set the last barrel down. "Let us talk like reasonable men, no need to shout at one another. I'm William Hanby. And you are?"

"Henry Corbin. And this is Johann Giere assisting me."

"Allow me to introduce my wife, Mrs. Hanby, and my niece, Miss Hanby."

Johann tipped his hat, conscious of his dust-covered face and arms. Mr. Corbin did not offer the same courtesy.

"Mr. Corbin," Mr. Hanby said. "I hope we'll have the opportunity to discuss your decision further. I can promise you I'll keep my head, which is why you may wish to come to me rather than some of my fellow townsmen."

"Ain't much to discuss."

"Well, we shall see." Mr. Hanby nodded. "A good day to you." When he tapped his cane on the wood and pivoted, his wife took his elbow. The young lady followed them, with a last glare at the wagon.

Down the street heads were turning. Fifty yards away a small cluster of men spied the wagon and headed their way.

If Johann did not leave quickly, he would be ruined as a potential reporter of this event. He must not be seen or they would think of him as an enemy and refuse to tell him anything for the paper. "Well, we have the barrels moved in for you, Mr. Corbin. And I must be getting back."

"Right, then. I'll come back to the brewery in a week to pick up more."

"Good luck." Johann ducked into the alley behind the Clymer building.

He made his surreptitious way to the station, sweat gathering on his neck in the late afternoon heat. Sometimes these coats were a bother in summer. It would be easier to go about in shirtsleeves, but no German businessman would chance being mistaken for a wage laborer. There was enough disrespect as it was from the so-called real Americans. Never mind that Johann was as native-born as any of them, with nothing to distinguish him from other young men whose fathers happened to immigrate from England or Sweden.

None of the others had come close enough to see him—none but the Hanby family. So his anonymity would be safe if he did not encounter the Hanbys again. And for all anyone knew, the story might be finished tomorrow. Corbin was in town, and so was his liquor. They couldn't very well force him out. It was all legal. But something about the determined stride of those townsmen down the street promised Johann he would be hearing more out of Westerville soon. And if he did, the *Westbote* would know before the *Journal* or the *Dispatch*, so Reinhardt would be pleased.

Johann was going to get the news first, even though he might be a part-time amateur and not a professional newsman. All he had to do was steer clear of the beautiful temperance crusader and any more of her ilk.

Five

"HANNAH NEIL MISSION FOR THE FRIENDLESS," UNCLE Will read from the brass plate. "Shall we go up and inquire?"

"Yes." Susanna's palms were clammy. The building was well kept, arching up three full stories to gabled windows, white columns framing its portico. She had imagined a prison, but this was a rich mansion given over to charity. The lawn was neat, the shrubs trimmed. Across the road the enormous estate of the Blind Asylum rested, peaceful in the pre-noon hours. A lone woman crossed the garden path from one wing to another, her bustled skirt neat, her hat just so. Only her white cane gave away her condition as she paced forward without a pause or tremor.

If a blind woman could forge ahead through her darkness, Susanna could be as resolute. Her uncle had been brave his whole life—she must not let him down. She mounted four stairs to the covered porch, where two rocking chairs sat empty.

She thought of her sister's well-worn rocker. Rachel loved to rock her babies and sing sweet bits of songs, for she could never remember the true words. She must sing for them again some-day—she could not have left them forever.

Susanna forced aside the thought and seized the brass knocker. She rapped three times. Uncle Will stood quiet beside her and rested his cane on the woven doormat.

The door opened and a plain woman in a white cap peered out. "Good morning."

Susanna's question was so large it jammed in her mouth. With a quick glance, Uncle Will seemed to understand.

"We are seeking some children who may have been admitted here this week," he said.

"You will have to speak to Matron, sir. Won't you please come in?"

The woman opened the door, and Uncle Will gestured with his free hand for Susanna to precede him. She gathered her skirt to clear the threshold and stepped up into the foyer just as the white-capped woman drifted out of sight into a side hallway.

The air inside was cooler, the ceilings high and elegant. The front parlor appeared just as it would in a private residence, graced with upholstered chairs and a settee by an unlit fireplace. Its gray flagstone invited Susanna to press her flushed cheeks to its cool surface, as she had in her father's house when the summer rolled around. But even more refreshing to summer-heated skin would be the white marble of this mantel, a luxury that had not adorned her family home.

"Good morning." A middle-aged woman in a dark-blue dress with a tailored bodice and neat bustle entered from the hall into the parlor. She held a brown ledger in one hand and moved with erect posture and measured pace.

"Good morning. You are the matron?" Susanna asked.

"Indeed I am. Mrs. Loomis is my name."

"And I am Susanna Hanby."

"Welcome. I understand you seek some children here. Are you a relation?" The matron's face was gentle and her skin luminous for one of her years.

"Yes, ma'am." Susanna took a steadying breath. The air smelled of lavender and a trace of baking bread. "The children are surnamed Leeds, and there are six of them, three boys, three girls. I am their aunt, their mother's sister."

"Yes." The matron's forehead wrinkled. She opened her ledger and looked down at it. "I wish I had only good news for you, Miss Hanby." She spoke softly, as if to cushion a blow. "I have admitted children named Leeds this week."

"But that is good news!" Susanna took a step forward, her heart lifting.

"I have only three Leeds children, not six. I am sorry. We were only able to take the three youngest, into our Nursery Ward. The other rooms were filled to capacity—more than filled, in fact."

"Where are they?" Susanna asked. "The oldest—Clara, Wesley, and Daniel?"

"They have been sent to the Hare Children's Home. It's in the central business area at Town and High. Not far, by the streetcar line."

Susanna sighed. "I had feared worse. At least they are in Columbus."

"Yes, well . . ." Mrs. Loomis closed the ledger and cradled it in her arms. "When you see the Hare Home, you will understand why I would have preferred to keep them all here."

Uncle Will shifted and his cane tapped the floor. "Mrs. Loomis, were the children surrendered to you by their mother?"

"Yes, sir." Her face sealed itself against further questions like hardening wax. "More than that I cannot say."

Then Rachel had given them away, just as George said. Susanna's heart deflated and her uncle looked equally downcast. Was the rest also true? Never. There had to be another answer.

She gripped her brocade handbag. "May I see the little ones? Della is the five-year-old. And little Annabeth, and baby Jesse."

"You may. Follow me, please." Mrs. Loomis led them to a back stairway.

"Uncle Will, if you need to stay here . . ." Susanna trailed off, conscious of his cane.

"I'm not so decrepit that I can't manage a few stairs." But he winced as he climbed the first step.

As they mounted to the second floor, a faint sound of infant cries reached Susanna's ears. The matron crossed the hall and opened one of the tall oak doors. Baby noise washed out into the hallway at greater volume, along with light. Susanna followed her inside at her nod. Judging from the marble floor, the room must have once been a ballroom. Now, instead of a piano or a table, numerous bassinets sat in rows. A woman in uniform dress and white cap held a baby against her shoulder and patted its tiny back. She was as tender as a mother. Susanna's heart cramped.

The matron called to the attendant, "Alice, will you bring me Jesse Leeds? He is the newest."

"Yes, ma'am." The baby she held ceased its crying and she laid it down in a bassinet. She strolled to another bassinet on the end and murmured to the baby as she lifted it out.

It was Jesse, with his little shock of reddish hair. He began the soft, hiccoughing cry that meant he wanted his mother—she remembered it well from helping Rachel. Susanna unwound the strings of her handbag from her fingers, flexing them against the unexpected ache. She had pulled the strings so tight that they left white marks on her hands.

The matron gave her a sympathetic look, and when the attendant approached, she indicated with a nod that baby Jesse could go to Susanna.

She held him under his arms and looked into his face. He was like Rachel, as all the boys were, with his auburn hair and big round eyes. She gathered him close and he nuzzled into her neck. At the baby smell of his hair like sweet, fresh hay, tears collected in her eyes. She turned away so the others would not see her weeping. Droplets fell from her face to vanish into his rough baby gown. Why, why, had her sister married George? No one else had ever married so badly in the Hanby family, no one had married a drinker. They were Hanbys, and so no one in her family ever touched a drop or associated frequently with those who did. Only Rachel had taken it so lightly as to think she could marry whom she liked, whether he shared their values or not. And now Rachel was gone, and her children were in danger of vanishing too. She held Jesse close.

After a few minutes she hefted Jesse in one arm, wiped her face with the other sleeve, and turned to Uncle Will, whose troubled eyes gave away his internal battle.

"Jesse must come back with us," she said.

The matron's brow creased and she crossed her arms over her ledger. "Miss Hanby, you are unmarried?"

"Yes. But my aunt and uncle have been married for decades. They live in Westerville, and I am staying with them to attend college."

"I don't mean to be rude," the matron said. "But, sir, you are in your"—she pressed her lips together—"golden years. And I presume your wife is as well?"

"Yes." Uncle Will smiled gently as if he forgave the reminder of his cane and white hair.

"And forgive me for prying—but have you significant means to provide for this child and the others?"

His smile slid away. "No."

"I am sorry, but our Women's Benevolent League has established certain policies to protect the welfare of the children we shelter. And one of those policies is that our outplacements must be to young families, both spouses living, with demonstrable means to provide for children."

Susanna put a protective hand on Jesse's head. "But they are my nephews and nieces." The baby stared at her as if he knew something strange was afoot.

"Miss Hanby, it is difficult, but we must consider their futures. These three are so young—" She looked at the ledger again. "Jesse, Della, and Annabeth will find excellent homes in which they will want for nothing. Childless couples will value them as the children they never had."

"Will they be together? In the same home?"

The matron paused. "It is unlikely. We have a family who has been waiting for a young infant, a boy, for months. And another who would take a darling two-year-old like Annabeth. The five-year-old will go to a different home."

She could no longer listen. "The children mustn't be separated." She bowed her head over Jesse, who grabbed a lock of her hair and twined his fingers in it.

"I will send for the girls so you may see them."

Susanna looked up to see the matron whisper to another attendant, who had come in behind them. She finished and turned back to Susanna and her uncle. "Our policies exist to protect the children, and you have no way to support them, from what you tell me. There is one way you might reclaim the children, but I can't recommend it under the circumstances."

Susanna stayed mum, arms wrapped around Jesse's comforting weight.

The matron continued. "If their father were to come and take them back before they were placed out to new homes, we would be bound to return them to him. But, Mr. Hanby, I beg you to pray on it long before you take children you might not be able to feed."

Uncle Will nodded, his brow heavy.

Jesse was falling asleep in her arms, his breathing regular, his face round as a cherub's.

The door opened to admit two little girls in cream linen. So the home had furnished them with clothes better than the disgraceful ones George had kept them in. Annabeth and Della held hands.

Della's eyes grew big. "Aunt Susanna!"

Susanna handed a startled Jesse to her uncle, who took the baby in one arm with ease, shifting his cane to lean against his leg.

Della dragged Annabeth toward them and jumped into Susanna's arms. "Have you come to take us home?" Her blue eyes grew watery. "Mama left us here."

"I know, Della." Susanna must not weep when the girls needed her reassurance. "I know." She hugged Della's little body and knelt to the floor to gather Annabeth in her other arm.

Annabeth's dark hair was pulled in two short bunches behind her ears, her cheeks dimpled. "See Mama?"

"No, sweet girl. Mama has gone away for now."

"I want Mama." Annabeth's lower lip drooped.

"Everything will be all right, girls, I promise." She longed to tell them they were coming home with her, but she wouldn't make that promise until she could keep it.

"Miss Hanby, I suggest that you go to the Hare Home and see about the others," the matron said. "We will not place these children out for at least three or four weeks. They need time to gain weight and grow strong."

Guilt lanced through her. How could she explain about George and Rachel, and the children's thin and pale look?

"Thank you, Mrs. Loomis." She embraced the girls again, longing for her arms to be a shelter from what lay ahead. When she released them, they clung to her. "I must go," she said, touching Della's cheek. "Be good and take care of Annabeth. I will be back to see you."

"I want to go with you!" Della pleaded, tears sliding down her face.

"I know. But this is a good place. Be patient, and I'll be back."

She had to refuse their clutching hands when all she wanted was to hold them. The nurse eased the girls back a few steps.

"Say your prayers, and eat all the good food, including the vegetables." Susanna forced a cheerful tone, but she would lose her composure if she did not leave soon. Uncle Will relinquished baby Jesse to the nursery attendant.

She felt their eyes on her back the whole way and Della's pitiful sniffs following her. When the double doors closed behind them, she reached for Uncle Will's free arm and walked close to him, clinging to any human comfort. She thought she would rip in half.

They bid the matron farewell and walked down to the street. Uncle Will guided her to the omnibus line to wait.

"Can we afford the fare?" she asked him. If only she could use some of her tuition money to pay their expenses, but it was exactly enough for the year, and her uncle had insisted she must not touch it.

"Don't worry yourself on that account." He rattled a few coins in his pocket. "We may not have much, but I'm still making harnesses, and we've put aside a few pennies. The children must come first."

When the streetcar came, Susanna settled herself on the bench next to her uncle and watched the scene outside the windows. So many fine homes—she had never seen the like. Any of those families who lived here might take the children, for they certainly had "demonstrable means." It was wrong—what could be plainer than the need of a family to stay together?

Once they crossed into downtown proper, the business establishments created a swirl of traffic and painted signs covered the buildings: Varner Jewelers, Ohio Stoves and Pipe, J. Hall's Fabric and Parasols. The storefront labeled Smithson, Undertaker featured a polished hearse carriage, two black horses hitched up and ready for death at a moment's notice.

"There." Uncle Will pointed. "High Street. We can walk from here."

He had surprising stamina, for a man of his age with a limp. Five minutes' walk down High Street didn't seem to drain his strength, though Susanna refrained from taking his arm in case that might be an additional difficulty.

A right turn on Town Street brought them past more merchants—a shop front full of sewing machines on the corner, and a drugstore beside it. Beyond that was a soot-covered gray building, its sides naked and ugly without the clapboarding that covered the stores next to it.

Uncle Will checked the address on the handwritten card the matron had given him. "That establishment is our destination."

Four stories high, the building was bleak and forbidding, its windows streaked with layers of grime so she could not see inside even at the street level. Sad curtains sagged behind the smoky glass, curtains that might once have been pink but were now gray as the windows and walls.

She tried not to let her trepidation show in her eyes and went up to the door. When she lifted the handle of the iron knocker, the whole contraption came halfway off the door and dangled down in the air. She shot a glance at Uncle Will, who moved up and knocked with his fist. The muffled thump did not sound loud enough to bring an answer.

In a minute, though, the door wedged open and a hostile face with small, piggy eyes looked at them through the crack. "What is it?"

"I am William Hanby," her uncle said. "We understand there are three children here by the name of Leeds."

"What of it?"

Uncle Will paused, his expression inscrutable. "We wish to see the children and ascertain that they are safe. This young woman is their aunt, and I their great-uncle."

"The children are indentured to this orphan home now. You understand that?"

"Yes," Uncle Will said, though a shadow flickered across his face.

The door opened a little wider, revealing a stout woman whose apron strained around her waist, her gray curls unkempt and wiry at the edges of her bonnet. "So you want to see them?"

"If we may." Uncle Will must have been quite a force of nature in his youth, for even with his snowy mane he was still capable of winning female hearts with his quiet deference.

The squat woman seemed to relent, with a grudging jerk of her chin. "All right then."

Uncle Will placed his cane over the sill and levered himself up. Susanna followed him into the dank hall and up two flights of stairs to the top floor. She saw the strain in her uncle's shoulders, but he made no sound as he ascended. It must hurt his knees to climb, since he was slow on the stairs but still so vigorous on the flat road.

The third floor was divided into only two large areas. She was sure this building was once a warehouse or factory, with such unwelcoming, bare rooms. Fragments of plaster lay like crumbled cheese on the ground. The ceiling was in dire need of repair, with holes and stains along the entire south end of the building.

"You have roof troubles?" Uncle Will asked.

"Our benefactor did not leave us with excess funds. We must make do," the woman said over her ham hock of a shoulder. "I am Mrs. Grismer, the housekeeper."

Cots huddled together at the far end, and on each sat a childish figure working on something in her lap.

"Leeds!" Mrs. Grismer said.

All the faces turned toward them. Then one sprang to her feet. "Aunt Susanna!" A young girl ran through the gloom, her thin frame and torn dress heartbreakingly familiar.

"Clara," Susanna said as she embraced her niece. "Are you quite well?" Clara's slender shoulders were shivering under Susanna's hands.

"Oh yes, oh yes." Clara's eyes were bright, though her voice was brittle. "Have you come to take us away?"

"No." The fat woman's voice was hard. "You belong here now, and we will determine where you go and how you may be useful. Those are the terms under which we accept children."

Susanna must be careful, very careful. "Where are Wesley and Daniel?"

"They've gone to help haul coal and earn their way." The housekeeper stood with her arms propped on her hips.

"I see." Susanna made her response as noncommittal as she could.

"How do the finances of this home fare?" her uncle asked.

"Terrible, just terrible." Mrs. Grismer fell into what sounded like a long-whined complaint. "We have only ten dollars for vegetables for the whole spring and summer. For thirty children, sir."

As her litany of woe continued, Susanna stole a glimpse at her uncle. He looked fascinated, which was odd. Oh—she should have known. He was distracting the woman to allow Susanna some private words with Clara.

Below the babble of the housekeeper's talk, Susanna whispered to her niece, "We will try to take you home with us, Clara, but not just yet. Be patient. And pray for us."

"I'm afraid. Daniel is coughing."

That was grim news. Daniel had always been the most fragile of Rachel's children, prone to a rattling cough at even the slightest chill.

"A piece of ceiling fell on a boy last night. His head was bleeding." Clara leaned closer to Susanna like a fawn seeking a warm side for comfort.

"We will not be long," Susanna said. "We'll remove you from this place one way or another, I promise." No matter what it took, Susanna could not leave them here.

The housekeeper's voice grew pointed and penetrated the gloom. "The girls must sew. They are sewing for their own suppers, you see."

Clara looked down at the scrap of material she still held in one hand. It looked like men's underdrawers. A flush crept up Susanna's neck. Clara was too young for so intimate a knowledge of men's undergarments. Was there no better task for the girls?

"Well, Mrs. Grismer," her uncle said. "Our deepest thanks for your kindness in allowing us to see our niece."

The woman harrumphed, but she looked self-satisfied. "If I say so myself, Mr. Hanby, the children would be far worse off without me."

"Indeed." Her uncle sounded remarkably sanguine.

Is that true, or is some of the children's food going down that woman's gullet? But Susanna would not speculate without proof.

"Visitors really aren't allowed, so you must be going," the housekeeper said.

"Yes," Uncle Will said. "Perhaps we shall stop by again and bring you some sweets for the children."

Light flared in Mrs. Grismer's small, thick-lidded eyes. "And you will be welcome, Mr. Hanby."

And with a few more pleasantries from her uncle, they made their way down the flights of stairs.

The comparative brightness of the street outside should have loosened her tongue, but she stayed silent all the way to the horse car. Uncle Will offered her his arm without comment, as if he knew that a young woman beyond tears was also beyond words.

Six

JOHANN TWISTED THE TAP AT THE BASE OF THE KEG and held the tin cup beneath it as amber liquid flowed out. He raised the mug to his nose and inhaled the aroma. This lager was ready, with just the right hoppiness to win his father's approval. He took a sip and let it linger on his tongue. Yes, it was well brewed— light and bittersweet with the color of honey, not sour like the lager some brewers tried to foist on unsuspecting customers.

He called to Heinrich across the cellar, "This is ready."

"*Sehr gut.* I'll tell the men to get to it this afternoon," Heinrich said.

His father's voice echoed down from the ground floor, "Johann?"

"Down here, *Vater.*"

Steps thumped on the wooden stairs and his father walked into view. The broad planes of his face gave him a permanent air of good nature, but now his brow was furrowed. "We have a small problem."

Henry Corbin stalked in behind him, his dark hair, olive complexion, and narrow features a sharp contrast to Johann's father with his fair openness.

"The Westerville temperance gang vandalized my property last night." Corbin's words were choppy remnants of fury. "They bored holes in the barrels and let all the beer run out on the floor."

"And the bottled liquor?" Johann needed details if he planned to write it up for the paper at some point.

Corbin took a packet of tobacco from his pocket. "Safe. They must not have thought of it, or else someone surprised them and they didn't have the opportunity." He stuffed a wad of chew in his mouth.

A few ruined barrels of beer were not news for Johann—not yet, anyway.

His father put a hand on Corbin's shoulder. "I will replace those barrels for you free of charge. But you will have to be careful and keep watch, because I cannot do such a thing more than once."

"That's neighborly of you, Mr. Giere. Much obliged." Mr. Corbin's tobacco made a lump in his cheek when he spoke.

"I believe in freedom, Mr. Corbin. And law. They cannot drive you out of a legal enterprise by criminal force, not in America." Johann's father turned to Heinrich. "How is the new brew?"

"Even better than the last," Heinrich said.

"Then let's send some off with Mr. Corbin."

Johann hoped Corbin wouldn't spit on the floor. It was unmannerly to chew indoors without a by-your-leave, even in the brewery. But then, he had no reason to expect Corbin to be a gentleman.

Heinrich walked to the double doors and yelled in German to the floor hands. They rushed in, shirtsleeved and suspendered, carrying barrels at top speed. His father looked on, smiling, as they chided one another in German.

"If you'd like," Johann said, "I can assist Mr. Corbin in taking the beer to Westerville."

"*Danke*, son. It's still as heavy as it was the first time."

And even more likely to cause trouble—and news.

He needed to get his wallet for the journey. It wasn't the first time he'd been glad they lived only two streets away from the brewery. His mother stood with her back to him at the baker's table in the large kitchen, a line of *Rouladen* forming beneath her hands. Johann watched her nimble fingers pick first a strip of bacon, then onion, and pickles from a jar. She piled them in the center of the steak, rolled it into a log shape, and tied it with a string.

He made his face very sad. "*Rouladen*, and I am not coming home for supper. And I am hungry. Life is hard."

"You poor boy." She clucked her tongue. "Whatever will you do?" She shot him a merry look through her veneer of cynicism. Her apple-cheeked face was rounder and heavier than ten years ago, but she wore it well in her neat lace-collared blouse and apron.

"If you don't save me one, I'll be inconsolable," he said.

"I'm sure Lotte will make you some if she hears you love them."

He shut his mouth quickly. In any conversation with his mother, it was only a matter of minutes before the charm, beauty, and talents of her best friend's daughter, Lotte, came to the fore. He would make no comment and hope the Lotte spell dissipated.

"Lotte is the best young cook I know," she said.

He sighed. "I must get my bag and go."

"Where?"

"On an errand for *Vater*."

"I will have pity on you. There are some *Broetchen* in the pie safe."

"Danke." He flipped open the door and seized one of the soft rolls. His mouth watered. Their soft, doughy sweetness was unmatched: his mother bought them from Kaufman's Bakery, who were the acknowledged kings of *Broetchen*, as good as any in Germany, his father said. He tucked it in his bag for the ride to the station. "Where are the girls?" He thought his two sisters would have been at home helping his mother.

"At the Turnverein."

Ah, that made sense. The girls had been spending more time at the social athletic club lately. Perhaps it was a sign of growing up and wanting to be around the young men. And with his mother as matrimony-minded as she was, she would prefer them to be out husband-hunting.

He walked out with bag over his shoulder and wished his mother good-bye. If they had the wagon loaded by now, he and Corbin could make the afternoon train. But he would not sit with Corbin if the man insisted on traveling in the smoking car. A businessman met his obligations, but stewing in foul-smelling cigar smoke was not one of them.

"We're just in time to catch the next train," Uncle Will said. He offered Susanna his hand and she descended from the horse car, her skirt sweeping through the dust around her boots. It was still so hot, as if Ohio's mild climate had been swept away by a fiercer summer from the west. The fabric on her shoulders scorched in the sunlight while she slowed her pace to match her uncle's.

The train stood in the station, huffing to catch its breath, proud of its dark-green exterior and gilt filigree trim. The whistle blew.

Uncle Will quickened his step, leaning harder on his cane. "We'll buy tickets from the conductor."

They made it to the closest passenger car just in time. The conductor held the last door for them, then climbed in after them and shut it with a twist of the brass handle. Uncle Will paused to get out his billfold while Susanna moved into the aisle and waited for him. While the train stood still, no breeze flowed through the clerestory roof vents and the heat was oppressive. Her uncle really should not pay the extra charge for first class, but she knew he would not let her ride in the lower-class cars with their rough assortment of passengers. He pressed the money in the conductor's hand, took their tickets, and waved her ahead down the aisle.

The first-class car was full of passengers, ladies' straw hats trimmed with black bands or flowers above the seat backs. Men had the wilted look of soldiers after a long march. There were no free seats.

"Try the parlor seating up ahead," the conductor called after them.

Susanna skirted the carved wooden divider with its fancy pillar and stepped into a little salon-style area of the car. Several seats adorned with tapestried cherubs faced one another quite like a room in a hotel.

Sitting in one of those rich, upholstered seats was the fair-haired brewer's son they had met in Westerville. He looked up at her from the newspaper in his lap and his blue eyes widened.

"Good afternoon," he said, getting to his feet. "Miss Hanby, I believe?"

She could not remember his name—something German and beery-sounding. And she did not want his attention or his company, no matter how civil he might be. It was worse when people who did immoral things like create intoxicating drinks were also pleasing in appearance, like him. Evil could seem very attractive. The way George had first appeared to Rachel, perhaps.

"Mr. Giere," her uncle said from behind her.

That was it. Gier-a, to rhyme with beer-a. She would not forget again.

She did not want to sit near him, but it would be ridiculous to brave the swaying platform between cars, especially with her uncle's cane and bad knees. But she did not have to speak to Gier-a. Perhaps he would read his newspaper and leave her alone. With the sharp memory of the children gnawing her from within, she wasn't fit to talk to anyone.

"After you, my dear," her uncle said, and indicated one of the seats across from the brewer.

Before any of them could sit, the whistle blew again and the train lurched. Her uncle braced himself on his cane, but Susanna staggered a step toward the young brewer. He reached out reflexively to steady her by the elbow. But she regained her balance and jerked away from his touch. "I am quite capable of standing in a train, thank you." She sat down, feeling stiff as an angry cat.

He took his own seat as her uncle also lowered himself into a soft chair. "I beg your pardon, Miss Hanby. I simply did not wish you to fall."

"I would not fall, because I am not drunk, you see."

"Susanna." Her uncle's gentle word did not soothe her.

"And neither am I," the young brewer said. "You are very perturbed, Miss Hanby." He seemed more curious than put off.

He had not the faintest idea. The sad faces of the children sprang back to her mind's eye. She stared at him as an ache clear to her bones threatened to make her weep. But she would not.

"I apologize, Mr. Giere," her uncle said. "My niece has received a shock recently and may not be quite herself on the subject of temperance."

"You do not need to beg his pardon for me, Uncle," she said, barely keeping her composure. "Instead, he should beg ours, and that of every family torn apart by strong drink."

Uncle Will raised his eyebrows but said nothing.

"I hate to differ with a lady," the young man said, color creeping up from his collar, "but I must point out that my family does not make or sell strong drink, but only lager, which is much more . . . temperate. Shouldn't that earn us some mercy, Miss Hanby?"

"None. Lager can be as dangerous as whiskey. I'm sure just as many beer-swilling husbands and fathers have returned home from the saloon to beat their wives or become lazy loafers and fail to provide for their children." The thought of George with his dissipated, shadowed eyes made her sick.

Why did she have to meet this young brewery man here and now? A twinge of conscience made her even unhappier. She had never been so rude to anyone before, but the pain had sharpened her tongue, and she did not seem to be able to dull it again.

Her uncle spoke into the charged silence. "Where are you traveling today, Mr. Giere?"

"To Westerville once again, sir."

"On business?"

"Yes, sir." He looked indecisive, then took a breath. "But to be honest, my heart is in journalism, not in the brewery." He darted a look at Susanna as if to gauge her response.

She twisted away to look out the window at the unrolling industrial scenery, the damp hair of her ringlets grazing the back of her neck. She could feel herself teetering on the brink of an outburst. She mustn't say anything more.

"Indeed, journalism?" Uncle Will sounded relieved at the change of subject. "And do you work in that profession too?"

"Not for a salary, sir. But I write articles for the *Westbote* once a week. Local crime, mostly."

"And will you ever leave brewing for the newspaper?"

He shifted and moved his hat from one hand to another. "I don't know, sir."

"A difficult prospect, with a family business to sustain." Her uncle was so even-tempered—perhaps working as a minister had made him immune to the shock of immorality.

"Yes, sir." Mr. Giere fell silent and looked out the other window, then unfolded his paper as if to read. But he stopped in mid-gesture and lowered it again. "I have a personal request to make of you, Mr. Hanby." He glanced at Susanna again, his gaze a flash of blue that veered back to her uncle at once. "And perhaps you will be willing to honor my request if you know that it's my opportunity to leave the brewing business." He looked cautious, or perhaps ashamed? Well, he should be. And he would not deserve credit for repentance until he actually left the business.

"What do you wish of me, Mr. Giere?" her uncle asked.

"I go to Westerville not only to do business but to find a story for the paper. If I find it, I may make journalism my profession." He spoke in a rush, as if to force it out before he could change his mind.

"I see." By the lift in his voice, her uncle was clearly intrigued, and despite her inner chaos of feeling, so was Susanna.

She pinned Mr. Giere with a stare. "And you expect to find this story in Westerville?"

"In Henry Corbin's saloon. I don't think your town will take to it."

"I'm afraid you're correct, Mr. Giere," her uncle said, a pensive look in his eyes. "Let's hope Mr. Corbin will go peacefully. But you still haven't told me your request."

"If I'm to find the story, I mustn't be known to the townsfolk as the brewer's son. They will not talk to me openly if they see me as an enemy."

"Which you are, in this matter," Susanna said.

"I'm not the one opening the saloon, Miss Hanby. We aren't even supplying the majority of his goods. At any rate, I hope you will allow me to do my reporting without unmasking me."

"If it leads you out of your father's profession, then we are bound to do all we can to assist you." She heard the edge in her own voice, and the young brewer must have too, for he looked away.

Her uncle sighed. "It's not my affair, Mr. Giere, and thus, you may conduct yourself as you see fit. I won't interfere, though of course I won't lie if I am asked about you."

"Of course not, sir," the blond man said, looking uncomfortable. "And you have my thanks." He rose, hat in one hand, newspaper in the other. "As my presence is disturbing Miss Hanby, I will take my leave." With a formal nod, he turned and strode down the car to the end door, then went through to the next car.

"Susanna." Her uncle tilted his head in her direction and looked sad.

"I am sorry, Uncle. I'm not myself." Tears gathered at her lashes—she hated to disappoint him with her behavior, but her nieces and nephews would not leave her mind. She blinked the water away and bowed her head.

She felt her uncle's touch on her shoulder. "Be gentle, my girl. Striking out at others will not help."

She knew he was right, that one wrong did not justify another. But she could not be gentle or peaceful with those who made the poison that turned George Leeds into a monster. If Rachel had left her husband, Susanna would not blame her for escaping her suffering. But how could her sister abandon her children? It would be so selfish, as selfish as George's indulgence in drink. She would not believe it. She would maintain Rachel's goodness to her last breath.

The wheels clacked and the train windows rattled, and for a moment she wished George under the wheels of the train.

A shudder of self-loathing went through her. *Lord, Lord, take my thoughts and heal them. Am I really so wicked as to murder a man in my thoughts? Am I not only to lose my family but my kindness too?*

Her uncle seemed to sense she was struggling for composure, and he left her to pray and sit in silence for the rest of the journey.

Seven

THE TISSUE PAPER LAY IN HER OPEN VALISE, VIVID even in the dim upstairs bedroom. It was too hard to see this reminder of the children every time she came up here. Susanna gathered it up and went downstairs. Looking around, she spied her aunt in the parlor doing some needlework.

"Do you know anyone who might have a use for this?" She brandished the delicate folds of color toward her.

Aunt Ann looked up. "That's lovely paper. Why do you wish to give it away?"

"Because . . ." She swallowed. "I had planned to use it to make paper flowers with the children."

Her aunt stuck the needle in the fabric and laid it on the chair next to her. "My dear." She stood and approached to lay a hand on Susanna's back. "You must keep it, for when we bring them home."

"How, Auntie? Even if the orphanage would let us, we have no money to keep them, not six of them. I would gladly give my tuition money, but it's not nearly enough."

"Your uncle would never permit that—your education is too dear to him. But he has some other plans that might reassure you.

He's in the barn if you'd like to talk." She tilted her head. "And it would do you good to get outside, maybe take a walk even."

Susanna struggled against a troubling sensation that her arms, shoulders, and face were encased in lead and could barely move—she was overcome. She must be stronger, more like her aunt.

"I'll go see Uncle." Maybe she could store the tissue paper in one of the drawers in the saddlery, at least keep it out of sight.

When she walked in the side door of the saddlery, Uncle Will was bent over his saddling bench deep in concentration. His hands darted quickly to and fro with the chisel and hammer. At the flash of sunlight from the door, he stopped and looked up.

"Hello." His attention went to the paper in her hands. "What's that you have there?"

"Something for the children, when they come home." She forced herself to sound confident. "Is there somewhere I can keep it?"

"You can just put it on the table. I'll clear a space in a drawer when I finish this."

She did so and turned back to him. "Auntie said I should speak with you. About your plans for the children?"

"Oh, yes." He put down the tools, rubbed the creases from his forehead, and stood up. "Come look."

She followed him to the doors that led to the other half of the barn, where they kept their cow and their one horse. When they went through, she was surprised to find a dark hallway at least twelve feet long, an unexpected space between saddlery and barn. They were below the hayloft, she realized after a moment.

Uncle Will opened the door wider to let in more light. He went to a locked door set in the side of the aisle and opened it with a quick twist of a key from his pocket.

Inside was a large storage area, piled high with boxes and bags. Rows and rows of shelves were crowded with jars.

"This is food we collect at church to distribute to the needy," he said. "I asked yesterday if the church would be willing to use these foods to support the children this year, if we brought them to live here. They agreed. After that, we'll have to trust God to provide, but at least one year is already possible."

A little hope flared inside her. "Will it be enough to convince the matron at the Hannah Neil Mission?"

"I doubt it will persuade her to let us adopt the children." He closed the storage door and locked it. "But it's all we have, so we must hold on and pray that Rachel comes back or George retrieves the children and gives them to us. At least we would have a way to feed them."

The relief was like a breath of air blown into a sealed vault. "Thank you!" She threw her arms around his neck.

When she stepped back again, he smiled at her. "It's really the church we need to thank."

"Of course. I'll write a note to all of them, if you will read it on Sunday."

He nodded. "The other part of the plan requires me to increase my leatherworking, particularly in harnesses. The harvest is coming and more teams will need to go out in the fields, so I plan to get their business." He looked critically at a saddle sitting on a wall rack. "If only I had my father-in-law's skill, my work would garner a higher price—but I have yet to see his match in saddlecraft."

"But you already work so hard." An idea seized her. "Can I help you?"

"You will already have enough work of your own with your studies and your housekeeping for the college."

"I can do it—please, teach me. If you work late into the night, I will too."

"We'll see. I can't let you neglect your studies." He tried to look stern, but a quirk at his lip gave him away. She could tell he was pleased to think of having her company while he worked. Maybe he would relent. He returned to his bench and picked up his chisel again.

Her mind spun with questions—she must find Rachel, because now everything would be set right if they only found her.

Her aunt had suggested she take a walk. Maybe that would give her uncle time to relent, and he would teach her some of his craft later today. Now his dark eyes were narrowed, his keen attention on the strap in his hands. She watched him with secret affection. Flesh might sag and hair might whiten, but his stubborn goodness was the same as she had always known.

She would walk, then, while he was absorbed in his work. She must have faith in the children's return, that there would be beauty and order again and all would be as it should. In fact, she would go look for flowers to use as models for the paper ones. She would need a blue flower. Blue vervain, perhaps . . . they were in bloom now, most likely to grow by water. "Uncle, I think I will walk to the creek."

"That's a good walk." He was only half listening, lost in his work.

She took a sheet of her blue paper and borrowed a pencil off the table.

The heat was still oppressive, but the sunlight lifted her spirits. Better hot and sunny than hot and gloomy. She walked briskly, feeling her blood pump through her limbs, not minding the moisture that gathered on her skin. She passed the shops and turned onto the college avenue.

Where could she look for Rachel? She turned over the possibilities in her mind.

After crossing through the college quadrangle and beyond, she reached the path to Alum Creek, on the west side of town. Water glinted through the trees.

The banks were still green, nourished even in the summer heat by the water in the soil, though the creek looked shrunken and had left a muddy flat at its edge. As she had predicted, a whole host of blue vervains collected near the bridge. *Verbena hastata*. The Latin name sprang to mind as she scrambled down the bank beside the bridge, clutching the blue paper. The children would love this flower, and it would be very challenging to reconstruct. Perfect.

In her handbag she kept a little pair of scissors for just this reason.

Taking her scissors in thumb and finger, she stepped to the patch of blue flowers and began to hunt for the perfect specimen. Hopeful lyrics crept into her thoughts, a hymn, and as she walked between the long stems, she began to hum. The song quieted her soul and strengthened her resolve.

She would not give up—she would make this flower template because she expected right to prevail in the end. And she would do her utmost to ensure it did.

gedddddddddddddddd

Johann strode along the path to the dairy farm. Time to gather some local opinion on the saloon, and he knew just where to get it.

The surrounding trees thinned into open air as he crossed the creek bridge. What was that sound rising from below? Someone was humming—it was a melody he knew, a hymn. He looked over the rail. A young woman in a straw hat and plain green dress stood with her back to him, her trim form surrounded by tall candelabras of tiny blue flowers. She looked as if she had walked into a French country painting. At the sound of his steps, she looked over her shoulder.

It was the temperance girl—Miss Hanby.

Not again! Her opinion of him made no difference. He should not react with any kind of embarrassment, but the sting of her accusations returned at the sight of her. He looked away and walked on: he did not want to endure another attack.

"Mr. Giere."

To his surprise, she climbed up the bank toward him, still holding a bunch of the blue flowers and a pair of scissors. She might try to stab him with those scissors—it wouldn't be a surprise. Still, he couldn't help but appreciate her beauty, the hazy mystery of her green eyes. But her face was unusually rosy—from heat, or was she about to fly into another fit of anger?

Trying not to show his reluctance, he paused and braced himself for whatever might come. "Yes, Miss Hanby? May I assist you in some way?"

She shuffled and looked down at the flowers she clutched. They were spiky wands with bursts of blue blossoms along their length. "I would like to apologize." She did not raise her head or look at him. "I was very rude to you on the train. Though I still detest your business, that is no excuse for me to abandon all consideration."

"Thank you, Miss Hanby. I admire your candor." And he did. A humble apology was a sign of grace and maturity many could not muster.

Silence strained the air.

"That is all." She turned without meeting his gaze, but he glimpsed the shine of tears in her eyes as she moved away. He felt sorry for her now. Clearly something was troubling her to make this young woman so mercurial. She did not seem harsh by her nature, and she had a conscience.

"Miss Hanby."

She turned over her shoulder, blinking the tears away.

He followed her by a few steps. "If you don't mind my asking, what are you doing down there?"

"I am on a botanical quest." She said it with such seriousness that he restrained his urge to smile.

"Oh yes? You are a botanist?"

"An amateur."

"And have you found what you sought?"

"*Verbena hastata*." She held up the blue flower wands.

"What will you do with it?"

"Take it apart, piece by piece, and study its structure."

He liked the matter-of-fact way she said it, as if it were not at all unusual to dissect a flower instead of putting it in a vase. She was an intelligent girl, if a little eccentric. "I see," he said. "Is that the chief appeal of flowers for you, study?"

"Flowers always follow universal principles by which God has designed them, Mr. Giere. They have much to teach us."

He rose to the slight challenge in her tone. "They are a moral lesson? Aren't they beautiful as well?"

"That is the moral lesson. Their adherence to heavenly principle is what gives them their beauty—it deepens the beauty we can see on the surface."

"Until you cut them to pieces, of course."

She almost smiled. "But I'll make a new flower of paper modeled after the first."

This conversation was growing odder at every turn. "Why?"

She paused for a long moment, her expression shifting through several cryptic changes. She held the flowers close to her bodice and took a quick breath. "I must ask you once more, Mr. Giere—please don't help the saloonkeeper by supplying him with beer."

Why on earth must she go back to the subject when they had just managed an interesting, if awkward, exchange? Apparently her apology would not restrict her single-minded crusade, even if it improved her manners. He couldn't hide the annoyance that colored his tone. "That's not my decision to make, Miss Hanby. You will need to address Mr. Corbin, not me."

Her eyes went cold and opaque as jade. "Good day, Mr. Giere." She turned her back and walked down the bank again to her patch of flowers, her green skirt swaying. He stole a glance around the end of the bridge as he continued on his way.

She seemed to have forgotten him already. She pulled one of the lush floral spikes close on its stem and examined its blue blossoms with wide eyes and an intent, analytical stare.

She was prickly and opinionated, but what an interesting

mix in her character—sometimes cool, scientific, but also tender-hearted. Still, it was plain that he and she would never be on good terms.

That was for the best. If Westerville provided him with his news story, Susanna Hanby was sure to be in the thick of the action, judging from her vehemence.

For now, he needed to go meet his friend.

Mr. Bergen, a widower, lived on the far west side of the creek, where he kept his small herd of dairy cattle. He welcomed Johann in, opening the red farmhouse door wide. *"Ach, mein Freund,* it has been too long. You did not bring your father to visit me?" He beckoned Johann into the kitchen.

"Not today, Herr Bergen."

The stocky man in overalls gestured toward the table and Johann took a seat at it. "I'm here to seek your opinion."

"For the *Westbote*? Am I so famous?" He grinned.

Johann smiled back. "Your opinion about Westerville. You've lived here a decade, you should have a feel for the town, yes?"

The farmer sat down opposite him and leaned back on his chair. *"Ja."*

"Will there be a story in this saloon opening, or will it all blow over in a week or so?

Mr. Bergen raised his brows to his hairline. "Oh, *nein,* there will be no blowing over. The people of this town are good people, but some are very stubborn. There will be big trouble when the saloon opens tomorrow. Everyone says so."

Johann pondered. "Then perhaps I'll stay in town this evening."

Mr. Bergen wiped his brow, which was moistening in the afternoon heat. "Mark my words, son—this will be something no newspaperman would want to miss."

Eight

A THUNDEROUS CLANG STARTLED JOHANN FROM HIS sleep. He scrambled out of bed, blinking in the morning light. Where was he? The din dazed him in his bleary state. Bells. It was the sound of church bells, resonant, deafening, echoing through the walls.

The sight of the four-poster bed and simple porcelain wash-stand brought him back to his senses. He was in Westerville, at the Commercial House Hotel. He had stayed overnight to see what would happen to Corbin's new stock of beer. And he had succumbed to sleep when he meant to stay up and watch the street. Some big-city reporter he would make.

He looked out his second-floor window, wincing at the vol-ume of the pealing bells. It sounded like every church in town was ringing an alarm. Across the rooftops he could see bells swinging away in three steeples. Below in the street, men and women hurried to the intersection of College and State, which was rapidly clogging with scores of pedestrians.

He had to get down to the scene, whatever was happen-ing. He pulled on his trousers and buttoned them, then checked himself in the looking glass and brushed pillow-lint off the trace of blond stubble on his face. No time to shave. He grabbed his hat and ran down several flights of stairs to the main doors of the hotel.

Outside, a buzz of excited and angry voices joined the clamoring bells. He descended the hotel steps and blended in with the crowd. They had gathered outside the Widow Clymer's building, only a block from his lodgings. State Street was so packed he could make progress only by sidling close to the windows of the confectionery and the timepiece store. Finally he reached a good vantage point—he was only yards from the door of Corbin's saloon, standing in an alley where the saloonkeeper would not be able to see him. Johann didn't want to be called upon for support and exposed as some kind of ally—it would ruin his story-gathering. He had already done his duty to his father by delivering the lager—he had no duty to the crude proprietor of the new saloon. Now he could be a reporter.

"Henry Corbin, show your face!" a man in a black hat and clerical collar called from where he stood front and center of the crowd, directly across from the saloon. The clergyman appeared to be in his midforties, ruddy, square-shouldered.

"We're not leaving, Corbin," another man shouted behind him. "Open up and account for yourself."

No response came from the shuttered windows.

The minister addressed the crowd still expanding behind him. "He appears to be ashamed to answer for his actions. Perhaps his shame will encourage him to pack up his whiskey and leave." He appeared determined but in good humor.

"You tell him, Reverend Robertson," a man cried. A few women echoed with "Amen!" and "Hear, hear."

Hundreds thronged Main Street. If it wasn't the whole

town, it was all the able-bodied adults. Johann began to run through headlines in his mind. "Temperance Town Takes to Streets Against Saloon." Not a crime headline for the New York job, perhaps, but a dramatic story for the *Westbote*.

"Come out, Corbin!" the reverend repeated to the window.

The crowd cheered and whistled again. Across the street, under the sign for Dusenberry's Shoes, Johann noticed a slender figure in a pale yellow bustle dress and straw hat, standing beside a familiar white-haired gentleman. The Hanbys.

Miss Susanna Hanby was not cheering. She had her arms wrapped around herself, a handbag dangling, forgotten, from one wrist, her forehead creased in worry. No doubt she would continue to blame him for Corbin, for drunkenness in America, and for ruined families, despite the fact that he didn't even want to be a brewer. But there was nothing he could do to change her mind, or alter the opinion of anyone else who thought Germans were Sabbath-breaking corrupters of public morals. He could hardly take her to church and show her his family at worship, and he should not need to do so. Prejudice was an ugly thing, even in a beautiful woman.

But perhaps he was unfair. She had said nothing about Germans—only appeared single-mindedly committed to her cause, which she believed to be good. The fervor for pursuing good was not wrong; her passionate belief would be attractive, if it were not so adversarial.

The red saloon door opened and Corbin stepped out, a horse pistol in each hand, the gun barrels pointed at the sky. He elbowed the door shut and grimly faced the throng, showing no reaction as he scanned its expanse from left to right. A silence fell over the street.

"You won't bully me," Corbin said in his flat, rough voice, "be there a hundred of you or a thousand. With my lawful right to bear arms, I will defend my right to open a legal business in this town." He brandished the pistols.

The reverend in his clerical collar fell back a step, and the crowd murmured.

"Put away your guns." A calm voice came from the back. William Hanby limped through the crowd, which parted as if he were Moses with a staff, not an old man with a walking cane. "Corbin, these people are not brutes. They simply wish you to hear them."

Corbin looked uncertain and lowered his pistols, but he did not holster them.

"Your business threatens the existence of Otterbein College," Mr. Hanby said evenly. "Many families here gave their life savings to rebuild the college after the fire. This college is the lifeblood of Westerville. And for twenty years, churchgoing parents have trusted Otterbein because there is no drinking establishment in town where innocent sons can be led astray in deadly habits."

"Men make their own choice to walk through a saloon's door," Corbin said. "I will not be dragging them. And before I fret about the children of others, I take care of my own children. They need to eat, and this is how I will put food on my table."

"You're a selfish man, Corbin," a guttural voice called. "Get out of our town!"

Mr. Hanby turned toward the interrupter, as if to hush him, and Corbin's face tightened.

"We'll fight you to our last breath," a woman cried. Johann looked around to see a hysterical-looking plump woman waving a round fist at Corbin. The rules of propriety had rushed away with the sound of the bells.

"He won't listen to us," another man said to the rest. The crowd murmured and moved toward Corbin like a wave, some faces worried, some angry, some looking as if they were pushed along on the tide and would really rather go home.

Corbin raised his pistols, cocked them with two loud clicks, and waved them toward the crowd. Some shifted nervously as the dark holes of the barrels wandered past them.

"You're a bunch of zealots," Corbin gritted out. "And I won't back down to the likes of you. You knock-kneed, hymn-chanting hypocrites and un-American thugs! You self-righteous, narrow-minded sons of . . ." The stream of insults continued and grew profane, and men looked at their wives in consternation. Johann darted a surreptitious glance at Susanna Hanby, who had gone pink over her delicate cheekbones. He fought the instinct to step forward and tell Corbin to shut his filthy mouth in the presence of ladies.

With a last curse, Corbin went back inside and slammed his door. Locks thudded into place.

Abashed by the profanity, the men and women looked around in the hush.

"It doesn't appear he's going to listen to you, Mr. Hanby," one matron finally said.

"I say we go in and throw him out by force," a young man yelled to a handful of amens.

William Hanby held up his hands. "Let's not be hasty. None of us should lay hands on any other man—we are called to peace."

At this, some looked relieved and others grumbled.

The pastor spoke up. "The power of prayer is mighty. We should do nothing without it."

"Amen!" a man said. The crowd stirred and rumbled.

"Let's go have a meeting at the Methodist church, sisters!" a handsome, middle-aged woman said to the assembled group. "We'll pray and we'll sing until we convince all Ohio to boycott this saloon."

"Men, you heard the ladies! We can do no less," Reverend Roberson urged. "All men to the Presbyterian church for a prayer meeting and discussion! All men are welcome, regardless of creed." Some men moved through the crowd toward him.

The handsome matron linked arms with another woman next to her and walked up the street. She opened her mouth and sang in a rich alto: *"Come friends and sisters all unite, hurrah! Hurrah! . . ."*

He knew this tune—everybody did, "When Johnny Comes Marching Home." But apparently many of the townspeople knew a new set of words. *"Come out and take the Pledge tonight, hurrah! Hurrah!"* Twenty others joined in, *"Come out and join our Temperance band, and nobly to our colors stand!"* Now half the crowd was singing, moving their feet to the rhythm like a small army, men and women separating into clusters like leaves on the surface of a pond, milling toward the steeples at the end of the street. They did not seem angry now, but joyful and determined.

The men were going to the Presbyterian church. Johann should be able to fit in quite easily, given that there would be several hundred men there. He followed the crowd as it flowed on, but he did not sing, though the pulse of the music pulled at him and the melody swirled in his head. He didn't know the new words, and even if he did, he wouldn't pretend to be an ardent teetotaler just to get a story.

He looked at the spot where Susanna had been as he passed. She was still there, just taking her uncle's arm as he returned to her. She stared at Johann in surprise. Was that a touch of disapproval in her glance? He turned away with a flash of irritation and walked on. Let her think what she wished, he did not care, as long as the Hanbys did not advertise his identity here in Westerville.

The straight brick lines of the church bell tower rose against the green treetops behind it, its crenellated top like a castle battlement. The tower was incongruous in front of the humble, low-roofed church behind it. For such a plain building, it had a very grand bell.

At the front doors the men jostled in like a herd of horses, some calling friendly greetings and striding around the pews with the ease of long familiarity, others moving more gingerly into a strange house of worship, gazing at the rows of dark pews, the low roof rising to heavy support beams. It was not as elegant as Johann's church, St. John's German Independent Evangelical, with its stained glass and polished organ pipes. But Westerville was a small town and the simple starkness of the church had a beauty of its own. Besides, Johann's church had incurred a debt of twenty thousand dollars in its construction, a debt that weighed on his father and the other founders. There was something to be said for a more frugal approach.

The pews filled, and Johann remained at the back with a score of others who did not find seats. This mixing of congregations was very convenient—no one noticed him as an outsider. Half the men there were outsiders, at least at this church.

The reverend rose and cleared his throat. "Gentlemen, the time has come to rise in defense of our families." He spoke for ten minutes, an impassioned, sincere outpouring with just the right pacing and build so the men hung on his words and punctuated them with "Amen" and "Preach it, Reverend Robertson!"

He paused. "In our very midst . . ." His eyes skimmed the pews. "We have living examples who can witness to the terrible destructive power of intoxicating drinks. One of those men has had the courage to confess and turn from his past, and I know he will have no reluctance to testify for us today. I would like to ask our brother Arthur Pippen to come forward."

Halfway down the aisle, a slight man stood up in a pew and walked to the front to ascend the low platform and stand next to the reverend. He wore a coat shiny at the elbows from wear, but his hair was neatly combed back, his face alive with the urgency of his thought. "I am not ashamed to tell you that my Lord Jesus Christ delivered me from a drunken, wasted life a year ago in this very church." His voice hardly carried to the back doors, but it was firm. "And by doing so, he saved my wife and children from hunger and misery."

"Praise be," another man said from the front pew with pent-up feeling. Reverend Robertson turned, murmured something to Mr. Pippen, and shook his hand.

After a moment the small man continued. "Through an unwise friendship with some farm laborers, I fell into the habit of taking strong drink, and before I knew it, the demon had taken residence in me. I thought of nothing but that glass of whiskey from the moment I awoke until I obtained it. I lost my good position at Mr. Jones's farm." His face sagged. "Were it not for the charity of the good ladies of Westerville, my wife and children would have had nothing to eat, and even as it was, they suffered—" He faltered and swallowed visibly. "Don't let Henry Corbin open a saloon. The temptation is too great, especially for young men who follow their friends through the swinging doors. I have cast out my demon by God's grace, but I beg you not to let others fall by the wayside."

"We won't!" someone called from the back.

"God bless you, brother," the reverend said. As Mr. Pippen took a seat, the black-clad minister held up his hands. "Let us pray."

After the prayer the men drew hymnbooks from the pews and held them with long familiarity as they sang loud and stirring hymns, men's voices lifted together in strength and vibrance. Johann sang, but quietly, so his voice would not attract attention. He sang second tenor with the German men's choir, the Maennerchor of Columbus, and he knew from experience that people would stop to listen if he sang out. Even in his own church, he was careful to blend in so as not to distract from the worship.

Another pastor from elsewhere stood to give a speech. After a few more fervent declarations from individual men about the sad effects of drink on men they knew, the Reverend Robertson dismissed them. "Go and serve the Lord, and ask everyone you know to oppose the saloon."

A few men strode out with the preoccupied look of those who have business to attend. But many remained, talking in knots scattered through the pews.

"Good morning, brother." A man with pox scars on a friendly, broad face extended his hand to Johann. "Are you new to Westerville? I don't recognize your face."

"Yes, sir. Here on temporary business. John Green, pleased to meet you." Johann felt a pang of guilt. He did not like to misrepresent himself, but the name Giere was too well known for him to risk using it.

"Well, I'm mighty glad to see you here. It's an urgent cause."

"Yes, sir." Johann listened as the man went on to tell his own story about a grandfather ruined by drink. Close behind them, another small group of men was talking, and Johann found himself distracted by their mutterings.

"It's not right," one of them said in an intense half whisper. Another shushed him and the conversation fell quieter for a minute before rising to be audible again.

"What if Corbin won't leave?"

"There are ways to ensure that he does. The survival of the college may depend on it."

"Some men are more stubborn than others. He looks like an obstinate one who won't be persuaded easily."

"Then we persuade with fists. Or other forceful means."

Johann stole a look behind him at the men, then turned back and nodded as if fascinated by his own conversation with the pock-faced man.

The mutterers behind him were young: in their early twenties at most. Perhaps that was not so surprising. Young men were full of big talk.

One of them paused but then continued after Johann turned away. He had the kind of nasal baritone that carried farther than intended, a voice for whom a "whisper" was another man's normal volume. "The law does not give us enough recourse. It should not be legal for him to open here, against our will, and thumb his nose at the citizens."

"And at Otterbein too," another added. "Some situations call for emergency measures."

Were they Otterbein students? They certainly spoke like college men, all formal phrasing and pretty speeches while they discussed the use of force.

"Let's go outside," another said. "It's too close in here. We need to speak further." They went out, putting on their neat bowler hats, exiting into the early heat of the summer morning.

Johann considered following them. No, it would be too obvious and he would not overhear anything more if they saw him. He smiled at the pock-marked man and thanked him for sharing his thoughts, then took his leave a few moments later.

Outside, the sun beat down on his shoulders and made him thirsty for a glass of lemonade from his mother's kitchen, or a crisp, light lager straight from the cool barrels at the brewery. He had no taste for the harder liquor these men despised, and he understood why they hated it so. It was designed for intoxication in its potency and could turn the strongest men into despicable animals. But lager was not the same, no matter what Susanna Hanby said.

He quickened his pace and headed back toward the hotel. He must get back to Columbus and turn in an initial report, but he would be back as soon as his brewery duties allowed. The story of the saloon was getting more interesting by the hour. He would not forget the faces of those young men in the church, at least the two he had seen in his quick glance backward. That clique bore watching.

Mr. Reinhardt put on his glasses and inspected the article. After a minute or two, he laid it on the desk and tapped on it. "Excellent. Concise but vivid, unusual, with a whole town up in arms. I'll run it tomorrow and also wire it to the *New Yorker Staats-Zeitung*."

"What?" Johann leaned forward in his chair and took his writing back just as Mr. Reinhardt made a futile grab for it. "It's not a crime article."

"But it shows your talent. You want to get your foot in the door as a candidate so they don't hire someone before you."

"I do?" Johann asked dryly.

"Your talent is too great to hide under a bushel. I'm doing it for your own good. Give me that back."

Johann hesitated, then handed over the article. "Very well. But don't tell anyone."

Mr. Reinhardt chuckled. "You'll have to tell them when you're packing your bags."

"A very unlikely event." The mixture of adrenaline, longing, and guilt made him twitchy and he got to his feet. "I must go back—our brewmeister wants to talk to me."

"Give me just a moment more." Mr. Reinhardt took off his glasses and laid them on the desk. "You love reporting the news. I know you do."

"Yes, sir."

"Why?"

"Because people need to know what crimes and injustices are happening around them."

"Why?" Mr. Reinhardt prodded.

He masked his irritation. "Because we live in a democracy,

and the people can't govern themselves well if they don't know the truth about the world we live in. What if our rich citizens never hear of the poverty and suffering of the rest of the city? Why should they ever give to charity or vote for reform?" He had grown emphatic and fervent, which made him feel foolish when he stopped for breath. Mr. Reinhardt knew him too well.

But the editor smiled. "Very good reasons. And why would you want to be a brewer?"

Johann was silent.

"There is only one answer—to please your father. I am right, yes?"

Johann stood up. "It's more than that. My father already lost one brother in the War, and another long ago in Germany. I'm the only Giere left to carry on the name."

"Your uncle Fritz was my friend too, God rest his soul. But you can't let his sacrifice turn you away from a God-given gift and path to serve."

"Who's to say it's God-given? God asks me to honor my father."

"Men are not given talents so they can bury them."

This line of argument made Johann uneasy. It was true—his allegiance to God was higher than even his duty to his father. But discerning the will of God for his future was no easy feat. "How do we know that we aren't simply using the Almighty as an excuse to justify our own selfish desires?"

"You watch and you listen and you pray." Mr. Reinhardt sounded gruff, as if the topic had become too personal. He stood and began to collect pages from the top of his desk and the cabinets behind him. "I'm confident it will become clear."

Johann opened the office door and stepped out.

"You're not a brewer, Johann." Mr. Reinhardt's voice carried out to him over the clack of the press.

Johann closed the door as if a flimsy piece of wood and glass could shield him from the lure of New York.

Nine

June 30th, 1875

To George Leeds
Union Center, Ohio

Dear George,

We have found the children and wish to take them in as our own. In order to do so, we ask you to come assert your paternal rights to remove them from the orphanages. We will pay your train fare and all expenses to Columbus. Please write and let us know when you will arrive. Also, please inform me if you have any news of my sister's whereabouts. Have pity on my distress at her disappearance.

Best,
Susanna Hanby

July 3rd, 1875

To Susanna Hanby
Thirty-One State Street

Westerville, Ohio

I got your letter. I'm not going to do what you want. Your sister left the children with the orphanage and it is not my fault if she left her own children. Let them go to better mothers who dont run off like loose women. She didnt tell me nothing about where she went.

Geo. Leeds

She folded the letter once, twice, three times, into a tiny square as if she could fold it out of existence.

"What is it?" Her uncle held out one strong, knobby hand for the letter.

She handed it over, and he unfolded it and scanned the creased paper in silence.

"What will we do?" she asked. "He refuses. They'll send the children away and we'll lose them." The thought seared her like a hot iron. And how dare George speak of her sister so, in writing, even? Loose woman, indeed. Susanna would swear in a court of law that she did not believe her sister would do such a thing. The more she reflected on it, the more likely it seemed that no other man had been involved at all.

Her tight-laced corset was hurting her and she could not get enough air. She just prayed Rachel was still alive.

"Don't be too dismayed," Uncle Will said, his deep-set eyes gentle under white brows. "They won't send the children out for at least a few weeks, maybe longer. We'll think of something."

"I must visit them again. They can't think I've left them to stay there, especially in that horrible place where they're keeping Clara and the boys."

"We'll go visit in three more days. The Independence Day celebrations are over now, and the traffic in and out of the city will be thinner. But we can't go too soon or we will look overly eager and arouse the housekeeper's suspicions—the one at the Hare Home. If she thinks we're trying to take the children, she'll ban us from the premises completely."

"I feel as if I'll burst with the wait."

"Why don't you go down to the store and get some candy to save for our visit? Remember, I told the housekeeper we would bring her some. We must stay in her good graces. Then I'll get one of our hams and we can smuggle some in for the children. Candy for the matron, but real food for the children."

"You're very good to us." She was subdued at the thought that he would also be sacrificing a good chunk of one of the two smoked hams she had seen in the cellar. But he had told her several times that there was a year's harvest in the barn, what with all the church contributions.

"You're my family, and so are Rachel and her children."

———•◦•———

The confectioner's window brimmed with colorful candies: gaily wrapped toffee, chocolate bars with curlicued logos, powdered jellies and peppermints, green and blue lollipops. Inside was a child's magical world of neat boxes, bins full of hard candy, and tantalizing treats stuck up on countertops.

"The children will love it in here when we bring them

back." Auntie's delicate face brightened under its fine overlay of wrinkles.

How Susanna wished she had the same strong faith in the children's return—she had tried to summon it, but fear kept slipping into her thoughts. It was so hard to wait. She had to try to be more like her aunt.

Susanna poked through the bins by the window, scooping at the candies with the wide paddles, watching the swirl of their pink and white wrappers. "Can we bring a little toffee? Wesley likes it."

"Don't be disappointed if the children don't get the sweets."

"I'll hide a few pieces in my pocket." Susanna would not let that housekeeper eat it all. She shoveled ten pieces into a paper bag and folded down the top.

Outside the window three children had crowded up to watch with hungry interest. They were thin and dressed in old clothing, their sleeves frayed, the boy's breeches too short.

Susanna turned to her aunt. "I want to give them some candy too." She nodded toward the faces pressed against the window. "Who are they?"

"The Pippen children," her aunt said in a low voice. "They may not have a lot, but they're getting along all right now that their father is abstaining from drink. I know their mother. We can give them some peppermints if you wish."

The store bell rang and a woman entered, dressed in old, faded clothing like the children. She couldn't be above twenty-five, but she looked like she had been wrung out against a washboard too many times, her lips pale, her coloring wan. Still, she was not unhappy-looking.

"Good afternoon, Mrs. Hanby." Her smile momentarily

brightened her face, but her teeth were brittle and chipped, as if she had gone without milk and meat for long stretches.

"You're looking well, Mrs. Pippen," Susanna's aunt said. "Healthy and happy this fine day?" There was another question beneath the one on the surface, a woman-to woman question.

"Oh yes," Mrs. Pippen answered. "It's Mary's birthday, and she is getting a peppermint stick." The glow with which she pronounced the words made the rarity of such a treat clear. She smiled in the direction of the little towheaded girl outside, who was standing on tiptoe looking over the sill.

Susanna exchanged glances with her aunt. They would not give any candy to these children today and risk spoiling the pleasure Mrs. Pippen took in buying her own single piece.

"How lovely," Aunt Ann said warmly. "And I'm making muffins later today. I will have to bring Mary some. I know she loves them."

"Thank you," Mrs. Pippen said with the humility of one who has learned not to turn away offers of food.

She handed her money to the shop girl, who put her single candy in a small brown paper bag. "We'll see you later, then?" Mrs. Pippen asked Susanna and her aunt with a duck of her head.

"We'll stop by to visit," Aunt Ann said.

The door closed behind the wan woman, and Susanna saw her give the red-and-white candy to the beaming girl. The first thing the little girl did was break it in three and share it with her brother and sister. A pang struck Susanna as she watched them traipse down the street until they turned the corner.

Her aunt paid for the two small bags of candy for her nieces and nephews. A few minutes later they followed in the Pippen family's footsteps over the hard lumps of the baked street. The overcast day held in the heat, and the air swelled heavy on the brink of a storm.

Susanna took a handkerchief from her handbag and blotted her damp brow. "Do the Pippens have enough to eat now?"

"Yes, though a loaf of bread every now and then helps."

"But what about the saloon?" A whisper of headache slid across Susanna's temples. "Is their father likely to be tempted?"

"I certainly hope and pray he won't be."

"Well, I will pray the saloon meets an inglorious end and Corbin leaves town." Susanna took a breath and realized she had unconsciously crumpled the top of her paper bag in her fist.

"Try not to worry. You have enough on your mind." Her aunt placed a light hand on her shoulder. "Let God take care of it."

"Perhaps he'll take care of it through the good people of Westerville."

"Yes, perhaps." Her aunt looked preoccupied, rolling the top of her bag of candy as she walked.

"Some of the citizens seem very determined." Voicing the idea brought Susanna some relief. She couldn't object if they stopped Corbin by any means necessary, if it meant they would protect families like the Pippens.

The Pippen children shook her, in their thin, ill-dressed state. They were fragile, like her nieces and nephews. The similarity hurt her so keenly that she could only bear it with a fierce resolution. If she could not yet help her sister's children, if she had to bear this torturous wait, at least she could help these little ones. She would help her aunt bring them food and do anything she could to oppose the saloon.

Her return to the house brought a welcome surprise: Uncle Will took her out to the barn and showed her how to stitch leather.

"I'll punch the holes," he said, "and you can stitch the pieces together. But only until the school term starts in September—after that, it will be too much work for you."

She agreed to it, but only to pacify him. Whatever she said now, she would work as long as it took to support the children.

The double-needle technique took some practice but was not that difficult, especially with the pinprick holes he had already made for her. He pointed out how to get the stitches tighter with more tension, and she redoubled her efforts until he nodded.

"Very good," he said. "I can see the Hanby blood in you." He chuckled. "Have you had your fill of leatherwork yet? It must be getting close to midday."

"I'm just getting good at it. Will you go in and see if Auntie needs me? If not, I'll finish this before lunch." She indicated the jumbled heap of leather at her feet.

"Don't overexert yourself," he said gently, and left through the propped barn door.

It took her another twenty minutes to stitch the loops and the "keepers" for the ends of leather straps on the bridle. If she did this type of work for her uncle, he could double his production of harnesses.

A shadow fell over her. She started and looked up.

A young man stood in the doorway. "Good day, miss." He was about her age, with a boyish, freckled face and prominent front teeth.

"Good afternoon." She rose in surprise, still clutching the bridle in her left hand.

"You are a saddler?" His surprise was almost comical.

"I'm just helping my uncle with something simple."

"Your uncle? Then you are a guest here, I assume." He removed his brown bowler hat and examined her from head to toe with open admiration. Flustered, she hung the bridle on the wall.

"Will you be staying with the Hanbys for long?" he asked.

"Yes, I'll be attending classes at the college."

"Then welcome." He crossed to her and sketched a little bow. "I'm a fellow Otterbein student, Abel Wilson."

"A pleasure to meet you, Abel."

He stood gaping at her for a minute. What did he want?

His face went rosy, briefly erasing his freckles in a wash of pinkness. "I hope you don't think too ill of our town, after the ruckus yesterday."

"Not at all. I understand perfectly why the town is upset. The saloon is dangerous. And it may ruin Otterbein's reputation."

"Exactly! You understand, then?" He looked as if they had just exchanged the greatest of confidences.

It wasn't quite as dramatic as that, but she did have a feeling of kinship with him. "I couldn't agree more, Mr. Wilson. I'll rejoice to see Westerville rid of Mr. Corbin's business."

"Miss Hanby, I promise I'll do everything within my power to achieve your wish." He looked exalted, in a silly but touching way.

This meeting was beginning to feel awkward. "Are you looking for my uncle?"

"Uh—yes. My father wants to ask about a harness."

Good. Just as Uncle Will had predicted, they would get more business. And now she knew how to help. "If you don't mind waiting here for a moment, Mr. Wilson, I'll fetch him from the house."

"Not at all, Miss Hanby." He was dreamy-eyed as she moved past him, reminding her of some of the younger boys from her school at home. She smiled to herself as she walked to the kitchen door. Charming, silly boys. How was it that even in their naïveté, they knew right from wrong, while the German brewer, with years more experience, couldn't seem to discern it?

One thing was certain—if she brought her nieces and nephews home, they would never need to be told that decent people should oppose drinking. They had already seen ample evidence of that truth.

The thought wiped away her amusement at Mr. Wilson, her thoughts smearing into a blur like chalky residue on a blackboard. No good feeling could last—gaiety would always crumble into dust until the children were safe. She did not think she could wait three more days to see them.

Ten

THE NOTE LAY ON HIS DESK, ONLY A FEW LINES BUT
enough to make his pulse jump.

> *I received word from the Staats-Zeitung today. They
> agree with me about your talent. Now they want to
> see a crime article. Get one to me by Friday evening.
> —Reinhardt*

Impossible as it seemed, the big New York paper was interested in him. No doubt it helped that German language reporters
were scarcer than English ones, but still. He had thought Mr.
Reinhardt far too quick to send off that article about the saloon.
The last thing he expected was to actually hear back, and so soon.
Would he pursue it? The thrill and the challenge were too great
to resist. Perhaps Mr. Reinhardt was correct and God intended
Johann to be a reporter. Maybe his father would understand—but
the unlikeliness of that outcome made his heart sink. He would
worry about it later. Odds were still very low that it would happen, even if he wrote the best article he could. So now he needed
to find a good crime.

"Johann, *komm hier bitte*!" His mother's voice drifted faintly from downstairs. She might need his help with lifting the sauerkraut barrel, if she had finished packing it—her back sometimes pained her after too much exertion. He laid his pen next to the ink well and left his article drying on the desk.

When he arrived in the kitchen, Mrs. Thalberg was there at the table, and so was her daughter Lotte, all blond tresses and curved cheeks. He should have been more cautious—his mother had been setting too many such snares lately.

"Good evening," he said.

"Good evening," Lotte said in almost accentless English, as her mother said, *"Guten Abend."*

"I am going to Hulda's house tonight," Lotte said. "I thought since you are going to the Maennerchor, we might walk together, yes?" Her brown eyes sparkled—she had unusual coloring, with her fair hair and dark eyes, and she never lacked for a partner in the waltz or the polka at the *Biergarten* dances.

"It would be my pleasure," he said. She was a nice girl, and he would not let her see anything but kindness from him. It was not her fault if their mothers schemed day and night about their future wedding and had probably even planned the wedding dinner. They had given Lotte the wrong idea about him.

"You're going to rehearsal soon?" Lotte asked.

"Yes, in just a minute." He stared at the cuckoo clock in the hall and wished for the little wooden bird to pop out and create a diversion. Nice as Lotte might be, she had an embarrassing habit of singing to him if they were ever alone. She would pretend to ask for help with her singing technique, but she always chose love songs. She had a nice voice and did not need his help. She just wanted to fix those brown eyes on him and croon in

German under the moon. This might be diverting if he had feelings for her, but instead it made him want to move to New York immediately and avoid the whole subject, avoid ever having to hurt her feelings by telling her he was not swept away by passion for her.

The cuckoo ran out on its platform. "Time to go," he said.

His mother grinned at him and then at Mrs. Thalberg. They looked as if they were both about to laugh. He repressed a sigh and turned to hold the door for Lotte. "After you." She glowed and sailed out, and he gave his mother an exasperated look, where Mrs. Thalberg could not see him. His mother waved impishly. He shut the door harder than he should have.

They had barely made it out into the street and Lotte had just taken his arm when another call came. "Johann!"

It was his father, heading in their direction from High Street. He was effusive. "Johann, I just learned there will be a bottling demonstration at the Centennial next year. You will go, won't you? I can't leave for so long, but you could go. Oh, hello, Lotte." His father gave Lotte a quick kiss on the cheek. She might as well have been one of his own daughters, and indeed, all the girls were friends. Good thing Johann's two sisters had not been home just now, but off at the Turnverein for their knitting club. Had they been in the kitchen with the mothers, there would have been even more elbowing and cackling.

"If you bring back the latest bottling techniques," his father said with hope, "we could leap ahead of Hoster and the other brewers in our bottled beer."

"Yes, sir," Johann said. What else could he say? Would he be gone to New York City by then? Even the thought almost paralyzed him with guilt. He had to get out of here—the expectation of his father and the clinging hand of Lotte on his arm were too much.

"We'll have to discuss this more, Father, when I return from the Maennerchor." He managed to sound agreeable.

"And is the Maennerchor accepting pretty young women now?" His father wiggled his eyebrows. Johann would have liked to shake him if he didn't love him so much.

Lotte laughed. "No, sir, I am going to Hulda's house, and Johann is kind enough to take me there on his way."

"A good excuse, son." His father smiled.

Johann abruptly averted his gaze. "Well, we must be going if I'm to be on time to rehearsal."

His father bid them farewell and passed beyond them on his way to the house, which was gathering the shadows of twilight in its eaves.

Johann escorted Lotte down the side streets between neat brick cottages tucked under the characteristic pitched roofs of the German settlement. Had his father been able to tell how annoyed he was? He hoped not.

"I have heard a new song," Lotte said.

"Indeed?" A fatal mistake—he should have kept her talking. Now he was too preoccupied by his father to think of an evasion.

"I will sing it for you, and you can tell me how to sing better." She composed her face in a serene expression of longing. *"Mein Herr, ich kanst nicht leben . . ."*

As they walked down the bricked street, she sang about how she could not love him any more because her love was as high as the moon and as deep as the sea.

He could not actually squirm while walking, so the impulse turned into an inner twisting of his gut. He would rather be with the angry Miss Susanna Hanby, who thought him a devil, than listen to Lotte serenade him. At least Miss Hanby's anger had a kind of bracing, truthful quality to it, while this had the sickly sweetness of stale marzipan.

She finished.

"Very nice," he said.

"Was my technique flawed? I know it must be, to the ear of a singer like you."

"I don't have much training," he said. "Only what we got under Herr Lang. And perhaps a little from our choir director."

She smiled, probably remembering the eccentric ways of their grammar school music master. "But you sing so beautifully, just as you do everything so well."

"You're too kind." How could he discourage her from such flattery? She deserved a young man who would return her affection, and if she would forget Johann, she would probably find five eager suitors waiting on her. She did not need to abase herself so. "I think your singing is quite good and you do not need my advice."

"Thank you." She grasped his arm tighter and walked so close that her skirts brushed his trousers. He could not move away without being rude—he felt warmth move across his cheeks and counted in his head to take his mind off it. *Ein, zwei, drei, vier, fuenf...*

He made it to *dreiundvierzig* before she spoke—of course, it would never be a whole minute.

"The Hosters are holding a dance next week," she said.

The silence was painful. He had better say something. "I . . . I don't know if I will be in town." Perhaps some reason would present itself for him to be in Westerville.

"Oh." She sounded like a little girl who had dropped a lollipop in the dirt.

"I'm sorry." He hated to see her so crestfallen—he must find a gentle way to let her know he was not the man for her. Polite neutrality had not worked as he hoped it would.

"There is Hulda's house." She pointed out one triangular roof in the row.

He guided her in that direction, still conscious of her skirt brushing his leg.

When they reached the bottom of the stoop, she stopped without releasing his arm and turned to face him, too close, her dark eyes adoring. "I'm sorry our walk was so short. I always enjoy your company." She tilted her chin up.

Meine Guete!—she wanted him to kiss her. What should he do? He mustn't seem startled—that would hurt her feelings. He froze for a moment, then patted her arm and stepped back. "You're a good girl, Lotte."

She cast her eyes down and then bravely looked up again and mustered a smile. "Thank you for escorting me."

"Gute Nacht."

"Auf Wiedersehen," she said, and climbed the stoop.

He wanted to run but disciplined himself to keep his steps to a quick march. In only five minutes he made it up the street to the Maennerchor building and slipped in the door. He could hear the men singing in the great room at the end of the hall.

He would just have to pray for an answer, a clear direction that would not gravely hurt either Lotte or his father. Perhaps Westerville would be the answer for both. If that little group of young men at the church vented its illegal impulses toward Corbin, Johann might get that criminal story from the saloon clash. And New York would not contain any matchmaking mothers. But then he would miss his family dearly. And his father would never recover from losing Johann as a business partner.

The men's voices rose, tenors strong like trumpets, basses like the drums beneath in their deep power. With a sigh he let his uneasy thoughts float away into the music and walked into the room already singing.

———◆◆———

> *Dear Uncle and Auntie,*
>
> *I have gone to Columbus. Don't worry, please—I will be careful. I will return this evening with some news of Rachel, I hope.*
>
> *Fondly,*
> *Susanna*

Distant shouts of street vendors drifted to her hiding place, along with the crack of driving whips and the occasional rumble of wagons. She lingered in the shadow of the orphanage's gray wall, her hat tilted low.

By now her aunt and uncle would have found the note on her bed—she hoped they would not be too upset. She had no other choice. She could not wait idly in Westerville and let precious time slip away. And since George had refused to claim his children, finding Rachel was her only chance.

Here at the Hare Home, she could try to gather more

information about her sister from the older children. But her uncle was right to warn her that they could not return here too soon, in case the greasy housekeeper became suspicious of their intentions. To Mrs. Grismer, they must take care to seem only like distant family members easing their consciences with occasional deliveries of food.

Susanna would have to remain out of sight and hope she was early enough to catch the boys headed out to work.

Minutes passed, her heart thumping faster every time a pedestrian clumped by. She should not be so nervous. Even if some stranger asked what she was doing, Mrs. Grismer would be none the wiser to her presence on the street. But the long solo journey by train had weighed heavily on her. Her uncle would not be happy that she had used a little of her tuition money on her fares, and her aunt would be very worried at the idea of Susanna wandering unaccompanied through strange city streets. She was not accustomed to being anything less than forthright, and it nagged at her conscience, especially after their kindness to her.

A din from the street made her jump, but it was only a vendor's cart passing with a clatter of iron wheels. She must have been waiting nearly an hour by now. Would she have to sneak into the building? She swallowed against the tightness in her throat. Trying to appear casual, she climbed the steps, laid her hand on the iron door handle, and pulled.

Locked. It would not budge despite her best efforts. A figure passed by on the street and she froze. When the man did not look her way, she let out a breath and hurried back down the stoop to seek its partial cover from any prying eyes.

If she could somehow let the children know she was there, perhaps they could make an excuse to come out. Even if Wesley and Daniel were out working, Clara would be there. As the oldest, she was most likely to know more about Rachel anyway.

She cast about the dirt alley for a few pebbles. The window on the third floor, directly above her, was the one closest to where she had seen the girls working. She breathed a silent prayer for protection and cast her handful of gravel up as hard as she could.

It fell short, bounced from the second-floor window pane, then rattled on the ledge of the first-floor window. *What have I done? Is that Mrs. Grismer's parlor window?* She put a hand over her mouth and crouched down as low as she could under the window, flattening herself against the wall.

The click of a window lock and the screech of wood against wood froze her rigid.

"Who's there?" came the voice of the housekeeper above her.

But after a moment she heard the window close. Perhaps the woman was too heavy to lean far out the window, or perhaps the noise had simply not been enough to prompt such exertion. It could have been a squirrel, after all, scrabbling on the ledge. Or a rat. She shuddered.

She didn't move for another two or three minutes, fearful the housekeeper was still by the window. Then she crept over to another patch of gravel by the wall.

Did she dare? The odds of discovery would be twice as great if she again threw badly. She must throw in such a way that the gravel would not drop straight down. A parabola. She pushed out of her mind irrelevant fragments of geometry and inched farther down the alley to her best guess for the right trajectory. She would have to throw like a discus athlete to make that distance. That she would never do without divine aid. Her cousins had told her she threw well when skipping stones, but only "for a girl." *Help me, help me, please.* She took a deep breath, blood pounding in her ears, kept her eyes on the window, and slung the pebbles upward with all her might.

They clicked against the third-floor window and dropped with a faint patter on the other side of the alley. Victory! But would it matter?

She would have to stand exposed if any child up there was to have a chance to see her. She stepped away from the wall and strolled down the alley at a snail's pace, then turned and did it again, praying Mrs. Grismer had ceased to pay any attention to the window or the alley. Still nothing as she gazed up at the empty window. Now what?

A small, pale face appeared behind the glass. Susanna waved, a small, jerky motion for fear of attracting more attention. She stopped and stared upward, willing the child to remember her, or at least her yellow dress from her previous visit. It might be the first time in her life she was grateful to own only two dresses.

Then a more familiar outline appeared at the dirty window. Clara! Thank goodness, thank goodness. The young girl held up one finger solemnly in the age-old gesture meaning "Wait."

And wait Susanna did, for another fifteen minutes, sequestering herself around the back corner of the building next to a high backyard fence. At last the side door opened and her niece came out with a chamber pot in both hands. With a face that gave away nothing, Clara spotted Susanna and walked down the alley as if the chamber pot were her only mission.

Susanna held her breath as her niece set down the pot, took a small shovel from her belt, and began to dig a small hole a few yards behind the back fence. Susanna stayed in her place, hidden from the main building, while her niece walked with her back to the orphanage.

"Auntie! What are you doing here?" Clara whispered. "Don't come any closer. She might be watching me from the window."

"I'm going to find your mother." Susanna kept her voice almost inaudible, but she could tell Clara had heard. Joy lit her downturned face as she dumped the nasty contents of the pot into the shallow hole and covered it over with loose dirt.

Susanna murmured, "You must tell me anything your mother said that might help me find her."

"I only remember something she said about children not being allowed on some boats."

Boats? Had her sister gone down the Ohio River to a different state, or even abroad? But steamboats allowed children, of course, as did transatlantic ships. "Nothing else?" she asked in a hoarse whisper.

"Clara!" a sharp voice called from the house.

She jumped up with a start and grabbed the pot to return to the building.

A powerful urge swept through Susanna to snatch her niece and run. Everything in her wanted to shout, *"Wait!"* She clung to the fence to restrain herself. The sight of Clara's dress vanishing from view around the corner of the fence was like a blow to the chest.

She stayed there for a good five minutes after the door thudded closed behind her niece. This was no time for hysterics or self-indulgence. She must think of her task, keep her goal always ahead of her. Any further attempt at contact with Clara today might jeopardize her chances of ever getting them home.

Boats. She would assume the best, that it was possible to find

Rachel and that her sister had not gone far beyond her reach. At least the mention of travel implied that her sister might have eluded George successfully and was still alive. That is, if Rachel had ever made it to the boats, whatever they were.

The Scioto River could not possibly be the location of those boats: it was practically unnavigable with its treacherous sand bars and the rise and fall of its waters.

Then the closest possibility would be the canal docks.

Susanna would have to be a fool to go there unaccompanied—from what she had heard, only one type of woman wandered alone near the docks. She would be placing her virtue and perhaps her life in danger, and if something happened to her, who would find Rachel?

She could do only one more thing, at least for today. She could pay an errand boy to go to the canal office and hope he was honest enough to make it all the way there. He could post a notice asking for information from any witnesses who might have seen a woman matching Rachel's description. Susanna could use her uncle's name on the notice, and his postal address.

Well then, she would do it. And though it made her want to beat her forehead against the fence, she had little choice afterward but to return to Westerville and solicit her uncle's aid to make any further progress.

At least Clara had given her somewhere to begin.

Eleven

HER NOTE AND ABSENCE MIGHT HAVE CAUSED MORE uproar, except for the new note that had shown up on their doorstep while she was gone. She found it when she got back, lying open on the mantel.

Shut your mouth, Hanby, if you know what's good for you. Stay out of this saloon affair, or we'll give you cause to regret it.

"Auntie, what's this?" She couldn't conceal her shock.

"Oh, you weren't supposed to see that. Will was supposed to put it away." Her aunt sighed.

"Who do you think it is?" Susanna asked. The lettering was ugly, aggressive. "Does Uncle Will have any idea?"

"No." Her aunt took the paper and crumpled it into her pocket. "We can't even tell which side it's from. It could be from whiskey lovers who think Will's too outspoken against the saloon, or temperance men who think he's too mild and peaceable about Corbin."

"What will Uncle do?"

"Nothing. He used to get death threats while working with fugitives. It never changed him or silenced him."

Later that night, in her room, she heard her aunt and uncle argue. She winced at the intensity of their voices, rising clearly through the floorboards up to her bedroom: the strained hush of genteel people at odds. She had not imagined such a conversation between them—was she responsible for it?

Her uncle spoke. "If there's any chance at all, I must go see if I can find Rachel."

"But it's such flimsy evidence, dear. There must be a better way than combing every dock in central Ohio. Especially with all that's going on in town. You know I love Rachel—I would do anything to have her back. But I don't want you to exhaust yourself in a fruitless chase."

"It's all we have."

"What about the Corbin situation—doesn't it need your attention? No one else seems to be succeeding in getting him to see reason."

"It can wait another day, can't it?" He sounded weary. No wonder her aunt was concerned for his health.

Silence fell. She could almost see him rub his brow.

"I suppose," her aunt said. "But every day the saloon remains here is another temptation for someone who might not be strong enough to resist." From the worry in her voice, Susanna knew she must be thinking of the Pippens.

"Still, we can't be hasty," her uncle said. "Or let our emotions rule the day. Too many in town are already drunk on their excessive zeal for temperance."

Who did he mean—what was "excessive" zeal? Surely not the ordinary citizens who opposed it. They had every reason to oppose it, and vigorously. Her uncle had always been a stalwart champion of temperance. He had been an example to her, to her whole family. Was his conviction fading? Unsettled, she got to her feet and went to the small table, where she had laid her uncle's botany book. She didn't like this inadvertent eavesdropping at all.

Good, they had lowered their voices to a murmur and she could no longer make out what they said. Well, she would look at the book anyway to take her mind off the whole painful mess and hope distraction would bring on sleep.

A page of the book rustled as she turned it, now the only sound in the late-night quiet of the house. The candle burned in its old-fashioned holder on her desk. She would buy more candles and lamp oil with her earnings once she started her housekeeping work for the ladies' dormitory. Without that cleaning position her uncle had obtained for her, she could not have afforded to attend college at all, not even with her meager savings.

The beautiful floral drawings in the book captivated her: the arc of a petal, the colors bright in one illustration after another. This must have been an expensive book, back when her cousins had to buy it for their studies. And now Susanna would get to use it herself. She could hardly wait to study botany when the semester began in the fall. But would Rachel be here to share Susanna's excitement at what she learned, her new knowledge of the things they could grow in the garden?

She closed her eyes and touched the tips of her fingers to her forehead to press away the ache of the sadness. She had to know about Rachel. When she and her uncle next went to the Hannah Neil Mission the day after tomorrow, she would ask the matron if Rachel had given any hint as to where she might be going. Perhaps there would be more than just the cryptic mention of boats.

She would never sleep if she did not think of something else. She kept reading. Linnaeus, the famous scholar of plants. Oh, this was interesting. He had designed a flower clock, something to do with the daylight and when each blossom opened. Apparently one could plant carefully selected flowers in a circle to mimic a clock face. According to the time of day, as the light grew or faded, the petals of each variety of flower would open in its turn—

A great clap of thunder shook the whole house and rattled the windows. She jumped so she almost slid off her chair. Wrapping her dressing gown around her, she rushed to the window of her bedroom. There was no lightning across the midnight black of the sky, no moon, no light at all—the inky clouds had covered everything.

Faint shouts sounded from the north side of the house. The commotion grew louder. Small orbs of light glowed behind gauze curtains and drifted across the fronts of neighboring houses, carried by dark figures.

"Susanna." Her aunt peeked in the bedroom door. "Can you see from here? What's happening? I saw the lanterns."

"I can't tell—just people hurrying up the street."

Her aunt raised the window so the sounds from below grew more distinct.

"The saloon!" one yelled to another. "Corbin's done something. We should have taken away his guns."

"Goodness," Aunt Ann said. "Perhaps we should go see. I hope no one is hurt."

"Yes, let's go." Susanna crossed to the old wardrobe, peeled off her dressing gown, and substituted a day dress and light shawl over her shift. In the dark no one would see that she was without a corset.

Her aunt did not appear perturbed by her makeshift attire. "I must go dress too. I'll meet you downstairs in five minutes."

"All right. And Uncle?"

"He told us to go ahead and he'll follow as soon as he's decent."

They joined the scattered figures converging on the intersection of State and College. Aunt Ann had brought a lantern that cast enough light for their feet when she held it low, though it left their faces dim. Streetlamps were few, as yet, even in the town center. Other lanterns blinked in and out of view along the street as they bobbed in the hands of pedestrians.

There were thirty or forty people gathered in front of Corbin's saloon. Susanna peered through the darkness as they approached but did not see anything unusual. There was a musty, strong odor.

"Gunpowder," her aunt whispered to her. "And plenty of it. Goodness."

The one black iron lamppost on the street near Corbin's door shed ghostly light on the building. The glass of all the windows was broken, with a few shards still poking angrily from each frame.

"What happened?" her aunt asked the woman who had waved her fist at Corbin the morning the bells rang against the saloon.

"Mr. Corbin appears to have had a lesson." The woman pointed up at the roof.

Susanna took in a breath. The whole roof had separated from its moorings and sat crooked, though it was still attached to the building.

"Blew up the roof a good four inches, I'd say," said the woman with a quick jerk of her chin toward the damage.

"Was Mr. Corbin hurt?" Aunt Ann looked concerned.

"No." The woman contemplated the cocked roof. "He must have been at the other end when the blast went off. And I suppose it's for the best—we don't want him dead, just gone."

"Well, I'm glad he wasn't hurt," her aunt said. "And really, it's too bad, to damage a fine building like that. Widow Clymer will be very upset when she hears."

"A building is worth less than the souls that might be saved if Corbin leaves." The woman spoke with conviction, and privately, Susanna had to agree.

Shrill curses rang out through the broken windows. Corbin was no more polite in his language than he had been before. A single faint light moved through the saloon. Then the tall, skinny man leaned his head out the front window and shouted to all the onlookers, "You may have broken the rum bottles, but the whiskey bottles are still here. I'll be open for business in the morning. I'm an American, and I won't be pushed around!"

No one responded. He retreated back into his building and the light continued to bob through it.

Reverend Robertson stepped out and turned to face the crowd. "Friends! This vigilante behavior is not the answer—we must be peaceful in our protest."

There was a murmur of agreement.

"Permit me to read to you the following petition drawn up by myself and several of the other ministers. We ask you all to stop by and sign it at the Methodist church tomorrow."

He unrolled a furled sheet of paper. The boy beside him held up the lantern to the page and the reverend read in a loud voice.

"We, the undersigned citizens of Westerville, hereby solemnly pledge that we will not patronize any dry-goods merchant, grocery man, physician, lawyer, mechanic, or any other businessman that will frequent, encourage, or furnish aid to a liquor saloon in Westerville."

A few spectators clapped. "I'll sign it!" "And I!" A buzz ran through the little crowd.

"We'll sign it, won't we, Aunt Ann?"

"Of course," her aunt said. "Much better to use legal means than vandalism if we wish Corbin to leave."

Susanna was not so sure about that. Yes, in principle, but with a man as bent on his own way as Corbin, a mere petition seemed a flimsy thing.

She was sorry for the old widow who owned the building, but she couldn't summon any regret that someone had given Corbin a very serious warning. It was worth the risk, if he decided to leave and stop endangering the weaker men in the area.

There seemed to be a lively debate going on among the clusters of townsfolk on the street as to the best way to proceed.

"Ann!" Her uncle made his way toward them through the gathered people. When he reached them, bearing his own lantern, he was slightly out of breath but still possessed of his dignity. "I've asked Reverend Robertson to come meet me at the house.

My dear, will you see if you can find the other ministers, plus Professor Hayworth and the college president? Any of them you can find, send back to the house."

"Yes, dear." Her aunt squeezed his hand, with a concerned glance at his tired face, and threaded a path through the crowd.

"Susanna, do you mind going back to the house and waiting for us there? That way someone will be at the door to receive anyone who arrives before I return."

"Of course, Uncle."

But as it turned out, her aunt reached home only minutes after Susanna.

"You should go back to sleep, dear." Aunt Ann shut the door behind her and hung her bonnet on a wall peg.

Susanna lit the lamp on the mantel. "I'm not tired, Auntie. Let me get some tea for the guests." With seven or eight esteemed citizens on their way, it was the right moment to open the special canister of tea. Any help she could offer eased the guilt of having burdened her aunt further by her unexpected trip to Columbus.

"Very well. Thank you." Her aunt stepped into the kitchen to get the mugs and Susanna followed. Was her aunt angry with her? She did not seem so, but Susanna felt like an ingrate nonetheless.

The townsmen stumped in one by one, some looking preoccupied, others alert.

Uncle Will came last, with Professor Hayworth and the president of the college. Susanna brought them their mugs of tea, which they received with nods or quiet thanks.

"Gentlemen, I don't like the mood of some of our citizens," her uncle said. "This conflict mustn't go any further."

"Agreed," the president said. He was younger than her uncle, a solid, middle-aged man with brown hair and old-fashioned side whiskers. "It can only hurt the college's reputation further if there is arson or scandal—Westerville must remain a peaceful, safe town."

"Not to mention the danger to anyone in the saloon." Reverend Robertson set his teacup down. "Driving out Corbin is all well and good, but not in a hearse, please."

A subdued ripple of chuckles ran through the room.

"I have another suggestion." Professor Hayworth tried to straighten his age-curved back against his chair. Bent or not, he was still impressive with his learned air and his rumble of a bass voice. "Corbin won't leave unless he is compensated—he won't be willing to take the loss. But if we offer to buy out his stock, then he will get his capital back to go elsewhere."

"I hate to throw good money to a peddler of ruin," one of the other ministers said.

Her uncle walked to the mantel to turn up the lamp, dispelling some of the gloom from the corners. "Still, buying him out may be our best chance to avoid a worse alternative."

The minister groaned.

"I'm afraid I don't have material resources to contribute to that effort." Her uncle's humble statement paradoxically gave him even more gravitas. "But I'll go present the offer to Corbin, should we elect to do so."

"I'll pledge half of the money," the college president said.

"Mrs. Hanby, may I borrow a sheet of paper?" Professor Hayworth removed the stub of a pencil from his lapel pocket. "And please accept my compliments on the fine tea."

Aunt Ann tore a sheet from the kitchen ledger to give to the professor. He scratched figures. "Give me a moment, gentlemen, while I estimate the cost of Corbin's goods."

The general conversation proceeded to planning and money contribution, until finally, the men chose her uncle and Professor Hayworth to present the offer to Corbin.

"No time like the present," her uncle said.

"I agree." Professor Hayworth stood and took his cane from the wall. "Not a moment to waste to keep this affair from escalating."

The men tramped out of the house, wished one another good-bye, and headed home through the deep night. Her aunt kissed her uncle on the cheek as he took a lantern and followed the professor outside.

When they had gone and silence fell once more, her aunt walked to the stairs. "Don't stay awake too long, Susanna," she called softly over her shoulder. "And don't fret. Your uncle is good at calming angry men."

Susanna seated herself in the rocking chair at the window and watched the lantern lights recede up State Street.

It wasn't fear for her uncle keeping her awake. She had faith in him. Nor was it even the faint smell of gunpowder setting her on edge.

She had more pressing concerns than the saloon. The day after tomorrow, they would go back to Columbus and see the children, bring them food, and reassure them. And on this visit, she must find out more about Rachel's whereabouts. If she did not, her time with the children would run out all too soon.

Twelve

Someone knocked at the front door. It was only eight a.m.—who could want them at this hour? Aunt Ann raised her eyebrows at Susanna and wiped her hands on a towel before removing her apron and walking down the hall. Susanna trailed a few steps behind.

Perhaps it was Corbin, reconsidering after further reflection. She hoped so. Her uncle had been quite downcast the night before last, when he returned from his midnight meeting and told them of Corbin's vehement refusal of their offer to buy out his saloon.

Aunt Ann swung open the door to reveal the face of a male stranger who wore a badge. "U.S. Marshal, ma'am. I have a message from Columbus."

The blood drained from Susanna's face. *Lord, not something about the children.*

Her aunt scanned the paper he handed her and also went pale.

"What is it?" Susanna could hardly get out the question.

"It's a warrant for Will's arrest." Aunt Ann's voice quavered.

"I'm sorry, ma'am. It may come to nothing. Just an arraignment—there may not even be a trial."

"But what has he done?" Susanna asked.

"Incited a riot, according to the charge. But it's not just him—there are six others too."

"Probably all the ministers in town." Aunt Ann folded her arms across her bodice and her eyes flashed, making her look younger. "Thanks to Mr. Corbin."

"I'm afraid so." The marshal sounded grave, but Susanna detected a hint of boredom beneath his formality. "Where is Mr. Hanby?"

"In back, working." Aunt Ann did not step out of the way.

"I'll just go around the house, then, and get him."

"No!" Her aunt's forehead creased and her chin firmed. "Let me tell him. I'll bring him here."

"Don't tell him to run, Mrs. Hanby. It'll make it worse."

"Don't be ridiculous." She didn't flinch from his gaze. "He has done nothing wrong and has no reason to hide or evade justice." She turned away, head held high, and walked back to the kitchen. The door rapped against its frame, and a few minutes later Susanna heard the rustle of their passage and the tap of the cane back down the hall. Uncle Will did not look concerned, though Aunt Ann's face was tight.

"Are you going to place me in handcuffs?" Uncle Will almost smiled.

The marshal at last looked ashamed of himself. "No, sir. I see you're not a risk for flight."

"I'll come quietly." Uncle Will chuckled, but Susanna saw tears in her aunt's eyes.

"Now, Ann," he said, "don't take on. It's nothing. I'll be back before you know it. In fact"—he looked at Susanna—"don't interrupt our plan to go to the orphanages. Both of you should pack the children's food and come with me on the train. No sense in wasting a trip."

"They will not be permitted to speak to you on the train, sir." The marshal sounded apologetic.

"They're probably tired of my talk anyway." He laid a hand on his wife's back. "Peace, my dear. I'll meet you at the station."

"It reminds me of the last time." Her aunt's hand shook as she handed his hat to him.

"Fifty years ago," he said. "Ancient history. And this judge doesn't use floggings." He took his hat and embraced her. She took his lined face in her hands and kissed him gently on the lips.

The marshal examined his shoes and cleared his throat. Uncle Will gave her aunt a last squeeze and stepped forward to maneuver himself down the stairs with his cane.

"Take heart, Susanna," he called back. "We'll get it all straightened out in the city."

Johann peered left and right out his front door. He had only a few blocks between his home and the streetcar stop, but Lotte had a way of springing out when he least expected to see her. Good, the coast was clear. With hurried steps, he made his way to High Street, looking over his shoulder to be sure no pretty blond girl was pursuing him.

When the horse car came, he paid the fare and sank into the hard seat. He would get to the *Westbote* soon, but first he had to run even farther uptown to speak with the police and get their weekly crime report. At Capitol Square he stepped out of the slow-moving omnibus and kept to a brisk walk up High Street.

The heat simply would not relent—still no rain for almost a month now. The leaves of the trees on the square were parched. He took off his hat and waved it at his face, but even that slight movement of air was hot and gave no relief.

A large group of people was approaching from the north, swallowing other pedestrians in their midst and continuing toward him. They crossed the street, causing a few shouts and protests from drivers who stopped their carriages rather than run the people down. There were about two hundred, he guessed. He walked as quickly as he could to intercept them. Now they were only yards away. The handful of men in front were being guided—almost prodded—by police officers. They were under arrest, it seemed, though not handcuffed.

The white hair and beard of one of the captives was familiar. Mr. Hanby from Westerville! And the man in the black-and-white collar next to him was the Reverend Robertson from the Presbyterian church there. What were they doing? He had missed some important news, by thunder, and he needed to learn it. They seemed to be headed for the courthouse. By tomorrow, whatever it was would be all over the *Dispatch*. Well, he would simply have to write a better and more informed article about it.

The crowd following them looked familiar too. Those were Westerville women, he was sure of it.

And there, marching with her head high, was the lovely and fierce Miss Hanby, together with her aunt, the petite elderly woman.

He stepped in line with them. "Good morning, Miss Hanby."

The young lady's delicate eyebrows rose. "You, sir. What a surprise."

Not the friendliest welcome he had ever received. "Is something the matter? I saw Mr. Hanby with the officers."

"He has been wrongfully accused and arrested by your confederate, Mr. Corbin."

He held up his hands to ward off her words, then said in a low murmur, "Don't forget your promise, Miss Hanby. I'm not Mr. Corbin's ally and must not be seen in that light."

She looked unrepentant. The elderly lady glanced at him sidelong.

"If you would be so kind"—he made himself very humble—"as to tell me the charges against Mr. Hanby and the others, I can ensure the *Westbote* gives a fair account of whether the accusation has any grounds."

"We have another errand as well, young man." White, tense lines grooved the elder woman's face. "We can't stay long."

She must be beside herself. How sad for a wife of decades to see her husband hauled off like livestock to a judge. He wished he could help in some way.

"Here are the charges," Miss Hanby said. "Corbin accuses my uncle and the other preachers of inciting a riot."

"That gathering I witnessed on State Street?" He couldn't help scoffing. Journalistic objectivity aside, that was a laughable claim, if it was indeed Corbin's intent.

"I'm not quite sure—it does seem ludicrous to call it a riot." The young woman tucked a curl behind her ear with a quick, uncertain motion. "But a charge of gunpowder went off the night before last and damaged the saloon. Maybe he intends to draw a connection between the initial meeting and the violence."

An explosion—a crime! The Westerville story had just turned criminal. While he had been scanning the mundane headlines in

LOVELIER THAN DAYLIGHT

Columbus, he had been missing the exact story he needed: not only a crime, but an unusual one. Was God sending him to New York, as Reinhardt said? The hairs on his neck prickled—if it were true, God was very close indeed.

Susanna drew her aunt closer and lifted her chin. "And now we must be going. We have much important business." She fiddled with the clasp of her handbag.

He might have smiled at the loftiness of her phrase, except for the sadness that shadowed her green eyes and belied the independence of her speech. Her straw hat framed her face in a rural way that would be charming were she merry, but instead brought poignance to her attempt to be strong and worldly.

"Are you not accompanying your uncle to court?"

"He has asked us not to—he says our business is more important and nothing will happen today as they are all innocent. I believe him," Miss Hanby said firmly. "And so I'll do as he wishes."

"Then may I escort you?"

"You may not."

Even half-expecting such a refusal did not remove its jarring effect. Her aunt turned her head away as if to watch the rest of the marchers, but he thought he saw chagrin on her refined face. She was surprised, then, by her niece's rudeness, which meant that as Johann suspected, such behavior was not typical of the pretty girl.

"I see," he said.

"I wish you did, Mr. Giere."

He glanced around, but no one seemed to notice her use of the name. If she were not careful, though, she would ruin his anonymity.

"Our errand today would not be necessary but for the effects of liquor on my sister's family." Miss Hanby's gaze held an accusation. What had happened to the conscience-stricken, eccentric girl he had quite liked, wielding her scissors among her blue flowers?

"I'm sorry to hear it, Miss Hanby." He resolved to kill her with kindness.

"Young man, will you do one thing for me?" the elderly lady asked, considerably more mannerly than her niece.

"Gladly."

"Will you indicate to me the exact location of the court so we may find my husband there after our business is done?" She looked pale, as if the last thing she wished was to leave her husband's side. But Mr. Hanby must have a reason for not wanting her there. Perhaps she wouldn't take it well should things go poorly in court.

"Yes, ma'am." He stated the directions for her.

"Thank you, sir." The two women swept away without a backward glance. After a minute of gazing after them, he pivoted on his heel and chased down the street after the rapidly receding Westerville delegation.

Inside the courtroom the atmosphere was charged. People lined up against the walls in tense silence while the judge ruled on several initial hearings and charges. Finally, he called for the delegation from Westerville.

The lawyer for the preachers stood up. "I ask your honor to dismiss these baseless charges immediately. There was no riot in Westerville, and therefore these men cannot have incited one."

"But I understand," the judge said, peering down over the edge of his raised desk, "that there was an explosive set off and damage done to the plaintiff's property. Where is the plaintiff?"

Another lawyer stood. "He was unable to leave his business to attend, Your Honor, especially after the losses he sustained from the riot."

"Riot?" one of the Westerville folk called incredulously from the back.

"Order!" the judge said, and banged his gavel. "I understand all you men are employed in the preaching profession. Stand up, please, those accused."

The seven men rose, Mr. Hanby leaning on his cane, the younger men more limber but less serene.

"You men of the cloth, are you persecuting this businessman because he does not share your faith?" The judge's face grew ruddy.

Himmel, that was not the most professional question Johann had ever heard from a judge. What could he be thinking, to ask something so loaded? Perhaps the judge was one of the so-called freethinkers, like Robert Ingersoll, who thought everyone should be free of the burden of religion.

"No, Your Honor, these gentlemen are not persecuting any-one," the lawyer for the defense finally said, looking stymied. "They committed no wrong and had nothing to do with the charge of gunpowder."

"Or so they say." The judge almost sneered. "I've heard about the good people of Westerville and their friendliness to unbelievers. Mostly United Brethren there, are you not?"

One of the preachers stepped forward. "Yes, Your Honor. But we are Methodists and Presbyterians too."

"Birds of a feather," the judge said. "I am going to set a

bond, one hundred dollars for each of you. Or you may serve time in jail until your trial."

The preachers seemed aghast, and Johann would have been too. That was a steep bond for men who made the unimpressive salaries of ministers.

"Well, can you produce the bond? Or shall I have the officers make straight your path to the jail cell?" The judge chuckled.

The lawyer for the ministers stepped forward. "Your Honor, I have assurances that the bond will be posted."

"Then I must see it. Right here." The judge stabbed at his desk with a hooked finger.

The lawyer turned to the courtroom. "You heard him, ladies and gentlemen. Those who spoke to me beforehand must now present the bond."

One by one, men and women moved away from the walls and shuffled to the front. One put a bill on the desk, another carried what looked like a bank check. After they had all filed up and back, Johann guessed there must have been forty of them.

The judge was left hunched and glum over a stack of bank notes and even coins.

"This seems to be adequate," he said. "I will have the treasurer make an account before they are released."

A ripple of indignation went around the walls. "They are innocent," a woman said in a voice that carried to the front.

"Order!" The judge rapped again, hard. "I'll have you locked up for contempt if you cannot keep order. This hearing is adjourned." He jumped to his feet and stalked out behind the bench, his black robe flapping around his ankles.

The officers took the seven ministers out through a side

door. Johann tried to follow, but they barred his way with a steely refusal.

He slipped back down the aisle and out the main doors. He would have to go tell his father that he was going to Westerville this evening. He could check on Corbin, after the news of the explosion. But more importantly, he would be on the watch for whatever came next.

Thirteen

SUSANNA RAISED A HAND AND KNOCKED ON THE door of Hare House. The loose knocker from their last visit had now ripped off its screws, leaving blank patches and holes in the gray paint.

"Yes?" The same suspicious voice greeted them when the door opened a sliver to reveal one small, fleshy eye.

"Good morning, Mrs. Grismer. I'm Miss Hanby—you remember, the aunt of the Leeds children? We have brought some candy for you to give to them as you see fit."

She waited anxiously for some response, then the door swung open to reveal the stout woman in her dirty apron. "Well then, Miss Hanby, you come on in."

They walked past her into the crumbling hall, Susanna repressing a shudder.

Gazing at the grim surroundings, Aunt Ann looked appalled, but after an instant she summoned a cheerful expression. "Mrs. Grismer, I don't believe I've had the pleasure, but you met my husband, Mr. Hanby, recently."

"Oh yes," the housekeeper said with a wide, greasy grin.

"Charming man, delightful." Her mouth gnashed up and down with every word as if she were chewing instead of speaking.

"Will you tell me more about the Hare Home while Susanna visits her niece and nephews? It seems like a cause in need of philanthropy. Perhaps I can speak to the ladies in our church about possible contributions." Mrs. Hanby was so gentle that the wary look on Mrs. Grismer's face melted away, to be replaced by something even less pleasant—avarice.

"That would be just fine, Mrs. Hanby. Let's go to my sitting room where you might be more comfortable. Miss Hanby, you remember where the children are?" Susanna suspected the housekeeper didn't wish to exert herself to walk up the stairs.

"Yes, Mrs. Grismer." Susanna would not wait for a further invitation. Pressing the large handbag against her side, she smelled the salty piquancy of the ham her aunt had cut into slices and wrapped in waxed paper. Thank goodness Aunt Ann had thought of a way to keep the delicious odor contained. Susanna couldn't be sure the ham would reach the children unless she personally saw them eat it.

The girls were at their pitiful needlework, though two or three of them sat together on a cot, speaking in hushed voices. They started and looked up with white faces when she entered.

"It's only I, Miss Hanby," she called softly. The room smelled of urine—poor girls. One of the smaller ones had probably lost control in the night—she knew how it happened with little children. She hoped the child had not been too harshly punished.

"Aunt Susanna!" Clara said, and jumped up. She stayed in place, though, as if frightened to leave her spot without permission. What had this woman been threatening to the children?

Walking over to them through the cavernous room, she embraced Clara. "Hello, my sweet girl," she said. "I have something for you." Clara knew better than to say anything about their last meeting.

"Where are Wesley and Daniel?" Susanna asked. "Out at work?"

"Wesley is at work. Daniel is too ill." Clara's face looked very gaunt. She pointed to a slight form slumped on a cot by the wall, yards away.

Susanna's stomach turned over and she grabbed Clara's hand. "Let's go see him."

When they reached his side, she saw that his skin had an unnatural grayish color and his eyes were closed. She couldn't see any motion but heard the faint rattle of breath in his chest. She hated to wake him, but he must eat while he could.

She knelt down next to his cot and laid her hand on his frail shoulders, glad to at least feel the slight rise and fall of his back. "Danny," she whispered. His eyelashes fluttered, dark against his pallid skin, and he looked up at her with Rachel's eyes. "Auntie," he said in a hoarse whisper.

Her eyes stung—*stop!*—the children were troubled enough as it was. She looked down and dug one of the ham bundles out of her bag. "Danny, you must sit up and eat, hurry." She reverted to his baby name in the surge of concern. He did not correct her—that worried her even more.

She helped him up and placed the wrapped ham in his lap, then handed a piece to Clara. "Try to eat it so the others don't see," she whispered. Her guilt threatened to swamp her. All thirty of the girls here needed this food badly, from their bloodless look. But she did not have enough. Perhaps her aunt would be able to convince Mrs. Grismer to allow the church to give them all a meal.

Clara turned her back to the other girls so they wouldn't see. She wolfed down the ham in shreds and gulps, not at all like the ladylike niece Susanna had known at the farm. "What about Wesley?" she asked when she had finished her piece. "And the other children?"

"I can leave you the rest of this for Wesley—and most importantly, for Danny. He must have meat to recover. I'm sorry we couldn't bring more, but we feared your housekeeper would take it from us." She wished she could have packed the whole ham in her handbag, but that simply would not have made it past Mrs. Grismer's vigilant eye.

Clara nodded. "Thank you." She leaned her head into Susanna's shoulder. "Can we leave here soon?"

She took a deep breath. "As soon as I can possibly arrange it." She wrapped one arm around each of the children while Danny continued to eat, picking at it with the impaired appetite of the consumptive. No, she shouldn't say that—it was not consumption, surely. He had coughed even on the farm, and he had never been around a consumptive, nor did his siblings appear affected.

The picture of her cousin Ben leaped into her mind, the handsome young man and brilliant musician whose cold-susceptible lungs had taken him too soon to the grave. And then Ben's brother Cyrus had died of a similar weakness the next year.

She would not accept the same fate for Danny—he was only a little boy. But a chill passed over her neck even in the stifling heat. She would never forget Aunt Ann's face, wracked with loss as she stood over her son Ben's simple coffin. His wife,

Kate, had left town rather than live with the painful reminders of Ben's presence. The next year Susanna hadn't attended Cyrus's funeral, and she was almost glad her aunt and uncle had preferred it that way—she could not imagine their agony at the second loss, so soon. God had gifted the Hanbys with many things, but not strong chests. And Danny was weaker than any of his cousins had ever been.

She hated the smell of rot and mildew in here—it could not be healthful.

"Can you put these in your pocket?" she whispered to Clara, holding out the other three pieces of ham.

"She might see it." Clara stared at the paper bundles. "I have seen her check pockets before. Here"—she took the brown bundles and tucked them in Danny's over-large trouser pockets—"if he lies down on them, I don't think she will find them. She never pays anyone any mind when they are sick."

A tinder flash of temper made Susanna press her lips together to restrain an indignant comment. It would do no good to make the children even more conscious of their plight. "Is Wesley still healthy?"

"He's hungry, but he's not ill." Clara's eyes were huge in her young face as she attempted to sound comforting.

That was even harder on Susanna's composure. She clutched her skirt and rose. "I must go, before Aunt Ann finishes her talk with Mrs. Grismer." She bent down and kissed first Clara's cheek, then Daniel's. "Daniel, be sure to hide that right away if anyone comes in."

"Yes, Auntie." He turned to the wall and lay down on his side to conceal the ham, pulling off a sliver and putting it in his mouth. He looked almost too tired to chew.

"Watch out for one another. We will come back for you." Susanna turned away, barely holding herself together, like a cracked egg that somehow manages to keep its shape.

"Good-bye, Auntie," Clara said. "Thank you."

She waved and blew them a kiss, then left through the splintered doorway and descended the stairs.

In the parlor she recued her aunt from the litany of Mrs. Grismer's complaints. They wished the housekeeper good day and promised to return with more sweets.

"But don't return too soon," the woman said. "I shouldn't allow you here, according to the regulations. I'm supposed to report visits like this so they can be stopped."

"Of course we won't make a nuisance of ourselves," Aunt Ann said in a careless tone quite unlike her. "Besides, too much candy would not be good for them. Perhaps we will return in a week's time? And then I could see if some of the other ladies might make a cake? Mrs. Clark makes a delicious upside-down pear cake that I know the children might enjoy."

"A week would be acceptable," the housekeeper said grudgingly. "I suppose I can overlook a visit once a week."

"Then farewell until next week," Aunt Ann said. "And thank you for all you do for the children." She took Susanna's hand.

When they made it down the steps, Susanna murmured, "She does nothing. Nothing but take what should be theirs." She began to tremble.

"Yes, yes," her aunt whispered. "But let's wait to discuss it. We mustn't talk here."

And indeed, the gray curtain twitched away from the window as they passed.

When they made it to the streetcar stop, Susanna said in a low voice, "Horrible, hateful woman."

"Yes." Her aunt looked grieved.

They were quiet all the way to the Hannah Neil Mission, which was as light and airy and comfortable as before. Jesse was laughing and Annabeth and Della were not as sad as the older ones, though they still asked for Mama. When Susanna finished hugging and holding them and Aunt Ann had given them some of the second bag of candy, they were sent back to their rooms.

"Matron, I must ask you something," Susanna said to the neat woman with her ever-present ledger. "Did my sister give you any indication at all of where she might be going? I need to see if she is in need of help." She did not say *or even still alive,* though the question hovered in her mind.

"I'm sorry, Miss Hanby." The matron looked her straight in the eyes with kindness. "It is not common for a living mother to abandon her children to the care of the county. I kept no record of it, to try to avoid any legal complications for either your sister or her children."

Would the county or the state throw Rachel in jail for what she had done? Susanna had not even thought of that, and she did not want to ask. But she could not give up. "Did she say nothing at all? Please," she begged.

The matron hesitated for a long moment. "She said something about children not living on the boats."

"That is all?"

"Yes."

There it was again, the boats. Yet no one had responded to the bill that had been posted in the canal docks' office—if the boy had in fact posted it. But at least it confirmed what Clara had heard. "Thank you. And please, if you could tell me how long until the children will be sent away?" Her voice caught at the last words.

The matron spoke even more quietly. "July thirtieth."

The thirtieth! Only three weeks from now! She couldn't speak and instead headed for the exit, her steps faster and faster.

She heard Aunt Ann murmur behind her as she pushed open the heavy main door and almost tripped down the stairs. At the street level she braced herself on the stone pillar and banister. A passerby regarded her curiously, but she did not care, bent over, wretched and dizzy from her tight lacing, clutching the stone.

A gentle hand on her shoulder and Aunt Ann spoke. "I know it's beyond what you can bear, child. You must not try to carry this alone."

The infinite compassion in her aunt's words made her tears pour out and she had to borrow a handkerchief. Her heart did not want to give up this burden, painful though it was, for she feared if she did, she would lose Rachel and her children. The crushing pain in her chest was all she had to tie her to them until they were together again.

She wiped her face and sniffed. "We should go back and see if Uncle needs us."

"Yes, let's go to the courthouse. I remember the directions." Her aunt did the best she could to hurry, but her walk was slow.

Susanna matched her pace and took comfort in her slight, warm presence next to her. Even if she couldn't find her sister, she must somehow get the children before the three weeks were up. That way, when she told her parents that Rachel was gone, they would at least have the consolation of their grandchildren. To lose all at once might kill her father, who was frailer than Uncle Will even though he was a few years younger.

Once on High Street, they passed shop after shop, but Susanna was too exhausted from her emotions to be curious. Her aunt did turn to look in several, and no one could help but notice the large signs everywhere: Hardware, Boots and Shoes, Coal, China, even a Ladies' Ice Cream Parlor. "Oh look," her aunt said in a pleased tone, peering through one expanse of glass. "So many cut flowers." She pointed. "Why don't you go in and look for a few minutes? The courthouse is only a block away—I'll go see about Will and then come back for you here."

Susanna glanced listlessly at the gorgeous blooms in the window: carnations, roses, irises. "I should stay with you. What if Uncle—?" She cut herself off.

Aunt Ann wasn't fooled, but she didn't seem alarmed. "No, please stay. It will do you good. We have nothing like this in Westerville—a shop where you can see such lovely flowers all gathered together."

Perhaps Aunt Ann didn't want her to come along right away. Her aunt might want some time alone with Uncle Will to discuss the events of the hearing. Maybe this was her gentle way of hinting so.

"Very well, I'll look in the shop," Susanna said. "Don't hurry on my behalf."

Her aunt smiled and took her leave with a gentle press of her gloved hand. Susanna pushed open the door to the flower shop.

The moment the heady perfume of mixed blossoms surrounded her, her fatigue lessened. She inhaled deeply.

"Good morning, miss." A hump-shouldered, weathered woman in an apron came out from the store's back room, her speech accented like Mr. Giere's, but much thicker. "May I help you with a selection?"

"I'm just a visitor today." She became conscious of the tightness of dried tears on her face and the puffy feel of her eyelids when she blinked.

"Be our guest. I am Mrs. Pfeiffer. If you wish to enjoy the flowers and rest for a moment, we have a seat for you." She indicated a cedar-slatted bench mounted on black iron legs.

"Thank you," Susanna replied.

The woman hobbled out of sight with a swirl of the shop curtain.

Susanna wandered from one bucket to another. Here was a deep purple iris with its lambent yellow streak, there a white cloud of carnations overflowing their container. They must do a great deal of business to stock so many lovely flowers. For once she did not think about leaf patterns, or sorting and labeling into categories. She simply soaked in the beauty and comfort of the soft masses of color. This was how Rachel loved the flowers—as heaven's gift to the senses.

Wood lilies by the window attracted a beam of sunlight that made their orange petals glow. Susanna crossed to them. They were Rachel's favorite, and the same ones George had trampled in the dirt of her garden. These flowers were perfect, their petals extended to curved points, the subtle ring of yellow in the center dotted with warm brown flecks. Susanna grazed the brown stamen with her fingertip and rubbed the dark pollen between her thumb and forefinger. Such miraculous design—it never lost its wonder for her. She leaned down, closed her eyes, and inhaled the scent, until she almost believed that she stood in her sister's garden, with Rachel an arm's-length away.

Fourteen

JOHANN STRODE DOWN HIGH STREET, SATCHEL IN one hand, police report in the other. Two murders, a body floating in the Scioto River. Gruesome, but nothing to catch the attention of the jaded New York populace, he was sure. The only story with any bite to it was the Westerville bombing. He would follow it closely now. And his father could spare him for a few days, since Heinrich was capable of managing the lager deliveries. Johann would balance the accounts and check everything upon his return.

Up ahead, the courthouse emitted a stream of people. Had all the Westerville folk stayed so long after the hearing? Apparently so, for there was the Reverend Robertson shaking another man's hand. No doubt they had many thanks to give to those who had posted their bond.

He passed the shoe shop and then the florist, where a ray of sunlight streaked under the awning and lit up the window in a blaze of purple and orange.

To his surprise, there in the window was the familiar face he had seen not long ago, the one that had preoccupied him in perplexing ways for the last two weeks. Miss Susanna Hanby. She leaned over some large blossoms, eyes closed, an expression of deep longing on her face such as he had never seen before on any woman. The faint marks under her closed eyes made it seem she had been weeping, but her loveliness struck him more than her sadness. The daylight streamed around her and spiraled in rings of gold down the curls of her brown hair. Her yellow dress and the orange blooms before her made her appear to be the source of the sunlight rather than its object. Her face was luminous in its keen desire for whatever lingered in her mind, her lips unconsciously parted in her reverie.

Why did he feel so drawn to her intensity?

There was nothing school-girlish about Miss Hanby, nothing silly like Lotte's infatuated singing. Maybe he should go speak with her.

He should not—she disliked him and everything he represented.

But she was intriguing, and besides, he needed to maintain his Westerville connections to get the most information for his article. He took his hat off, placed his hand on the door handle, and pushed, letting himself in with a ring of the shop bell.

She looked up, startled, and straightened her posture. Her face was more open and vulnerable than he had seen it before, as if he had caught her off guard and she did not know quite what to do about it.

An old lady scuttled out of the back—he knew Mrs. Pfeiffer, she lived a few streets away from the Gieres. She gave him a gap-toothed smile. "May I help you, sir?"

So she was going to be coy and pretend she didn't recognize him. "Not just yet, thank you."

She nodded and hobbled back behind the curtain with a knowing look.

He turned back to Susanna. Now what should he say? Perhaps he should have considered that before. "Your uncle was released on bond."

"Praise heaven." Relief softened her face but did not dispel the longing that remained in her green eyes like a distant echo of whatever had caused it.

"Was your errand successful?"

"Not completely." Her lashes veiled her eyes.

He should make a peace offering, something to show her he was not the uncaring devil she thought. "May I assist you in some way? I know the city quite well and I can help you find anything you might need here in Columbus."

Her faint smile bore a hint of rue, but he did not seem to be her target, for once. "I'm afraid you can be of no assistance, Mr. Giere."

"I'm quite good at digging things up."

"It is a private matter."

"But if I can help, might you share with me just enough to procure what you need? There are many, many shops and establishments in Columbus, and I'm familiar with them from my wanderings in the newspaper business."

Her eyes sparked. "What I want cannot be procured from a shop, Mr. Giere," she said in a tense whisper. "I want my sister, who has disappeared, perhaps harmed by her husband, who is a drunk." She leaned forward, clutching her handbag against her skirt, almost vibrating with emotion. "And her six children are now at city orphanages, and we aren't permitted to take them home. Nor do we have the means to do so." An arc of pain coursed over her face like an electric shock, but she kept her voice low. "Without their intoxicated father's consent, we can do nothing. And he's a slave to his drink, which has made him lazy and cruel. There. Now will you do as you said and procure me my sister?" Lips trembling, she turned on her heel and walked to the far side of the store where she faced the bright masses of white and red roses. She crossed her arms over her chest and her shoulders slumped.

Warmth spread over his cheekbones. No wonder she had been so unpredictable and thorny—she was in real torment, as anyone in her position would be. He walked over and stood close behind her where he would not be overheard by the shopkeeper. "I humbly ask your pardon. I should not have intruded."

In profile, she blinked and raised her head, then swallowed.

"But as I've clumsily blundered into your private affairs, I wish to make it up to you by helping. What's the name of your sister's husband, and where does he live?"

"George Leeds." She did not meet his eyes. "Union Center. He hates our family now—he claims my sister ran away with another man and abandoned her children. But I know she did no such thing!" The contradiction of her fervent talk and delicate beauty was mesmerizing.

"Union Center is not far," he said. "Maybe I will go speak to Mr. Leeds. Talk a little, buy him a beer, and see if I can improve his intentions."

Her eyes widened and lips tightened, though she did not look his way.

Before she could chastise him about the beer, he held up his hands. "Wait. You say he hates your family. But a man unrelated to you, a friendly man, can share a glass of lager and talk—Mr. Leeds might be more receptive to good sense and compassion under those circumstances."

She took a shallow breath and sighed. A minute went by while she stared at the soft curves of the rose petals. "There may be some merit in what you say." She looked at him directly, her lashes still damp and dark. "You would go there and speak with him, to help us?"

"No gentleman could hear your story or see your distress without sympathy." The words felt stiff—she might think him a fool, but it was true.

"I thank you for that." She said it simply, closing her eyes with her face still turned to the flowers. The lowering of her eyelids allowed a flood of pain into her face. He watched with sympathy as she took a breath and let it all drain away, restoring a polite expression. "Thank you."

"Then I will find you in Westerville," he said. "As soon as I have spoken to this man."

She laced her fingers together, seeming at a loss. "I must be going." She walked to the door. He quickly moved to hold it for her.

"Auf Wiedersehen." Why had he said it in German? He was off balance for some reason and reflex had taken over. "Till we meet again, Miss Hanby."

He nodded to her as she left. The bell rang again and the hunched woman peeped out to see if any new customer had arrived.

"Are you interested in a bouquet, Mr. Giere?" she said, curiosity perking her withered face.

"No—wait, yes, I am, if you have a boy who can deliver them immediately."

"I do. Edward!" she called into the back, and after a moment, a boy of about ten in plain breeches came through the curtain.

"Then I'll take those." Johann pointed to the ones he wanted.

"An interesting choice, sir. Like this?" She held up a bunch in her hands.

When he nodded, she grinned a snaggletoothed smile and began to wrap them. "I'll put them in damp cloth so they will last till they are vased."

"Fine, but hurry please."

In only a minute or two, the boy had his instructions. He took the wrapped cone of paper in his arms and ran out the door.

———•◦◄———

"Miss, miss!" a young voice called out.

"He seems to be calling for you, Susanna." Her uncle raised one finger to point behind them at the boy running up, out of breath, with a parcel in his arms.

Aunt Ann looked a little startled. "Do you know him?" she murmured as the boy hopped up to the courthouse steps where they stood.

"No," Susanna said, puzzled.

He stopped, puffing, and carefully held out his bundle. "With the compliments of the gentleman, if you please, miss."

Wrapped in pretty green paper, five perfect wood lilies seemed impossibly fragile, their orange bright and exotic against the street's grays and browns.

Lilies. Orange. The meaning of it seeped through her mind as a hot blush suffused her face and neck. "I should not take them," she said to her aunt.

"Who sent them?" Aunt Ann asked, her eyebrows tilting to her snowy hairline.

"Mr. Giere." Her face burned like fire.

"You should not turn away such beautiful flowers. I think you should accept them," her aunt said.

"Do you think so?"

At her aunt's considered nod, Susanna held out her arms and accepted the bundle. Auntie was too kind to want to see a gift rejected, but still . . .

She could not believe Mr. Giere had sent them, and still more shocking, that her aunt had told her to accept them. Surely Aunt Ann knew the meaning of this gift, as all lady readers of Godey's magazine would know.

In the language of flowers, orange lilies spoke only one word: passion.

Fifteen

THE ENVELOPE HAD NO RETURN ADDRESS. SUSANNA'S name was on the front, care of her uncle, Westerville, Ohio. She did not recognize the handwriting.

Susanna slid a finger beneath the flap and broke the seal, careful not to rip it despite the racing of her pulse. Was it from the Hannah Neil Mission? Or heaven forbid, the Hare Home? No letter from there could bring good news. But the house-keeper there would not write to the Hanbys anyway, so it could not be her. She bolstered her nerve to unfold the letter.

How odd. It was not written in the same hand as the address. It looked as if it has been printed, but imperfectly, the letters sometimes lighter and sometimes heavier, not always in a completely straight line. And it was all struck in capitals.

> Susanna, I am well but cannot meet you. do not look for me. Your Sister.

She snatched up the envelope and turned it to the light. A Columbus postmark. She stared at it for a long moment, then laid it down on her desk and dropped her head in her hands.

What was it? Did it really come from Rachel? It seemed to be made on one of those new machines she had seen in the papers, a Type Writer. But why would Rachel use one, and whose handwriting was on the envelope?

She raised her head and looked at it again. It seemed like a trick, as if a stool had been kicked out from under her and she hung in the air for the space of time before she hit the ground. If George had hurt Rachel—or worse—he could have such a letter created on a Type Writer and feign it was from her. Sickened, Susanna closed her eyes. He did not seem that intelligent or calculating, but the threat of prison might spur a man to many deeds. And there seemed no reasonable explanation that could require her sister to use a Type Writer, or even worse, to have an envelope addressed in a hand not her own. She would have to pray the Lord in his goodness would grant that this letter was real, and that she would find Rachel through it somehow.

Mr. Giere was going to find George, or so he had said. She looked up at the orange lilies in the plain glass vase on her windowsill. Several times she had started to throw them away, unsettled by their gorgeous perfume and lush petals as a reminder of him. But she could not make herself destroy them—they were also a memory of Rachel, and the blond German might only have bought them because he saw Susanna admiring them when he entered the florist's shop. He could not have known what they would symbolize—it would be practically a declaration of some kind, and he could not have intended that. His gesture was a kindness only, probably prompted by pity for her story. He could not be all bad, if his heart could be touched by Rachel and her children. Still, no feat of chivalry would soften her toward his father's profession. She would tolerate his assistance only because he intended to leave the brewing business.

Handsome is as handsome does. Reflecting on his physical appearance was not a good idea—nor should she admire the charm of his faint accent that only surfaced when he was flustered. These things were all deceptive, just like the initial cheer an alcoholic drink brought to men. One must look beyond surfaces to essences, beyond the frivolous things and into the moral principles, and Mr. Giere's principles were as yet undetermined.

She stood and plucked her crocheted shawl off the peg on the side of the plain wardrobe, tying its strings quickly. She could not stand to show the letter yet to her aunt and uncle. It seemed too menacing, too questionable. Her head ached and she could not think of all this constantly or she would lose her mind. She would go to the one place she had discovered for silence and healing—the library of the Philalethean Literary Society, in Towers Hall. No one was there in these summer months. It was her own private library—her refuge.

The quiet welcomed her to the soft, muted light of the Philalethean Room. Several comfortable upholstered chairs waited for her like friends. Her heels clicked on the wooden floor as she walked to the tall shelves and sought the book she had been reading with such pleasure. It was the only thing that took her away from this horrible, anxious mess and stopped the constant tumbling of her thoughts with George, Rachel, the children—oh, she could not think of them one more time or she would break down. Just half an hour of peace through reading.

There—the book she sought. She grasped its leather-ridged

spine and slid it out from the shelf, then went to the chair by the window and nestled into it sideways so her bustle would not be so uncomfortable. She drew her knees up under her skirt, like a girl, but then there was no one to see. Book cradled in her lap, she leaned against the back of the chair. The light fell on the title page from outside, diffused by the gauzy curtain.

The Sagacity and Morality of Plants: A Sketch of the Life and Conduct of the Vegetable Kingdom. Even the title made her smile. Somewhere in the world there were authors who thought even more of plants and flowers than Susanna did. She turned to her bookmark.

> It cannot fail to be noticed that the central Apple-blossom is often the only one which bears an apple. All the rest "take their chance," so that every cluster of such blossoms preaches the precious doctrine of altruism.

That might be overstating the case just a bit. But she enjoyed the author's parables of the plant kingdom, even if the real miracle was in the design, in the way that every flower was governed by a number, three or five—sometimes four or two—and the number manifested itself again and again in that flower, God's own pattern of perfection.

A knock at the door broke in on her reverie. She hastily adjusted her seat, lowering her feet to the floor and straightening in the chair.

The door opened and a freckled face showed at its edge. "I hope I'm not disturbing you, Miss—"

He came in and his eyes widened. "Miss Hanby! I didn't know it was you."

"Good afternoon, Mr. Wilson." She stood, closing her book with hidden regret.

The young man closed his mouth over his prominent teeth and swallowed. "It's a pleasure to run into you here, miss." His eyes were starry above his freckled cheeks.

"What brings you to the college today?" She had to make polite conversation, though her mind was still on the book hanging in her left hand.

"I'll tell you, Miss Hanby, if you promise not to tell a soul."

"Very well," she said, wishing him to hurry it up so she could get back to the chapter.

"I know of some folks who are going to ensure that Mr. Corbin strongly considers leaving town." He raised an eyebrow in confidential delight.

"I'm glad to hear it," she said. "How will they do it? He already refused the leading citizens' offer to buy him out."

"Everyone heard. So these folks are going to be a little more . . . emphatic."

"Should I ask what you mean by that?"

"Perhaps not." He grinned.

It gave her a queasy feeling, this innuendo, but she thought of the Pippen children. No wonder people were up in arms, with the history of what they had endured. And what about Otterbein? It had almost collapsed four years ago. Townspeople had given their own hard-earned money to save the college, but now Corbin threatened its precarious stability with this saloon that would make recruitment more difficult. It could truly bankrupt the college, which was never wealthy at the best of times.

"People will do what they have to do, Mr. Wilson."

"Yes, miss. Someone has to make sure that virtue triumphs and the innocent are protected."

The gleam in his eye had turned a little fanatical. "Yes," she agreed, uncomfortable, "innocents must be protected." That was true, whether he was over-excitable or not.

"I'm so glad you think so." He looked as if he might go to his knees in knightly gratitude. She hoped he would not—it was 1875, not 1475, and though that gesture might be romantic from another, it would only embarrass her from Mr. Wilson.

"If you will excuse me, I must get back to my studies," she said gently.

"Of course." He walked backward and inclined his head a few times on his way out the door.

She sighed and wished for a fleeting moment that he looked like Johann Giere. It would be so much better if Mr. Giere were the ardent temperance man.

She sat down again in her comforting chair and opened her book once more. She had lost her place and squinted at the chapter title, holding the book up to the light.

Robbery and Murder.

Oh. That did not sound as nice. But this author had been so humorous that she would find out what he meant—another witty comparison, no doubt. She bent to the page.

There is one kind of tree called the Sipo Matador, or Murderer Liana. It springs up close to the tree on which it intends to fix itself, and the wood of its stem grows by spreading itself like a plastic mould over the trunk of its supporter. In the course of time, it kills its victim by stopping the flow of its sap. The strange spectacle then remains of the selfish

parasite clasping in its arms the lifeless and decaying body
of its victim . . .

She slammed the book closed, shaken. *George.*

Where were her universal principles, beauty, and altruism?
Her botany book had brought her right back to the disturbing
letter from the Type Writer.

This was not what she wished to study today.

———•◦•———

"George Leeds is in there?" Johann asked the cart boy.

The saloon ahead of them seemed stuck together with tacks
and old lumber, all crisscrossed planks. Its rough-sawn windows
boasted rickety shutters open to the hot afternoon.

"Yes, sir," the boy said. "Mr. Leeds is in there all the time."
He flapped the reins of his tall pony and drove away down the
town's sparse version of a Main Street, including a general store,
a doctor's office, and the inevitable saloon.

Johann restrained a grimace and shoved open the door of
the shack. It was gloomy inside. Weak light from small windows
fell on a makeshift bar, which was just another plank propped
up with minimal carpentry skills. A saloonkeeper stood behind
the plank and a lone customer sat on a stool. Not surprising, as
it was two in the afternoon and only a shiftless man would be
drinking at this time. At least it made identification easy.

"Mr. Leeds?" he said as the black-haired man turned around,
revealing a sparsely bearded face and an unwashed appearance,
from his oily skin to his rumpled clothing.

"That's me," the man said. "What do you want?"

The frontier still lingered in the small towns of Ohio, where people were suspicious of strangers. And drunks were even more suspicious.

"I'm here to talk and perhaps buy you a beer." Johann took the stool next to him.

"A whiskey would be welcome."

Ugh—he did not want to do it. No decent man liked to buy a glass of rotgut for a drunk. But the welfare of six innocent children came before this derelict's health. He signaled the bartender to provide the whiskey for George. "And a beer for me, please." He looked at George but did not offer his hand—it was too much. "I'm Johann Giere."

George jerked his chin at him.

When the two glasses thumped before them on the counter, George picked his up and tasted the amber liquid, letting out a raspy sigh. Johann repressed a shudder. He did not want to drink with the man, but he must create the warmth of *gemuetlichkeit* if he wished to be persuasive. He raised his own glass and sipped it. Hoster lager. He could always tell.

"Mighty decent of you to buy a man a drink," George said. "You came here looking for me?" The glint in his eye made it clear he was hoping there was more where that first drink came from. Not if Johann could help it. He would have to get to the point.

"I'm here to talk to you about your children," he said.

George's face grew hard and pugnacious. "What about 'em?"

"Nothing to inconvenience you. I realize you've suffered a great shock, with the disappearance of their mother." He tried to sound sympathetic, and it appeared to work, for George lost some of his defensive posture and took another sip of his drink.

"It was shocking, yes it was." His words slurred. "She left

with another man, no reason given, and took 'em all away. With that kind of mother, I think they're better off where they are. If anyone wants 'em, they can ask *her* to go get 'em."

That sounded like a reference to Susanna—and not a promising one. Johann made a noncommittal sound. "So you have no idea why she vanished?"

George looked sideways and then at his glass. "Nope." Was that a tiny smirk on his face?

He rallied to a sober whine. "And it's been hard for me since she left. She was supposed to tend the farm while I worked, and now there's no one to tend the farm. So it's hungry times for me."

Obviously George was neither working nor tending the farm. What a miscreant. His wife had been feeding their whole family, probably by working herself to the bone with the help of the older children, and now George complained because his chuck wagon had pulled out of town.

"It sounds like a hard life," Johann said.

"It is." He looked morose.

"Well, in that case, I would be happy to pay for your train fare to Columbus."

"For what?" His breath smelled of whiskey.

"It would be better for the children to stay with family, and so I would like to ask you as a gentleman to come claim your children under the law and retrieve them. After that, your responsibility would end, and your relations would take care of them."

"You mean the Hanbys?" He smirked again, but openly this time. "They already asked me this, and I said no. And I say no again."

"I will pay your expenses for any travel and meals."

A light gleamed in his dark eyes. "Well, maybe I'll consider it. I need the travel money in advance."

It would probably be a waste, but even the smallest chance was worth it. "I'll give you the train fare and then buy you a meal when I meet you in town." He fished out the money and used the stub of a pencil to write down the address of the brewery on his notepad. He tore it off and gave it to George. "Come find me here and we will take care of business, then have a fine German feast."

"All right." But the ongoing smirk told Johann it was a lost cause.

With a short good-bye, he walked out and hurried down the street, putting distance between himself and the wretched scene.

Why had he agreed to do it? Oh, yes. Susanna. The stirring memory of her beautiful face in the flower shop dispelled at least part of the slimy feeling of talking to George Leeds, a sensation like handling a newt.

And he had to admit that there was a silver lining, even in this failure with George.

He would have a good excuse to return to Westerville and investigate further for his article.

And he would see her again.

Sixteen

THE SINGING IN THE CHAPEL WASN'T UNIFORMLY
tuneful, but it was sincere. The congregation sang the strong
rhythm of the hymn with extra feeling to chase away the shadow
of the saloon.

> Down in the human heart, crushed by the tempter,
> Feelings lie buried that grace can restore;
> Touched by a loving heart, wakened by kindness,
> Chords that were broken will vibrate once more.

From the corner of her eye, she saw a man enter through
the doors in back and stand in the back pew. She did not turn
around and stare, but his blond hair and deportment were
unmistakable—Mr. Giere. Her pulse quickened. He could
only have come with news about his meeting with George
Leeds.

> Rescue the perishing, care for the dying
> Jesus is merciful, Jesus will save.

The men singing bass thudded to a close and the people sat down once more to hear the final thoughts of Reverend Spalding. He dismissed them with an urgent call to continue opposing the saloon and all who did business with Corbin. As they filed out, the congregation maintained respectful low voices and did not really converse until they scattered outside into the quadrangle of the college.

Mr. Giere was waiting for them a few yards away, hat in hand.

Uncle Will had stayed to talk to the reverend and had not yet noticed their visitor. Aunt Ann called out, "Good morning, young man." She beckoned to Susanna and led the way toward him as he took his hat off to greet her.

"Good morning, ma'am." The brewer's son was respectful, and his manner was different from the practiced sophistication of the college boys. He was humbler, but somehow it made him seem older and more mature—wiser, even, for his time in the real world of work and human events. But why was she thinking of such things? His personal qualities hardly mattered compared to what he might have learned about the children and their future.

Susanna trailed with some reluctance after her aunt, trying to stave off the memory of the lilies that threatened to make her blush. She could not acknowledge them, of course. But she had to speak with him if she wished to hear the news.

"Thank you for coming all this way to help us," Aunt Ann said. Susanna had told her of Mr. Giere's plan to speak with George Leeds.

"I wish I had better news," he said.

It was like an elbow to the gut. Susanna tried to breathe. She had known there was no chance, but still—

"I'm very sorry I didn't succeed, Miss Hanby." He looked as if he meant it, but she wished he would not be so sympathetic. It made it harder to remain composed.

"I suspected as much." She had to leave soon before she gave way. "He will not help us?"

"No. He was friendly to me at first, but stayed hostile to you no matter how I tried to work on his better feelings. Apparently he has few to none of those." A brief expression of distaste melted into concern. "He told me that if anyone wanted the children, your sister would have to reclaim them."

"He did?" She couldn't think, stupefied. Her aunt placed a hand on her arm.

The young man looked as if he would like to do the same but instead glanced down and kneaded his hat brim. "I asked Leeds where he thought she was. At that point he became guarded and said he knew nothing."

"Thank you," she murmured. Should she tell him about the letter? No, he might think she was asking for more assistance. She had to bite the inside of her lip to keep from breaking down. After an instant of pure pain, she tasted blood and let up. Her aunt was thanking Mr. Giere and asking him if he would take lunch with them. Susanna would have to plead illness—she was far too upset to make conversation, and especially not with him.

"I think I'd better pursue my other business in town," he said, with a subtle look at her. He was certainly too handsome and probably used it to his advantage to get people to buy his father's beer. "But I would be glad to escort you ladies to your home, if you wish. Where is Mr. Hanby?"

"He's speaking with Reverend Spalding about the saloon," Aunt Ann said, a little warily. "We'll go home ahead of him, as we often do—he will arrive just in time for the meal after I heat it up."

Mr. Giere looked as if he would offer his arm but did not know to whom. Well, Susanna did not want that. She took her aunt's arm. "Shall we go?" she asked.

He looked properly chastened, clasped his hands behind his back, and kept an appropriate distance from them. He shouldn't be familiar—they weren't cousins or even friends.

"I'm glad to hear Mr. Hanby is trying to solve the saloon problem," he said as he strolled next to them, matching his pace to her aunt's. He had an educated way of speaking that only increased its effect with his occasional accented word. "I have no doubt that any plans of his invention would be strictly legal."

"That's true," Aunt Ann said. "Will's only law-breaking days were during the Fugitive Slave Act. He certainly doesn't approve of vandalism or intimidation."

"Or perhaps worse." Mr. Giere's face was thoughtful. "Which is why I'm staying here this evening."

"For a dramatic story?" Susanna didn't blunt the slight edge of the question.

"I'm only willing," he said with his trace of a lilt, "to go so far in seeking a story. I won't stand idly by if I think someone may be hurt or killed, and then grin while I run to the presses. That's the act of a ghoul, not a man."

A little liking for him flared in her spirit, even in its overcast gloom. At least he had principles in some areas. Should she tell him what Abel Wilson had told her? But she had promised not to tell. And besides, Mr. Wilson was not talking about killing anyone—just being "emphatic," whatever that meant.

"Do you think someone may be injured due to the saloon?" Aunt Ann gave him a keen look. "Have you heard something?"

"I can't say." He glanced away, diffident. "But I assure you I'll do my best to hear what I need to hear, especially if lives are at stake."

"But won't you ruin your story?" Susanna asked.

"My hope is that the story will be both dramatic and harmless." He gave her a rueful half smile.

The saloon lay in their path to the Hanby home, its roof still askew like a rakish hat. A couple of men went in as she stared. Horrible, to have their drinking so open, even on a Sunday. Was that legal? Were there not ordinances? If not, there should be. She would have to ask her uncle.

Another man slipped around the corner and crept into the saloon with a surreptitious backward glance.

"Auntie," she gasped, and stopped. Mr. Giere halted next to her.

"What is it?" her aunt asked.

Susanna clutched her sleeve. "I believe that man who just went into the saloon was Mr. Pippen."

"No." Her aunt paled. "We mustn't assume so—we could not see clearly from here."

"Miss Hanby is correct," Mr. Giere said. "I recognized him too."

"You know him?" Susanna asked, her temper flaring.

"I saw him testify in the men's meeting."

"But it still doesn't matter, I suppose, that you helped Corbin set up his saloon here."

He fell silent and did not look at her, gazing at the doorway that had swallowed the slight man.

Would everything be ruined for all these children whom no one could protect? Their lives and health destroyed? All by the effects of drink, whether beer or spirits, and the law would not intervene. And Mr. Giere would not denounce it, he would continue to deliver beer to lost men. She was about to lose control of her tongue. She gathered her skirts in both hands and ran down the street toward home.

Seventeen

THE TWO OLD MEN WERE WATCHING CORBIN FROM the porch of the hotel. Johann was sure of it. They had taken up positions in the old rocking chairs as if they intended to stay a good while. One had a pencil and a ratty, worn journal in his lap.

"Evening, gentlemen." Johann pulled up the ladder-backed chair not far from them and sat down, extending his legs as if he, too, had nothing to do but sit on porches in the twilight of this oppressive heat that refused to break.

He could not let Miss Hanby's outburst distract him from his Westerville story—he would continue to seek information, despite the shock of seeing Arthur Pippen fall off the wagon. He shouldn't feel responsible—it wasn't rational. Pippen had talked of an obsession with whiskey, not lager. But Johann could not forget the distress in Miss Hanby's green eyes before she ran off.

One of the old men grunted a greeting, the other simply scrawled in his book.

"Are you from the Vigilance Committee?" Johann hazarded a guess based on what he had heard in that night's rally at the church.

"Yep." The one not writing nodded with a look of significance. "I may be useless for most things, but I can still sit in a chair." He wielded a toothpick with long practice on teeth that seemed solid and healthy for one so old. "You new in town?"

"Just an occasional visitor, sir. I went to the temperance meeting tonight and also the first meeting after Corbin came in."

"Where you from?"

"Columbus. I travel back and forth on business." Johann stared at the tip of his boot and waited so as not to sound too interested. "What are you watching for?"

"Violations, boy, violations." The toothpicker grinned, talking out of the edge of his mouth with the toothpick clamped between his teeth. "Corbin will flout several rules soon, I guarantee."

"Such as?"

"He can't serve outside. He can't serve to men under eighteen. And he can't serve after nine p.m."

"And what happens if he does?"

"The mayor might have him arrested."

"I see."

A loud shout broke the dusky stillness of the street. Corbin's unmistakable flat voice reverberated from the open window of the saloon building across the street.

The toothpicker chuckled. "He must have found it, eh?" he said to his friend.

"I reckon so," the other man said, deadpan, but with a twinkle in his eyes.

"What did he find?" Johann asked.

Before he could answer, the door of the saloon rocked back

against the wall and Corbin practically jumped out. "I see you over there!" He stabbed a finger toward the old men, who must have seemed to be nothing but dark shapes in the fading light. Johann was glad Corbin could not see him.

The toothpick came out of the old man's mouth and he held it in his palm. "What of it?" he called. "We may sit here if we wish."

"I know you're up to your spying and vandalism," Corbin yelled.

"What is it, Corbin, got a bad smell in your back room?" Both old men chuckled hard at this.

"You sons of mongrels!" Corbin threw his arms down as if he would stamp in his rage, but then stormed back inside the saloon.

Johann murmured to the toothpick man, "What happened?"

"Word has it someone was planning to pitch a few rotten eggs through Corbin's windows this evening." The man smiled like a prankish boy beneath his wrinkles. "They'll stink up his saloon for sure."

A minute later two customers hurried out of the saloon, one with his hand over his nose and mouth as if about to be sick.

"See?" The old man laughed. "Did you get that in your diary?" he said to his friend. "Don't miss it now. This is the juicy stuff."

"Got it," his friend growled, battered hat pulled down over his eyes. "But I'm losing the light."

Even as he said it, the lamplighter came down the street igniting the few oil lamps with his long pole. The hotel had its own porch lamps: a maid came out and turned them up to brighten the porch.

As she did, a group of men strode out of the hotel's tavern—an alcohol-free establishment, of course, but providing fine cold cuts and potatoes for travelers. The young men seemed familiar to Johann—it was the Otterbein students from the church. Johann watched them go down the steps, speaking to one another in low, hurried whispers.

"If you will excuse me, gentlemen," he said to the two elders on the porch. "I will take an evening stroll."

"Mind your step. Our lights aren't the best."

"Thank you." He followed the young men down the stairs at a discreet distance. This might be silly, playing at intrigue in the dark. But the way they kept glancing at the saloon seemed to be more than just curiosity.

He had to tread with caution in the gathering darkness, feeling with each foot before setting it down so as not to step in a dry pothole and break an ankle. Westerville would benefit from gaslight. But then, he could not conceal himself so easily if the streets had adequate lighting.

He moved down the empty street like a shadow, straining to see. The young men were still whispering to one another, but as they left State Street and turned toward the creek, they hushed. He could still hear their footfalls ahead and hoped their collective noise would cover his.

His foot met no resistance and he stumbled and tripped. He caught himself on his palms, scraping them on the pebbles in the packed road. He froze there, listening, but they did not appear to have noticed. What an adventurer he was, blundering around at night like a clumsy schoolboy. He clambered to his feet again and followed.

They went into a large building, a storehouse or barn,

judging from the dim shape outlined against moonlit treetops. Perhaps they simply had a secret club meeting. But he would watch for a few minutes more.

It didn't take long before the dark blot of figures came back out the door of the barn, some of them holding an object between them. He could not see what they were carrying: it was larger than a bucket but smaller than a lager barrel. He should not go any closer or they would spot him. They filed around the corner of the barn and disappeared into the trees.

He debated whether to pursue them. The footing over there in the grove would be even more treacherous without light. One or two of them must be very familiar with this site to navigate it without a lantern. Johann would not have that advantage and would probably plant his face in the ground the minute a tree root popped up and he failed to notice. Then they might discover him.

It was wiser to give up the pursuit for the night. He could come back and look again in the morning. And it all might yet prove to be a wild goose chase: some college boys out for nothing more than amusement.

But his instinct told him otherwise.

The dawn drifted through the kitchen window and shed pink light on the food Susanna was packing in the basket. She could not yet go see her nieces and nephews—the endless prescribed week between visits had another four days left before she could go back to the Hare Home—but she and her aunt could at least go help the Pippens.

Aunt Ann came in with a plucked, headless chicken hanging from one fist and a few drops of blood spattered on her apron. She had the grim look of a woman who does a necessary but hated task—Susanna understood. She had been the resident chicken killer at her parents' home, because she was the fastest on her feet and could catch one and make it quick and merciful. But she always felt like praying after she had done it. It seemed a huge thing to take a creature in your hand and still the hum of its life and the brightness of its eyes, even a life as small as that of a piebald chicken.

Her aunt wrapped the chicken in paper without comment, then took off her apron and hung it up. "Shall we go?"

They walked past the shops in the muggy heat—would it never relent? A horse at the hitching post switched its tail, giving up the battle against the flies that crawled on its eyelids. Poor thing. The flies were awful too, this summer, as if they searched for any drop of moisture in the long drought.

A wagon rolled down the street and pulled up in front of the slant-roofed saloon. In it rode a hawk-nosed, dark-haired woman and four children with the same sallow complexions. The woman climbed down and lifted in her arms the youngest child, a girl who looked no more than three years of age. After her, two boys and an older girl jumped down to the dusty ground. The children gazed around at the shops and the street, their dark eyes snapping with irrepressible curiosity that made Susanna ache for her nieces and nephews.

She and her aunt passed near the family as they spoke to one another.

"Mama, this is a small town," the tallest girl said.

"I told you so," the mother said, and smiled privately in the way common to all mothers on a mission. "Now, grab a sack or a box and let's get settled." She hefted the three-year-old onto her hip and gave her a hearty kiss, which stopped the fussing. The little girl put her arms round her neck and pillowed her face in her mother's shoulder. Susanna took a sharp breath at the memory of Della and Rachel standing in the garden, in just the same pose, the last time she saw her sister.

Susanna craned over her shoulder and saw them moving their things into the Widow Clymer's building. It had to be Corbin's family.

They were children, not responsible for their father's line of work. What if Westerville succeeded in getting rid of Corbin? What would happen to the children? How would they survive, and where would the family go if they closed the saloon and had to leave town?

They would get along all right. He would simply have to find some other town, as Susanna had asked him to do that first day on the street. She could not soften against the evil of the saloon when it seemed certain that Mr. Pippen's family would be destroyed if Mr. Corbin succeeded and remained. The danger to Mr. Pippen's children was much greater than the simpler hardship for the Corbin children of moving and starting over. But still, she could not get their expectant faces out of her memory. Why wouldn't people simply do what was right? Corbin was placing his family in a very painful position, but that was not the fault of Westerville. It was pure stubbornness and contrariness to open a saloon in this particular town—Corbin was creating a crisis that need never have arisen had he considered his duty to his family and refrained from dragging them into a war.

She and her aunt walked up to a little house, barely more

than a shack, tucked back in the trees off Walnut Street. Her aunt knocked gently. Susanna slung the basket over her arm.

The little blond Pippen girl answered. "Hello." She spoke in the artless way of children, with no welcome, only a stare.

"We have come to see your mother," Aunt Ann said. "Is she in?

"She is in bed."

"Is she ill?"

"I don't know."

The other boy and the older girl came into view in the plain room behind her, with its cold stove and only one window.

"I'd like to go back and talk to her," Aunt Ann said. "I'll see if she is in need of help."

They said nothing, just watched with miserable faces as she went to the one flimsy door at the side of the main room. Susanna followed. These children broke her heart—they were transformed from the happy, young things they had been at the candy store window into older, sadder, and much quieter versions of themselves.

In the dark side room a rickety bed frame held a slight body covered in a flimsy quilt.

"Mrs. Pippen?" Susanna asked. She let her aunt take the lead in walking forward—Mrs. Pippen knew her and might take her intrusion better.

The figure didn't stir, but it had to be her, with that long, colorless hair down over the shoulder of her nightdress. Her aunt walked around to the side the woman was facing. "Mrs. Pippen," she said with the most compassion Susanna had ever heard in a lady's voice. "We're here to help. Can you hear me?"

Why did she ask that? Alarmed, Susanna skirted the foot of the bed to look in Mrs. Pippen's face.

She gazed at the wall, her eyes glassy but not with intoxication. It was something strange, something unnatural—a shudder rippled over Susanna's back. It was as if she had stepped out of life, her empty face refusing more sadness. But the pulse was still there, the life still running under her skin. Why was she a mere shell and unresponsive?

Her aunt took the woman's limp hand and patted it, then rubbed it. "Mrs. Pippen." The woman blinked but did not move.

The hair rose on Susanna's arms. The woman's shattered will seemed to have released her mind to oblivion.

Words of comfort seemed inadequate. But there must be something, some tie to this world to awaken Mrs. Pippen—she could not abandon her children, who needed her even more now. Should Susanna say so?

But she would not—she wasn't wise enough, she had never seen this before. She hoped her aunt knew what to say, what reason or scripture could get through to the stricken woman, to make her want to come back to a life that must seem broken and lost. The dashing of her family's dreams was all the crueler for their having once been resurrected.

"Put down that basket and help me, please," Aunt Ann said with an urgent glance at Susanna. "Help me sit her up."

Susanna hurried to the bed.

It was difficult—Mrs. Pippen was heavy, a muscleless, boneless slump, despite the apparent thinness of her frame. But eventually they each took one shoulder and propped her up.

"Hold her there," Aunt Ann said. She went to her knees in front of the low bed, and to Susanna's surprise, she put her arms around the woman and held her close. Still holding her, she stood, lifting Mrs. Pippen's limp form with her so the woman stood with feet trailing, completely supported by Aunt Ann's even smaller figure and Susanna's hold under her arms.

Her aunt did not loosen her embrace but began to sing to Mrs. Pippen in a low voice, a song like a lullaby, a wave of comfort and love that seemed to pass from her body into the other woman's. She did not tire when there seemed to be no reaction, but continued with another song, a sweet one that sounded Irish. After the second verse Mrs. Pippen twitched. Her eyes closed, hiding their strange stare. She raised her arms and put them around Aunt Ann. As she held on, her back convulsed, then she groaned and started to sob. It shook her whole body, that eerie mingled groan and weeping. The raw sound brought tears of sympathy to Susanna's eyes.

An intuition told her to leave Mrs. Pippen alone with her aunt, who was murmuring words of reassurance, fragments of prayer, as if she were a nurse or even Mrs. Pippen's mother.

Susanna would take care of the children. She retrieved the basket from the floor and went back into the common room with it hooked over her arm, closing the door behind her. The children waited there, huddled in the corner.

"It's going to be all right," Susanna said. "Your mother was ill, but she'll be better now. We brought you something to eat. I can cook for you, if you like." She did not know if Mrs. Pippen would be ready to cook just yet. There were a few broken lumps of coal in the hod. She took them out and struck one of the matches from the box on the ledge by the stove. After a minute, she had it lit. Thank goodness the stovepipe would take most of the heat out of the home. She crossed to the window and opened the shutters. Light spilled pale gold over the floor and the basket, with its clean cloth pulled back.

Susanna went back to it and rummaged for the offerings. "Here—bread for you. And some milk too." The children reached for them with their quick, small hands, their faces growing less desolate as they ate and drank.

She turned over the pieces of chicken in the pan with quick, perturbed pokes of her fork. The sadness in her spirit twisted and mingled with anger.

The world couldn't heal as long as human beings were so determined to place gain over virtue, so determined to lead others to ruin down the wrong path. Only the choice of righteousness could spare these poor children—and her nieces and nephews—from suffering. It was a choice that both George Leeds and Arthur Pippen had refused. Why? Who would choose dissipation over good, suffering over joy?

It made the right choice all the more urgent, now, for Westerville. She stabbed the fork into the chicken breast and slapped it onto its other side. She might not be able to see her sister's children yet, but in the meantime she would do what she could here against the saloon.

Henry Corbin must find another place to live and to wreck homes. Nothing could be worth the price the Pippens had paid for a glass of whiskey.

Eighteen

THE SOUND OF RAIN PENETRATED HIS SLEEP—TOR-rents of water gusted against the hotel window. Johann crawled out of bed in the dawn's gray light, rubbed his face, and walked over to the window. Over the eaves the rainwater boiled, cascading in a white plume to State Street where it splashed up mud to a brown foam. That muck soup all over the road would make for a messy walk to the station, but the trains would still run.

The saloon looked much the same from here, though its outlines blurred in the rainy glass. No unlawful act had called the citizens from their beds. For news gathering it was a wasted night. But he wasn't exactly disappointed. He did want to be present if news broke, but he didn't want anyone to be hurt.

A good spread at breakfast explained the popularity of the hotel: fried eggs, bacon, cooked tomatoes. He took his time while the rain softened to a patter and the light grew. Other travelers were adopting the same strategy, dawdling over their newspapers, taking an extra cup of coffee. None of them seemed to have brought umbrellas—it had been so long since a good rain that they were all defenseless against the elements.

He picked up his hat and satchel and went to the open door that led out on the porch. The old men of the Vigilance Committee had already assumed their seats to watch Corbin's place. But they did not look as relaxed and jovial as at their previous encounter. They were staring at something—he followed their gaze.

A man had been hanged on the sign of the saloon. Johann's pulse pounded.

No, it was not a real man but a rag dummy, rain-soaked into the heaviness of a real body. The figure had been made to look tall and thin, wore clothes like Corbin's and a hat that resembled his. Beneath the hat poked some kind of dark animal pelt to approximate the saloon-owner's black hair. The rope around the dummy's throat had been twisted into a hangman's noose.

Johann's stomach turned. A nasty threat, and not worthy of civilized people. The old men on the porch kept blank faces, neither condemning nor approving.

Johann had turned to navigate the slippery stone stairs when a coughing sound drew his attention back to the saloon. A boy of about twelve had come out and was tugging vainly at the feet of the effigy. The coughing came from the sobbing girl next to him, who wiped her face on her sleeve between horrified glances at the dummy. She had the black hair and pointed features of her father. He had seen Corbin's children walking with their mother yesterday, going into the general store and emerging with drooping shoulders. They had not been welcomed, and now this.

The boy yanked again at the dummy—its foot pulled off in his hand, which seemed to disturb his sister even more.

"Get it down," she choked out. The boy's motions became

more choppy and urgent, but he was not tall enough to reach the noose.

Johann set his satchel down on the steps and splashed across the street, ignoring the smell of manure rising from the mud. The soupy mixture covered the tops of his shoes and in a few steps he was wet to the shins. A few raindrops flicked his hands as he sloshed onward until he stood under the sign with the boy.

Arms over his head, feet waterlogged, he worked at the noose, which the rain had tightened into a damp, solid mass. It took a good minute of pulling this way and that to extract the neck of the dummy and throw the vile thing down.

The children watched him with big, dark eyes. The girl had stopped crying.

A good journalist should only observe, but a good man must sometimes act.

"Don't worry," he said to the children. "No one will hurt you." He picked up the dummy by its old jacket and trudged through the muck to the alley. He would throw the dummy far away from the saloon, where at least the children would not have to see it.

The alley was not as flooded as the street. He dragged the heavy rag body along like a giant snail through the veneer of slime. At the back of the alley was a livery stable that served the hotel. A middle-aged man walked out of the barn with a grain scoop in hand and dirt smeared on his face—a groom.

"Good morning," Johann said.

The groom stared at the grisly dummy.

Johann hoisted it in one hand. "An unsuitable thing to leave in the sight of children. I want to throw it out in the woods. Or on your manure heap to be carted away."

"I have no love for whiskey-sellers," the groom said, his brows bushing out, deep lines appearing by his mouth. "Whose side are you on?"

"The side of those who don't wish to torment children." Johann felt his biceps knotting as his temper rose. He would get no help from this one. With a huff of breath, he dragged the dummy on, past the manure heap, beyond the tree line. What if someone tried to rehang it by the saloon? A burst of ire fueled him as he tore the effigy into pieces, the wet, cheap material ripping between his fists. It lay scattered in white chunks all around the tree trunks. There, that would not easily be reassembled. He took its unrecognizable head and tossed it in the air, then as it came down he kicked it upward as hard as he could. It sailed into the treetop and stuck, a little tan sphere. He felt better. Maybe a bird would use it for a nest.

Corbin was standing outside by his sign when Johann retraced his steps. He tried to pass unnoticed, but the saloonkeeper beckoned him.

"Good morning," he said reluctantly, conscious of the old men staring from across the street.

"Mr. Giere. So you were the one who took the dummy down? My son told me it was a yellow-haired man."

"Yes, sir."

"This is the work of thugs." Mr. Corbin sawed at the noose with his penknife and cut it off the sign.

"Well, I must be going." Johann wanted to get away before his cover was blown.

"Wait a minute." Corbin turned with the sodden rope in one fist. "I have something to show you."

"I'll go around back," Johann said. Must Corbin insist? Johann couldn't afford to be seen going into the saloon.

Back down the alley he went and around to the back door of the Clymer building. Corbin was waiting for him there. "Come in."

He followed the saloonkeeper through the back room, which held a few crates full of bottles and still reeked of sulphur from thrown eggs. A few more strides brought them under the oak-beamed doorway and into the saloon's main room, with its bar and tables.

"You see?" Corbin said proudly.

Aimed at the door, propped on the bar, was a rifle. There was some odd contraption of string and rods around it. Corbin stepped over to it and hooked it up. "If anyone tries to come in at night," he said, setting a heavy iron on a ledge above the door, "this will fall and yank the string, which pulls the stick and fires the gun."

He dropped the iron and Johann heard the click of the hammer. Had the gun been loaded, it would have gone off.

"Ingenious, but very unwise, Mr. Corbin." He set his hat on the bar. "You mustn't do this. You have young children here. What if one of them accidentally set it off? Or stepped in the way?"

"They aren't stupid, and they know not to touch it," Mr. Corbin said. "And when my daughter saw my invention, she looked happy to be protected from the likes of them who hung me in effigy this morning." His chin went hard and his lower lip jutted out.

"If anything happens, you could go to jail."

"It's defense of my own property."

Johann had no reply. It was true, if someone entered criminally at night and was shot, Corbin was probably protected by self-defense law.

"But you will escalate the danger for your family if your enemies discover this."

"They'll know I mean business." The set of his jaw did not change.

"Don't do it, man." Johann's voice softened. "Think of your wife and children. Don't put them in the middle."

"I haven't put them in anything. My actions are legal. I won't be bullied by religious vigilantes." But Corbin's eyes were troubled.

"Consider it carefully, that's all I ask." Johann took up his hat again. "I must be going. I've been absent from the brewery for two days already."

"Tell your father about all this. Maybe he'll feel inclined to stand up against such intimidation. It's bad for his business too." Corbin's voice had an edge of desperation.

Johann sighed and walked back the way he had come, skirting the bottles and boxes and making his way back out into the wet back yard under the gray sky.

He had a good story to file for the Westbote about the effigy, but it did not ease his worry about Corbin's children. He had a feeling this would not end with rotten eggs and dummies.

He passed by the steps of the hotel to retrieve his satchel and headed for the station.

How should he angle this story of the effigy on Corbin's sign? The bald truth was not flattering to the temperance crusaders, whether or not most of them approved of such tactics, which meant any story would not be favorable to Susanna. He did not want to bring more criticism upon her family. But if he still wanted to submit his work to the *Staats-Zeitung* in New York, he had better make it a memorable scene for readers. So he would write the truth and send it to New York.

Then he would see if Mr. Reinhardt was right that heaven would make a future path clear.

Nineteen

THE WATER WAS ALREADY DRAINING INTO THE THIRSTY
ground. It wasn't so bad along this side of the street, though on
the other side a wagon driver had stuck fast and was swearing
loudly until he saw Susanna and moderated his tone.

She picked her way along the edge of the morass, her boots
well-edged with mud but her skirt lifted above it. If she could
get a chest remedy from the apothecary, she would be able to
bring it to Daniel in only three more days. The thought quickened her pace. The store was another block along, closer to the
train station.

As she neared the drugstore, a man came out of the general
store, almost running into her. It was Mr. Giere, his gaze fixed
on something far away. He stopped as he took in her presence
and tipped his hat. "Pardon me, Miss Hanby."

"Good morning." She noticed the crystalline quality of his
eyes, even in the dreary morning light. She wondered if he had
sent the flowers out of pity, or if—

She needed to address the essential subject. "I went to visit
the Pippen family, Mr. Giere."

"Indeed?" A shadow fell over his face.

"They are in dire circumstances. Mrs. Pippen has almost given up hope."

"I'm sorry to hear it." He seemed truly sad.

"Then might I impose upon you to do something for me?"

"With pleasure." His expression brightened.

"Ask your father to stop supplying beer to Mr. Corbin's saloon."

His eyebrows knitted together, light brown, a shade darker than his hair. "Miss Hanby, I would do much to oblige you"— his tone was intimate, and a shiver went through her—"but not that. I can't ask my father to sacrifice his business. And it wouldn't prevent Mr. Corbin from operating his saloon." He stepped closer and lowered his voice. She had the unsettling thought that he might take her gently by the arms to convince her, and that would be very strange, especially because it wasn't completely repellent. Some nameless impulse urged her closer, as if she, too, could persuade by proximity.

She took a step back instead. "Anything might help. Even the slightest show of resistance might discourage Corbin and make him move away. You should have seen the Pippens!"

"I can imagine their plight, I assure you. I understand why you are so disturbed by the saloon. I don't like the effects of habitual drunkenness any more than you do."

"Then tell your father to stop causing it."

"He's not causing it." He said it with feeling, then paused. She noticed the healthy color his light skin had taken in the summer. His fair hair could use a trim, as it brushed over his ears and touched his collar in a disheveled poet's style, streaked with light and dark gold.

He regained his calm. "My father's business is not the cause of drunkenness, any more than Christ making wine at the wedding at Cana."

Her thoughts ground to a halt. What did he mean? She had never heard someone speak as if the Lord himself were a wine merchant—and was Mr. Giere well versed in the Bible, like a true believer? Maybe he had just learned to argue with Christians.

"Are you being irreverent?" she asked. A flicker of indignation made her stab a finger at his top button.

"Not at all." He smiled, took her hand, and wrapped it in his. "Stop pointing and listen to me."

Her nerves vibrated. She should not let him do it—he was holding her hand. The memory of the flowers spun in her mind and she could not meet his gaze.

"You're a compassionate woman, Miss Hanby. I know you are greatly troubled by the suffering of others, which is an admirable trait in this often hard-hearted world. But you don't understand the correct use of lager—"

"There is no such thing!"

"Wait. I'll prove to you there is. Are you going back to see your nieces and nephews soon?"

"In three days."

"Perfect—a Friday. Then I would like you to come with me that evening to a German gathering, with your aunt as a companion, of course. You won't understand unless you see it with your own eyes."

He was still holding her hand. Her knees felt unsteady and she pulled away. "I shouldn't go."

"Are you afraid to have your prejudices unseated?" His lips curved. They were fuller than she had noticed before, but strong in their contours like a man's should be. She sought another object for her attention. She was coming apart inside, not acting like herself.

"No," she said. "I'm not afraid."

"Then I dare you." He smiled outright.

"I accept your challenge." She took a deep breath and looked him full in the face, but found him too close and had to blink and gaze sideways at the storefront again.

He let go of her hand and rummaged in his inside pocket. "Good." He pulled out a small journaling book and a stub of a pencil and scrawled a few words. "Meet me at this address, with your aunt and also your uncle if he wishes—it will all be quite correct." There was a teasing look in his eye that made her stomach turn over. "At six o'clock in the evening. It will be a party. And then we'll have a proper debate. And if I don't change your mind, I'll offer this forfeit: to persuade my father to stop supplying Corbin."

"You will lose, Mr. Giere." She knew she sounded haughty, but he needed to be put in his place. "Done." She extended a hand like a man would, and he shook it with a smile, clearly humoring her.

"Good-bye." She kept her tone cool.

"Until then." He put on his hat and strode away, humming something.

He was a shade too sure of himself—it was provoking. Never mind. When Aunt Ann heard about the mission, she would be happy to come along and show him the error of his ways. And what a prize—to cut off Corbin's supply of lager and withdraw the Gieres' support! It was too good to pass up.

Twenty

THE THREE DAYS HAD CRAWLED BY, BUT SHE HAD finally made it to the orphanages and even managed to keep her composure through the meetings with the children. Seeing them had been as upsetting as the last time. But nothing compared to the shock of seeing Rachel.

She was sure it was her sister, that woman who walked around the corner of a large warehouse, toward the docking basin for the canal boats. Her exact posture, her auburn hair, the soft line of her neck and her profile. This was it—the entire reason Susanna had insisted on walking this way. She had found her.

Susanna broke into a halting run, hampered by the luxurious fabric and bustle of her borrowed dress. Behind her, Aunt Ann called something inaudible.

But by the time Susanna turned the corner, there was nothing to be seen on the dock, only a couple of freight wagons unloading. Sweating river men in rolled-up sleeves worked by the squat, many-windowed boats that lay moored in a line down the canal's edge. She stood, scanning the crowd. Was it Rachel? Or was it a hallucination of wishful eyes?

"What is it?" Aunt Ann caught up, panting for breath.

Maybe she shouldn't even confess it. "I thought I saw Rachel."

The flicker of shock in her aunt's brown eyes dissolved to pure sympathy. "Did you?" she asked softly.

"Yes. It was so like her I can't have been mistaken. And the matron at the orphanage said that Rachel had mentioned boats."

"Where did she go?"

"I lost sight of her." Her voice trailed away.

"I'm sorry, my dear."

She could not give up. "Let's go to the dock office and ask if a woman answering to that description frequents this area."

Her aunt considered. "I don't know—I have a responsibility to keep you out of unsavory places."

"We should be safe together." Susanna's heart lifted and she turned toward the small shack on the wharf below them, where a man seemed to be regulating boat traffic. "How do we get down there?" The brick levee wall dropped a sheer ten feet from where they stood to the water level.

Aunt Ann pointed back down the waterfront. "There's a set of stairs."

A minute's walk brought them to the stairs in question, and another minute's navigating past coal, stacked lumber, and refuse brought them to the office. A mustached man yelled instructions to the boat at the head of the line, which was hitching to the horses that would draw it up the canal.

He paused. "Excuse me, sir," Susanna said. "We're looking for a missing woman, auburn-haired, about my height, in a gray dress?"

"Sorry, miss," he said. "Ain't seen anyone like that."

"Not today, or not in the last few days?"

"Not at all." He raised a hand at the second boat in line. "All clear!" he shouted.

Susanna glanced at her aunt. They were dismissed, and there was nothing more she could do now about the woman. It was maddening to be so close and not find her. She peeped through the office window. There! Her notice was on the wall—she saw the headline she had given the errand boy: "YOUR CHILDREN NEED YOU." Had this notice prompted the letter she received? Or was it all foolishness to think so?

"Let's go," Aunt Ann said. "We'll ask on the upper level if anyone saw her pass. And then we must go to meet Mr. Giere. It's almost six." The light was fading and purpling into evening—it would not be wise to stay by the docks any longer.

"It may not have been Rachel," Susanna said, defeated.

"Maybe, maybe not," her aunt said. "I did see men in crowds who looked so like Ben a few times in the month after he passed. But I don't mean to discourage you." She looked stricken, a deep wrinkle appearing in her forehead under her white fringe of hair.

"It's all right, Auntie," Susanna said, though a sharp pain felt like a blade through the ribs. "I mustn't give way to fancy."

"Neither should you give up hope. Come, let's go back and ask a few of the wagon drivers if they saw her."

But the three men in their rough work aprons—the laundry man, the fish man, and the coalman—had not noticed the auburn-haired woman either.

"I'm sorry," Susanna said to her aunt. "I shouldn't have insisted we walk past here. It put ideas in my head."

"It was on the way. No need to apologize, dear. Let's tell Mr. Giere about it and see what he thinks we should do."

That was a comforting thought. Mr. Giere specialized in this city, as a journalist. He would know whom to ask about the riverboats and their traffic.

She would be sure to ask him about it before she crushed his arguments about temperance, just in case he decided to hold a grudge.

———— ❈ ————

"*Hoster Biergarten*" read the arched sign over the pathway, painted in pretty calligraphy. On either side were flickering lamps, their flames still ghostly in the evening light.

"Oh," Susanna said, looking at the address on the paper in her hand.

"Let's go in."

"I don't think I can." Susanna fought back revulsion. A *Biergarten* was a German version of a saloon, and she couldn't patronize such a place.

"You can't win your prize without entering the battle." Her petite aunt sallied ahead, her light-blue gown trailing over the green lawn.

Susanna followed reluctantly. Inside the walled enclosure were trees and bushes, some of the bushes forming a hedge so tall it created a second wall inside the first. Which way should they turn. Along the hedge or around it into the center?

Her aunt continued straight in. On the other side of the green bushes, a large number of wooden picnic-style tables formed a perfectly ordered grid of rectangles. About ten of the tables were already taken by large families, grandmothers with grandchildren, husbands and wives holding babies, young women talking in girlish secrecy to one another. Lanterns on posts stood waiting to be lit all around the garden. Flowering plants bloomed at intervals, mostly roses in white, red, and pink, carefully tended and trimmed.

On a raised wooden platform at the other end of the space, beyond the tables, musicians were setting up next to lanterns and music stands. A cellist plucked his strings, a double bassist lifted his massive wooden instrument from the ground. Two violinists tuned up. They were all dressed in elegant light coats, as if to play for a ball. Susanna was glad, now, that she had worn a borrowed dress, nicer than her everyday yellow one.

"Mrs. Hanby. Miss Hanby."

Mr. Giere walked up behind them, smiling in welcome, his usually disheveled hair combed perfectly into place. His eyes looked even brighter against the black of his coat and his white collar. "Thank you for coming." He took her aunt's hand and made a slight bow over it, then did the same for Susanna. "A pleasure."

"We shall see about that," she said.

He chuckled. "Yes, we shall. Mr. Hanby could not come?"

"He is speaking to the men at a town meeting this evening," her aunt said, "but sends his regards."

"What's his subject?"

"He cautions them against rash and unchristian action against Corbin." Her aunt said it with wifely pride, but a hint of anxiety lurked in her eyes.

"A good idea, don't you think?" he asked.

"Unless he makes the aggressive ones so angry that he incites such action." Aunt Ann sighed.

"But he's a persuasive man," Mr. Giere said. "I don't think that likely."

Her aunt assumed a discreet quiet, her lips sealed together.

"Some of them are easily angered," Susanna said. "We've had proof."

"Susanna." Her aunt crossed her arms over her bodice. "Let's speak of more pleasant things."

"I'm sorry to miss Mr. Hanby this evening." He held out an arm to her aunt, who took it with grace, and then he offered the other to Susanna, who accepted with significantly less warmth. "Did you see the grounds yet? This is the largest *Biergarten* in the South End. The Hosters are our hosts this evening. I'm sure you're familiar with the name."

"Yes," Susanna said stiffly, thinking of the brewer's name on several lager wagons they had seen in the streets.

"Allow me to show you." They strolled around the hedge, past more beautiful rose bushes, to the end of the garden. Here a pond reflected the oblique light of the setting sun, its silver surface broken by scores of green lily pads like polka dots across the surface.

"It's very pretty, Mr. Giere," her aunt said. She raised a fragile hand toward the pond. "The lilies have closed up for the evening, I see."

The water lilies had tightened from their open lotus-shapes into small bunches of green and white. Susanna thought of the flower clock. "They'll open again tomorrow morning."

"Yes," the young man said. "They're lovely in the daylight. Like God's grace notes on the water."

She looked at him, surprised. She had not heard many men speak with such eloquence—perhaps only her uncle, when he spoke about spiritual matters. And Uncle Will did not count, as preachers were known for that sort of beauty of speech. But this was a brewer's son.

"Are you a musician, Mr. Giere?" her aunt asked. "You speak of grace notes as if you know such things." She could not disguise a look of pinched grief well enough to evade Susanna's notice. Yes, a musician would remind her of Ben—poor Auntie. Bad enough to lose a son, but to lose a son like Ben, who struck everyone who met him as extraordinary and had changed the hearts of the nation about slavery . . . and then Auntie lost Cyrus too.

"I'm not much of a musician." He looked a little shy. "I don't play an instrument or even read music very well. I only sing in the chorus."

A singer. She wondered how his voice would sound. "It's peaceful here," Susanna said.

"Yes," he said, giving her a deeper look until she turned her head away, stirred and uncomfortable. What did he think he saw in her?

"Most *Biergarten*s are not so garden-like, especially here in America." He folded his arms across his coat. "From what my father tells me, though, there are beautiful ones in Bavaria, sometimes with acres of land."

"Your father's homeland," Aunt Ann said. "Would you like to go there someday?"

He paused. "Of course I would like to go." His accent gave melody to his inflection. "But I love this country. I'm American. My family has shed its blood for America, and we belong here now."

Susanna held her tongue. She did not know him well enough to ask who had died in the War, though she was sorry for the loss evident in his distant look.

He focused again on them. "And I don't want to spend my

life talking of Bismarck and the Kaiser like some of the old men in their *Lederhosen*." He grinned.

She was glad she knew who Bismarck and the Kaiser were, but then anyone would who read the paper even once a month.

"Let's go find a seat," he said. "The music will be starting, and I don't want you to miss it."

Susanna's chest tightened. Now he would want to prove to her that drink was acceptable. He could never do it. As soon as all the German men started reeling around drunk, singing their beer songs, waving their steins, she would have to leave. All the other women would as well. The German women were probably accustomed to it—Susanna could take her cue from when they left the *Biergarten*.

Dusk was falling over the garden and the tables like a gauzy mist. The chamber ensemble struck up a waltz. Susanna's heart began to soften—it was calming to listen to such beautiful music in the open air, surrounded by families.

She mustn't let her guard down. This was only the early part. Ah, see, several maids had come out with trays loaded with steins and began to pass them out to those at the tables. This evening could turn into a very sad spectacle. The smiles on the men's faces as they drank and talked and watched their children twirl on the brick floor were the smiles of the unwitting lured to their fate, like the story of the Pied Piper of Hamelin—that was German, wasn't it?

"It's not so bad, is it?" Mr. Giere said. "Shall we sit down?"

"No, thank you. The night is young," she said in an ominous tone.

He laughed. "It will be much the same, all night long. It's not like an American saloon, Miss Hanby. Lager is taken with food and among family." And, indeed, out came the maids again with trays of sausages and breads piled high.

"I don't like your American saloons, you see," he said in a confidential tone. "They are places for men to sneak away and rebel against their lives and their work, a place to toss down drinks and escape from family. No wonder they have caused such heartbreak." He looked pensive. "But a *Biergarten* is a place for the whole family, for brotherly and sisterly fellowship, *gemuetlichkeit*, we call it. It is not a place to run from one's duties, but a place to open to laughter and music and family and appreciate the good things God has provided."

Several couples stood up and headed to the open space where the children were twirling.

"You see?" He nodded toward the dancers. "They do not have to be young to love the dance." It was true, the women and men first on the floor were older, some even stout, but wreathed in smiles and good nature as they moved to the sweeping rhythm of the waltz, their steps lighter, wives more graceful, husbands more gallant. The lanterns had begun to glow in the dusk.

"My father," he said. "You must come meet him!" He escorted them over to one of the tables, where a genial man with ashy hair was seated next to his wife, a fairer blonde with apple cheeks and a dimple to make her round face and figure sweet even in middle age.

"Father," the young man said. "I would like you to meet my guests, Mrs. Hanby"—he nodded to her—"and her niece, Miss Hanby."

The older man rose to his feet. "A pleasure to meet you." He spoke with a much thicker accent than his son but with appealing verve. "Johann had told us he was expecting some guests, but kept very mysterious about them." He pursed his lips and looked sideways comically. "I see you were hiding the beautiful women, son."

The younger Mr. Giere smiled, but his mother lost her warmth and looked with a trace of wariness at Susanna. She tried not to squirm under the assessing regard. Why was his mother so interested? He should have told her there was no romantic intent, only an argument to be won. But then there was the matter of the flowers.

Susanna blushed as her aunt carried on polite conversation. So Mr. Giere the younger bore the Christian name Johann? It suited him, made him less formal than the "mister" she had known until now. Johann. He was a likeable man, and he had been kind to her, but he would not win this debate.

A maid brought over a tray of steins and set them on the table in front of each of them. Susanna stared at the foamy liquid. "I won't drink it," she whispered to her aunt. Her aunt also made no move to take it by its white handle.

Johann beckoned to the maid. "Birga, will you bring some lemonade for my guests?" She nodded and whisked the steins off to the kitchen. "Will you try some of the bread?" he asked Susanna. "Or this, the *Weisswurst*?" He glanced at her aunt.

"It smells delicious." Aunt Ann skewered a piece of sausage with the wooden fork on the table and tried it. "Oh, it is."

Susanna hesitantly tasted it and had to admit to herself it was excellent, with its smooth, creamy consistency. The dark bread was sweet, and she ate it in a few bites.

Johann was looking at her. Had she been gobbling it? Her ears tingled.

But he looked pleased, not repulsed. "You see the good things God gives us," he murmured so no one else could hear. "We are made to enjoy them."

The yellow liquid that appeared in the steins this time when the maid brought them was paler and thinner. Still, Susanna felt odd drinking lemonade out of a beer stein. For a moment she relaxed and let herself enjoy the pulse of the music, the stars coming out through the trees overhead, the lantern light, and the delicious food. But the people were drinking intoxicants. How long would it be before they were raging drunk? Well, Johann would not do such a thing—she knew him better than that. But others would. Her shoulders tensed and the fabric pulled tight across them.

"You are enjoying yourself?" he asked, his expression hopeful in the lantern light.

She did not want to give him the satisfaction. He might use it as a debate point later.

"Come," he said in the face of her silence. "Would you like to dance?" His expression was curious.

"No," she said firmly.

He looked disappointed.

"I would like to dance," her aunt said, surprising her.

"Do you know how to polka?" he asked. "It's easy." The people on the floor had started a sashay step like a slow, elegant skip.

"I can do it," Aunt Ann said, watching closely. "I did much harder steps in my day." She smiled.

He held out his hand to her with a mock courtly bow and they strolled to the floor. He seemed very solicitous. She liked how he guided Auntie, protecting her from the energetic youthful dancers if they came too close. It was sweet to see an elderly woman treated so kindly by a very handsome young man who could have his pick of partners. In fact, one blond girl over by the entrance did not seem to be able to take her eyes off Johann Giere, drinking in the sight of him as deeply as the men pulled at their steins after a good dance.

He brought her aunt back. She was puffing a little for breath, but Johann was not winded at all from the gentle pace of their dance.

"Now you see how easy it is," he said to Susanna. "Will you try it?"

As there was no open drunkenness yet, the music was so transporting and the night so inviting, maybe she would try. She was unlikely ever to repeat such a scene with an unusually charming man and the opportunity to dance under the stars by lantern light. These things did not happen at church, where dancing was condemned by many.

She took his hand. It was warmer than her own nervous, chilly fingers. He folded her smaller hand in his own while they stepped onto the brick dance floor. Gently he placed her left hand on his shoulder. She stared at his shirt buttons, then raised her eyes to his. If she had ever thought they were an attractive blue before, she had underestimated their hypnotic effect by the glow of lamplight. The intimate, inquiring look he gave her made her feel as if she were too close to breathe. He circled his hand around her and held it against her back. Her body felt light and her skin warmed at his touch. No wonder some of the church folk objected to dancing. But, at the same time, she did not want to leave the floor.

He guided her into the flow of the dance. She concentrated hard on the steps at first, afraid to make a mistake, staring over his shoulder and counting silently. But it was so easy that she was soon able to stop her counting and simply follow his lead. She looked up to see his gaze fixed on her, then flushed and looked down, then at him again. *Like a moth to a flame*, she thought, *I must be careful*. But it was hard to keep up her guard after the kindness he had shown her, even in response to her rudeness. There was a great deal about Johann Giere that was heavenly, whatever his opinion about drinking.

When the dance ended, they stood together, still in the dance position, at the far edge of the crowded floor where they were shielded from the watching eyes of the spectators. Something had shifted and changed. She did not want to let go of his hand.

"Johann!" A woman's voice startled her and she let go with a guilty flinch. Johann looked taken aback at whatever he saw over her shoulder.

She turned to see that the pretty blond girl from the other table stood right behind them.

"Johann, I thought you were out of town."

He looked at Susanna, then back at the blond girl. "Lotte, this is a friend of mine, Miss Hanby. Miss Hanby, Miss Thalberg."

"I have lacked for a partner these past two dances." She eyed him with a flirtatious pout.

"Then I must have the next dance," he said, as any gentleman would under such open coercion. "Allow me to escort Miss Hanby back to her seat, and then I will come for you."

He led Susanna back with a subtle glance of apology, but as she prepared to sit, his father stood and offered her his hand. "Miss Hanby, may I have this dance?"

"Thank you." She took the older Mr. Giere's hand. It

sounded like another polka, so she thought she could do it. And then she would not have to sit and watch Johann dance with the blond girl who made her oddly twitchy. No young woman should be as forward as the blonde, but then, maybe Johann liked it or was accustomed to it. They might even be sweethearts. She didn't look back at him as she walked out to the floor again with his father.

After a few steps of the dance, Mr. Giere spoke. "My son likes you."

Were all Germans so blunt? Well, she could be equally direct. "But we differ in our opinions, sir, which is why I'm here this evening." There, that would place the discussion on more familiar turf.

"Indeed?" One eyebrow quirked. "And what are those differing opinions?"

"I do not think gentlemen should drink."

"How about ladies?"

Of course no woman should drink—no one ever even discussed such a thing. But that was not the point. "I've seen too many families destroyed." Could he tell how deeply it hurt to say it aloud?

"By whiskey, gin, rum, yes. By lager, not so often."

"That is what your son says."

"What can I say? He is my son." The self-deprecating charm was clearly a family trait. She could not help but like him, just like his son. So wrong, but not bad at heart.

"But if even one family is destroyed by your business, Mr. Giere"—her eyelids prickled and she blinked—"is it worth it?"

He looked sober, even as he carefully kept her from having her toes trodden on by a burly young man and his dance partner. "I pray about my business, Miss Hanby. Does that surprise you?" He asked it as a simple question, without rancor.

"Yes."

"I consider my duty before God every day, and I do see the articles in the paper about the drunks and their poor families. But though drunkenness is sinful, so is gluttony. Will you prevent all merchants from selling bread and meat because some take too much of it and place their stomachs before God and all else?"

She fell silent for a moment. "I mean no disrespect, sir." She followed his step, one-two-three, two-two-three.

"Of course not. I can tell you are a sweet woman and you mean what you say. And I am glad you say it straight out, to let a man answer to your charges." He smiled again and spun her around with an expert hand so that before she knew it she had done a neat turn step.

She smiled at the unexpected pleasure. "I have never been accused of a failure to speak plainly, sir."

He laughed out loud. "And I admire that in a woman." The music flourished to an end in a run of violins, and he released her and bowed. "Thank you."

When they headed back to the table, Johann had also just returned from escorting the blond girl to her seat. He looked harried.

"We mustn't stay much longer," Aunt Ann said. "The trains will stop."

"I wish you didn't have to go." He looked straight at Susanna.

She noticed his mother had walked to the blond girl's table to speak with another older woman. Both matrons were watching them with a keen eye.

"I should take you to the station," Johann said.

"I will have Heinrich do it," his father said. "He hates dancing." He beckoned to a one-armed man who came over, listened to his whisper and nodded with no apparent resentment, then headed out the exit. "He can take you in the carriage," Mr. Giere said.

"Thank you, sir," Aunt Ann said. Her natural refinement reminded Susanna of the stories she used to tell about Pittsburgh and its fine houses and dinner parties, the manners and wealth. Her aunt knew how to speak in the finest circles when necessary, but was just as gracious here in the German part of town where no one needed to stand on pretense.

"But I didn't show you the fountain," Johann said. "Why don't we walk to it while Heinrich gets the buggy?"

Susanna and her aunt took his arms again and this time walked the other way around the hedges, where the buzz of the people faded, a gentle whisper of water started, and the lanterns lit a quieter path by more rosebushes. Another corner brought them face-to-face with the source of the trickling rush: a stone fountain that sprayed water to all points of the compass from the mouths of four leaping fish.

"It's beautiful," Aunt Ann said, and let go of Johann's arm to go inspect it more closely. "I will throw in a penny and make a wish." She dug in her handbag.

Her aunt must be almost giddy—Susanna had never seen her so girlish. Johann turned his head toward her, the lamplight shining in a streak across his gold and brown hair. "Have I changed your mind, Miss Hanby?"

"No," she said, stubborn. "I must think on it."

"A good enough response," he said. "We will call it a draw, until we next meet." He put his free hand on top of her hand, where it lay on his arm. She looked at him in wonder. What was all this? He seemed equally drawn by some nameless force between them, a power not their own at work. She wanted him to embrace her and hold her. She thought of kissing him where the line of his jaw made a shadowed hollow on his neck.

She had never thought such a thing. She pulled away just as her aunt threw her penny in the fountain and looked up at them. "A wish, so silly." Aunt Ann's laugh made her look very young, as if her white hair were just blond, silvered by the moonlight.

That was it. Susanna's head had been turned by the moonlight, just as her aunt was acting in a way she had never seen. They must get back to Westerville.

"I'm sure your friend—Heinrich?" Susanna could not quite remember if that was the right name in her distracted state. "He must be waiting for us."

"Yes," he said softly. "Let me take you to him." He put her hand through the crook of his elbow, and they went to collect her aunt and walk back out of the garden.

He stopped them by the hedge. "We'll wait out here on the road." He pointed to the exit under the sign. And as he said it, a clatter of hoofs announced Heinrich's arrival in a stylish black four-seater buggy.

Aunt Ann headed out the gate with a quick good night.

Johann slipped both of his hands around Susanna's as if he shook it on a business deal, but much more gently, which sent a tingle up her arms. *"Auf Wiedersehen."* The look he gave her was intense, as if the thought of a kiss had passed through his mind as well.

Her breath caught. "Good-bye." She turned to follow her aunt.

She climbed into the carriage with Heinrich's help.

What was she doing? She was supposed to win an argument, and instead she had begun to imagine kisses.

She had known it might happen from the start. But she no longer seemed to be able to stop whatever had begun, and her skin still warmed from the pressure of his fingers.

Well, no matter what his personal charms, she would not forget that he and his family sold beer. She would not give up her principles, no matter how he made her heart pound. She was a woman of her convictions, and she could resist.

But wait—why was she thinking of him at all, or dancing in a garden as if she had not a care in the world? The purpose of this evening was to stop the beer to Mr. Corbin's saloon. Her convictions were no good if they didn't help others, especially the children.

She must do better. The next time she saw Johann Giere, she would tell him that he had lost his bet.

Twenty-One

THE PRESSES CLACKED AWAY, AND EVEN AS HE SAT IN the back room with his article, the rhythm was like her name, *Susanna, Susanna* . . . He could not get her out of his mind. Her heated fervor for her ideals wrapped in her soft, womanly skin was a contradiction that drew his thoughts back to her again and again.

"Giere." Mr. Reinhardt poked his head around the door frame, peering from behind his glasses. "I need to show you something."

"Yes, sir." He laid down his pen.

Mr. Reinhardt came and stood in front of him, practically bursting with some news. "You see?" He thrust out a piece of paper.

"I can't see it, sir."

Mr. Reinhardt stepped beside him and handed the paper to him.

Giere is our man. Tell him to finish series on saloon and then we will expect him in New York by end of September. Terms to follow.

"They will give you a good salary, by newsmen's standards," Mr. Reinhardt said. "What did I tell you?" He looked as if he would skip around the newsroom and burst into triumphant song at any moment—Beethoven's Ninth.

Johann read it, then read it again. He had received a job offer from a New York paper. He could go off to the adventure of his greatest dreams. He had to blink and clear his throat. "Thank you, Mr. Reinhardt. Thank you for recommending me."

"And you will take it, yes?" Mr. Reinhardt leaned over him as if holding his breath.

"I don't see how I could refuse such an opportunity." Johann heard the ambivalence in his own voice, but his editor either didn't notice or didn't care.

There was his family to consider—and then he would hate to think of leaving Susanna alone in her plight, especially if she lost her nieces and nephews. But he could not let that stop the move, if Mr. Reinhardt was correct and God himself had opened the door for this career he loved.

"You must tell your father, then," the editor said.

"That will be hard." Could he even do it? He would have to if he wished to take this unforeseen opportunity, which did seem like a gift from heaven.

"Don't delay too long. Give your father time to adjust before you leave. He has Heinrich, he'll be fine."

Johann nodded, but he didn't think Mr. Reinhardt understood. His editor had five sons. His father had only one.

And because of that, he must go home and consider carefully how to break the news and when.

"Son?" his father peeped around the frame of the bedroom door. "Are you writing?"

"Yes. But it can wait if you need something." His father was always so polite and encouraging about the newspaper, which made it all the worse to think about telling him.

His father came in and sat at the end of the bed on the handmade blue-and-white quilt, wearing a preoccupied, hesitant expression.

Johann swung his knees around to sit sideways in his chair. "Is something wrong?"

"Not really. Well . . ." His father examined the bedpost as if checking it for flaws. "You've never brought a guest to a dance before."

"Yes." He had known it would come up sooner or later.

"A beautiful young woman, Miss Hanby. And with a good mind."

"Yes."

"And you have come to know her through your newspaper work?"

"We happened to share a train car on the way to Westerville when I escorted Henry Corbin and his lager."

"I see." His father rubbed at the post with his thumb. "She is a teetotaler."

"She spoke with you about it?"

"When we danced. She didn't pursue the subject—I did."

That was a relief. She might be ardent, but he wouldn't expect her to be rude to her host.

His father looked at him. "I see you like her very much."

Johann scratched a sudden itch on the back of his hand.

"Your mother saw too. She asked me to speak with you because she is concerned."

"About what?"

"Your heart. She doesn't think a Westerville woman who hates all drink would be a happy match."

Johann avoided rolling his eyes with effort. "Mother only sees one match for me—Lotte—and you know that well. That's the real source of her concern."

"Ja." His father smiled. "You do not like Lotte?"

"I like her, Father. But she is like a little sister, except awkward to be around. She's just a girl."

"And Miss Hanby is not just a girl."

"No."

"What do you see in her?" His father's intent look meant there was no sidestepping this topic—he was determined to ferret out the truth.

Johann stood up and walked to the window to look out on Wall Street where a few women in aprons headed north to the market. "You should get to know her, Father. She is very intelligent, scientific even. But a caring woman too."

"I liked what I saw, except that she is so narrow-minded about our business. But she did appear to listen to my perspective, which is more than I can say for most women of her convictions."

"She has good reason to be passionate about the subject. Her sister is married to a cruel drunk and recently vanished. The husband claims she ran off to a lover, but in truth, she may not even be living. Their six children, Susanna's nieces and nephews, have gone to institutions. It's only two weeks before three of them will be sent away forever to new homes. And the Hanbys can't adopt them because they haven't the money to support them." He realized he had been tapping his pen on the desk and spattering ink droplets. He sighed and wiped them away with one finger. "So you see, she's sensitive on the issue of drink, as she's about to be deprived of the children she loves."

His father swiveled to gaze at the framed artwork on the wall, something Johann's sister Maria had done at the Turnverein last year, a painting of their new church. He was quiet for so long Johann wondered if he would speak.

"That is a tragic story." His father's voice was husky. "I'm sorry for Miss Hanby and her family."

"Yes." They both looked at the painting, the lambent glow of the stained glass that Maria had captured in rich colors, the church lit up at night.

"You know Fritz and I lost our little brother in the rebellion of '48," his father said.

"Yes, sir." Of course he would never forget this story. Through his childhood, his father and his Uncle Fritz had each lit a candle once every year, on the night Louis had gone missing at five years old in the chaos of a popular uprising in Bavaria. But when Uncle Fritz died in the War Between the States, his father had stopped lighting the candles, as if his loss was too deep for one vigil flame to bear without its twin.

His father cleared his throat. "Where are the children, her nieces and nephews?"

"In the Hannah Neil Mission and some other charity called the Hare Home."

"I know of the Hare Home." His father looked troubled and rose to his feet. "If you'll excuse me, I must go inspect the cellar."

"I'll be there in half an hour."

His father walked out and pulled the door closed with a soft click.

Good. Perhaps his father would explain it to his mother and she would also see Susanna in a different light.

But now he must finish his article, or Mr. Reinhardt would not have time to give it to the typesetter.

He could not sacrifice objectivity for even the most captivating of women. He laid the nib of his pen to the page and let the ink flow.

Twenty-Two

SUSANNA'S FEET FELT HEAVY ALL THE WAY DOWN State Street, though the mud had dried and her shoes were clean. The weight was in her spirit—the knowledge that it would be six more days until she could see the children, and the frustration of seeing a woman so like Rachel, but having to wait for her uncle to make more inquiries. Aunt Ann agreed, now, that Uncle Will should go ask after the auburn-haired woman at the docks, but he had told Susanna he had to finish a saddle first. That money was vital if they ever hoped to get the children. So Susanna had been helping him with every free moment, counting every hour of the two days until they could go back to Columbus to hunt for her sister. And even then she still would not be allowed to see Clara, Wesley, and Daniel. The thought cramped her heart— the children might think she did not care, that they had been left to the Hare Home forever.

The stores were full of activity on this Saturday, all the women and travelers out buying what they needed before the Sabbath quiet of tomorrow. She eyed the saloon ahead of her with distaste. Even from yards away she could hear the hubbub of voices. Corbin was infuriatingly successful with travelers and laborers from the outskirts of town.

She hurried her pace as she drew alongside the saloon. She did not look toward it as her shoes clanked on the boards of the sidewalk. A roar of noise from the revelers inside made her flinch.

Something hurtled into her, knocking her sideways. She landed hard, half on the walk, half in the street. She wheezed against her corset and pushed herself up to her hands, half-dazed.

"Miss Hanby!" A young man's voice called out, and after a moment Abel Wilson knelt next to her and helped her up.

Angry words flew behind them. She looked over her shoulder and saw a small knot of young men, all students from the look of them, standing over a drunken laborer about their own age, who was struggling to his feet and snarling at them.

"You owe this lady an apology!" one of them shouted.

"Get away from me, college boy. If she tries to walk into a saloon, it's her own fault."

Susanna gasped. Before she could defend herself, Abel spoke through gritted teeth at the tousle-haired farm boy. "How dare you? You flew out of it like some kind of demon and knocked her down."

A rough-looking man swung open the door of the saloon and looked out. "And good riddance to you!" He growled at the farm boy, who flushed even redder and staggered toward the older man, raising a fist.

One of the college men pushed the farm boy down on the sidewalk, where he scrabbled for footing. "First you hurt this lady, and then you would brawl in front of her? You, sir, are no gentleman."

"And you, sir, are no man at all," the farm boy slurred. He reeled to his feet and grabbed the college man by his shirt, slinging him against the wall.

"Miss Hanby, come with me!" Abel Wilson took her arm and hurried her into the nearest store—Dusenberry's Shoes. She heard oaths and thumping behind them as the door closed.

"Stay in here, please, miss," Abel said. "We're going to make him answer for this. We can't have young ladies assaulted by drunks on our own streets."

"Don't risk yourself on my behalf, Mr. Wilson."

"I will stand up for you, Miss Hanby, and for every other lady in town, and for Otterbein. You see if Corbin doesn't answer for it. He's ruining our town." The fury and distress in his voice washed through the room even after the door slammed behind his running feet.

"Do you need to sit down, Miss Hanby?" It was Mrs. Dusenberry, the handsome woman who had first suggested the women's prayer meetings against Corbin. She wore a neat jacket and bustle, as befitted the wife of a storekeeper who must wait on customers. She pulled up a chair and Susanna sat, catching her breath.

"A glass of lemonade?"

She nodded, still feeling almost deaf and dumb. What was happening? She didn't want to be in the center of it, and yet the college men were right, they had to do something about Corbin.

Mrs. Dusenberry brought a cool glass of lemonade from the back room to Susanna. "I'm sorry, my dear—I know it must have been frightening. I saw through the window."

Susanna was glad the older woman did not seem as angry as the boys. Every thump and yell from outside made her more unhappy. "I don't want them to fight." She sipped the cool liquid. The glass soothed her scratched hands.

"I know, dear. Neither does anyone. Or at least, no one I know. We all just want it to go away."

"The saloon?"

"Yes."

"So do I. But not through force."

Mrs. Dusenberry sighed. "What happens is not completely up to us. Most of the townspeople are good folk, but some are too rash. Your uncle won't be able to hold them off forever."

"He's trying."

"I know. We'll have to keep praying for his effort."

She brought a cool cloth and washed Susanna's abraded hands. When the noise died down and the street was empty, Susanna slipped out the door and hurried home. She did not want to see anyone else—only to be left alone. Her troubles were mountainous enough without taking on the whole town's.

❖

The setting sun threw the familiar contours of the Westerville train station into silhouette beside the train. Johann could not have stayed away longer, not with both the pull of the story and his desire to see Susanna again. He should go see if he could offer any more assistance, or invent some plan to delay the inevitable at the orphanage.

But first he must go to the hotel and put his small traveling case in his room.

He ascended the stairs and headed for the dining hall and common area. A quick bite to eat and then he would use the details Mrs. Hanby had mentioned at the *Biergarten* to find his way to the Hanbys' house.

Despite three visits to the hotel, he was still unaccustomed to the odd spectacle of a dining hall without lager or wine, the diners quiet, not conversing but eating in silence, some reading newspapers.

He had almost finished eating when a cluster of young people at a far table stood up with a scrape of chairs. He held up his own paper to disguise his interest and then peered around the edge.

It was those students—the would-be dashing young men who had been so full of bravado in the church, the ones who had stolen out at night on some mysterious errand when he followed them. They looked grim and simultaneously excited. It was not a reassuring combination.

He waited until they had filed out across the plank floor and stomped down the porch steps. This time he would stick closer and see what they were doing.

It was no surprise that they walked once again through the shadows down the avenue and to the same large building as before. But when they emerged this time, they were not carrying anything. He remained in his vantage point, hidden by the darkness, until their rustling and footfalls had disappeared back around the corner onto State Street.

He would not be dissuaded easily tonight. He stole over to the door they had used. What was this place? No way to tell, though it clearly provided storage. A tile facility? Inside the large main room, stacks of tile towered ten or more feet in the air, piled against walls, red-brown where the light fell on one stack through a window.

The students could not have been thieving—what idiocy that would be, to throw away their future as college men to purloin a few tiles as a prank.

He made his way slowly around the perimeter. At the far end, he found a stone stairway, steep, cut down into what must be the cellar. He glanced around once more, then took his matches from his pocket and lit an oil lamp that hung on the wall by the stairs. Down he went, only the small flickering light battling against the dark hole of the cellar.

It was a tiny cellar, not good for much but a little storage. Odds and ends were piled up so he could hardly move more than a step from the bottom of the stairs.

But something caught his eye.

Two small barrels labeled gunpowder sat right there within arm's reach, where one could pick them up and run away. And they were just the size of the object he had seen the young men carrying a few nights ago.

Well, he would ensure this gunpowder would do no evil tonight. He didn't know who owned it, but as the young men seemed to know of its existence, it was suspect. He would not feel guilty for taking something that might be used illicitly to harm others.

He put the lantern down and scooped the barrels into his arms. Now he could not carry the lantern. He blew it out and left it, feeling his way up the stairs with the aid of memory. At last he made it to the floor where the moonlight from the windows helped him find his way out.

The powder was heavy, and it must be very dense in there. Its acrid smell was not confined by the barrel and he might have powder smears on his shirt tomorrow. Merely hiding the powder would not be good enough. He had to ruin it beyond use, given what he had already seen in this town.

After only two minutes' walk through the trees, he saw the glint of light on water. The creek. He climbed down the bank and opened the plug of the first barrel with his pocket knife.

A stream of peppery powder poured out when he inverted the barrel and held it over the water. When it was empty, he floated the barrel in the sluggish current until it bobbed under the bridge and vanished. He repeated his work on the second barrel and then dusted off his hands.

If those young men were the vigilantes who had damaged the saloon, they would not have the help of explosives. He could go see Susanna with a clear conscience and talk to her about her nieces and nephews. Corbin would have to deal with the rest of it himself.

Twenty-Three

A KNOCK CAME AT THE HANBYS' DOOR. SHOULD SUSANNA answer? Uncle Will was out at the men's meeting, where they were celebrating the exoneration of the Westerville ministers by the Columbus court. And he was also speaking out against illegal action, yet again, which had Aunt Ann worried. She was rinsing one of Uncle Will's collars with extra vigor in the washbasin in the kitchen. And it wasn't even washday.

Susanna had better go to the door. She hoped she would not find another note on the doormat like the one that had come yesterday.

This is your last warning, Hanby. No more about the saloon, or we'll harm you and yours.

The memory of the black, hostile lettering still gave her pause. But she couldn't become so afraid that she refused to answer the door—what next, refusing to go out of the house? Susanna set her knitting on the table beside her, then glanced in the small brass mirror on the wall to make sure she was presentable.

When she opened the door, the sight fell on her like a load of logs, stunning her into silence.

"Evenin'." George Leeds stood on the stoop, his shirt and hat as crumpled as ever, his beard still oily-looking.

"Hello."

"Aren't you going to invite me in? I have news I think you'll like."

Rachel. Susanna's pulse quickened and she took a breath.

He grinned through his sparse, oily beard. He looked as if he had a lost a tooth or two since she last saw him, probably from falling facedown in a drunken stupor. He had the rotten, nutty odor of the chronic drunk, though she didn't smell the sharpness of fresh liquor.

"Come in." She twitched away from his coat in disgust as he brushed by her.

"Susanna, who is it?" her aunt called.

She did not respond, looking warily at George. He threw his hat on the table, seated himself in Uncle Will's chair, and propped his legs on the footstool, just as if it were his home. If only Uncle Will were here, George would not dare behave so insolently. But her uncle was off at the temperance meeting.

Susanna perched rigid on the edge of a ladder-back chair, feet on the ground, hands in her lap, and stared at her sister's husband.

Aunt Ann came out of the back, wiping her hands on her apron. "Oh." She stopped on the threshold of the sitting room.

"Miz Hanby." George did not get up but lolled against the chair with his head back. What a rude, sorry excuse for a man. And with his oily head, it was a good thing her aunt had cotton doilies on the backs of her humble furniture.

"An unexpected visit, Mr. Leeds." Aunt Ann amazed Susanna with her ability to seem unruffled.

"I was telling my sister-in-law here that I have news I think you'll want to hear."

"Indeed?" Aunt Ann kept a calm façade but stroked the arm of the chair almost absentmindedly as if using its brocade to steady herself.

"I have reached a decision that will interest you." He balanced the heel of one boot on the toe of another, as if sitting outside with another man talking of chickens, not talking about a missing wife with her two grieving female relations.

"It hasn't been an easy decision to make," he drawled.

Susanna wanted to scream but continued to breathe in and out in steady channels of air.

George scratched his chin. "But if you still want me to sign papers and get the children back so you can keep 'em, I will."

What? She rehearsed his words again in her mind, a balloon of unreality about to burst into joy, rising, rising—

He put both feet back on the stool again. "For a thousand dollars."

What?

"What?" her aunt asked simultaneously. "I must have misheard you, Mr. Leeds."

"No, ma'am." He shook his head with solemnity. "I have many expenses in my farm business, and so this is a way we can all get what we want and need."

Hot tremors raced up Susanna's arms like flames up a dry tree. "You listen to me, George." She stood up.

"Susanna," Aunt Ann whispered.

She did not look at her aunt. "My sister is a good woman

whom you neglected and took for granted. She and her children often went hungry because of your lack of character and fondness for drink. And now you come here asking us to pay you for your children?" Her voice rose, edged by fury. "None of us has a thousand dollars to give to anyone."

"Everyone always claims they ain't got it, but they do." His sideways look reminded her of a fox.

"We don't!" Her cheeks felt full and hot. "But even if we did, we wouldn't give it to a miserable excuse for a human being like you! What would you do with it? Nothing but drink!"

He got to his feet. "Don't you disrespect me, Susanna. I'll make you wish you hadn't." Little flecks of spittle came out on the hard ring of his lips.

"Tell me where Rachel is! I believe you know something about it!"

Over George's shoulder her aunt's face had whitened.

"She's a bad woman who can go to the devil for all I care. Maybe she's already with him." George smirked.

Susanna drew back her hand and slapped his leering face.

He exploded in a blur of motion. A hard blow to her chest threw her back against the wall, her head hitting with a thud. The room collapsed into a bleary whirl around her and she would have fallen, but his hands wrapped around her neck, cutting off her breath, so hard her throat crushed in agony. She opened her mouth but nothing could come in or out, only the waves of pain at her neck.

She batted at his arms but had no strength against the determined glee of killing in his drawn lips and bared teeth. She heard Aunt Ann shouting but it was fuzzy.

The room dimmed, disappearing from her sight.

Twenty-Four

JOHANN PAUSED NEXT TO ONE OF THE OIL STREETLAMPS
and examined his shirt in the faint light. A black smudge of powder marked the place where the barrels had touched him. He
buttoned his lightweight blazer, hoping to hide the worst of it.
There. The Hanbys probably would not notice. Good thing his
trousers were black so any hand-wiping done by the creek would
not have left a trace. He could still smell it though.

He passed Corbin's saloon, which had five or six hardy drink-
ers inside on stools from what he could see through the window.
He hoped one was not Arthur Pippen.

He shoved his hands in his pockets as he walked. Should he
really go visit Susanna? Yes. By now she would be almost frantic
about the youngest children and their adoptive placements. He
could at least talk with her and together they could try to produce some new solution.

But when the white frame rental home Mrs. Hanby had
mentioned loomed ahead, he had second thoughts. He continued
walking, on past the house down State Street, nerving himself.
What if the enchanted quality of the night in the garden was only
an effect of the music and the beautiful setting? He might walk

into her house and be greeted with cold hostility if she regretted her venture into German life—or her dance with him.

He was ten yards past the house. *Don't be a fool. Go talk to her.* He stopped, spun on one heel, and strode back toward the door.

Within steps of the front porch, he stopped again. *You are going to New York and it will all be a moot point.*

But as he dug his heel in the grass, the sound of a woman's voice raised in fear came from the house, accompanied by loud thumps.

"Don't, don't! Let go of her!"

It was Ann Hanby crying out. Something was wrong. He sprinted up the stairs and hurled himself at the front door, crashing it open.

Against the far wall of the parlor, a dark-haired man pinned Susanna by her throat. Her hands weakly pushed at him, her eyes dulling into unconsciousness. Her aunt pulled the man's hair, trying vainly to drag him off. He threw the elderly woman off with one blow, and she staggered back and fell against a chair.

Johann charged across the parlor and yanked the man backward by one shoulder. As he spun around, surprised, mouth open, Johann swung one fist around with all his strength and connected hard with the man's temple. He went down like a felled bull, his head swinging back and forth. George Leeds.

With a roar he rushed up from the ground and swung wildly at Johann. He missed, grabbed for Johann's shirt, and clutched him in vise-like hands. He shoved hard. Something slammed into the back of Johann's knees. He tumbled backward over a chair, hitting his head hard on the floor.

In an instant George was on top of him. Johann heaved him over and thrust his knees in his chest. The other man gasped, totally winded, paralyzed. With a deft twist, Johann wrapped his arm behind him in one of the holds from wrestling at the Turnverein. Thank the Lord for physical education.

The only sound was the heaving of breath—Johann's, Susanna's, and eventually George's, when his mouth stopped working in silent agony.

"You swine!" Johann forced his arm farther up, bringing a wince from the greasy-haired man. "What do you think you're doing?"

George did not answer.

Susanna and Ann staggered into his line of sight, the older woman supporting her niece. Susanna tried to speak, then put a hand to her throat with a grimace.

"It's all right, dear," her aunt said. "Don't talk right now."

"What happened?" Johann asked Ann.

"He wanted us to give him one thousand dollars for the children. Susanna flew into a temper and slapped him, then he attacked as you saw."

"I, too, probably would have hit him after such an offer," he said, pitying the humiliation that filled Susanna's face.

He spoke down at George. "Have you no shame at all?"

George said nothing, his teeth gritted, face inches from the floor.

"Well, perhaps you'll feel more comfortable conversing outside." He hauled the man roughly to his feet and pushed him toward the door. "If you'll excuse us, ladies," he said grimly over his shoulder.

When he had marched George a good thirty feet behind the

house, he hooked George's legs out from under him with a practiced sweep and put him down on the ground again, facedown.

"So you come here blackmailing these women who want nothing but to take care of your children?" he asked. "What's wrong with you?"

"I don't even know if they're my children," George said. "If she ran off with another man now, how do I know she wasn't loose before and I just didn't find out?"

The ludicrousness of it staggered Johann. At least some of the children had to be George's, no matter what kind of woman Rachel Leeds was. "Unless you prove her false and the children bastards, you have a responsibility to support them, which includes signing them over to family, not allowing them to be sent off to strange cities and separated."

"If you knew what she was like, you wouldn't judge me, Giere." George's voice turned bitter. "Always nagging, always complaining, never satisfied. And always pregnant, popping out more babies so we couldn't keep up."

"I assume you contributed to her condition or you would have known her faithless for certain." He couldn't keep some dryness from his voice.

"That woman ruined me. She drove me to drink and then blamed me for it. I could have made a good life for us. I had talent."

"At what?" Johann tried not to scoff. The more George talked, the more chance he had of learning something useful about Rachel.

"At acting. They all said so, all the traveling players after I recited for them."

Johann had visions of a drunken George spouting ballads.

George took on a boasting tone. "They said I should come

with them, join their life. But by that time we already had three children and she nagged, nagged, nagged. Then when she heard I wanted to go with the actors, she went to them and told them I was married with three children. They told me they couldn't support a family man, not for the bit parts. So they withdrew their offer. She ruined me." He paused, breathing hard.

The pride and selfishness was too much to answer. "Be that as it may"—Johann could hardly disguise his loathing—"you just attacked a woman after an attempt to blackmail her. The only reason I don't haul you straight to the police in Columbus is because I retain some faint hope you will come to your senses and reclaim your children on Susanna's behalf."

George sneered. "Maybe I will, maybe I won't."

Johann stood up. "Get out of here. Go straight to the train station and get on board, or you'll regret it. And keep in mind that there will be bullets in the Hanby home, always, with your name on them, should you ever repeat such a command perfor-mance. And it would be self-defense should any of them shoot you dead in your tracks."

"I don't have any money," George whined, scrambling up.

Johann kept a wary eye on him, though George looked like a classic bully—no fight when faced with an equal oppo-nent. He took out his billfold and sighed. "This is the fare." He threw it at George's feet in the road so George could not use it as an opportunity to take him by surprise. George went to his knees and patted the ground until he found the coins. What a despicable creature. Was it his nature or the drink? Drink alone could not make a good man bad, could it? Perhaps it could, but he did not think that had been the case with George. The man was a poser and a lover of self, as shallow as a pie plate.

George stood up with the money in his fist and hurried up State toward the station.

Johann watched him the whole way.

Five minutes later Johann gave a polite knock before he walked back in the Hanby's front door.

"What happened?" Susannah asked. Her voice was hoarse, a wisp of its usual self. She was holding a mug and sitting beside her aunt on the one padded bench against the wall of the sitting room. Her aunt's arm circled her waist.

"We had a discussion about the law and the rights of a man defending the lives of others."

"You mean," Mrs. Hanby said, "you told him you'd kill him if he came back?"

"Essentially. Or you would, with the gun that will now be waiting for his return. And I punctuated it with the reminder that we already had more than enough reason to put him in jail. But I know you want him to get the children for you, so I stopped short of hauling him there tonight."

"And he's gone?" Susanna said.

"He slunk off to the train station on my orders. And on my dime."

She set down her mug on the brick hearth beside the bench. "I see." She leaned her head back against the wall and closed her eyes. "I don't know how we will get the little ones now."

"I'm sorry. Should I have behaved differently?"

Her eyes popped open in surprise. "No—no. I'm grateful to you, Mr. Giere."

"Johann."

She sighed. "Johann." She looked very young, gazing at him with dark shadows under her eyes.

Her aunt looked hesitant but did not object. He had guessed correctly that saving a young woman's life qualified them to speak on a first-name basis.

Aunt Ann turned to Susanna and rubbed her shoulder with a considerate hand. "It would not have mattered, Susanna. We did not have the money, and that was all he wanted."

Johann went quiet. "Would you have given him the money if you had it?"

Susanna touched a hand to her forehead as if it pained her. "No. He could have come and taken them away at any time and demanded more money."

"An astute point." As she sat there struggling to hide her distress, he wanted to console her in his embrace.

Instead he walked to the door. "Ladies, I will make sure he has left on the train. Then I will do my best to bring you some better news within the next week." He did not know how, but he would figure it out. Anything to make her happy, to see her eyes light up. Even if he was leaving for New York within a month.

"You are very kind." Susanna set down her tea and stood, as if she could not decide whether to follow him to the door or stay where she was. He returned to her in a few steps, took her hand, and kissed it. He felt the blood rush to his cheeks, but it was worth it because she did not pull away—her eyes just went wide and her lips parted in surprise.

"Good night." He nodded to her aunt and left.

He usually hated blushing in front of others, but tonight the heat in his face was oddly pleasant. All the way up State Street, the tingle in his skin reminded him of her.

Twenty-Five

"JOHANN GIERE IS A NICE YOUNG MAN." AUNT ANN was deceptively casual as she washed Uncle Will's shirt in the laundry tub.

"Yes." Here came the question she had been dreading since yesterday. Susanna dolloped out batter into the muffin pan.

"He seems to think highly of you."

Susanna smoothed off the batter with a spoon.

"Which is understandable, for you are a lovely young lady." Aunt Ann soaped the shirt and rubbed it against the board. "But it's curious too."

"Yes. We differ on many things. I would think he'd hate me for how frankly I've spoken. And sometimes rudely." She remembered the soft brush of his lips on her hand and a shiver ran up her arm. To hide it she grabbed a rag, opened the stove, and inserted the pan.

"It's a good sign when a man likes frank speech in a woman. It isn't common."

"His father said he liked it too. Johann must have inherited the trait."

"I respect his father." Aunt Ann twisted the shirt and wrung it, then looked at it again. "Men with good fathers have a good start in the world, whether their fathers are rich or poor. It's the character that matters."

Where was Aunt Ann leading this? Yes, Johann was very attractive, and yes, she had discovered that he had many good qualities. But they were from two separate worlds and his family still made beer. Time for a new topic of conversation.

"It's the nineteenth today." Susanna deposited her rag on the kitchen table and wiped her hands.

"Yes. Only a few more days until we may visit the Hare Home." Her aunt was too compassionate not to guess immediately why Susanna would mention the date. "I'm sure the children will be fine until we see them. Even getting a good meal once per week makes a difference."

Susanna wished she could trust it was enough. She paced around the kitchen, straightening jars.

The front door opened and Uncle Will let himself in, locking the door behind him. They were more careful since what had happened with George. Uncle Will had been conscience-stricken not to have been home with them, despite their reassurances that nothing could have been done. And indeed, despite his good intentions, he was too frail to have stopped the attack. It was a blessing that he had not been present, for he could have been seriously injured when he went to their defense, as he surely would have.

"I had some success at the docking basin." He walked in and sat in his chair with a sigh, not even stopping to lean his cane in the stand.

"What happened?" She approached, took his cane gently from his hand, and replaced it before taking a seat. Aunt Ann took the other one with a soft rustle.

"I asked many men whether they had seen an auburn-headed young woman in a gray dress. Every man on the docks, I think, and probably some of the mules." He closed his eyes and Susanna had to smile. Then she realized she was perched on the edge of her chair. She shifted back, reminding herself to stay calm and behave serenely. Like Aunt Ann.

"Finally someone told me he had seen a woman like that. He said she came in on one of the packet boats—he didn't know which—and went out again every few days. So I asked the visiting wife of one of the packet boat captains in the basin."

"What did she say?" She could hardly contain herself, and Aunt Ann looked breathless too.

"She said she was certain that woman is the wife of one of the other captains, a man who boats a regular route up to Cleveland and back."

Her heart dropped out of her middle and left a clanging emptiness under her bodice. "Was that all?" She heard the plaintive tone in her voice and felt guilty. He had done his best. "Thank you for trying to find out, Uncle."

"I'm sorry I didn't make more headway. But I think we should still try to find more information about this auburn-haired girl. One wharf-woman's opinion is not conclusive."

"That's true." Her spirits rose somewhat, so at least she did not feel like a gutted fish.

"What is that delicious aroma?" Uncle Will asked.

"Corn muffins." She smiled faintly. "This batch for us, the next for the Pippens."

"Good, good."

She sat with him in silence. How much she loved him—and her aunt too, of course—how grateful she was to both of them. Without their counsel and comfort, she could never have gone so long without telling her parents what had happened. And yet she was convinced that this was the kindest thing to do. She would not tell her parents unless all hope was lost for the children. Her two letters home since her arrival had been full of little inconsequential things as well as some information about the saloon, as she knew they would probably hear about it in the papers. And thus far, they had not asked about Rachel. But that would not last. In a week or two they would certainly have begun to wonder, especially if they'd written to Rachel and received no response.

Her aunt stood up, crossing to Uncle Will. He had fallen asleep right there in his comfortable chair, his head propped against the wing. He did that sometimes. He worked so hard and never stopped until sleep stole up and took him by surprise. Aunt Ann kissed him and glided out to the kitchen.

An hour later, when Susanna was finishing her baking, a knock came at the door. Uncle Will made a snuffling noise and woke up. She could see him stirring in his chair from her place at the kitchen table. "Would you like me to answer the door, Uncle?"

"I'll get it, dear." He grabbed his cane, which Aunt Ann had propped on his knee during his nap. As soon as he stood, he was dignified again, leonine and assured. He crossed to the door.

"Who is it?" he called.

"Arthur Pippen," came the reply.

Uncle Will raised his eyebrows and turned to look at Aunt Ann, who hurried up behind him. He unlocked the door and opened it. "Good afternoon."

"Hello, Mr. Pippen." Aunt Ann gave him a smile so loving that Susanna thought it could have lifted a heart of pure lead.

And he was not immune, for he smiled back at her even though his eyes looked bruised and his cheeks hollow. "Hello, Bishop Hanby, Mrs. Hanby."

"Won't you come in?" Uncle Will said.

He shuffled in, looking around as if he didn't dare take a seat.

"Sit down." Uncle Will indicated his own comfortable chair.

"I'll just sit here, sir," Mr. Pippen said, taking one of the slat-back chairs.

"Would you like some tea?" Aunt Ann asked.

"No, thank you." He looked haunted. "I'm here to express my gratitude for what you've done for my family, Mrs. Hanby."

Aunt Ann pulled up a chair next to him and sat down, minding her bustle. "You're a good man, Mr. Pippen."

He said nothing. How many people had her aunt helped with her kind words? Mr. Pippen seemed so broken—Susanna's heart ached for him.

She put a kettle on, listening from the kitchen so as not to intrude. He would probably like a cup of tea, whether he admitted it or not.

She listened to murmured words about temptation and sickness, and the power of God to remove guilt and to heal, from both her uncle and her aunt. She felt very young and callow. They seemed to know exactly what to say, where she would have been stumbling and inept. Her faith was still so immature compared to theirs. Perhaps in another fifty years she would be as full of love and wisdom as they. She hoped so. She probably would have talked to him about rightness and responsibility had she been in their place. That would not have been the best approach, and she could see that now.

"I'm thinking of moving my family, if they'll forgive me and come with me," Mr. Pippen said. "Out where there's no saloon nearby."

"If it's too much temptation, much better to move. But how will you escape other saloons?" her aunt asked.

"Farming," he said. "Just me and my wife and children, out with the animals and crops under a big sky. Where I can work hard and be a good father and husband. It's all I really want." His voice caught.

"Some may mock it as running away, Arthur," her uncle said, "but don't listen to them. We must all choose the life that allows us to walk with God. If the saloon is too much, right down the street from you, then I applaud you for your willingness to do what it takes to get away from it. And don't let anyone make you feel small. They haven't walked in your shoes. Or perhaps they have, but they're not strong enough to choose a different way."

Mr. Pippen held out his hand and shook her uncle's. "I'm going to choose it, sir. And I pray the Lord will help me love my family more than anything but him."

"You already do," her uncle said, and clasped his hand.

Twenty-Six

"HE ATTEMPTED TO BLACKMAIL HER. FOR A THOU-sand dollars. He demanded it as his fee to retrieve his children from the homes and give them to her." Johann poked the fork at his breakfast cutlet as his mother attempted to shove more eggs on his plate. "No, thank you, *Mutter*."

"How awful," his sister said, her blue eyes huge. "Poor woman."

He liked Maria's soft heart—she could never hear a sad story without sympathy.

"Yes," his father murmured, gazing out the window with the unseeing eyes of a man struck by memory. Johann knew he must be thinking of Louis at five. How hard it would be to have a brother so young vanish at the height of his innocence and never return.

Maria swallowed a mouthful of egg and put her fork down. "I thought she seemed very nice at the Hosters' dance." She grinned, her dimple flashing. "Aren't you glad I didn't come over and pester you?"

"Yes." Johann smiled despite his preoccupation. Maria could always amuse him.

Veta, his younger sister, was ash blond like his grandmother and just as practical, or so his father always said. "Are you courting that girl?" She seized the butter from beside him and took a pat to slather on a roll.

"Girls, leave him alone," their mother said, very stern as she sliced her pork.

Johann reached across and stole the butter back. "How about you, Maria? I saw you with Peter Adler. Kissy, kissy."

She smacked his arm lightly with her hand. "Don't be so silly."

His father grinned, but it faded. "Are you finished eating, son?"

"Yes, sir."

"Come with me to the garden."

Johann stood. There was always a good reason if his father requested his company. "Kissy kissy," he said over his shoulder at Maria, making Veta giggle.

They went out through the kitchen in back to the little flagstone area where his father had ordered several large decorative boulders hauled in from a nearby quarry. His father took a seat on one and felt in his pocket for a cigar. Johann sat on the boulder nearest him and looked up at the morning haze over the high wooden fence. The green ivy climbed up the wood and softened its outlines, as did the dark-green shrubs around the courtyard.

"One thousand dollars he wanted?" His father put the cigar in his mouth.

"Yes."

"A worker's wages for a year." He struck a match and puffed several times.

Johann didn't say anything but waited for his father to continue.

"Perhaps we should offer to give this man the money."

"What?" That was not what he had expected. "But it's extortion."

"It's also the lives of six children at stake."

Johann let out an exasperated breath. "But I think Miss Hanby is correct that he will continue to try to extort money from her—or anyone in her vicinity."

"But time is short now, and once the children are gone, it will be too late. Why not get them out of the home and then worry about their worthless father later?"

Johann rubbed the rough granite beneath him as if he could uncover an answer. "I would have to ask her, put the situation to her again in those terms."

"I think you should." His father lit another match and puffed. It was only an occasional indulgence for him, the cigar, and a sure sign that something was weighing on his mind.

"Let me consider it," Johann said. "I'll go work on the accounts this morning and think about it."

"Good." His father looked relieved. "And then, after you have thought about it, you can decide you agree with me and go to Westerville."

His family was so endearingly blunt. Ordinarily he would have joked back at such a statement, but he would not today. Too much was at stake. And his father was probably right that he would end up in Westerville tonight. If he finished the accounts, he could make the last train and stay over at the Commercial House Hotel to speak with the Hanbys in the morning.

———◦•◦———

The crickets chirped in the darkness of the hot summer night. Susanna stood outside the barn door looking in at Uncle Will, working late as he had many times since she arrived. It was past midnight and here he was, his white head bent over a saddle in the light of a lantern. All because of the children. She must help him more, try to learn some additional leatherworking skills.

She leaned against the door frame to watch, but he looked up. "Hello, Susanna."

"Hello." She slipped in and sat on the stool a few feet away, her dressing gown much easier to arrange than a bustled dress.

"You're up late." He peered at his stitching and inserted the double needles again, one after the other.

"I couldn't sleep."

"Because of your sister?"

"And the children. Only ten days left until they leave the Hannah Neil Mission."

He silently continued his stitching. He was so quiet she wondered if he was praying, with that intense, faraway look in his dark eyes.

"Perhaps we should go back to Columbus tomorrow," she said, hesitant. "And ask more about the red-haired woman—"

Something boomed like a cannon, so loud it shook the air and hurt her ears. She started as the ground vibrated under her feet. Uncle Will stood too, dropping his needles.

"Good heavens." He swung his leg over the bench, unhooked the lantern, and took his cane. He hitched quickly toward the barn door.

She was afraid he might lose his balance, rushing so. "Let me take that." He paused and she took the lantern to free at least one of his hands.

"It's the saloon," Susanna said. "It must be." She had never heard anything like it.

"Let's get your aunt," he said. She had never seen him walk with such quick and jerky strides. She raised the lantern to light their way back to the house.

Aunt Ann flung open the kitchen door, holding another lantern, and held herself back when she saw them coming. "Oh, Will—it can't be good."

"No," he said. "Come, we must see if we are needed."

She hurried down the steps, dress bunched in hand, and they rounded the house to State Street. Others ran past them, lanterns swinging. A woman was screaming and male shouts carried through the darkness. Susanna grew cold and had to force herself to keep to a pace slow enough for Uncle Will to match. An overpowering smell of sulphur and charcoal filled the air, hazy with smoke. Her eyes stung.

When she caught sight of the corner of State and College, she gasped. The Clymer building lay in ruins, collapsed on itself. The roof had come down and the second story crushed the first beneath it. In the front the building was completely annihilated. Only a shaky pile of wood and brick survived in back. Men rushed toward it with buckets, throwing them on several small fires burning in front.

Where were the children? The screaming came from behind, seemingly out of the wreckage itself. The fear and pain in the woman's voice brought a knot to her throat. Only a mother could sound like that—a mother calling for her children. Susanna took a shuddering breath and prayed the only words she could summon. *Lord, spare them, Lord, please spare them.*

The blast had removed all debate and conflict like a layer

of skin, leaving people's hearts exposed. The men throwing water on the fires looked stricken and determined, even as they coughed from the floating smoke. Women stood with hands pressed to their mouths, still in their dressing gowns, some heads bowed. In the back, the heartiest and most courageous of the men edged their way into the building, soaked kerchiefs tied over their faces. After a minute, two emerged carrying the older girl Susanna had seen on the street when they came to town. Her face was covered in black dust, but she was conscious and sat upright in their chair grasp. Behind her stumbled first one boy, then another, coughing and rubbing their eyes.

Now she saw Mrs. Corbin, whose anguished calls had been coming from behind the building, not under it. The woman flung herself forward to embrace her three children, her black hair tumbling in a braid over her shoulder all the way to the ground where she knelt and hugged them, sobbing out loud to the men. "Please, please," even as she held the children close. "Where is Oralie? Where is Henry?"

No one answered—only the ominous crackle of flame and thudding of boots from the men fighting the fires, the splash of a bucket of water, which was lost as soon as it flew into the fire and soot.

The men headed back into the building.

Uncle Will made his way toward Mrs. Corbin around the pieces of glass and blackened wood. Aunt Ann and Susanna followed. Someone must be with her for whatever came next. It was a terrible vision—hypnotic flames reeking of sulphur. Something knocked against her shoe and she looked down. She had almost stepped on a daguerreotype of the Corbins flung this far from the building by the blast—perhaps an engagement portrait. Their serious faces were obscured behind a maze of cracks in the glass.

A groaning went up from tortured timbers. Several onlookers cried out, "Get out! Watch the wall!"

Would the building collapse in the haze and flame?

A burly man picked his way out from behind the rubble, straining under the weight of the tall body of Henry Corbin flung over his shoulder. Several people rushed over to help, including a man in a black coat. Thank heavens Dr. Amos was here.

Another man, the last of them, emerged cradling the little girl in his arms. Her eyes were closed and she was blackened with soot, her streaked white nightdress making her look like a ruined doll.

They laid both Corbin and his youngest daughter out on the ground. Mrs. Corbin released her other children and staggered through the debris toward the prone figures. She almost tripped on splintered sticks and pieces of fabric—the sad remains of what must have been a family chair.

Aunt Ann touched the shoulder of the one of the boys. Uncle Will took the hand of the other as if by unspoken agreement. "Stay here, sweet," her aunt said to the older girl in a firm tone. The girl looked uncertain but obeyed.

Susanna did not know what to do—the girl looked so shattered and scared. She walked over and put an arm around her. It did not matter whether it felt strange. She had to show what human kindness she could. The girl began to shake as the doctor laid his fingers to the necks of the unconscious forms. Even the small pool of lantern light showed Mr. Corbin's head wet with blood.

"They're alive," the doctor said. "Bring them to my office,

and be careful." He led the way, and the other men took up their burdens again to follow him.

Mrs. Corbin sat blinking on the ground, as if unable to move. Aunt Ann released the boy she was holding to Uncle Will, so he held both of the boys' hands. They seemed as stunned as their mother and made no effort to resist.

"Mrs. Corbin," Aunt Ann said. "I want to take your children to a safe place where we can care for them. May I take them to Professor Hayworth's house?" The professor lived only yards away from the intersection where they stood.

Mrs. Corbin nodded, silent.

"And will you come with us? We should give you a cup of tea, something to wear—" Mrs. Corbin's clothing was only a night gown, which was torn. But the black-haired woman shook her head and stayed where she was.

Aunt Ann darted a worried glance at Uncle Will.

"I'll stay with her," he said. "Susanna, will you go with your aunt and help?"

"Of course."

They took the boys and walked a few paces away, the girl following.

"Don't touch me!" Mrs. Corbin shrieked at the top of her lungs. Susanna whirled around to see that Mrs. Corbin had risen to her feet and was screaming at Uncle Will, who did not appear to have touched her and stepped back, alarmed. She waved her fist in his face like a madwoman. "It's you and the others who caused this! You're full of hate. You claim to be good Christians but what have you done? We did nothing to earn this! Look at what you've done! Look!"

She rushed at Uncle Will. He raised one arm in defense,

the other still braced on his cane. She landed one furious blow on his lifted arm before two men ran in and grabbed her. She collapsed from the elbows, hanging in their grasp, sobbing and shouting at them.

Aunt Ann had stiffened and looked as if she would go to him, but Uncle Will waved a hand in an unmistakable signal that she should take the children away. The boys had started to cry, but the girl looked too frightened to move.

Susanna turned back to her. "Will you come?" she asked gently. "We must let you sit down and have some tea."

"I want to stay." Her wide eyes would not leave her shouting mother, who was running out of strength and breath.

"Then I'll stay with you." She remained with her arm around the girl while Aunt Ann walked away with the boys and Uncle Will. What would it be like, to see your mother reduced to screaming rage and hysteria, after your home had been blown to rubble? A pain burrowed deep in her heart at the sight of the girl's stricken face. The haze floated on around them, making it difficult to see figures clearly more than twenty feet away, turning men into hazy gray shapes slipping through the night, throwing the water on the still-burning pyres.

After a minute Mrs. Corbin fell silent. The men murmured to her and she answered more calmly, though still with hatred in her voice. They let her go and she rushed to her daughter and yanked her away from Susanna.

"Don't try to act like a saint," Mrs. Corbin said between her teeth. "The time for help was before, not now." The light in her eyes was pure fury. She marched away with her daughter toward the doctor's office.

Mrs. Corbin might be right. Her words had stripped to the

bone, as if Susanna could see herself clearly for the first time. What had she said to Abel Wilson?—her words could have contributed to this awful scene. The horror in the children's eyes, the memories that would never leave them, and the real chance that they might lose their father or sister, or both.

She could not avoid it, though she wanted to rip away the knowledge and stuff it in a hole. It burned like the fires of the saloon had scorched her inside. She bore some of the blame for this breath of destruction, exhaled over Westerville like a demon's laughter.

———

Johann wearily set down his bucket and wiped his sleeve across his face. One fire out, though it was hard to feel it an accomplishment in the rubble of the Clymer building. He picked it up again and walked out from behind the building. It was his first venture away from his firefighting spot since he had run to the scene from the hotel.

Susanna stood in the midst of the soot and scattered debris that had once been a parlor. The expression on her face mirrored his own state—sick at heart, her eyes full of sorrow. What evil mind had done this and claimed it as righteousness? And Johann had failed, after all his satisfaction in finding and destroying that gunpowder. He should have done more. The little girl might die, and he had not acted as he should. He should have told more people about the veiled threats, the stash of gunpowder.

He stepped over to her. "Susanna."

She registered his presence with the complete lack of surprise that marked the wake of disaster.

He stood close enough to her that they could have held hands, though he did not presume such a thing under the circumstances. Together they watched the men pick through the wreckage, trying to salvage what few possessions might remain.

"All the windows on State Street are broken," Susanna said.

She was correct. The buildings around it were damaged. It would cost thousands to repair the stores and homes scarred by the blast.

"It's not right," she said. "It's evil. I don't want them in my cause. I didn't want this." Her eyes pleaded for forgiveness.

"You are not to blame," he said quietly.

But she hung her head and would not look him in the eye.

"We should go to your aunt and uncle. There's nothing more for you to do here."

It was true. Mrs. Corbin and her daughter did not want her help, and she could do no more than the men to find any of their goods. They were all soot-blackened, anyway, and most would be beyond rescue.

"Let's go." He held out his arm and she put hers through it, almost reflexively, and fell in step with him.

Susanna showed him the Hayworth home, an unassuming frame house with neat window boxes of pansies lit by a lamp sconce beside the door. At his knock Mrs. Hanby came to greet them. "Oh, hello, Mr. Giere." She opened the door and beckoned them in. "The professor has gone out to an emergency meeting. But he told us to make ourselves comfortable. The boys are upstairs lying down. They're young enough to sleep from pure exhaustion, thank goodness."

It must be almost one o'clock in the morning. They headed

down the hall and into the sitting room, where Mr. Hanby sat with a Bible in his lap, pale from fatigue.

"Uncle, you aren't hurt, are you?" Susanna approached and sat in the chair closest to him.

"No, dear," he said.

"What will happen now?" she asked.

"We'll have to go on and do the best we can to help. Given Mrs. Corbin's sentiments toward our town, they probably will not allow us to give them much assistance. I expect they'll leave, and I pray God will restore both Mr. Corbin and his daughter to full health eventually."

"The Columbus police will come to investigate," Johann said. "They'll probably take reports from practically everyone in town, but certainly you, Mr. Hanby."

"I will be glad to assist the police," he said.

"As will I," Johann said. "I have some information I hope might help them to apprehend those responsible."

He paused. The Hanbys seemed very dispirited, and little wonder at that. "I came here tonight with the intention of discussing something with you tomorrow morning. As it's already morning and I will have to go back to the city in a few hours, I would like to raise the subject."

"Please do," Mr. Hanby said. His white hair was grayed by soot.

"It's about the children."

Susanna's green eyes focused on him, the pall of shock and guilt on her face lifting for a moment. "What is it?"

"My father has offered to pay George Leeds his blackmail money in order to prevent the children from being sent away."

Susanna went very still. Mrs. Hanby's mouth dropped

open. Mr. Hanby listened, though he leaned his head back against the chair.

"You told him?" Susanna asked.

"Yes, I hope you don't mind."

"No—that's generous of him. I don't know what to think."

"He wishes you to consider the fact that once the three youngest children are gone, you will be unlikely to ever retrieve them. Better to give in to a corrupt man's demands now, as my father has the money and can spare it."

Mr. Hanby smiled a little. "A funny thing, to 'spare' a sum like that."

Johann kept quiet—awkwardness was inevitable in such a strange situation.

"Your father makes a good argument," Mr. Hanby said. "But it requires time to consider. And I believe the decision must lie with Susanna."

"All I know," Susanna said, "is that I'd like to see the children right away."

The sorrow and worry creased on her forehead tugged at Johann's heart. He could tell she was thinking about the little girl's limp form coming out of the remains of the saloon. It haunted him too. "Then come with me, when I go back on the train," he said. "All three of you."

"Will, I think you're too tired," Mrs. Hanby said before her husband could answer. "Please stay and rest."

Johann had to agree. The older man looked worn to a thin shadow of his usual energetic self.

"All right," Mr. Hanby said. "I'll see if I can help the Corbins in any way while you're gone." He closed his eyes.

"And I'll escort you to the orphanages," Johann said to the women.

"Thank you," Mrs. Hanby said. Susanna did not respond, but she looked relieved.

He was so glad to have eased her burden that it took some of the sorrow from his heart, but nothing could erase the pictures that night had painted in his mind. "I will go to the hotel. And at eight o'clock"—he fished his watch out of his pocket—"that is, in seven hours, I will meet you at the train station." He rose. "Good night. Or good morning, I suppose." On another day it would have been a gentle witticism, but now it was a simple observation.

"Until then," Mrs. Hanby said.

He left, his footfalls loud on the oak floor in a silence like a house during a wake. *Lord, keep death away from this town tonight.* He prayed silently for Corbin and his daughter as he closed the door behind him.

Twenty-Seven

THE DARK OUTLINE OF THE HARE HOME TOWERED ahead. Susanna took unexpected comfort in Johann's steady presence at her side, his measured stride. He had stopped only to deliver his article to the *Westbote*, and then he had escorted them straight here. He was so gentle about it—he didn't appear to mind at all.

This time Susanna would find a way to ask Clara for every detail of what had happened when Rachel gave up her children. There had been no time, when they last brought the ham, and part of her shrank from making her niece describe whatever had passed between Rachel and George. But if there was any chance to find Rachel, she must take it. Giving Mr. Giere's money to George was a last resort, and one she would resist until the last possible moment.

She held the heavy basket in both hands as Johann knocked. Mrs. Grismer opened the door and scowled out at them. Her expression lightened when she registered Susanna and the basket. "Good morning, Mrs. Hanby and Miss Hanby," she said. "You're early." She looked crafty. "I didn't expect you for another three days."

"Yes, ma'am," Susanna said. "But since we had strawberry pies, we thought we should bring two for the children." Johann had taken them to the German bakery and purchased the pies to ensure their admission.

"Very well." She was gruff, as if relishing her power. "And who are you?" she asked Johann.

"A friend of the family, just seeing them here safely, ma'am," he said.

Susanna thought he seemed very appealing in his humble and polite response, and Mrs. Grismer must have thought so too, for she opened the door. "Come in."

"Why, Mrs. Grismer," her aunt said. "We should offer you a piece of pie first of all. Will you have one with me?" With magnificent aplomb her aunt pretended to enjoy that prospect. Susanna admired her self-control, but she did not feel like giggling at it today as she would have a month ago. She felt empty of laughter. The gunpowder had blasted it out of her like the broken glass on State Street.

"How kind, Mrs. Hanby." Mrs. Grismer leered and waddled toward her sitting room.

Her aunt took the basket and followed.

"We'll go visit the children for just a few minutes," Susanna said, and Mrs. Grismer did not appear to notice, obsessed with the immanent appearance of flaky crust and sweet red filling.

Johann offered his arm and she took it shyly. She had done it so often in the last week that it felt natural, as if her place on his arm was no longer alien but a sweet moment of refuge.

They climbed the stairs together, he holding the banister with one hand, she on his left side.

"Appalling," he said under his breath. A surge of warm

liking for him made her hold his elbow more closely, and she didn't care if he felt it. Not many other men would care for the children of strangers and how they might be treated in an orphanage.

"The three here are indentured to the charity," she whispered to him. "I don't know how we'll get them out, even if George reclaims them."

She saw the thought sink in, and he looked reflective.

"But at least they won't be sent away," she added.

They stepped into the large room with its crumbled plaster and musty odor. Clara did not notice them until they were almost upon her, so absorbed was she in her sewing, peering at the small stitches.

But when she did, she jumped up and embraced Susanna, clinging tightly around her waist. And this time Wesley and Daniel were both there. In moments, her arms were full of skinny, poorly dressed children. Tears ran down Wesley's face as he held on without speaking, and Susanna had to take a breath to restrain her own. It was such a relief to see him, after all this time. His reddish-brown hair was long and scraggly around his small neck, his dark eyes almost as shadowed as Daniel's, though he was taller and seemed sturdier than his brother.

Johann watched her over their heads. His eyes glistened brighter, then he blinked and looked away, holding his hat over his chest.

"Come over here by the window. Let me see your faces properly." She led them to where the sun shed a rectangle of light through the one window at the end of the large room, and Johann followed them. "This is my friend." She nodded at Johann. "His name is Mr. Giere."

Neither he nor the children spoke—introductions and hand-shakes were for grown-ups and Johann seemed to understand their childish reticence.

"I've brought some more ham." She passed it out quickly, retrieving the paper bundles from her large pocket as Johann took several from his coat pocket and handed them to her. "But we haven't much time. I need you to tell me everything that happened when your mother brought you to the Hannah Neil Mission, that first place where the little ones stayed. I'm trying to find her and I need to know everything."

"She left us there. She said we would be safe." Clara unwrapped the ham but left it in her lap untouched.

"I know this is a sad subject, but, Clara, you must eat even if it makes you sad. We don't know if the housekeeper will take the food away."

Reluctantly, Clara took a bite.

"What did she mean, that you would be safe?" Susanna asked.

Wesley swallowed—he had wasted no time in digging into the food. "I think she meant from Father."

A chill passed over her even in the musty, close room. "Why, Wesley?"

He had always been the least intimidated by their father, and had born the bruises for it more than once from being taken to the woodpile. Now his eyes flashed with resentment. "Because he said a couple times when he was drunk that he was going to kill all of us children and that would show her."

Susanna heard a sharp intake of breath from Johann behind her, the sound of a man ready to fight. She glanced at him and saw his jaw line harden. But he kept quiet.

Susanna addressed all three children. "Do you know why she left just then? Did anything unusual happen?"

"She cried a lot," Clara said. "At home, and then when she had to leave."

"She cried at home because Father hit her," Wesley said. "When he was drunk." He said the word with loathing.

"But she didn't give you any hint of where she might be going?" Susanna asked.

"No," Clara and Wesley both said at once. Daniel stayed quiet, as if the effort of speaking was better left to his brother and sister. His nostrils flared with effort when he took a breath. It hurt her as if it were her own straining lungs. She placed her hand on his shoulder. "Keep eating, Danny." She left her hand there and he obeyed, soothed by her touch.

"Don't worry, I'll do everything I can to find her." Now that she had stirred them up, she wanted nothing more than to reassure them before they had to leave. "Tell me what your work is like," she said to Wesley.

Though his story of the long hours of labor made her ache inside, at least he and Daniel were not being struck or otherwise abused. She continued to urge them to eat, glancing at the stairs from time to time to be sure Mrs. Grismer was not there.

Johann asked Clara about the other girls, whether she had any friends. He had the easy manner of a man who is comfortable with young children. While he listened to her, Susanna's gaze drifted out the window. The street looked gray and faded, even in the morning sunlight, but at least the children had something to watch, if Mrs. Grismer was not around. Down on the street the morning traffic swirled around, men on work errands stepping around slower women carrying baskets or bags. A vendor selling cutlery had parked his wagon by the curb, and the driver of another cart yelled at him to move it out of the alley where he was stuck.

In the shadowed alcove of a doorway there by the alley a woman stood. She was wearing a hat that shadowed her face, but where the sunlight hit her dress near the hem, it was gray. Susanna could not see her eyes, but it seemed to her that the woman was watching them. The conviction that it was Rachel rushed over her. She beckoned Johann, but when she turned back to the street, the woman had slipped away.

He looked at her with a question in the slight lift of his brows.

"We have to go," she murmured. "I saw someone outside who looks like my sister." She broke away and picked up the papers that had held the ham, folded them with quick motions, and slid them into her pocket. No evidence of the food must be left. Her movements were quick, as fragmented as her thought. They must leave before that woman disappeared.

She wished the children good-bye, with assurances of her return as soon as possible. Her steps were quick all the way to the stairs, her skirt swaying around her ankles. She must go see if that woman was still on the street.

She clattered down the stairs, hearing the soft thump of Johann's footfalls behind her. It did not matter if Mrs. Grismer saw—not now. She ran out the front door, down the stoop, and around the corner.

A wagon barely missed her. She pulled back with a startled exclamation, then hurtled across the street. Johann was a step behind her the whole way.

When she reached the alley, it was vacant. Her heart sank. She was too late.

"Susanna." Johann was breathing hard, looking concerned as he paused a few steps away. "That wagon almost hit you."

She did not care. She felt her lip trembling.

He moved closer, laid a gentle hand on her arm, and looked down the alley as if he could summon back the phantom of her sister for her. "It's all right. We've missed her today, but we won't lose the children."

His face was so near to her in profile that she saw his lips part to take a breath. He turned to her, the curve of his lower lip only inches from hers. Something went through her like a thirst, but in every atom of her body, a craving. She did not move.

"You must promise me you won't run into streets without looking," he said.

She was practically in his arms, both of them motionless, though alarm still lingered in his eyes as she was sure sadness marked hers. They were both breathing fast.

"You could have been hurt," he said.

She said nothing. She should move away. But she wanted to be close to him so keenly that she could only stand there with her face tilted up to his.

"You must be careful," he whispered, not taking his gaze from hers. He slipped his hands under her elbows and the warmth of his fingers made her feel faint. He lowered his lips toward hers and she closed her eyes, half-afraid, her pulse pounding. The gentle touch of his mouth on hers replaced the fear with an even fiercer longing and she held him to her in a rush of passion and kissed him back. She was aware of nothing but the softness of his lips, the pure bliss of being in his arms. He pressed kisses to her mouth and trailed them down her neck, kissing the tender spot below her ear so she gasped. After a turbulent moment, she heard him draw in a breath. An intense mix of feelings warred on his face as he pulled back, his eyes closed, head down, but he kept one arm around her in a protective clasp.

Susanna started. What was she doing? A wave of guilt crashed down on her and she pulled away and raced back to the street, though she paused to look both ways this time. As she crossed, she heard the rustle of his coat against his shirt behind her, the light tread of his shoes. The tingling in her lips would not stop—the more she willed it away, the more she thought of his kiss. *Stop! Go back to Aunt Ann! This is not the time.*

Aunt Ann was waiting for them in the lobby, with Mrs. Grismer beside her. "Why did you run out?" the housekeeper asked suspiciously.

"I thought I saw someone I knew." She tried to make it sound light, like a scatterbrained young woman.

"I feared she'd be run down in her excitement, and I was almost proven right." Johann knew just what to say—he was too intelligent to jeopardize their contact with the children. Aunt Ann tossed out a few pleasant sentiments and Mrs. Grismer answered in grunts.

"You came back for this visit three days early." Mrs. Grismer ushered them out the front door. "That means you must wait longer the next time. Ten days."

Susanna's temper crawled in twists of heat up her neck. Some people were such petty tyrants when given the slightest bit of power. Why did they seize upon every opportunity to torment those who depended on their whim?

She stifled her retort. "Yes, ma'am," she said, humble as a schoolgirl.

She wished this woman would face a reckoning for her selfishness. But that was the least of her concerns. She went down the stoop of the building and waited for her aunt at the bottom, trying not to meet Johann's gaze, though she sensed it on her. He made a few congenial comments to the housekeeper— she admired his composure, though she could not summon it herself. She peered around the street and took a few steps back toward the alley. It was still vacant.

She returned to meet Aunt Ann on the stoop. Her aunt's quick glance was assessing, as if she sensed something unusual afoot. Susanna felt warmth creep from her neckline to her cheeks. But her aunt said nothing and waited for Johann with ladylike calm as he came down the stoop after them.

"The Hannah Neil Mission is next. We'll need to take the streetcar," Susanna said.

"I'll go with you, if you like." Johann seemed very serious. Could her aunt hear a new intimacy in his tone? Susanna folded her arms and did not meet either of their gazes.

But she did not want him to leave. "Yes, that would be welcome."

She longed to take his arm again, waited on even that formal touch with anticipation. When he offered, she felt the same lift of the heart as when they kissed, but also a new, deep reassurance from his unflagging regard and care. It eased her spirit a degree, even in the absence of Rachel, the plight of the children, the awful memory of the Corbins.

She felt she would go with him anywhere, and he with her.

Twenty-Eight

"Is Mr. Giere here?" The low, male voice came from the front of the *Westbote* office, down the hall.

"Yes, sir," the boyish treble of the newsboy replied.

Johann walked a few paces and emerged into the main printing room. A man with salt-and-pepper hair and a mustache was standing just inside the front door.

Johann approached the man, offering his hand. "I'm Johann Giere."

"Ronald Brundish." The man shook his hand with a firm grip. "Reporter for the *Dispatch.*" He appeared to be in his fifties, from the creases on his forehead.

"Ah, yes, Mr. Brundish. I've seen your articles. A pleasure to meet you in person."

"Likewise. I read your piece on the saloon bombing this morning."

"You read German?"

"My grandparents came over from Bavaria."

Interesting that Johann had not seen him at German events— but then, some men didn't want to claim their heritage.

"My congratulations on scooping the rest of us," Brundish said.

"Any time."

They both grinned, though Brundish's held a hint of rue. No reporter missed a story without pain.

"As you were the only member of the press to witness the scene in person, I'd like permission to write an account for the *Dispatch* based on your eyewitness account."

"With appropriate credit?"

"Of course."

Johann considered. It did not matter, really, if Brundish wrote the article, as long as he gave credit. And Johann was behind on the brewery accounts again after spending the day yesterday with the Hanbys. He had no time to draft another article right now. "Yes, that's acceptable," he said. "If you'd like to walk out with me, I'm afraid I must get to another appointment." An appointment with his overdue ledgers.

"Certainly." They exchanged professional courtesies as they walked down High Street. The horse car trundled toward them— Johann wished Brundish good-bye and swung himself up into a bench seat.

The *Westbote* building receded from his peripheral vision and he sighed. Never would he have thought he would be so ambivalent about the newspaper. But the heady aroma of gaslight and crime that hung around the New York position now had a rival in the soft, sweet-smelling hair of Susanna. And he must be honest with himself—he had thought of her a hundred times since they parted company yesterday, with a sharp yearning to hold her again and kiss her as he had on the stairs. Their subsequent walk to the Hannah Neil Mission had been charged with that unexpected intimacy, though of course Susanna became completely absorbed in the children once they arrived. That was a mercy, because her aunt had sensed something and was observing him more closely than he liked. He did not mean to conceal anything, but who knew how Susanna's relations might react to an open courtship. And he could not truly court her, anyway, if he were going to New York.

Donnerwetter, what a mess. Guilt seeped down to his gut. He should not have kissed her, not if he meant to leave. It wasn't honorable—he was ashamed of himself for losing his restraint. And still, a little whispery voice said he could choose to stay, try to convince his family and the Hanbys that he and Susanna were a good match.

But why would God have arranged the way to New York so neatly unless Mr. Reinhardt was correct? What were the odds that a national crime story would happen in Westerville, Ohio, of all places? It could not be coincidence. If God did have a plan to send Johann to New York, then was Susanna merely a distraction? If so, she was the best one ever created.

At the very least, he would not rest, he could not leave until he had helped her do everything possible to bring those children home to the Hanbys. It was one thing to know of her situation— quite another to see in person the sad faces of the Leeds children, the real possibility that they would be separated and the little ones would never know their siblings. It had torn at his heart, standing there in the orphanage, until he had to turn away and wipe his eyes when she wasn't looking. No one could fathom the impact on those children should their family be utterly destroyed. It was bad enough that their mother had disappeared to parts unknown.

He was so lost in thought he barely noticed the passing

scenery, and he realized with a start that he had almost missed his corner near the brewery. When the horse car slowed again, he jumped out to the pavestones. He strode down Brewer's Alley and crossed Wall, then Front. The entrance to the brewery lay a few yards ahead. He rounded the corner of the wooden fence.

"Giere." To his right, a man loomed very close to him.

Johann jerked away by instinct, opening a few feet between them.

It was George Leeds, hair tidier than usual, clothes smoother, beard trimmed and clean. But the fumes of whiskey still drifted from him in a noxious cloud.

"What brings you here?" Johann did not make an effort to sound friendly. It was too odd to have the man spring up at his elbow.

"I'm here to tell you my offer still stands, but only for four more days. I knew who you were when you told me your name." He pointed to the brewery. "And I know you can afford it."

Johann gritted his teeth and waited.

George puffed out his unhealthy chest. "I got a part with the traveling troupe. We leave for the South on Monday." He beamed with pride as if he expected congratulations. "So if you want the children, I could use the traveling funds. And I won't hold anything against you."

Monster. Johann's pulse sped up and his fists tensed. But richly as this man deserved it, a trouncing was not going to solve the problem. "Understood," he said reluctantly. "And where am I to find you?"

"Here." He handed Johann a card, garish and new. On it "George Leeds" was printed in elaborate lettering, with "Actor" beneath it.

"I need an address."

"On the back," George said smugly.

The address scrawled by hand was on Rich Street near the river. Not a good part of town, but Johann expected nothing else. "I'll find you if I need to find you," he said with disgust, and walked on into the yard toward the building.

His stomach turned. What a sickening display of ego and pride—a man to whom a wife and six children meant nothing, but the chance to strut on a stage was life itself. It was as if he had tossed seven human beings on a ragpicker's wagon without blinking and had them hauled away.

When he reached the brewery office, no one was there. He sat down and opened the ledger, but he gazed at it for a long time with unseeing eyes, too churned up inside to work.

Twenty-Nine

She daydreamed of him while she washed the pots and pans, while she stitched harness, while she helped Aunt Ann sort pieces for a quilt.

Her preoccupation lasted all afternoon. She boiled blackberry preserves, the canning steam rising high in the air, moisture gathering on her forehead. If she had cost her aunt and uncle money, she could at least help them store up new supplies. The work of canning was hot, but she didn't mind the solitude that left her free to remember blue eyes and those breathless few seconds in the alley. She might as well do something useful with her time—it was better to stay busy. And she did not wish to go outside, where she would have to see the hideous, blackened hulk of the saloon with its roof lying to one side on the ground.

Someone rapped on the kitchen door. That was odd. She peered out to find the freckled face of Abel Wilson at the window.

"Good afternoon, Miss Hanby."

"Hello, Mr. Wilson. Are you looking for my uncle?"

"No, I came to look in on you and see if you were recovering from the shock—you know, of the saloon and all." He looked ill at ease.

"Thank you Mr. Wilson, but I'm quite well. I'm more concerned about the Corbins."

"My concern is for you first."

She didn't want to hear declarations of affection from Mr. Wilson, and it also seemed in poor taste, with a child and man lying injured in the doctor's house. "Have you heard anything about the Corbins' health?"

He waved an impatient hand. "Aren't you glad that the saloon nightmare is over?" He looked bizarrely expectant. What did he want?

"I don't think it's over, Mr. Wilson."

He recoiled. "Why not?"

"Every time I see that building, I see the town's nightmare continuing."

"I thought you wanted it gone as much as I did." His eyebrows knit together in a wounded twist.

"I was wrong. What happened was terrible. My uncle will be preaching on it. Every preacher in town has asked him to come help, to console the congregations. Don't you see how awful it's been? People won't even look each other in the face. They won't walk down State Street." She realized that she was wringing the dishrag in her hand until drops ran down her wrist.

He bit his lip with his big front teeth, resembling a worried young rodent. "I don't think your uncle should preach on it."

"Why not?"

"He's been too critical, using the Bible as if no one in Scripture ever had to fight an evil, as if it's wrong to take up arms and fight."

She stared, dumbstruck. Did he think blowing up children belonged in the same league with a knightly joust? "If you don't mind, Mr. Wilson, I'm in the middle of chores."

He added resentment to the parade of expressions moving across his boyish features. "I see, Miss Hanby. Good day."

Even the canning steam couldn't dispel the cold that had slithered into her stomach.

Twenty minutes later her aunt walked in from the backyard. Her cheeks had more color from the walk, her white hair twisted in a neat chignon below her straw hat. "They've gone to Columbus."

"Who has gone?" Susanna asked.

"The Corbins." Aunt Ann removed two long hatpins and hung her hat on the wall. "Mr. Corbin and his baby girl will recover, they say. Praise God! But they won't be back, and I can't rejoice in the wicked act that prompted their departure."

"I suppose we should be glad that Arthur Pippen won't have to leave, and other men will be safe because there's no saloon." Susanna's voice was weak. Abel Wilson's visit had shaken her, and the strangeness of what he said would not leave her mind.

"The benefits can't outweigh the injuries and evils," her aunt said. "Have you seen this?" She laid a newspaper on the kitchen table. "It's causing a stir over at the hotel and in the post office."

Susanna walked to the table, curious. It was the *Daily Evening Dispatch*. At the top, it said "General Telegraph News"— in other words, a piece that would go all over the country, to the *New York Times* and other major papers.

BLOWING UP A SALOON
COLUMBUS—At last the people of Westerville, a small village in this county, have succeeded in blowing Henry Corbin, the saloonkeeper in that

town, high and dry out of his building. All kinds of persecution have been resorted to in order to rid the village of a saloon. The majority of the villagers support temperance and belong to a religious sect know as the United Brethren. They fight Satan as well as all others not of their belief, and an outsider is considered and treated as little above the most degraded.

"Oh goodness," Susanna said. Her heart sank. "Has Uncle Will seen it?" What an awful piece, to tar the whole town and attack the United Brethren for the violence of a few. And to call the Brethren a sect, as if they were some strange, eccentric people instead of just another Christian church. Her uncle would be so hurt. Perhaps they could hide it from him.

"Yes." Aunt Ann's brow was furrowed. She picked up the tongs and began to place lids on jars with assured, quick motions. "Did you read the last part?"

Susanna scanned the rest of the article, mostly a description of the explosion, the two kegs of gunpowder discovered missing, and the damage and injuries. But then another sentence caught her attention.

While the citizens profess to be indignant and claim that they will investigate and bring the guilty to punishment, little confidence is had in such statements. It is a well-known fact that any person not in league with the United Brethren sect cannot hope to live in peace, but is harassed until he either departs on his own or is blown out.

She laid a hand over her bodice, pressing without effect against the ache that had started there. Oh, Uncle Will. He had given his whole life to the church and worked so hard to serve.

The last line of the article read:

We are indebted for this article to our German colleague at the *Westbote*.

What? She glanced at her aunt, then back down at the page as if she could rearrange the lettering by her will alone. "Johann did this?"

She picked it up and held it closer to read the telltale line again. How could he? It was too monumental to even take in.

"I don't know, dear." Lines of worry etched across her aunt's brow. "Perhaps it wasn't he." She took the pot of steaming water and set it aside to cool.

Aunt Ann was being too generous. There was no other reporter at the *Westbote* who had covered the story. It was Johann's story—Susanna knew it.

The lock clicked in the front door and her uncle entered. He seemed older, his shoulders slumped, his face sagging.

"Hello, dear," her aunt called.

He did not speak but went upstairs one slow step at a time.

Susanna tore off her apron with shaking fingers and threw it down on the table.

Her aunt held out a hand in caution. "Now don't let it upset you too much." But her eyes glittered with unshed tears and she turned back to the stove.

Susanna grabbed her handbag from its hiding place in the

pantry and hurried to the door. Her tuition money was inside—it would pay her fare.

"Where are you going?" her aunt asked across the sitting room.

She did not answer—she did not want to be stopped. She pulled the door closed and headed to the train station.

———•◦•———

Johann bowed his head and rubbed his aching temples. Too much work, too little rest. He had spent several hours looking for Rachel Leeds by the docks and in nearby businesses, but no one knew anyone by that name. And the auburn-haired description brought up the same information that Mr. Hanby had told him: a captain's wife, in and out of town. As a result of his investigations, he had stayed up late into the night finishing the books for the month, balancing accounts. Sometimes he wished he did not have such a good head for figures, but he was the best bookkeeper, and so his father liked him to look everything over. It was the wise thing to do, in a business as complex as the brewery.

Heinrich stuck his head around the door frame. "Johann. You have a visitor." He winked.

It must be Lotte. He suppressed a comment and rose to his feet.

"In the front yard," Heinrich said.

The last thing he wanted with this aching head was to hear another love song, but he could not be unkind. He already felt guilty about taking someone else to the dance. He had most certainly hurt her feelings.

He skirted the mash tuns where the brew fermented, then exited through the double doors. A light sprinkle of rain had begun and pattered in tiny circles on the dirt of the yard. And it was not Lotte, but a much more welcome visitor, standing in the yard in her green dress.

Susanna. The sight of her delicate features under the brim of her hat melted him at once, though she wore a look of strain around her eyes that he had seen too often. He wished he had some news about her sister to ease her worry.

"Good afternoon." He smiled.

But she did not return his smile or his greeting. She brought up a newspaper in her hand and showed it to him—the *Dispatch.* "Did you see this?"

"No." He hadn't yet found the time to look at the other papers today.

"Here." She held it out.

What had prompted such a clouded expression? He unfolded it and looked at the first page. She stabbed her finger at the telegraph news column. He read it. *Meine Guete,* it was harshly worded. He could see why she was so perturbed. He read through the description of the facts—yes, Brundish had it all straight. But it was harsh—he felt her distress and he must console her for it. Then he read the credit at the bottom. He raised his eyes to meet her gaze. She was about to burst, her green eyes smoldering.

"How could you do it?" she said with restrained intensity. The accusation in her face stunned him.

She took a step toward him. "Why? Why would you ridicule us in this manner? Were we just figures of fun to you the whole time, the crazy United Brethren? You must have laughed to see us so taken in by your charm at the dance . . . and elsewhere." He knew she was thinking of the alley outside the Hare Home. She was so bitter he could not summon a response. Her words went into him sharp and deep as a lance and stuck there, skewering him in silence. She thought so little of him? She should know him better after their time together and his efforts to help her.

"You do not seem to wish to hear an explanation," he said, his own temper rising like stirred coals. "Do you? Because perhaps there is something you're overlooking."

"There's nothing to explain. It's all clear." The rain was harder now, covering her straw hat in a net of tiny droplets.

"You are very hard in your judgment. Perhaps you should ask more questions and make fewer—"

"I don't want to see you again, Mr. Giere." Her words were quick and cold, but as she turned to walk away, her severe expression cracked into pieces. She hid her face as she hurried away, her bustled skirt brushing over the rapidly dampening yard.

He watched her leave. What had happened? She had judged and sentenced him without a single question, without an atom of grace to lessen her fury.

It was too much. Her outburst was so unexpected, as if she had ambushed him, hacked away, and left him bleeding in the dust. Her temper was no excuse for a lack of compassion or mercy for a friend.

He could have wept at the injustice of it, at how badly he still wanted to go after her and embrace her and make everything right and kiss her again. But nothing he did could make her heart right—it was poisoned against him.

He was still holding the paper, rolled up. He muttered an

oath and slapped it against his palm so hard it stung. He stormed back inside.

"May I come in?" His father stood at the bedroom door.

"Please do," he said. The telegram offering him the New York job lay facedown on his desk—he shoved it in the desk drawer as his father approached and sat on the bed.

"Have the Hanbys decided whether they wish to give the money to George Leeds?"

Johann hesitated. He picked up his pen and doodled on the blotting paper. "They have not told me."

"But there are only two days left, correct? And then the man leaves town?"

"Correct."

"And they are aware of this?"

"No."

"You haven't told them?" His father's brows were raised, Johann knew it without even looking around.

"A problem has arisen," Johann said.

"Of what nature? No matter what, you must tell them."

"Miss Hanby and I have fallen out. Did you read the article in the *Dispatch* today about Westerville?"

"No. Only yours in the *Westbote.*"

"Well, here's the *Dispatch* version." He handed it over.

Silence followed for three or four minutes. His father did not read quickly in English. Johann wanted to drop his head on the desk and close his eyes, but he would not give in. He kept doodling.

At last his father made a harrumphing noise. "And the writer credits you."

"Or discredits, in this case."

"I can see why your friend is hurt."

"She is furious."

"It's all the same." The bed creaked as his father stood up. He walked around to stand at the side of Johann's desk, his back against the wall. "This does not change the fact that you must tell her about George Leeds before the opportunity is gone."

"You seem eager to spend your one thousand dollars." Johann sounded gruff. He did not mean it—he wanted to rescue those children even more than his father did. But what would his father think if he gave the Hanbys the money and soon after, Johann informed him he would be leaving for New York? His father would feel deceived as well as abandoned. It made Johann feel sick at heart.

If Susanna ever recovered from this attack of unjust hatred, could they marry and move to New York together?

No, though a reporter's salary would support a small family, it wouldn't support all of her nieces and nephews. And it was a logistical impossibility—she would never leave Ohio while her sister's children were here. But he really wouldn't have her any other way. Her deep love for her family was one of her best qualities.

His father stood up straight. "The future is too important to risk on a lover's quarrel. For that's what this is, yes?"

He felt himself blushing. "No, it's more serious—she won't listen to reason or even ask for my explanation. She won't forgive this article."

"That is always what lovers think." His father's look was astute. "And you are in love with her."

Johann's ears grew hot and he looked down at the page in front of him. "I will ensure that she knows about Leeds."

"*Danke.* You will not regret it—I have faith that the Hanbys will choose to accept the money. No one will let children go if there is any choice."

"Except George Leeds."

"Yes. But Miss Hanby is a decent woman who loves her nieces and nephews. Time heals all, regardless of what bitterness she feels now. They will take the money and get the children. After a few months—perhaps even a few weeks—the two of you will be as before, and you can bring her back to another dance. I did like her." He patted Johann on the shoulder and walked out.

After a few months I will be gone, and you will be one thousand dollars the poorer, all for a woman who now sees me as an enemy.

To stay or to go—it was an impossible choice.

Thirty

THICK, DARK SMOKE HUNG EVERYWHERE, CHOKING her as she ran through it.

Susanna awoke in the darkness of her bedroom, faint moonlight glowing behind the curtain. She lay there with her heart hammering. It was a dream, nothing more.

But she smelled smoke. She rubbed her nose and inhaled again. Was it her imagination? No. She swung her feet out of bed and slipped into her dressing gown. Alarm prickled over her shoulders as she padded down the stairs.

There was nothing amiss downstairs. The stove was cold. A faint hissing came from the back door. She walked over and opened it to look out.

A column of smoke billowed up from the barn and a light danced behind the small window.

"Uncle! Auntie!" She ran to the door of their room to see them sitting up, eyes wide, scrambling to their feet. "The barn is on fire!"

She ran back into the kitchen and grabbed a bucket, then flung herself out the door. She barely felt the kitchen steps fly by as she bolted for the barn, the empty bucket swinging.

She snatched the side door open, grateful for its wooden handle. *Dear Lord, help us.* Flames engulfed the hay and storage area above the saddlery at the far end of the barn. A large stick of wood in the middle of the hay pile burned with an unnatural ferocity, like a torch.

A terrified whinny went up from the other side of the barn. Thank heaven for the partition between the saddlery and the stalls: it might have saved the horse and cow. She dropped the bucket and ran to open the front door of the barn. Inside, she snatched the halter and lead rope from its nail. The smoke stung her eyes.

The roan gelding showed the whites of his eyes as he plunged around his stall. Haltering was out of the question—if she went in the stall, he would crush her. She slid back the bolt, stepped out of the way, and swung the door wide. He shot out at top speed and vanished into the night.

In the other stall, the cow was standing in the back, her wide nose to the wall as if she could hide. Susanna threw the horse's halter aside and grabbed the cow's. But when she had slipped it on and buckled it, the cow stood with her feet planted and would not move no matter how Susanna tugged at the rope. She whirled around, searching wildly for anything to help.

The slim figure of her aunt hurried through the barn door. "I'll get her." She slowed as she neared the cow, put on the appearance of calm, and took the rope. Susanna retreated out of the stall—animals responded best to those they trusted most. Sure enough, at her aunt's urging, the cow pivoted and followed on its rope. Susanna rushed out the wide door ahead of them. Her aunt turned toward the house—she would take the cow to safety on the other side. "Go help Will!" Aunt Ann called back to her. "I'll get the neighbors!"

Susanna raced back toward the burning saddlery. She almost collided with her uncle coming out the door, coughing. He had picked up two buckets.

"The water trough," he said. She took one of the buckets from his grasp and hurried toward the trough in the small paddock behind the barn.

She plunged her bucket deep into the trough and pulled it out with both hands, bracing her knees. She staggered back to the barn carrying it, some of it sloshing on her toes. There was so much flame, and so little water. The heat was so fierce she could no longer enter the barn, and the flames began to lick up the outside wall close to her. She emptied her water on the wall—at least it smoldered out in that one small patch. Another bucketful of water from Uncle Will hit the wall.

The faint shouts of neighbors meant they were running up to the house. But sprouts of flame grew into long tendrils up the walls. It was too late to save the barn. Their battle would be to hold the line and make sure the fire did not take the house as well.

An hour after dawn the house had fallen quiet, the neighbors gone, the condolences given for the loss of the barn, the meat, bread, and pie left for them in the pantry or on the shelf. Uncle Will was sleeping in the back room, exhausted. Aunt Ann had gone to Mrs. Hayworth's house just to escape the scene for an hour or two.

Susanna was worn thin as cheesecloth, but she could not sleep. Pressing her fingers into her sore temples, she breathed deeply but the air was saturated with the odor of smoke. She hunched on the back stoop, her dazed mind still refusing to accept the reality of what she saw.

The ruin of the barn was like a half-shell. Even the surviving side was blackened in streaks. She stood and walked to the destroyed end. The saddlery was covered in soot and what had been the storage room beside it was barely a skeleton of itself. Glass lay all over the floor from stored jars of food that had exploded in the heat. Sacks and sacks of supplies had burned beyond recognition. Even her uncle's tool bench and racks had not been spared: most of the tools had wooden handles that had blackened to charcoal.

What would they do? All the church's collected food, which would have supported the children. And the very means of his livelihood, his tools, all taken away. Was this what the threatening notes had meant when they arrived on the doormat for her uncle? Did this unknown enemy even know what it had cost them, the burning of the barn? Or was it simply the easiest act of destruction? The arsonist had stolen their last hope for the children.

She walked through the ebony bones of the building, covered in flakes of ash that stirred in the slightest hint of breeze.

Her uncle had also seen the torch lying in the center of the hay pile last night, its oily burn so different from the lighter flame of wood.

And this morning the neighbors had started wondering, once the smoldering had stopped.

"I know Corbin had something to do with it," one had said. "Tit for tat."

Another man she did not know rested, arms weary from lifting buckets on top of the paddock fence. "Seems unlikely to me," he said. "But Mr. Hanby was pretty strong in denouncing the bombing of the saloon. What if it was them, the same folks who used gunpowder the first time?"

The angry, indignant whispering went on. But Uncle Will stayed quiet and did not contribute to the discussion, his face craggy with fatigue.

She should go see if he had awakened. At least she could take care of him, bring him some of the food the neighbors had brought. She retraced her steps to the house, walked through the kitchen, and rounded the corner, moving quietly so as not to disturb him. She turned the handle of the door and knocked lightly as she pushed it open just enough to see if he was sleeping.

Uncle Will was sitting in the chair in the far corner, his head leaned back, his feet propped on the footstool. Had he fallen asleep in the chair? Or else—a stab of fear went through her and she glided toward him on tiptoe. Thank the Lord—his chest rose and fell gently with his breath. He was cradling something in his hands where they lay in his lap. She looked closer. It was a picture of her uncle and aunt and their children, in a simple wooden frame. It must have been taken years ago, before she was even born. Uncle Will was in the prime of life then, his hair still dark, as was her aunt's.

Their children stood and sat around them—all eight of her cousins. Amanda, Anna, and Jenny stood on the back row, Amanda looking off to one side with a genuine smile on her face as if someone had made her laugh. That someone was probably Ben, who stood there between his sisters perfectly straight-faced, as he often did after saying something funny. He was handsome, dark, and intense as she remembered him, but even younger, and healthy and strong, probably not yet plagued by the cough that she remembered when he laughed. This portrait must have been made just before he married Kate.

In the middle of the photo, her cousin Cyrus looked miffed

with his arms crossed, envious of Ben's quip, no doubt. There were so many funny stories about Cyrus and Ben. A pang struck, sharp and keen, for what her uncle had lost, and her eyes filled. She blinked the tears away. She should remove the picture from his hands and put it somewhere safe so he would not accidentally drop it when he woke up.

As she leaned down and reached for it, she glanced at his face to be sure she was not waking him. His cheeks shone in the diffused light from the window. They were wet—he was weeping. Could people shed tears in their sleep?

"Uncle," she murmured.

His eyes opened, too aware for one who had been dreaming. He had been awake the whole time.

How she ached for him. She had never seen him weep, and it wrung her heart. "Are you in pain? Can I get something for you?"

He turned his head to the window. Perhaps he was embarrassed by his emotion.

She wished she had not disturbed him in such a private moment of grief. "Anyone would mourn, Uncle. It's no shame." She knelt on the rug beside him and laid her hand on his.

"I'm not weeping for what I've lost, Susanna," he said, so quietly she had to strain to hear. "I'm just grateful to the Lord, grateful that he gave me so much." He wiped his tears with the back of his hand, though they continued to flow. "I could have died at eighteen on the floor of my master's barn. I would never have known the love of my wife, or the joy of my sons and daughters. Praise the Almighty God for what he gave me, for such love and such joy."

The lump in her throat deprived her of speech. She got to her feet and bent to kiss him on his cheek, weathered and rugged beneath his white beard. Life had engraved such beauty in those lines of age and wisdom, more graceful than even the designs of his saddles.

She had so much to learn.

Thirty-One

JOHANN WALKED PAST THE CONFECTIONER'S SHOP AS the blasted heap of the saloon rose ahead of him on State Street. Little wonder Susanna was discouraged and quick to anger, with such a disturbing scene facing her every time she ventured from the house of her aunt and uncle.

He felt for the letter in his pocket. It was there, all set in writing about George Leeds and his demands in case Susanna would not see him at all. He said a quick prayer that this would go well. But even if it did, New York still awaited, with all its messy allure.

This was no time to let that distract him—the children had to come first, then he would sort out the rest.

There was the Hanbys' home. He could not think of anything else but the opening of the front door and whether it would be her face behind it.

It was. She looked even more tired than when he had last seen her, her face drawn. Instead of the anger he expected, hurt filled her eyes as she looked into his. It was worse—he would rather she had raged at him or slammed the door. Despite the unfairness of her conviction about him, he still hated to see a beautiful and spirited woman beaten down by her circumstances to helpless pain.

He took a deep breath. "I have something I must tell you. About the children."

"What is it?" She stood halfway behind the door as if she could hardly stand to look at him. A lock of her light-brown hair trickled down her neck to touch her collar.

"George Leeds has told me that we have only two more days to accept his reprehensible offer, as he is leaving town. My father urges you again to accept his assistance."

Her lips closed and her eyelids lowered. "Mr. Giere . . ."

An extra stab of regret that she would not call him by his first name.

"Even if we wished to accept your father's offer"—she stressed *father* as if to make it clear she would not accept help from Johann himself—"we've found that we're no longer in a position to even consider taking the children." Her face twitched and gave away the pain she was trying so hard to hide.

"What do you mean?"

Without responding, she opened the door farther and stepped out onto the doorsill. He gave way to let her pass him.

"Come with me," she said.

He followed her around the end of the house.

The barn was a burnt wreck, at least the back half, the saddlery they had shown him before. It took his breath away. What else could happen to this family?

"We can't take the children." Her tone was final. "Because as you can see, my uncle and aunt have been left with hardly anything but the clothes on their backs and the food in the pantry. With the barn's stores, we might have done it. Now it would be foolish. And my parents are in no position to help. My cousins are either off on missions or struggling to make ends meet. None of us escaped the recession with any significant means." She had no pride; her confession was simple and honest.

It tore at him. He laid a hand on her shoulder.

She stiffened, then pulled away and put a few steps between them. "Now you have your answer about George. Please take your leave." Her shoulders had tensed.

It stung, and he struggled with a moment of anger. But he must be patient. She had taken such blows, one after the other, that he must grant her time to recover, as his father had said.

He nodded to her. "Then good afternoon." Was that flicker in her eyes regret or longing? He turned away and walked up State Street again with his head up and shoulders squared. He was innocent of her accusation and would not slink away like a guilty Judas.

But neither his innocence nor her anger would help her nieces and nephews. His father was right—the children must come first.

Thirty-Two

THE BOX JINGLED WHEN SUSANNA SHOOK IT GENTLY. It came from an address in Columbus. Could it have something to do with Rachel? She forced herself to slow down and open it with care. A letter lay on top of a folded bundle of green material. With unsteady hands, she tore it open.

> Johann Giere
> 30 Wall Street
> Columbus

Miss S. Hanby
21 State Street
Westerville

Miss Hanby,

My father has been informed of your family's current situation after the loss of the barn. Please accept his offer of assistance. If you agree to give George Leeds the money, my father will assist you to find a way to support the children. He knows many employers in Columbus, some who pay well, perhaps for a nurse or tutor. It would *mean the end of your college plans, and thus I hate to write it. But I know you would not accept an outright offer of charity, and even my father cannot offer to take on a decade's support of six children over whom he will have no authority. He does wish to assist you, and to keep your family intact, as he was not able to keep his own together.*

I myself am sending the enclosed package as a token of my esteem for your uncle and aunt, in the hope that it will be an encouragement to them after their recent loss.

Sincerely yours,
Johann

If it had been a gift to her, she would have thrown it away unopened. Her chest hurt, and a knot began at the center of her brows. He had betrayed her trust, after convincing her with his every action—and kiss—that he would care for her. It did not make sense, but she had heard men sometimes behaved so. She had been very foolish to let him kiss her and to give him a piece of her heart. If it hurt to breathe when she thought of him, she had only her naïveté to blame.

She would see what he had sent to her uncle to be sure it was not offensive in some way. She took out the green bundle and unwrapped it.

Shining in the folds of the cloth was an awl. Needles, a whole case of them. Mallet, chisels, embossing stamps.

Johann had sent her uncle a new set of leatherworking tools, some with the same beautiful, polished wooden handles that had been ruined in the fire.

The mingled gratitude and confusion made her want to cry.

Why did he continue to do such kind things? Of course it would be an encouragement to Uncle Will and Aunt Ann.

She rose, gathered the bundle in her hands with a clink and went to Uncle Will's bedroom door. "Uncle?" she called.

"Come in."

She pushed open the door with her elbow.

He was reading in his chair, his spectacles on.

"Look," she said.

"What is it?"

"Mr. Giere has sent this to you." She brought the bundle over and laid it in his lap. He set his book on the side table and unwrapped the cloth. A soft sigh was his only response at first. He touched the metal with his fingertips, picked up the awl, and hefted its weight in his palm. His eyes brightened.

"An unusually thoughtful gift," he said at last, laying it down and picking up the case of needles. "How did he come to know about my tools?"

"He came to visit and I showed him the barn."

"And his purpose?"

"He wished to persuade me to use his father's money to get the children. He said we had only a few days before George would leave the state and our opportunity would be lost."

"And I suppose you told him we are no longer able to consider that generous offer from his father?"

"Yes." The silence was heavy. "But he sent me a letter today with this new suggestion that I consider taking a position his father might procure for me, a position with an income that would allow me to go forward with the plan to reclaim the children through George."

He looked up from the tools, his brown eyes fixing on her

face. "And what is your opinion? You would have to give up your studies."

"That seems a small thing now." She knotted her fingers together. "It's not why I'm reluctant to accept."

He paused and gave her a keen look. "You don't want to accept it from him, from Johann Giere."

"No." The hurt flashed in her heart. "He has betrayed us once. I'm afraid he might do so again. What if it's all for the newspaper, some new scheme?"

"It does not appear that way to me," Uncle Will said, musing. "Not in the least. Have you ever thought, Susanna"—and his voice was gentle and warm—"that perhaps you are a bit hasty and intemperate in forming some opinions?"

"Yes," she said quietly.

"Once we know our own weaknesses and temptations, it behooves us to work against them and understand when they are most likely to blind us." He took off his spectacles and folded them.

"Yes." She looked down at the rug at his feet. "I'll try, Uncle."

She turned and went out, her face hot. Did he know or suspect what had passed between her and Johann? If he did, perhaps he would understand why she could not easily be as calm and rational as he.

But she would stop excusing herself. She would face her weakness, be more careful, and learn the truth, whatever she had to do. But she would need to act quickly, for the time to pay George was running out like sand.

The German bakery was fragrant with fresh rolls, sugary pastries, and pretzels. Susanna's mouth watered at the delicacies on the loaded trays. But there was no money for any extras—even train fare had become risky, an investment rather than an everyday expense.

"May I help you, miss?" A man in a white apron with a cheerful red face greeted her with the expected accent, though without the elusive, musical quality of Johann's speech. "A poppy-seed roll for you today?"

"No, thank you," she said. "I have a favor to ask of you, instead, sir." She had already been turned down twice by other merchants on High Street. But she would keep asking all day, if necessary.

He stopped in his reach for a tray and straightened up. "Yes?"

"I know you often wrap purchases in newspaper. Do you by any chance have the issue of the *Westbote* from July twenty-third?"

His faint eyebrows arched and he shuffled behind the counter, bending down to open a drawer. He rifled through papers. "Ah, yes. Here it is. You would like it?"

"Yes, sir." She peered at the sheets in his hands. "Just the front page."

He separated it from the others, folded it, and handed it across the counter. "You read German?" The note of surprise made it clear that he did not think so.

"No, sir. But it has personal value to me." For better or for worse, depending on the outcome of her mission today.

"Very well." He smiled.

"Good day."

"And to you, miss."

The shop door chimed and she once again made her way up High Street, dodging more impetuous pedestrians. She would not take the lumbering horse car, now that every penny must be saved just to get through the winter. Walking was no real hardship, not through the orderly, wide streets of Columbus.

The florist's shop was as perfumed and vibrant with color as she remembered. She let the door close gently and approached the counter.

"Orange lilies again, miss?" The old woman from before hobbled out, impeded by her curved spine, but bright faced, even mischievous. How did she remember one single purchase from two weeks ago, not even made by Susanna herself? It was disconcerting—especially given the nature of her errand. But she would not falter.

"I have a request to make of you, ma'am." She pulled out the newspaper sheet and unfolded it. "I hope you will forgive me, as a total stranger, but you are the only person I could think of who spoke German but was not involved."

"In what, young lady?" The woman sounded almost teasing.

Susanna felt her ears burning. "I cannot say. But I would be grateful if you would read this one short article for me." She prayed the woman could read, and that she would not offend her by asking.

"Let me see." The woman braced her elbows on the countertop and leaned over, running her finger over the words. She hesitated on the name under the article and darted a quick glance at Susanna, but said nothing. After she had finished tracing a few lines silently, she spoke. "I can translate it for you, sentence by sentence. Is that what you wish?"

"Yes, please." Susanna might have been on trial and waiting for a verdict, for how her palms moistened and her pulse raced.

The woman began, reading the German silently to herself

and then translating in halting English as she searched for equivalent words.

And there was nothing but a statement of the events that had occurred. No railing against the United Brethren, no scorn for Westerville. With every sentence closer to the end, Susanna's chagrin grew. Her uncle was correct—she had rushed to judgment and lost her temper. Johann was loyal; he had not been a Judas. It was the *Dispatch* reporter who made the cutting remarks that placed their faith and the temperance movement in such a bad light.

She could hardly stand to see her faint reflection in the polished surface of the countertop. She had been low and mean to accuse Johann when she had received nothing but assistance and compassion. The truth overturned her mind like a rock, and she could not bear the ugliness she saw wriggling there underneath. And what was worse is that he must have seen it at once, with the clarity of innocence accused.

How had he been so patient with her after bearing the brunt of her harsh words? It reminded her of her uncle for a moment— how Uncle Will spoke so gently, even during an argument, even when strongly opposed to something like the saloon. She knew very well what Proverbs and the book of James said about taming the tongue, and if she believed, why did she not also speak in love, as God had asked her? She felt herself crumbling inside.

Johann had even pleaded the children's case with his father on her behalf, after what she had done. She could still accept the position Mr. Giere had offered and agree that he could pay George in order to get the children for her. There was no trick or betrayal here, except the trick she had allowed her own assumptions to play on her judgment.

Her face flushed and downcast, she thanked the florist and left the shop. Even in her shame, relief swept through her like the breaking of a dam at the thought of the children, home at last.

But first she had a very humble apology to make, in person, at the Giere Brewery.

Thirty-Three

THE POLICE REPORT SAID SUICIDE. SUCH ASSUMPTIONS were always subject to question and often led to good stories. Twice before, Johann had discovered an apparent suicide to be a murder, when the report came from the bad part of town. And Mr. Reinhardt loved those stories, so Johann's task was clear.

Johann looked at the address on the paper in his hand. Yes, this was it. A rundown saloon near the river, faded to brown, chunks of mortar showing all across its façade where bricks had fallen out over the years. The door was faded wood, rough and shabby. He took hold of the doorknob with care so as not to end up with a splinter in his knuckles.

Inside, the saloon reeked of mildew. He approached the bar. A small man in suspenders was puttering with bottles on the back shelves and did not look up until he had switched them to his satisfaction and checked the labels.

"A drink for you?" he asked with a brusque tone.

"No, thank you." It was eight in the morning.

The barkeeper shrugged. "Suit yourself. Whaddya want then?"

"I'm a newsman. I want to ask you a few questions about the death here yesterday."

"I don't talk to newspapers. Too much trouble comes of it."

"But the police report said it was a suicide. Surely that can't be any trouble."

"I didn't have nothing to do with it."

"I'm sure you didn't. How did the man die?"

The barkeeper's mouth stretched in a thin line and he turned back to his bottles.

Not promising. And strange, because barkeepers were usually garrulous and up for any excitement.

He had botched the approach—he should have come in as a customer and drawn the man out gradually. He would have to look elsewhere for his answer.

The city morgue was a familiar place, with its sharp alcohol odor and the trace of garlic that signaled arsenic in the embalming fluid. Perhaps the stench had been worse before the war made embalming so popular. Still, it was gruesome how the cadavers lay there with blue feet and hands, many unwanted and unclaimed except by doctors and schools of medicine. They would pay handsomely for embalmed cadavers to dissect.

He had only been waiting ten minutes in the front room when the coroner's assistant came through the door. He was a young man in a brown suit, Mr. Jeffries the name, or so Johann thought he recalled. The man had been wearing the same suit the last time Johann came here for a story. Brown. It would be the appropriate color to disguise blood stains. The thought made his stomach churn—or maybe that was just from the strange odor.

"Mr. Giere, you have a question?" Jeffries looked rushed today.

"Yes, I'm seeking the suicide brought in yesterday."

"Suicide . . . suicide." Jeffries rolled his eyes in reflection, his mustache twitching. "Ah, yes. That body hasn't gone out yet, though it will go to the medical college this afternoon. Do you need to see it?"

"If you would be so kind." Though it seemed strange to refer to the exhibition of a body as a kindness. "And perhaps I might follow it to the medical college to see what they conclude?"

"Their conclusion will be the same as mine and the coroner's." Jeffries led Johann back through the door and into the main room. Several large mortuary tables with marble tops bore cadavers. Johann tried not to look too closely at the one dissection already in progress. Crime was one thing, medicine was more chilling, with its scientific coldness.

Jeffries led him to a body that lay unscathed on the farthest table. "Here it is."

Johann restrained a shudder. They seemed inhuman, these inert corpses waiting to be flayed and pinned. He moved to within a foot of the body and looked at it.

He felt the blood drain from his face and he stood rooted to the spot.

It was George Leeds.

"Go closer and you'll see what I mean," Jeffries said with authority. "The man reeked like a distillery when he came in. Our embalming merely finished the fine pickling he had already given himself. Drank himself to death in an alley. We see 'em every week."

George's eyes were open—no loved one had witnessed his death and closed them. They stared glassy and vacant at the ceiling. His mouth hung open and rigid.

What would he tell Susanna? Even if she decided to agree

to his father's solution, her last chance was lost. His stomach, already roiled at the sight of the messy dissection, threatened to revolt. He certainly wasn't about to bend closer to sniff the corpse, as Jeffries had suggested.

"That is all I needed to know, Mr. Jeffries. Thank you for your time."

"Good afternoon."

"Oh, one more thing." He turned at the door. "I'd like to look at some of your records before I leave. For some of our city institutions."

"It's public information. Ask the clerk to show you the files, then come back to me if you have any questions." The coroner's assistant took no further heed of him and went to the wall to retrieve a brown-streaked smock hanging there.

Johann hurried out, trying not to inhale more of the smell.

As soon as he finished here, he must tell his father about George, and perhaps gain his advice.

But he could not imagine any wisdom that would soften the blow for Susanna—the loss of yet another hope, whether she had chosen to pursue it yet or not. He would have to pray that in her stubbornness, she would find some other way to retrieve the children, without asking his father to pay George. Because heaven had taken that choice out of her hands.

"George Leeds is dead."

"What?" His father dropped the pen in his hand and spun around in his chair.

"He poisoned himself with whiskey."

His father leaned back against the seat with a groan. "He is one of those men who ruins others whether he lives or dies."

Struggling to master his anger, Johann sat in the chair against the wall, next to the desk, where he could see his father's face. "A selfish man." Johann couldn't keep the bitterness from his tone. "Consumed by his own vanity. I suppose it's natural that he wanted to go onstage."

"Not all actors are prideful beasts," his father said. "Your Uncle Fritz once wanted to be an actor, more than anything in the world. He loved the words and the creation of a vivid dream onstage. He wanted to write as well as act."

"He did?" Neither Johann's father nor his uncle had ever discussed this. "Why didn't he do it?"

"We experienced so many partings, Fritz and I. The loss of our brother, the deaths in '48, then all those we left behind to come here." His eyes fixed on the wall ahead of him, which bore a map of Bavaria. "I believe it taught us the value of our family, of dedication and sacrifice, of the illusions of success when one has lost those who would have shared it. We had heard it so often in sermons, but life taught us its truth."

"If only George Leeds had learned a similar lesson." Johann crossed his arms and bit back the additional comments that threatened to spill from his lips. Imprecations would be of no use—the man was dead. "What will I tell Miss Hanby?"

"We have done everything we can."

The finality of the words was like a punch in the gut. The faces of the Leeds children were real—they were not characters in some sad fairy tale, but human souls about to be torn from their true family and given over to strangers. And if the strangers were unkind, the children would have no recourse, no power to resist cruel treatment.

"I must attend to some work." Johann rose abruptly to his feet. His father nodded, sympathy softening his face.

Back at the house, Johann heard his sisters and Mother talking while they worked, but he skirted the kitchen and climbed the stairs. He did not feel up to conversation.

He went straight to his desk and pulled out a sheet of paper. The chair scraped as he adjusted its position and began to write. Minutes passed and blurred into an indeterminate time, until two sheets were covered in his even, neat handwriting. He dotted the last period and puffed out a breath. He would submit it to Mr. Reinhardt and see if it could be published as an editorial. Perhaps it might prevent more drunkards from ruining their families.

A painting of his family hung on the wall. Uncle Fritz had still been there when that portrait was made. The likeness was good. Johann regarded his own ten-year-old self, staring out of the portrait, a blond boy with no idea what awaited him over the next decade. The older Leeds boy had looked to be about the same age.

He did not know what to do. He bowed his head until it rested on his clasped hands and prayed for guidance.

Thirty-Four

"MR. JOHANN'S NOT HERE," THE ONE-ARMED BREW-meister told Susanna. "He went home to look over the accounts."

Now what? A young lady could not call on a gentleman, let alone unescorted. "I must speak with him on a matter of some importance. Is there any way you can assist me to contact him, sir?"

"We have errand boys here."

"Is there a respectable place nearby where I might tell him to meet me? I don't wish to disturb your work." It was humiliating, and her face must be scarlet, but she had brought it on herself.

"Yes, miss." He pretended not to notice the impropriety, or perhaps they were not quite as strict in the German part of town. "There's City Park, about a mile south. There's always lots of folk there."

"Thank you, that will do admirably."

He gave her directions. "And, miss, if you don't mind my saying, you had better pick a place in the park to visit. It's very large."

"Do you have a suggestion?"

"The Greek statue. They just installed her a few years back

as a drinking basin, south of the brick cottage. You'll see her near Stewart Street, miss."

"Thank you—Mr. Heinrich." At last she remembered his name.

He winked at her. Oh, the mortification.

It was a bit of a walk, all the way down through the South End, but the park was beautiful and green, having refreshed itself since the drought. Tall shade trees towered thirty feet or more on well-kept lawns. She skirted the park until she saw Stewart Street, then turned onto the path toward the brick cottage Heinrich had mentioned. She was glad washing day was yesterday: her yellow dress was still clean and neat despite her travels.

There was the statue, bronze and graceful in a Grecian drape above a hollow basin. And standing next to it was Johann, in a cream linen coat and casual tie that made him almost as elegant as the statue.

How had he arrived so quickly? She looked around, her heart pounding. There should have been more time to prepare. She should have been the one serenely awaiting him by the statue.

Ten yards away, behind him, she glimpsed a dun horse standing tied to a hitching post. So that was how he had done it.

She forced herself not to falter, to keep a steady pace toward him, even though her palms had begun to moisten.

A good six feet away she halted, placing the statue between them like a mediator.

He still bore a trace of hurt, a careful expression in his blue eyes. He took off his hat, giving his gold-brown hair its usual slightly disheveled charm. "Miss Hanby."

"Mr. Giere. Thank you for coming." She felt disjointed, unsure. "I hope I didn't interrupt you."

"It's a welcome interruption." He still didn't appear at ease.

The more gentlemanly he was, the more the guilt stabbed at her. "I owe you an apology. I was hasty in assuming the nature of your contribution to the article."

"It's nothing. Please think no more of it." He looked down at the walkway.

Why did he seem hesitant? Nothing seemed more important than earning his forgiveness, not just for the children's sake, but to restore their former intimacy, to heal the wound. He could be excused for being reluctant, after her behavior.

"If there is anything I could say or do to take back my words, I would," she said, stepping closer. If she had to plead, she would. "I wish to accept your father's kind offer."

He closed the distance between them with another step or two so they both stood directly in front of the bronze figure of Youth. "Susanna." The stillness of his eyes held regret.

"You can't forgive me?" she whispered.

"Of course. I forgive you completely." He still looked so sad. "But . . . I have bad news for you. George Leeds has died of acute alcohol poisoning."

"What?" She grasped at his coat sleeves as the ground seemed to shift under her, throwing her off balance. "He's dead?"

"I'm afraid so." He supported her, rock-solid while the rest of the park swung madly. Finally her head cleared.

"Then I have lost my chance. And the children's." Her throat tightened and she barely choked it out. "With my stubbornness and foolishness." She pivoted and walked away, head bowed to the ground. She loathed herself. The grass flew past under her feet, then she was back on the path. Her boots rapped on wood and she slowed, realizing she was on a footbridge over the water.

A hand caught at her elbow. "Wait." He had run after her and she turned reluctantly to face him. They stood together on a rustic bridge of crossed logs, over a narrow section of lake, so limpid and placid compared to the stormy thoughts that lashed at her. Trees surrounded them on all sides—not a soul in sight.

"It isn't your fault that Leeds died." His voice was soft.

"But had I not been so quick to judge and so strong-willed"— she gripped the bridge handrail to steady her shaking—"I would have accepted your father's offer in time."

He put a comforting arm around her shoulders and they stood side by side, looking out over the water lilies.

For a moment he was silent as the warmth of his arm cradled her. The lilies were profuse, scattered at the edges of the water, full white blossoms almost glowing in the afternoon light.

"You are as fresh and natural as those lilies," he said. "And they open in God's time, to receive the light he pours down on them, but they close in the darkness. If you were stricken and closed by the darkness around you, I can't blame you. That's how God has made you—sensitive and passionate. He made you lovelier than any change of the light, whether I see you in darkness or daylight."

No one had ever said such a thing to her. She was not worthy of it in any way. Her eyes dampened. "I do not feel lovely." She turned to face him, but could not meet his gaze.

She felt a gentle touch, his fingers brushing her cheek, and looked up.

"You are." He leaned toward her and she closed her eyes as his lips touched hers, softly, his hand sliding around her shoulders.

It was a painful sweetness, to be kissed just then, and to feel his care through the gentleness of his touch. Through her sense of loss rose a warmth, a longing to be closer, to dissolve into the kiss and let him hold her.

He drew back, but kept her in a loose embrace. "I don't make a practice of stealing kisses. My intentions are serious."

She stared at him, her heart beating fast.

"If we marry, I could support the children with my salary at the brewery. You could go to college."

"But—but—" She could not pick one of the many objections, they swarmed so fast through her mind. Finally she seized the closest. "We still have no way to get them from the home, not without George."

"If we are married and have the means to support them, we may be able to change the matron's plans for their future."

"But if we don't, you will have married me for nothing."

He laughed. "For nothing?" His face grew sober and his voice lowered to a murmur as he held her closer. "This is not a marriage of convenience, Susanna. I love you. I have every intention of being your husband in every way, and I hope you would want to truly be my wife."

A tremor went deep through her, and she realized she would want that, would gladly share his home, his name, and all the things that made her blush hot in his embrace. What better man had she ever known? No one had done for her what Johann had done, out of the goodness of his heart. Except—

"We could never marry," she said.

"Why not?" He did not appear taken aback and did not release her.

"Because of the beer. I'll never be able to see intoxicating drink in my home without thinking of George and Rachel." Real distress sliced through her. Only now did she realize how much she wanted to say yes. And yet she would be even more foolish than Rachel to marry a man who drank, who made alcohol his living, after what had happened to her sister. Her sister had chosen infatuation over righteousness, and look what it had done.

It would tear her apart to refuse him, but she must.

He drew one hand up to caress her hair. "And you think I would adopt six children for your sake and theirs, but refuse to give up a glass of lager, if that's all that stands between us?"

She blinked. "You would give it up?"

"Without any regret."

She paused. What now? An inner tremble began. "But you would still be employed by the brewery."

"Yes. Without it there would be no way to support the children."

She pulled away and clattered a few steps backward on the bridge, her feeling of panic rising. "I can't do it. It's a devil's bargain." Her moral conviction had to be stronger than her longing for him, which was more powerful than she ever wanted him to know. But tears washed her face, exposing her.

As if what had happened already were not enough, now she had somehow allowed herself to want the one thing that would be sure to continue this pain, in some way—a man who would inevitably make alcohol a part of her life, because her family's survival would depend on his selling it, even if he vowed to keep it out of their home. She could not be stupid. Rachel's lesson was all too clear.

He pulled a handkerchief from his inner pocket and gently blotted her face. She felt him kiss her gently where the tears had been, then he murmured, "You must take at least a little time to think. Don't throw away this last chance for the children."

"It's not the last chance." She turned away and walked off the bridge.

"What else is there?" he called after her in clear frustration, his accent resurfacing.

She did not turn around but continued down the path through the tall trees as the sunlight shone white off their glossy leaves. "God will provide another way. He will. I will find my sister, whatever it takes."

Thirty-Five

THE OFFICE WAS ALIEN, GLOSSY AND DARK, ITS HARD-
wood furniture carved and polished to a high shine. A luxurious
carpet pillowed the hem of her skirt as she sat in the waiting room.

"Miss Hanby?"

She rose, looking at the slight clerk quizzically. "Yes?"

"Mr. Piper will see you now."

She followed him back to the majestic office in back. A
middle-aged, gray-haired man rose from his enormous desk to
greet her.

"Miss Hanby." He extended a warm, strong hand. "I'm Ernest
Piper. Welcome to our practice."

"Thank you." Could he tell from her clothing that she was
not the type of client who usually patronized lawyers?

"You have a case to describe to me?"

"Yes, sir." She gave him a quick summary of everything that
had happened with Rachel and her children.

"And you wish to know if you have legal recourse to gain
custody of the children?"

"Yes, sir."

"Well, you will not have any legal rights, but you may be able to appeal to the mercy of a judge."

"Is that often successful?"

"That depends." He hesitated, tapping his pen on the desk. "These things your brother-in-law said about your sister running away with someone else. You are sure they are false?"

"I would stake my own honor on it."

"Good." He leaned back in his chair. "Then there may be a chance. The court will not have any mercy on morally bankrupt mothers."

"But they might help me, given her innocence?"

"Yes. Of course, if you wish me to advocate for you, I will need a retainer, as I will have to do some research and file some papers."

"How much will you need?"

He named a sum. It was practically all of her tuition money. "Is that acceptable to you, Miss Hanby?"

"Yes." She opened her purse. "Here it is." She counted it out, hiding any emotional reaction. She must not mind if her uncle was disappointed. Even he must admit that life came before study. If she wished to give up her college chance for the children, that was her choice.

"Very good. Now, I will begin work, and you will hear from me in a week or so."

"Thank you."

"Just be aware, Miss Hanby, that the retainer is not refundable."

"I understand. Good afternoon."

"Good afternoon."

The clerk came back and ushered her out.

Now there could be no going back. She had taken the last step in her power to find her sister. But her heart still ached at the thought of Johann.

The lawyer would find a way to get the children back to her. No one ever had a bad word to say about Rachel. If good character could bring mercy from a judge, her sister's long-suffering at George's hands must be a certain win in court. Susanna's sacrificed tuition money was nothing in such a cause.

———————

"I'm sorry, Mr. Reinhardt. I appreciate your recommendation, but I can't go."

"Johann, what changed? You were practically packing your bags." Mr. Reinhardt grew lines across his forehead. "You will throw it away, just like that?" He spread out his arms in a shrug and leaned back in his chair behind the office desk.

Johann hated to see him disappointed. "Sir, you said that God may have a plan for us, yes?"

"Yes. And what about your talent?"

"I can still use it, sir, if you'll keep me on part-time. But I think God sent me a messenger this week."

"An angel?" Mr. Reinhardt did not quite scoff, even in his disappointment.

"A dead man."

"The one you wrote about in your article."

"Yes, sir."

"Ach, I can't argue with that." Mr. Reinhardt picked up the

Westbote and opened it up with a flap. Johann was apparently dismissed. He turned to go.

The door from the street opened, across the room with the printing presses, and a woman came in, veiled heavily for summertime, in black hat and dress, clearly in mourning. She looked around with an air of confusion, then saw Johann and made her way toward him, a black handbag on one arm, a newspaper folded in the other hand.

"May I help you, ma'am?" he asked, eyeing her veil curiously.

"I'm seeking the original author of this article." She held the paper toward him. The *Dispatch*, of course. But to his surprise, the article she indicated with her crocheted black gloves was titled "The Tragedy of a Drunk," a translation of the title of his article about George Leeds. And there beneath the title was his byline and a credit to the *Westbote*.

"Excuse me for one moment, please," he said to the lady, and walked back into his editor's office. "Did you give permission for the *Dispatch* to translate and reprint my article?"

"Yes, Brundish asked. He likes your writing."

"Is he going to pay you? Or me?"

"We'll see." Reinhardt did not put down his newspaper. Still irritated by the New York refusal.

Johann walked back out to the lady. "I'm the author of that article."

"I must confirm it with you. This man"—she pointed to the name George Leeds—"was from Union Center, and left six children, with a vanished mother?"

"Yes." He stared at her hard, but could not penetrate the blur of her veil.

She pulled it back over her hat, revealing a pretty, half-familiar face, and when she took off her hat completely, he knew. Her hair was auburn.

"I'm Rachel Leeds," she said. "And I need your help."

Thirty-Six

SUSANNA TOOK THE IRON OFF THE STOVE, DIPPED her fingers in the water next to her, and flicked drops on the flat black metal. They hissed into steam. The rain lashed against the windows, its din broken by an occasional thunder clap and flash of lightning. She applied the iron to the collar of the shirt, taking care to move quickly so as not to scorch it. Professor Hayworth and his wife had agreed to allow her to do some ironing to make more money for her train fare. She would finish as quickly as she could today so she could return to Columbus and the boat dock.

Uncle Will was working in the cellar, where he had set up his saddlery. Aunt Ann was at the church with a group of ladies knitting for orphans. They would take the scarves and mittens to Columbus the next day to be stored up by charities for winter.

A return to Columbus to look for Rachel—but Johann would not be with her on this search, not offering his steady arm as he had last time. She had to breathe deeply against the ache of refusing him—it was just her susceptible heart, her weak flesh that wanted to be his wife. And if her chest hurt like she was cloven in two, it was her own fault for letting down her guard and falling in love with someone unsuitable. Heaven would never intend her to marry a man whose business was so destructive, so there must be some other answer, even if it seemed impossible to save the children in only two days.

She adjusted the shirt on the board and pressed the cuffs. Why did her traitorous mind insist on conjuring forth these visions of herself and Johann, as if it were his shirt she ironed and he would walk out of the back hall, put his arms around her, and kiss the back of her neck, as if they were married? She summoned the image of George, oily and drunken. That would cool her ardor. Sickened, she placed the iron back on the stove to reheat.

A loud clap of thunder made her jump. In its wake came a rap on the door. Who was out in this weather? Aunt Ann would not knock—unless her arms were full. Susanna rushed over and flipped the lock, pulling the door open to a shower of raindrops on her face.

A couple stood on the stoop.

No, not a couple—it was Johann and a veiled woman. He held an umbrella over her, but it was little use against the blowing rain. Rain dripped off his hat and his face was wet, his clothing hanging with sodden heaviness. The woman was not as drenched as he, but her veil hung limp and the hem of her dark dress was covered with light-brown mud.

"Please, come in," Susanna said.

"I have business to do in town, but I've brought you a visitor," Johann said. "I'll return in half an hour."

Susanna stepped aside to allow the woman to enter as Johann strode off, his umbrella buffeted by the wind. Why did he leave so abruptly? This was hardly the weather in which to do business—he should have come in to wait out the storm. And he did not even introduce her to the stranger, who had now come in and was standing in the parlor. But the open door was letting in the gale, so she shut it firmly against the wind and turned to the woman.

"Please come into the kitchen and dry off, ma'am," she said. "The stove is warm and you are damp—I wouldn't want you to catch a chill. May I take your hat?"

The woman removed a hat pin and took off her hat and veil together.

It couldn't be real. She raised her hands to her face, gasped for breath, rooted to the floor. When her heart started again, she held out her arms. "Rachel!" The name from her lips released tears that sprang freely from her eyes. She staggered forward, taking her sister in her arms and holding her fiercely, not minding the dampness seeping through her light sleeves. She sobbed, pain and joy pouring out of her together.

She clung to her just to stand up. When her tears had run their course, she held her sister at arm's length so she could see her again, to reassure herself that it was true.

Rachel was also weeping, her brown eyes swimming in tears, her pretty face reddened. "I'm sorry," she said in a choked voice. "I was afraid George would find me and harm the children. I'm sorry I couldn't come to you."

"It's all right," Susanna said, barely able to speak. "Everything's all right." And it was—her prayers of the last weeks had been answered and everything would work out just the way it should, without an unwise marriage. So why in her joy did she feel a twinge of regret, still? Just her fallible heart, longing for Johann. And how selfish, when God had been so gracious and her family was restored. The thought brought more tears and she held Rachel close, her love and relief washing away all else.

After she could breathe again, she led Rachel into the kitchen. "Let me take your wrap." Her sister wore a loose shawl that had taken the brunt of the weather's wrath. Its black fringe dripped on the wood floor.

Rachel shrugged out of it and gingerly handed it to Susanna, who hung it across the back of one of the chairs.

When she turned back to look at Rachel, she froze. "Oh. Oh."

A noticeable bulge rounded the front of her sister's dress.

"You are expecting again—is that why you left?" She did not know what to think—it made it even more shocking.

"Let's sit down." Rachel looked reluctant—but then so would Susanna if she had a tale of woe to tell.

Susanna moved the two kitchen chairs close to the stove and took a seat in one of them. Rachel did the same but remained silent with a pensive shadow on her face.

"You can tell me, whatever he did," Susanna said. "I'm your sister. I can bear what you've borne."

Rachel took a deep breath. "Yes, I left when I realized I was expecting. But the baby is not George's. He and I had not known the marital relation in months."

Susanna blinked. The sentences her sister had just spoken jumbled in her mind. She must not have heard. "What? I don't understand."

Rachel's voice was faint. "I broke my marriage vows."

Susanna's mouth fell open as order and meaning fell out of the world and she struggled to put it back together. The baby—not George's.

Was it all true, what George had said? That Rachel was a loose woman?

"Then you did leave your children to run away with another man?" Susanna could hardly get it out.

"No! I only left them because I knew they would be in danger with me. George had sworn to kill them in front of me, the morning I ran away. I had to get them somewhere quickly. It was only afterward that I went with Richard. I had nowhere else to go, and he promised to care for me."

Rachel had a lover—she had brought all this suffering and grief on all of them with sin. Susanna started to her feet. "Who is this Richard?" Her shock bleached the words dry.

Rachel looked down, shame falling over her face. "He's a traveling vendor. He came by the house once in a blue moon . . . and then more often."

"And so George discovered the two of you?" Susanna's voice shook. All this mess, the children placed at risk, Daniel's worsened lungs, a family broken. What would happen now? The lawyer would say they could not reclaim the children, no doubt. After Susanna would have staked her own honor on her faith in her sister's virtue.

"George suspected." There was a pleading note in Rachel's voice. "That's when he threatened to kill all of us. And knowing I was with child, I had to leave before he found out. I'm sorry for what I've done . . ." Her voice trailed off into silence.

"So why did you come back?" It was an accusation. Why hadn't she just stayed with her lover?

"Richard decided not to leave his wife. I saw George was dead. I knew it was safe. And"—her eyes welled up again—"I love my children."

"Not enough, apparently, to keep them." She felt as if Rachel had thrown her under a streetcar, for how much it hurt. Like her bones were snapping, one by one, under the heavy wheels of this new, unwanted knowledge. "I can't speak to you right now."

Rachel's face crumpled.

It maddened her—what right did Rachel have to expect anything from her? If she did not leave, right now, she might scream or slap her. Something was shaking loose in her and about to get out.

Susanna whirled, threw herself against the door, and splashed out into rain that whipped against her face. She did not care, the sting in her heart goading her one. Buffeted by the wind, slipping and sliding across the street, she could hardly see for the rain streaming down in her eyes, mixing with her tears. She ran on behind the shops, across the quadrangle, stumbling, holding up an arm to shield herself from the gale. At last she reached Towers Hall. She sought the shelter of its arches and let herself in. Her drenched clothing stuck to her skin, her bustle felt as if it weighed a hundred pounds as she staggered down the hallway, raining droplets on the wood floor. She was sobbing and did not even care who heard. She would have given anything for Rachel and the children, but Rachel had walked away from virtue for her own gratification and cast them all into chaos.

When she reached the literary society library, she sat on the floor with her back to the wall, then slumped over on her side, the tears still running out her eyes, over the bridge of her nose, down into her soaked hair. What could she say? Should she tell Rachel the full consequences of what she had done, that she had cost Susanna her tuition, and more importantly, cost her children their chance at a family by abandoning what was right?

And then, unbelievably, the door opened. She felt a flash of desolate rage—could she not even be alone at this time, in this storm? Was it Abel Wilson?

The head that peered around the door frame was blond, and as wet as hers. She sat up—he could not see her like this. But his presence was like cool cream on a burn, easing the hurt even if nothing could fully heal it. He had come to look for her, and that mattered.

"How did you know I was here?" Her voice was thick with tears. She must look awful, with her hair plastered down around her brow and ears. Not that it mattered anymore.

"Your sister told me you ran toward the college." He came in, dripping, and sat down next to her.

"I went to a lawyer yesterday. He told me the only way we could get the children back was if Rachel's conduct was unquestionable. I swore it would be."

He put an arm around her, warming her shoulders in the chill of the draft. "It's hard when people disappoint us."

"Why?" she burst out. "Why can't they just do what's right? Why is everyone so determined to do what they wish at the expense of children?" Her question was ragged, full of all the pain of the previous months. "How can we ever help all the children they're hurting with their selfishness?" She let it pour out while he sat there absorbing it, as if he would willingly take her sorrow, share its ache.

"You've done your best, my sweet." He cradled her close.

She leaned into his shoulder and wept, choking out words. "I've wanted to be like my uncle and aunt and my cousin Ben my whole life. They're such good people. I wanted to be like them, the Hanbys who were brave and who stood for righteousness against those who did wrong."

"Was that what they did? Is that what you've seen in them?" He stroked her shoulder.

She remembered her aunt with Mrs. Pippen, and her uncle with Mr. Pippen. What had they done? How had they stood for righteousness while she had been here?

They hadn't, exactly, not in the way she always thought of them, the heroic Underground Railroaders fighting against injustice and wrongdoers. Instead they had put their arms around the suffering and spoken words of love, words of encouragement and faith.

"It's not how I thought it would be." She sounded to herself like a bewildered child.

"What will your aunt and uncle say to your sister?"

It hurt to think of it—they would not behave as Susanna had. They would not reproach Rachel, or run away in fury, hurting her sister more, making her feel rejected and despised.

"I don't know if I can forgive as they do," she admitted. She had stopped sobbing, but tears still leaked from her eyes, a silent confession.

"You can," he said. "I've seen your love for your family. Forgiveness comes from there. You have an unselfish heart."

She could not speak but wiped her eyes. "I suppose we should go back."

He helped her to her feet, both of them bedraggled and out of place in the refinement of the library. The wind had slackened, but they were drenched again within a minute of leaving the doorway of Towers Hall. He shrugged off his light jacket and wrapped her in it, his white shirt clinging to his shoulders.

He thought she had an unselfish heart. But she must have

a very stupid brain to have so completely misunderstood all these years.

The world had not broken from a lack of righteousness.

It had broken from a lack of love.

Her aunt and uncle knew this, cousin Ben and his wife had known it, her missionary cousins in Sierra Leone had crossed the sea for it.

But Susanna had not found that truth in herself, always too busy looking for righteousness.

Johann took her hand as they passed the ghostly shrouds of the saloon. Its blackened beams and broken walls stood like a silent reproach.

Why had she never realized that the architecture of a heart could be just as ruined and blasted from a lack of love?

She held tight to Johann's hand as the truth rolled over her and threatened to sweep her away.

Should she continue in her rage at Rachel, in her desire to punish her sister, Susanna would be as culpable as anyone who ever set match to gunpowder.

———— ·•· ————

Her aunt and uncle had resolved to go into Columbus to the Hannah Neil Mission as soon as dawn broke. Johann stayed overnight at the hotel, where he also engaged a room on another floor for Rachel, as if sensing that the sisters still needed time apart.

The train journey into Columbus the next morning was tense. At the station Uncle Will and Aunt Ann spoke quietly to one another, sitting a few feet removed from the others on their own bench. Johann read the paper and leaned against the wall as if glad to avoid the awkward curtain of silence between Susanna and her sister on the second bench. Rachel stared at the tracks with the sad eyes of an exile.

They had waited for five minutes, in silence, when two new arrivals made Susanna look up, startled, and catch Aunt Ann's eye.

Abel Wilson and another male student walked through the station with deliberation, shoulders hunched under their coats, muttering to one another out of the sides of their mouths.

The freckled young man was within ten feet of them by the time he noticed their little party.

He blanched ghost white and stepped sideways as if he could escape, bumping into his companion. When the other young man saw them, he, too, flinched and stared across the station.

She would not let it go unchallenged. "Mr. Wilson."

He nodded, trapped by their proximity. "Miss Hanby. Mr. and Mrs. Hanby." When he said their names, he looked as if he would faint.

"You are headed into Columbus?"

"Much farther than that," the other young man interjected with a stiff grin. "To Washington, then abroad."

"Really. How exciting," she said faintly, as her mind worked. "A recent plan, Mr. Wilson?"

"Yes—John offered to take me to Paris and London for the year. How could I refuse?" He looked like a dead man trying to talk, his jaw hardly moving.

"Of course."

Her aunt murmured good wishes to them as they hurried to the far end of the platform and stood there as if they would melt into the brick wall. What could she think, but that Abel

Wilson was petrified with guilt or fear? And yet the authorities had questioned Abel and everyone else in Westerville to no avail—there was no evidence, and at least twenty people had been named as suspects by other townsfolk, until the police said they wouldn't be starting another Salem witch hunt and closed the case.

She tried not to look at them. At least they would ride in a separate car. She simply could not spare the mental effort when so much lay ahead of her family that day. She was fighting her own giant.

The train pulled in, and as they mounted into the car and took their seats, Susanna struggled with herself, plumbed deep to remember her love for her sister, their childhood affection, all Rachel had endured that had led to her situation.

Forgiveness did not come easily, no matter how much Susanna wanted it. The others were reading, Johann still engrossed in his paper—or pretending to be, to avoid the silence. Uncle Will and Aunt Ann shared a *Harper's Monthly*. Rachel had her eyes closed, pale, leaning into the corner where the seat met the wall.

Susanna took her pocket Bible from her bag and opened it in her lap—Uncle Will had recommended Proverbs.

A fool gives vent to his anger, a wise man holds it quietly in. She stole a glance at Johann. Like her uncle, he had proven himself patient and self-controlled—in sharp contrast to her own behavior.

A hot-tempered man stirs up strife. She turned pages again. *Death and life are in the power of the tongue.* She closed the Bible. It was painful to look in this mirror. She hadn't considered the consequences her speech might carry for the Corbins. Her lack of love led to her support of driving them out of town by any means, which might have encouraged the unknown bombers to violence and injury.

She could no longer ignore this lack, this missing grace in her heart. Why didn't she just throw her arms around Rachel as she had on their first reunion? Johann could accept her sister, but she could not?

She could and she would.

"Would you like to read this?" Johann folded the newspaper and handed it to her. Always so observant, so considerate. She wanted to be as patient. Maybe after the children were home and this relentless twisting of her nerves was over. And this trip to the Hannah Neil Mission was only half the task—then they must discover if anything could be done to break the indentures of the Hare Home.

One giant at a time, or she would surely falter. One at a time.

They sat in the parlor of the Hannah Neil Mission, waiting. No one spoke. The maid had told them that the matron would be with them shortly.

She walked in a minute later, neat and orderly as usual. Her eyes widened only a fraction when she saw Rachel sitting in one of her chairs, but she disguised it well. Johann and Uncle Will rose to greet her.

"Good morning," the matron said. "To what do I owe the pleasure of this visit?" She seated herself in the only vacant chair.

"As you can see, ma'am," Susanna said, knotting the fabric of her dress in her fingers, "my sister has returned, and is ready to reclaim her children."

"You are in mourning, Mrs. Leeds?"

"My husband passed away." Rachel's face was white and stiff.

"I see." The matron took a subtle glance at Rachel's rounded belly, not disguised by her dress and shawl. "I'm afraid I must speak plainly. Forgive me." She shifted in her chair. "When living mothers give up their children, we have found that these mothers are usually motivated by their wish to pursue a life of . . . pleasure . . . unrestricted by the little souls they brought into the world."

Rachel grew two spots of bright red in her cheeks.

Susanna crossed and uncrossed her feet beneath her skirt. That was not fair and went beyond "speaking plainly" to be sure. Rachel was not a woman of the streets. Susanna should tell the matron so. But the proverbs she had read on the train circled in her mind and slowed her tongue. She must not lash out and ruin it all—she had done too much of that.

"Mrs. Leeds has always been a good mother prior to this occasion, and has every intention of being so again," Uncle Will said. "That is why we came with her, to vouch for her maternal qualities."

It must be agonizing for her sister to sit there like a criminal and be discussed. Pity swelled in Susanna's heart. Clearly Rachel could not defend herself, and someone would have to speak for her.

"Please," Susanna said. "We would like to take the children with us today, to be with their mother, as is right and good for them."

"The families awaiting these children are upstanding, moral, and kind," the matron said. "I have no doubt they will be well cared for in their adoptive homes, with plenty to eat and both mother and father in the house. I do not have that assurance with you, Mrs. Leeds. I am sorry."

A cold shiver went right to Susanna's bones. "Are you saying we may not have the children returned to their mother?" She willed herself to keep her tone moderate. She prayed the lawyer was only right about the mercy of judges, not about the mercy of matrons.

"You may not. I am sorry. They are scheduled to leave in only two days. And I cannot release them to Mrs. Leeds."

Rachel grew so pale she looked as if she might faint.

Susanna wanted to scream, to beat her head against the wall, but she kept perfectly still and held her tongue by looking at the pattern on the carpet and counting silently. Discretion. Persuasion.

She heard Johann clear his throat. "Then I must make a suggestion. Miss Hanby and I plan to be married very soon."

Susanna looked up at him in astonishment and had to close her mouth. Uncle Will and Aunt Ann swiveled like stick puppets in his direction.

He was leaning forward in his chair, intent on the matron. "If we were to take the children, we would certainly provide as good a family for them as any of your other candidates."

"I'm sorry, sir, but I did not catch your name."

They had indeed forgotten to make introductions in the tension of the meeting.

He stood and gave her a nod that was almost a bow, with perfect manners. "I am Johann Giere, ma'am. My father is Conrad Giere."

She looked impressed, even in her strictness. "Conrad Giere, of the South End?"

"Yes, ma'am. With my work in our family business, the children would lack for nothing."

Susanna could hardly breathe, pummeled by contradictory emotions. He dared too much—it was not true—and yet she wanted to throw her arms around him and thank him for the determination with which he stood his ground and fought not to lose her nieces and nephews.

"You have seen that Miss Hanby is dedicated to their welfare," he said. "And that she is a virtuous and compassionate woman. And I can produce character references for myself and my family."

The matron was silent. She steepled her fingers in her lap and contemplated them, then looked back at Johann. "I will have to see a marriage certificate, or witness the marriage in person. The issue at hand is too vital for mistakes."

Susanna's heart thudded hard and fast. She did not know if she could bring herself to do it—it was a rock and a hard place, and she could not choose. But she would be discreet this time and hold her tongue.

"That can be arranged." A slight smile chased Johann's words, though he did not look at Susanna. Aunt Ann was still wide-eyed across the room, and though Uncle Will had laid a hand on her back, he sat stoically without comment. Rachel had tears rolling down her cheeks. Yes, it must be awful to be told one was morally unfit to raise one's children. Susanna thought of all the love she had seen Rachel lavish on her children, all the hard labor of diaper cloths and burping, the sleepless nights with no help. Her love for her sister surged through her and obliterated any other feeling. She quietly handed her a handkerchief from her handbag. Rachel let out a shuddering sigh and blotted her face with it.

"Then, if you'll excuse me," the matron said, "I must tend to the affairs of the mission."

"Of course. We will plan to see you tomorrow." Johann was

completely assured, the perfect man to convince any suspicious matron of his worth and solidity.

"Lucy will show you out. Good morning." The matron turned and paced out into the hallway and up the stairs.

They all sat and regarded one another, though Rachel would not look up and clutched the handkerchief with a shaking hand.

"Well, we should take our leave," Johann said. He crossed in a few steps to Rachel and held out his hand. "Mrs. Leeds." She looked up and took his assistance to stand, gratitude spilling from her eyes.

If Susanna had not loved him before that moment, that alone would have been enough—his tender understanding that Rachel needed his respect.

But the question of whether she loved him was no longer at issue. It was the marriage that loomed over her head like a pot of boiling oil about to tip. The past had proven that when it came to marriage, sentiments were deceptive, principles were not.

Lord, what should I do?

She let her uncle and aunt go ahead and followed them out.

Thirty-Seven

J OHANN UNLOCKED THE SIDE DOOR OF THE M AENNERCHOR building and stepped back to hold it open for his guests.

Mrs. Leeds entered the hall first. She looked so young for one who had been through such trouble—hardly older than Susanna, though he knew there must be almost ten years between them, judging from the age and number of her children. She deserved compassion, not additional humiliation. Life and sin had inflicted enough sorrow on her already.

Mr. and Mrs. Hanby followed, gazing with interest at the dark woods of the foyer, the many coats of arms blazoned on the walls for the towns of Germany. The Maennerchor was renowned all over the state and well supported; there was nothing cheap about Germania Hall, which resembled a small opera house.

Susanna trailed after all of them, avoiding Johann's gaze, her beautiful face pensive, hair curling at her brow in the air still humid from yesterday's rain. What would she say? He could not tell her mood from her averted face. It could be anger or simply shyness. He would have to wait and see.

"So no one will disturb us here, Mr. Giere?" Mr. Hanby asked. "I thought it was quite the social club."

"The mornings are usually quiet. It's the evenings when the men gather." Johann gestured toward the stairs. "The meeting rooms are upstairs, if you care to follow me."

He passed them and led the way. The first room at the top of the stairs was a library, furnished with leather chairs and a sofa, shelves lined with the dark spines of German, Latin, and English classic works. "Here is a place where you may rest. There is another small salon down the hall, should anyone need to speak—in private." It was awkward. Should he speak to Susanna alone? Perhaps she would want to speak to her family first.

"I would like a word with you in private, Mr. Giere," Mr. Hanby said. "It won't be long."

"Of course, sir." It was a relief, in a way, to postpone the inevitable moment of decision when Susanna would have to answer. They had run out of time—there could be no more consideration. "We'll leave the ladies here to browse the shelves if they wish." With a nod to the three women, he ushered Mr. Hanby out and closed the doors.

Once inside the salon Susanna's uncle remained standing, leaning on his cane, one white eyebrow hooked at an inquisitive angle. "Rather a surprising announcement, Mr. Giere."

"Yes, sir."

"And was my niece aware that you would be announcing your engagement?"

"No, sir." He could feel himself flushing, but did not look away. "She has not agreed to it."

"Indeed." Mr. Hanby gave him an appraising look. "Admirable of you to seize the moment, but extremely unorthodox."

"I understand, sir. In the press of the conversation, I was forced to assume that she could still refuse me once we were alone, but if I did not speak then, she and Mrs. Leeds would certainly lose the children."

"Your motive was honorable. Shall we be seated?" Mr. Hanby took a few steps to a wing chair set at one corner of a square oriental carpet that dominated the small room.

Johann took the chair on the opposite diagonal. The decor of this room had a Moroccan flavor—red-and-cream carpet, red divan, gold curtains—which lent the conversation the atmosphere of a meeting with a very imposing sheikh. All Mr. Hanby needed was a turban. As if Johann was not already trepidatious about the outcome.

"From what I understood, Mr. Giere, your heart was set on becoming a journalist. Did that change in the last few weeks?"

"Yes, sir. In some ways."

"Ways that allow you to continue working for your father, I presume."

"I can write without making it my sole living, sir."

"And what led you to that conclusion?"

"I think it was heaven-sent. I had some qualms about my future, sir. It did not seem right to leave my father, who depends on me to carry on his legacy."

"You are his only son?"

"Yes, sir."

"Practically old-fashioned of you to care for such things, in this modern world. What about your own legacy? You don't wish to leave one in journalism for any sons you may have?"

"My legacy is not distinct from my father's. They are joined."

"But your father is not the only reason for your change of heart, I gather. Did your feelings for my niece enter into it?"

"Yes, sir." His cheeks were scarlet, he was sure.

"One of my sons once wished to change his profession for the sake of a woman. For him, it would have been a mistake. Are you not concerned that love may have blinded you to your real calling?"

"No, sir. I'm more concerned about blind ambition. Love makes men foolish, but ambition makes them cruel. George Leeds demonstrated that well."

"I admire your sincerity."

"I can do good work as an amateur newsman here in Columbus, where we certainly have no shortage of news. What is there in New York journalism that I could not find here? Only personal gratification and the opportunity for the most noticeable achievement. But that has nothing to do with the quality of the work."

"That is true. But will you be miserable working at your father's business? A miserable man does not make a good husband."

"The work there has its own rewards. It's not my passion, but there's much camaraderie among the men, and we have known each other my whole life."

"Well." Mr. Hanby stood up. "I was already convinced of your merit, Mr. Giere, and I'm now assured of your motive. But I'm not the only one who needs convincing."

"Yes, sir." Johann stood.

"Then I suggest you go to her. Time is short."

"I agree, sir. And thank you." He reached out his hand, and Mr. Hanby shook it with a warm, dry clasp. Johann wished his fingers were not cold—it gave away his nerves. But Mr. Hanby just smiled again. "Let's go find her. She may yet decline your proposal, and that would be her right."

"Susanna," Aunt Ann said. "This is a very unusual situation, to be sure. Would you mind coming with me for just a few minutes? Rachel, if you will excuse us—we'll return shortly. And you won't lack for reading material." She opened the door and slipped out.

"Where are we going?" Susanna felt as if she should whisper in the long, empty hall with its plush red carpet.

"We'll find some nook where we can speak." Her aunt glided down the hall and Susanna followed. Two doors down they heard the murmur of Uncle Will's voice, though his words were indistinct.

At the end of the hall was a set of double doors. Aunt Ann listened for a moment, then turned the knob and peeked in, her white head tilting around the sill. "It's unoccupied." She forged on.

It was a ballroom with a black-and-white marble floor and white-corniced walls. Susanna could picture beautiful gowns swirling around it—she had never seen such a place in person, but only read of it in newspapers.

"A very large room for a small conversation." Aunt Ann's voice echoed across the smooth floor, bouncing back from the walls. "But we have a pressing matter to discuss." She walked to the wall, where chairs lined the perimeter of the dance floor, and drew one of them around to face another. "Please, come sit."

Susanna complied. When they had both taken chairs, their skirts were only inches apart. Susanna took comfort in her aunt's nearness, especially in the cavernous room.

"Mr. Giere was not quite accurate in what he said in the Mission, was he?"

"No. He was . . . improvising."

"I suspected as much. Have the two of you ever discussed marriage before?"

"Yes. And I told him it was impossible."

"On what grounds?" Her aunt was mild, a proper lady at all times.

"Auntie, he works at a brewery and will inherit it."

"Yes, the thought had given me pause as well when I realized that he was growing attached to you."

"When did you realize that?"

"The flowers were a rather broad hint." She smiled.

The lilies. If they weren't appropriate then, she couldn't deny their true meaning now, after the passionate kiss they had shared. Susanna looked at the floor to wait for the surge of emotion to pass. When she lifted her gaze, she was steady again. "But any feelings aside, his profession is immoral." She could hear tension in her voice. "Surely you think so too, Auntie. You are as ardent in temperance as I am."

"I've given it hours of reflection, my sweet. You see, in the absence of your parents, I must be a mother to you, and no female relation could ignore her responsibility in this situation."

"And you must agree with me." Susanna realized she was compulsively opening and closing the catch on her handbag. She stopped with a twitch and laid her hands flat in her lap.

"About the evils of liquor, yes, and so does your uncle, as you know. But I have more years on this earth than you, and so I must weigh the virtues of Mr. Giere against his profession."

"What virtue can compensate for the promotion of vice?"

"He is a man who believes deeply in fulfilling his duty. He is compassionate and generous. He thinks far less of himself and more of others than most men. And he loves children and values family above all but faith. In short, he reminds me quite a bit of your uncle. And that kind of man is a rare find. I didn't even know the full extent of my blessing when I married Will. It has unfolded over the years, as I've seen the marriages of others and how often they are marred by pride and selfishness."

"But Uncle Will was a minister, not a maker of intoxicating drinks." Her protest sounded weak—could her aunt tell how hard it was to resist, when all she wanted to do was marry him?

"It's easy to see a ministerial profession as ideal. But Will's work was the most difficult aspect of our life together. I did not regret it, but it was not easy, all the travel that took him away from me and our eight children. And then there was the bickering, dissension, and sin that can infest communities of worshippers."

"But if I married Johann"—she felt a painful twist of her heart—"I would be taking a great risk, don't you think? Just look at Arthur Pippen, or George."

Aunt Ann sighed. "Marriage is probably the riskiest proposition in all of mortal life. I do not argue that this is easy, and you must do as you think best. But I did wish to share the thoughts that have collected in my mind over the past weeks. And I wish to share them"—she looked deeply into Susanna's eyes—"because I do not want your well-developed reasoning ability to be the enemy of your heart and your happiness."

"Oh." She looked away, confused. Was she that transparent?

"Would you refuse to marry a man because he owned a gun factory?"

Susanna fell silent. "But, Auntie, one could argue that guns do good as well as evil. Alcohol does only evil."

"That isn't true, I'm afraid, even though I believe that abstinence is the safest approach. For one thing, God did not give us guns, nor are they mentioned in Scripture. They might be seen as a purely human invention that twists God's bounty into something wicked."

"But God did not give us beer and liquor."

"He gave us grapes and barley, and there is much mention of wine in Scripture. It is one of the earthly substances that commemorates our Savior. He would not have chosen it for his supper had it been purely evil."

"I didn't expect this from you." She stood and wandered to the window. It almost felt like a betrayal, to have Aunt Ann make the issue more complex. Where could she turn now? She had hoped for a simple decision as clearly drawn as the squares of the floor. But her aunt had made it much more difficult.

"Do you love him?"

She paced around the floor, following the tiles in a rectangle, not wishing to confess it face-to-face. At last, "Yes."

"He is a good man, and he cares for you, truly. Do not throw it away without much consideration. You might go far before you meet another like him. I have only met a handful of men in my life with such character as Will and this young man. He will place you first, after God. Few women have that privilege and grace from their husbands. Few men can love like that."

Susanna broke out of her rectangle and hurried to the window. It opened on a hinge: she turned the latch and pushed it out, breathing in the outside air. It was no cooler than inside—but it was an excuse to open the window.

"Susanna"—her aunt had come up behind her and laid her hand on hers where it rested on the window ledge—"marriage is not a trap, not with a good man. You mustn't let what happened to Rachel rob you of your own joy."

Susanna closed her eyes, her brow tense. "Thank you, Auntie. I know you speak out of love."

"I'm glad." Her aunt patted her hand. "Will you pray with me?"

Susanna nodded, and they bowed their heads. Aunt Ann prayed for a wise choice, whatever that might be, and for Susanna's peace of mind, and thanked the Lord for his constant protection and care. "Amen," she finished.

"Amen," Susanna forced out. She was so anxious she could hardly speak.

The door at the end of the room opened, and Johann stepped in.

Thirty-Eight

"AM I INTERRUPTING?" JOHANN ASKED. THE TWO
women stood together near the window, where the sunlight fell
on Susanna in her pale-yellow dress.

"No, we had finished our conversation," Susanna's aunt
said. She walked toward him with the careful grace of age. "The
two of you will need to speak, so I'm sure my niece will wish to
remain."

Susanna did not stir from her place by the window, her eyes
wide under the brim of her straw hat, clutching her small handbag in front of her.

He held the door for Mrs. Hanby, who gave him a nod as
she left.

When he turned back, Susanna was still there, as pale as a
figurine. Should he go to her? She seemed so nervous that he
didn't want to upset her further.

"First," he said, approaching only halfway, to the center of
the room, "I must apologize for placing you in such an awkward
situation."

"You did it for the children," she said in a small voice. "I
understand."

He did not want to go to her and make her feel cornered by the window. "Will you come speak with me?"

She was so hesitant, not at all her usual spontaneous self. But she inched toward him across the black-and-white tile until she was only a yard away.

"Susanna," he said with a wave of tenderness for her. "You don't have anything to fear. It's just your adversary Johann forcing you to marry him against your will."

She laughed and her face relaxed.

"I can't promise you will never feel discomfort about the brewery. I can only promise to be a good husband to you all my life." It felt strange to stand there and say such things in the midst of a ballroom. He stepped so close that he could smell the faint sweetness of her hair, like a trace of peach. His urge to hold her was overwhelming him—he fought for control. He must not press her, she must decide freely. She had lowered her eyelids and looked very conscious of his nearness as well.

He dropped his voice to an intimate murmur. "There will be difficulties—my family may appear to have strange customs at first—but with mutual respect and love, we can overcome them. And I promise, there will be no drinking in our home, if you don't wish it."

"Thank you," she said, then took a breath as if to fortify herself. "It is very sudden to have to make this decision."

"Yes, it is," he said. "I'm sorry for the circumstances. And I don't wish you to accept unless you truly think you can be happy as my wife. If I were not so certain myself that you could be, I would never have suggested it."

She put out a hand and he instinctively brought up his own to hold hers. "But you aren't afraid?" she asked. "To take responsibility for all six children? Rachel will be with them, of course, but we will have their legal charge. She might even have to live with us."

"I know." He did not underestimate its gravity—a woman under their roof with a seventh child on the way. Six souls already to be guided and nurtured, as if he were a stepfather. "If you can learn to care for my family despite our differences, I can do the same for your sister."

Her eyes glistened and their green darkened. "I can care for your family," she whispered.

"Can you be happy with me?" He barely said it, his pulse in his ears deafening him. The whole world hung on her next words.

"I think I can," she said.

She *thought* she could? Was it enough to build a marriage upon?

She smiled. "I would certainly be desperately unhappy without you."

The warmth of his relief seeped into a smile of his own. "Should I understand that you love me, as I love you?"

"You may understand whatever you like." Her lips twitched but she kept a straight face.

"I like this." He leaned down and gently kissed her, reveling in her soft nearness. She slid her arms around his waist and returned his kiss with her own. *Donnerwetter*, how he loved and wanted her. He held her close.

"You seem to have reached an agreement." Mr. Hanby had entered without Johann hearing and stood in the doorway, looking pleased. Johann released Susanna and straightened his linen coat, feeling like a schoolboy caught kissing the prettiest girl in class.

"I have accepted, Uncle." Susanna sounded happy—it made his heart lift.

"Then the next stop must be the courthouse. Come along." Mr. Hanby sounded pragmatic, but his eyes were dancing and his white hair looked almost rakish over his brow.

Susanna walked to her uncle with a resolute and confident step.

Johann had never seen anything so beautiful as her form gliding in the yellow dress across the black-and-white floor. He followed with rising joy. *Thank you, Lord.* Beyond that was too deep for words, like a brush with heaven.

———

Susanna could not dispel the cloud of unreality that followed their small party through the streets to the courthouse, blurring the events there. Thank goodness Uncle Will had married hundreds of couples and knew the legal requirements well. They made their way to the probate court, where a judge asked her to swear that she was over eighteen years of age, not previously married, and not closer than a second cousin of Johann's. She answered in a clear affirmative. Similar words were addressed to Johann, who stated his eligibility to marry. The judge inscribed their names on a license, signed it, and handed it to Johann. Both Aunt Ann and Rachel were solemn. Susanna felt like shaking her head to get rid of the daze, but she took Johann's arm and walked out like any other young affianced couple.

When they had descended the steps of the courthouse to the

street, he turned to her and stopped. "Would you like to see the license?" He retrieved it from his inside pocket.

A stamped drawing of a family surrounding a couple adorned the top of the paper. Two cherubs with bows and arrows flew around the edges of the page. She would have smiled at their absurdity except for the sobering sight of their names written together, Susanna M. Hanby and Johann C. Giere. Below the judge's signature were the words "Marriage Certificate" in gothic lettering and more empty spaces to be filled in.

Johann pointed to it. "Whoever marries us will be our witness, here, to the marriage. Mr. Hanby, should you do the honors?"

"It depends on where you wish to take your vows." Her uncle adjusted his hat and looked down the street. "I presume my niece would rather not be married here in the middle of a Columbus thoroughfare. Where is your family's church, Mr. Giere?"

"Not far, sir. A few blocks. Would you like to be married there, Susanna?"

"Oh, yes." She had not considered it, but much better to be married in a church than anywhere else—especially for such a hurried wedding. At least it would be in a place dedicated to God. "I would like that."

Uncle Will spoke up. "Then, Mr. Giere, you should ask your pastor to marry you."

"Yes, sir, an excellent idea. We worship at St. John's Evangelical. It's only two city blocks from here." Johann turned to look at Susanna. "I would like to make some arrangements, if I can," he said. "Do you mind if we part company, perhaps for two hours? I will send you, your sister, and your aunt on a mission while your uncle and I go to speak to my family and our pastor. You will not miss your chance to be a bride before you are a wife, not if I can help it."

She could not speak, touched by his tenderness, but nodded.

He fished a gold watch out of his coat pocket. "I will return here for you at three o' clock. And I will give your aunt something for you to do in the meantime." He looked mischievous and stepped away to speak to Aunt Ann, who was standing with Rachel by the curb.

Uncle Will rubbed his forehead with one hand, bracing the other on his cane. "I only regret that your parents will not be here. But it cannot be helped."

"Better for them to miss a marriage than lose their grandchildren," Susanna said. "They will find out soon enough." She could not even allow herself to think so far ahead. They would marry today, and go to get the children tomorrow. Afterward they could handle her parents and the rest of the arrangements.

Johann returned, slipping something back in his pocket. His billfold? How strange that he could now purchase anything for her family with complete propriety. Sure enough, Aunt Ann was closing her handbag with a glad snap that spoke of excitement. Even Rachel had brightened and was smiling at Susanna, her veil thrown back and stirring in the light breeze that cooled the sunny street.

"I will be back for you soon," Johann said. He hesitated as if he would like to kiss her, but with a glance at her family, he refrained. She was both disappointed and relieved—it still felt so strange and new to kiss him at all, let alone in public.

"Thank you," she said.

He caught her uncle's gaze and they set off eastward toward Third Street.

"We have an errand or two to perform," her aunt announced, making Rachel grin more broadly, looking like the girl Susanna had known at home. "Shall we be off?"

The shops of High Street produced one mysterious box after another until Rachel was weighed down with several bags, and Susanna too. Aunt Ann had been keeping Susanna at arm's length, sending her to the other side of the street with Rachel so she did not even know which shops her aunt had visited.

"So I must carry these, but I can't know what you've purchased?" she asked, fizzing inside with thrill and anxiety.

"Yes, that's a good girl." Aunt Ann opened her handbag, took out a bill, and handed it to Rachel. "Now, take Susanna to that ice-cream parlor please, and have something delicious there while I finish up with Mr. Giere's instructions."

The ice-cream parlor was cool inside, and Susanna watched the people go by on the street, letting the sweet vanilla cream linger on her tongue. She hesitated before murmuring to Rachel, "Have I lost my wits, to do such a thing?"

"No, you haven't," Rachel said. "He is a good man. And I assure you I won't shame you or be anything but a model mother to my children." Her gaze dropped and she let her spoon clink against her bowl as if she had lost her appetite.

"I have faith in you," Susanna said. She touched her sister's hand, and their eyes met. The flood of warmth in her heart felt like sunlight.

Aunt Ann entered with a small flat box in one hand. "Time

to go back to the courthouse." She was glowing with pleasure. If she could be so enthusiastic about the marriage, Susanna knew she herself should not worry. Her aunt was a discerning woman.

When they stepped off the High Street horse car at Mound Street, the courthouse towered over them again. Waiting in front of it was a black, shiny buggy drawn by two gray horses, with Johann sitting in the driver's seat. "Ladies," he said, and taking the reins in one hand, jumped down to help them up. Susanna stroked the burgundy leather seat in admiration as he climbed back to the front.

"Do you like it?" he asked. "It is ours now. My father has given it to us."

She could not help a gasp. "That is very generous." Another thought struck her. "What does your mother think?"

"Oh, she is not covetous. And besides, he will get another for them."

"I mean about the marriage."

He looked a little rueful. "She will accustom herself to it. It's a bit of a shock. But she is a kind lady and she will treat you politely."

He clucked to the horses and the buggy wheeled smartly around the corner. In only a few minutes they pulled up before a large church with arched windows and stained glass rosettes over the front doors. Johann pulled into the side lot, jumped down, and hitched the horses to one of the posts there. He returned to hand each one of them down. The ardent look in his eyes and the light touch of his hand sent a shiver through her.

He gathered bags in his hands, grinning at the quantity, and led them to the front door. "Reverend Purpus told me you could prepare in the vestry."

He somehow managed to open the door, even loaded down as he was, and held it for them. As soon as they were through, he followed and set down the bags against the left wall of the small entry room so he could offer her his arm.

As they walked into the church, she caught her breath.

Flowers adorned every niche and blanketed the altar railing in soft whiteness. Roses, lilies, chrysanthemums, all in bridal white, pure and delicate. Where the light from the stained glass fell on the ends of the railing, the clusters of flowers were radiant. Tears came to her eyes and she blinked them back. "Did you do this?"

"With the help of friends." As soon as he said it, she noticed over in one pew the bent figure of the lady from the flower shop and her messenger boy.

"I know you love flowers," he said. "Come." He led her to one side so they walked around the edge of the pews and up the three or four stairs in the far corner of the church. When he opened the dark, polished door, the first thing Susanna saw was his mother, blond and neat in a well-cut blue dress.

"Good afternoon, Miss Hanby," she said with an effort, but it was real warmth in her eyes. "May I stay with you and help you prepare?"

"You are very welcome to stay. Thank you." Susanna spontaneously walked forward and kissed her on the cheek.

The blond, apple-cheeked woman smiled. "It is a surprise, but it is still a happy surprise."

Mrs. Giere was very gracious. No mother could be entirely happy to have her son marry a stranger on a moment's notice.

Aunt Ann made introductions while Johann went to fetch the bags and boxes. He returned and handed them through to the older women. "Do you require anything else?"

"No, Johann. Go ready yourself," his mother said. She and Aunt Ann were already opening packages, but fending Susanna off when she tried to come over to look.

"I have something for you," Mrs. Giere said. "If you like it." She went to the large built-in wardrobe and opened it. White satin gleamed in its recesses and she lifted out a dress.

Susanna's hand flew to her lips. It was silk brocade, a cuirasse bodice with tiny covered buttons from the waist to its square neckline. Silk satin ruched around the neck and shoulders. She had never dreamed of wearing a dress like this. "Where did it come from?" She reached out and felt it with her fingertips.

"The Hosters' daughter married last month, and she was willing to lend her dress. What a blessing they hadn't yet re-cut it for a ball gown. I knew she would be close to your size." Mrs. Giere eyed Susanna with an experienced mother's eye. "Let's put it on."

Aunt Ann helped Susanna remove her yellow polonaise and skirt, until she stood only in her corset and petticoat. Together Mrs. Giere and her aunt lifted the brocade skirt above her head and settled it over her bustle.

"Almost," Johann's mother said with satisfaction. "Just a tiny gap at the waist. But it won't show under the bodice." She reached for the cuirasse and handed it to Aunt Ann, who slipped it over Susanna's arms and shoulders. The sleeves ended in the same elaborate satin ruching that bordered the neckline. The back of the bodice extended over the bustle, giving an even richer effect as the brocade contrasted with a tiered fall of silk satin to the short train.

Aunt Ann fastened the bodice and stepped back to admire the effect. "My word. And we're not even finished." She turned to one of the bags and rummaged in it for the largest box. Lifting the lid, she took out a dainty white hat adorned with tiny white satin roses and two narrow, gauzy strands of veil trailing behind. "I knew this would be to your taste," she said.

"It's exquisite." Susanna could not stop smiling as her aunt pinned on the hat with long hat pins, hiding them in Susanna's thick hair. Rachel brought white satin gloves and slipped them over Susanna's hands.

For this last-minute wedding in a borrowed dress, she would be attired more beautifully than she could ever have been with a traditional engagement. God seemed to be blessing their marriage already. But of course he would bless Johann—how many men would take in this brood of children and their mother, with such generosity?

They fussed over her hair and adjusted her train until a knock came at the door.

"Is the bride ready?" It was Uncle Will's voice.

Aunt Ann opened the door. "She is. And the groom?"

"Ready and waiting."

"Then we should take our seats," Mrs. Giere said. She, Rachel, and Aunt Ann went out past Uncle Will, leaving him alone with Susanna, looking her up and down. "You're more an angel than a woman," he said, his courtly dignity never more touching. "May I have the honor of escorting you down the aisle?"

She just smiled, afraid she would lose her self-possession if she said anything.

"This way," he said, pointing with his cane to the back of the vestry. When they rounded the wardrobe, a side door came into view. "Mr. Giere told me about this exit," he said.

She turned and bent to pick up the train of her dress, holding it carefully away from the floor. If they must walk around the side-walk, she would ensure that nothing happened to spoil the hem. Not when the Hoster heiress had been kind enough to lend it.

The sunlight was warm on her face, but her hands were growing cold with nerves. It was about to happen. Holy vows could not be broken, and there would be no going back. They turned the last corner and Uncle Will opened the door for her.

She stepped inside. As her eyes adjusted to the diffused light of the stained glass, she saw Johann waiting at the front with two others. A small cluster of people sat in the front pews. They rose to their feet when they saw her.

Uncle Will offered his left arm, still using his cane with his right hand. She placed her hand on his sleeve and they began to walk down the aisle. The silence was deep, more reverent than any music—even the muffled sound of their feet melted into the hush. She could hear the silken whisper of her train against the floor.

She could see now that the man beside Johann was his father, looking very serious, as any father might whose son was taking this leap of faith. The reverend stood in the center with his prayer book in hand.

There was the matron from the Hannah Neil Mission, standing behind the others, watching impassively as if to register the event in her ledger. Susannah was glad when she passed by her and could only see the florist and family members, Johann's sisters and his mother, her aunt and Rachel.

Uncle Will stopped at the head of the aisle. The reverend asked in a resonant voice, "Who gives this woman in marriage?"

"I do," Uncle Will said, and stepped aside to return to the pews. He needed no training in wedding custom—he had seen more than his share.

Johann moved close to her and they stood facing one another. The reverend said some things that slipped past her, as she saw only Johann's eyes, steadying in their blue depths.

"And now I ask you to repeat after me," the preacher said. Susanna repeated the time-honored words, and hearing them fall from her lips shook her. She was making a vow to God. She had never said anything as important or binding—her hands started to tremble in Johann's, but she took a deep breath and went on. She would not weep; it was too sacred a moment for that. She made it through, looking only at him. She could trust him. Then it was his turn, and he vowed his lifelong love and honor for her with no hesitation.

It had gone so swiftly.

"You may kiss the bride," the preacher said.

Johann leaned down and touched his lips to hers for a long moment—it was not the fiery, passionate kiss he had given her before, but like an echo of the promise he had just made, a seal between their hearts.

"I present to you Mr. and Mrs. Johann Giere."

They walked down the aisle as if it were a dream to the scattered applause of their families, smiling at one another. It was done. A burden lifted from her heart. There could be no turning back, and that was good. They would go forward together, she and her bridegroom.

Thirty-Nine

EVEN IN THE LIGHT HAZE OF HALF-SLEEP, JOHANN felt her warmth against his side. He opened his eyes and turned his head on the pillow to the wash of light pouring across the hotel bed. Susanna lay so close he could smell the sweet, fresh tumbled hair down her back and see the curve of her body under the sheet. He slid a hand across to the pool of her light-brown, gold-glinting tresses on the white linens and stroked it with his fingertips, marveling at its satiny softness, its vivid color, at his freedom to take joy in the beauty of his wife while she slept beside him.

But he would not wake her. He rolled to the edge of the mattress, with an even motion so as not to shake the bed. He lightly rose, leaving her undisturbed, her face serene, the top of her shoulder just peeking out from under the sheet and her cotton gown. God had smiled on him. He wanted to take her in his arms and feel her breathe against him, see her shy smile and her dark eyelashes fluttering down to hide her intense emotion.

But he had something to do for her this morning, even before they went to the Hannah Neil Mission to claim the children. And he would not fail his bride in this.

The Hare Home was a short ride away by horse car. He was struck again by how gray and dirty it looked amid the brighter buildings on the street. He raised a fist to the old door and rapped three times.

The broad face of the housekeeper appeared in the window, then the door opened. "What is it?" Mrs. Grismer did not appear to recognize him, her piggish eyes narrowed in unfriendly slits.

"Good morning. I came to visit last week. I'm here on business pertaining to the orphanage."

"Yes?" She did not move to let him in.

"I must speak with you in private."

"I'm busy at the moment."

"It's an urgent matter."

She still did not budge and regarded him with an insolent spark in her eyes.

He pulled a folded piece of paper from his vest pocket. "Perhaps you recognize these names? Sarah Eddy, Dick McIntyre, Martha Daggett, Edward Clark?" He shot a look at her whitening face. "Shall I go on?"

She opened the door and turned on her heel with a swish of her grimy, wrinkled skirts, leaving him to follow her into the dim hall.

She turned inside her small parlor and glared at him. "Well, sit down. Apparently it is a matter of some weight." Her tone could have frosted a window but did not deter him. He sat in a chair covered with grease spots and adorned with a few crumbs in its seams. She closed the door of the parlor with a sharp push and snatched the paper he still held unfolded in his hand. "Where did you get these names?" She scanned the list.

He kept his tone neutral. "The city morgue."

"Ah, the poor children." She changed her tone abruptly to a cooing lament, though her face remained flat and hard. "You know it wracks my heart to lose even one. Such a pity we get them in ill health and we can't restore them, despite our best efforts."

"All twelve of those children died in this home last year."

"As I said—" She spit out the words.

"I heard you, madam." He held up a hand and she sputtered to a stop.

He pointed to a portrait on the wall above the fireplace. "Is that not Mr. Timothy Hare, the benefactor of this home?"

"Yes." She shifted from one foot to another, her bulk swaying from side to side.

"And he is deceased?"

"Five years ago, God rest his soul." It sounded more like a curse from the woman's tight, ungracious lips.

"And his estate now manages the finances of this orphanage."

"Who are you? What business is it of yours?"

"I am a news reporter."

She went even whiter, an oily, fish-belly paleness.

He kept his voice level. "I imagine Mr. Hare's trustees are not as involved with the management of the home as he might have been himself."

She kept silent, her eyes like dull black marbles, a few droplets of perspiration on her upper lip.

"But it appears to me, from an examination of the society pages of the *Dispatch*, that more than one charity ball has been held for the benefit of this institution over the past five years. And those events have raised a significant sum of money for Mr. Hare's cause, in addition to the very generous legacy he left this home in his will."

"What paper do you write for?" She rasped out the words.

"The *Westbote*."

"Oh. Nothing but a German paper." A grin crawled across her face and twisted into disdain. "Who will ever read anything you have to say?"

"May I remind you, madam, that our mayor is German and well known for his interest in the welfare of indigent women and children."

"What do you want?" She lumbered over to a cabinet in the corner and opened the door to reveal an iron safe, built into the wall. She began to turn the dial.

A wave of disgust stopped his words until she had actually fumbled it open. "I do not seek money. I simply wish you to release to me three of the children in your charge."

She stopped and peered over her thick arm at him. "The children are indentured to the home. They are legally bound."

"As you were legally bound to use the funds of the home in their support."

She gazed at him with a gray, nervous face, the fat jiggling at her throat. "Which children?"

"Wesley, Clara, and Daniel Leeds."

The light of comprehension dawned in her eyes. "You were the one with the Hanby women."

"A friend of the family." And now a member of the family, in a manner of speaking, but no need to mention that.

She reached into the safe, pulled out a cashbox, and set it on the desk, then retrieved a small portfolio. She braced it against her ample bosom, ruffled through it with thick fingers, then whipped out three pages, one at a time. She threw the portfolio back in the safe and crammed the cash box after it, then slammed the door with a heavy click. "Here." She snarled it, revealing her yellowed teeth as she thrust the papers toward him.

He examined them. They were indeed the documents of indenture, signed by the matron of the Hannah Neil Mission. Of course—she would have signed, as Rachel had never been here.

"And the children?"

"You will not write on this subject, now or ever, in your paper?"

"If you bring me all three children now, and forget you ever saw them."

"Very well. But you must swear on your immortal soul that you will not write such an article."

"I will not swear on my soul—that's no vow for a Christian. But you have my word as a gentleman that I will not write on the subject."

"Then wait here and I will bring them down." She hobbled out the door and shut it again, leaving him alone in the parlor.

He had given his word. He could not be the one to expose her corruption, which had caused the starvation, illness, and death of so many innocents. The coroner's assistant had told him how those poor children left the Hare Home wrapped in sheets and ended up in his city morgue.

But even if Johann couldn't write an article about the home, he also couldn't permit such a crime against humanity to continue.

So on the way back to the hotel, he would have to ask the three Leeds children to be patient and wait in the carriage while he made a quick visit to the offices of the *Dispatch*.

He was sure Brundish would welcome such a juicy and humanitarian story, especially as the *Dispatch* reporter seemed to enjoy using Johann's leads.

This was one favor Johann had no reluctance to call in.

Forty

CLARA WORE A CORNFLOWER BLUE DRESS THAT FLUT-
tered around her as she led the roan horse around the lawn beside
Uncle Will's house. Annabeth clung to its mane, giggling, seeming even tinier than usual as she perched on the horse's back.

Susanna carried the bucket of water past them, stepping out
of the way as men streamed across the grass carrying planks and
stacks of tile. State Street was crowded with wagons, twenty or
more of them.

Danny held baby Jesse, who was waiting his turn to ride,
his wisps of auburn hair lifted by the breeze. Susanna reveled in
their bright faces, the color returning to Danny's cheeks, their
neat clothing and unworn shoes. How far they had come, in just
a few weeks, from the sadness of June and July.

The bucket of water was getting heavier—she lurched over
to the kitchen steps and set it down.

Inside, Aunt Ann greeted her with a smile over her shoulder
as she placed a pie carefully in the pie safe. Her aunt's forehead
was moist in the heat of the kitchen. She had tied her hair back
under a kerchief, as had Mrs. Pippen, who stood at the table
stripping the husks from sweet corn.

"Susanna, where's your mother?" Aunt Ann asked. "She shouldn't exert herself too much."

"She won't be outdone," Susanna said. "She's picking wild blackberries over at the Hayworths."

Aunt Ann and Mrs. Pippen both laughed.

Rachel rounded the corner carrying a bowl of mashed potatoes. "Are the children staying out from underfoot?" Susanna was relieved that the strain around her sister's eyes had eased in the last few weeks—she even smiled more, almost like the old times, before she ever married.

"The girls are playing with the horse. Wesley is with the men, but don't worry, they won't let him up on the roof."

A shout echoed from the men outside. Was anything wrong? Susanna hurried to the door and peered at the hubbub of activity surrounding the new barn. From high on the pitched roof, Johann was grinning down at the other men, who were yelling good-natured taunts about the fact that he had finished his row of roof tiling first. Well, that was a relief—everything was going smoothly.

"We are good at this in Bavaria," Johann called down.

The other men groaned and someone threw an apple up at Johann, though it fell far short. Johann's father chuckled as he received a pail full of nails handed down from the living chain of men that led to the top of the roof. "Everything's better in Bavaria," Mr. Giere said, to more friendly heckling from the others and shouts of approval from the other German men who had come to help, including Heinrich and a dozen of the brewery employees. On the train there had been much good-natured complaining about the absence of lager, or so Johann had told her, but now they were very polite about the prospect of lemonade. They knew what the town had been through, and they seemed to be kind people.

Uncle Will carried a crate full of saddling tools into the barn, his lined face practically glowing under his fringe of white hair.

"It's all over but the sweeping," Reverend Robertson shouted as he climbed down the ladder. "Strike up a tune!"

One of the townsmen walked to the table where someone had set his fiddle case and took out the instrument. He tuned it with a few twists, then launched into a quick, merry tune, an avalanche of notes falling from his seesawing bow.

Rachel came down the kitchen steps, careful with a tray held over her rounding belly, first in a line of women bearing baskets and bowls. Just then, Susanna's father walked out of the barn, shoulder to shoulder with Uncle Will.

Father had not lost the air of slight confusion that surrounded him whenever he looked at Rachel, as if he knew he was missing part of the story about one daughter's widowhood and another's sudden marriage. But they would tell him everything, eventually, when Rachel was ready and he had come to know Johann better. For now, Susanna's joy was deepened by the very knowledge he lacked: how close he had come to losing his grandchildren, and the miraculous goodness of God in restoring them.

All the children swarmed after the procession of women. They stood on tiptoe to peek over the rims of the baskets and see what delicious feast was in store. But their skipping turned into capering to the heady rhythm of the music, and the adults had to call them back with mock firmness to keep them from bouncing into the food and overturning the dishes on the tables.

Even called to order, they could barely contain their glee. Baby Jesse burbled as if he had caught the excitement from the older boys and girls. Susanna wanted to go over and kiss him, but she would have all the time in the world to do that now—his whole life, or at least until he grew manly enough to object.

The men had gone in clusters to wash up, using a pile of hand towels loaned for the day by their wives. They came back two and three at a time, rejuvenated by the music and the prospect of food. One man began to sing and clap to "Bluetail Fly," and a few others joined in, but most were eyeing the food.

As Susanna arranged serving bowls, arms went around her waist in a welcome, familiar embrace. "Does it make you glad?" Johann whispered in her ear, sending a thrill down her neck. She smiled at the tickle, then nestled back against him and turned her head to murmur back, "So happy, love. Thank you for helping."

"It's good for a town to build together."

She knew what he meant, having witnessed those many strong hands working together driving dowels, sawing timber, lifting beams to shoulders on the count of three. Every plank raised built back the spirit of the town, their confidence that strife and destruction could give way to love and charity.

The fiddling ended and Uncle Will cleared his throat. "Shall we pray?" Heads bowed across the lawn, the men's hair still damp from their quick washing at the pump, the women colorful in their bright kerchiefs and aprons.

He offered a short, heartfelt prayer of thanks for the barn and the hands that built it, choking up only once and continuing with determination and a steady voice. "And, Lord, thank you for the love of our neighbors and for this food. All that we need, you have provided. Amen."

"Amen," they all echoed in a ripple, and happy chaos began, mothers ladling food onto tin plates, little children sitting on the grass together chewing unself-consciously with open mouths. Even that made Susanna smile, as Danny chomped on a biscuit with the blithe innocence of youthful table manners.

She took a more ladylike seat on the brick stoop, and Johann came to join her. When no one was looking, she laid her hand on his, and he turned his palm up to cradle hers.

The music began again, jaunty but pretty, a three-beat fiddler's polka. A few couples rose and danced by the edge of the yard, where hollyhocks bloomed in profusion along the neighbor's fence. Johann squeezed her hand for some reason and lifted his eyebrows in a subtle signal—she followed his gaze. Heinrich held blond, smiling Lotte in his one strong arm as they danced together, completely besotted and glowing. Susanna looked sideways at Johann and saw him trying not to grin. She knew it was a relief for him, that Lotte had recovered from her infatuation, and even better, that she and Heinrich made one another so happy, her bubbly youth lightening his dry, experienced humor. He had even overcome his loathing of dance for her. And now Lotte would sing Johann no more songs. Susanna clamped down a giggle. Johann had given up the fight and was grinning broadly. She knew he was thinking the same thing.

His eyes met hers, and they did not have to say anything at all. He stood up, keeping hold of her hand with a more intimate look.

"May I have the pleasure?" he asked.

She rose with him and danced, while the little girls twirled by the flowers. Several other couples joined them, but she only looked at her husband. His gentle hands guided her just as he had in their first dance together. She would never have dreamed this trial would end in such happiness.

As the tune came to a close, the fiddler began to play something else—it was familiar. Where had she heard it before? Oh—Cousin Ben had written it and played it for the family, not one of his most famous tunes, but a light, happy dancing song. She did not begin to dance at once, but glanced at her aunt and uncle—they held hands, and she saw tears sparkle in her aunt's eyes but they did not fall. Uncle Will smiled at her aunt with the tenderness of fifty years' married love.

She remembered Johann's murmur in the garden that lantern-lit night when they last danced. *You see the good things God gives us . . .*

And her uncle's words after his barn burned. *Praise God for such love, and such joy.*

Yes. Yes. Her heart swelled to overflowing as she watched her family, the children dancing, Rachel smiling at them from the stoop, and her uncle and aunt holding hands.

Gratitude made her feet light. Like the beautiful blossoms of the hedge, no earthly joy could last forever, but she hoped that like Uncle Will, like Ben, they would leave their seeds behind. She would dance with her husband, dance for their love, and for the legacy they would pass to the children.

Afterword:

History and Fiction

WHEN I SET OUT TO WRITE *LOVELIER THAN DAYLIGHT*, I knew it would be an unusual novel for the inspirational market, unusual in its frank look at the wide variety of opinions and behaviors that surrounded the Westerville Whiskey Wars of 1875 and 1879.

In this novel, people of faith grapple with difficult questions about the use and abuse of alcohol, questions that still cause controversy and divide families and churches. My aim was to depict all of these opinions and show how one family might have handled the decisions that faced them under the circumstances. I did not try to advocate one point of view or elevate one believer above another, but instead aimed to hold up a mirror to a historical event that still has the power to cause us to examine our moral choices.

My characters are imperfect, as we all are. I expect their experiences will generate lively discussion among book clubs! I love my heroes and heroines because they so deeply desire to help others and do good, even though they fumble their way through occasional bad decisions and lapses in self-control as they seek to

347

follow Christ's example of love. If they were not as flawed as the rest of us, they would only be fairy tales. So to do justice to the real people behind my story, I must write them to be real, and to grapple with the richness of life and Scripture.

Ben Hanby, famous composer and hero of my novel *Sweeter than Birdsong*, had a real cousin named Susan. She was the niece of the real William Hanby, who appears in *Lovelier than Daylight* fifty years after we first met him in *Fairer than Morning*.

During my research in the Westerville Public Library's archives, I discovered that Susan Hanby had an older sister named Ruth Ann Hanby, who married a man named George Lehman. When Ruth Ann died at a young age, George Lehman gave their six children to the Hardin County Infirmary in Kenton. Unlike the fictional Leeds children in *Lovelier than Daylight*, the Lehman children were separated from one another and scattered across the state. I was struck by this tragedy and the motive of any father who would give his children away, as well as this puzzle: why did none of the Hanbys have the power to rescue these children, who were Susan Hanby's nieces and nephews as well as the grandchildren of William Hanby's brother?

I was fascinated by the potential resonance of this true story about the abandoned Hanby cousins with the events of the Westerville Whiskey Wars. Out of that resonance, *Lovelier than Daylight* was born, with the fictionalized Susan Hanby appearing as Susanna Hanby. Some of the family details have been changed, but most of the information about the Hanby family adheres to the historical record.

Henry Corbin was the real entrepreneur who foolhardily tried to bring alcohol to Westerville, a center of the temperance movement. No one ever found out who bombed Henry Corbin's saloon, either of the times he tried to open it. For the sake of clear narrative, I condensed the events of the Whiskey Wars into one year. I am indebted to Harold Hancock's *Our Ancestors of the Westerville Area: A Genealogical History* for its in-depth description of the confrontation between town and saloon through the diary of Isaac Speer, an eyewitness. I also relied on newspaper accounts of incidents in the war, and most of the dramatic events in this novel are true: the ringing of the bells and profane argument in the street between Corbin and the townsfolk, the church meetings, the bombings, the hanging in effigy.

William Hanby's barn was actually burned, perhaps in retaliation by some unknown person he offended through his outspoken behavior during the saloon battle. The words that I have placed in his mouth in the scene after the barn burns reflect what the real William Hanby said on his deathbed, praising God through tears for all his blessings, though he had been abused as a boy, saw two of his sons predecease him, and died practically penniless. His compassion for others and gratitude through hardship have inspired me throughout my years of work on the Saddler's Legacy series.

Westerville and the United Brethren church were shamed in the local and national press for what the vigilantes did to Corbin. The harsh, mocking text that I have used and attributed to the fictional Brundish of the *Dispatch* was published in an article without a byline by a reporter at the *New York Times* on September 16, 1879.

Johann Giere and his family are fictional, but closely based on the great German American brewing families of Columbus, including the Borns and the Hosters. The German population of Ohio was industrious and successful, and brought many cultural benefits to the area in music, the arts, and the physical education of the Turnverein. The historic Columbus Maennerchor to which Johann belongs was founded in 1848 and still sings in German: I had the pleasure of visiting them and received a very kind and memorable welcome during the research for this book.

The City Park in German Village where Johann first proposes to Susanna is a real place now called Schiller Park, and beautiful historical photos exist of its rustic bridges and pathways.

Many other events and locations in the novel are real, but those who are interested in learning more may visit the historical sites, libraries, and museums that contain more information about the Hanbys, German Village, and Columbus. These include the Hanby House museum, the Ohio Historical Society, the Columbus Metropolitan Library, and the Westerville Public Library.

Ohio has a rich and inspiring history, and it is with pleasure, a thankful heart, and a twinge of regret that I finish the last novel in the chronicle of the Hanby family and give it to you. I hope their story will bless you, reader, in all the thorny and joyful ways that it has blessed me.

Reading Group Guide

1. Why do Susanna's nieces and nephews end up in the orphanage? Is it due to the choices of one parent or both? Are there parallels between the 1875 situation of these children and the reasons why children end up as wards of the state in twenty-first-century America?

2. Susanna has a strong antipathy to alcohol that affects her behavior toward Johann. Is her attitude understandable? Many people have painful personal histories that may color the way they see complete strangers. Have you ever observed or experienced this kind of pre-judgment? What are its consequences?

3. What dilemma faces Johann throughout the novel? Why does he choose one way of life over the other? What is admirable about his character?

4. In this novel, Will and Ann Hanby are fifty years older than when they first appeared as teenagers in *Fairer than Morning*. Do you enjoy a story that follows characters throughout their lives? How can that story differ from one that shows only a year or two in the life of a character?

5. The temperance movement of the nineteenth century resulted in the twentieth-century legal prohibition of alcoholic beverages, which is generally seen as a failure. Why do you think legal prohibition failed? And why is there no organized, high-profile temperance movement today as there was in the nineteenth century?

6. Some characters in the novel are willing to do whatever it takes to get Corbin's saloon out of Westerville, even resorting to violence or bloodshed. How does this conviction match up with their Christian faith? Is violence ever justified in the name of morality?

7. How are George Leeds and Arthur Pippen different, despite their similar addictions? How would the novel change if one of these characters were edited out—if we saw George's story without Arthur's or vice versa?

8. The town of Westerville is publicly shamed in the press for the events that take place there. This is not uncommon today: an entire community or group of people may be vilified for the actions of a few. How does this media stereotyping show up in our own time? What can the Westerville Whiskey Wars teach us about how to read the news?

9. The housekeeper in charge of the Hare Home seems to enjoy demonstrating her power over others just because she can. In what areas of life does a petty tyrant make people miserable? Does power corrupt everyone, most people, or just a few people? How can faith serve as an antidote to the temptations of power?

10. How does the wisdom of older people affect the younger generation in *Lovelier than Daylight*? What advice or counsel do older people give that helps Susanna and Johann? Why

do the younger people listen to their elders instead of ignoring them? What does that teach us about how to give advice and build character in the young?

11. Reading a book about a controversial and sometimes painful issue like addiction can stir up deep feeling and strong opinion. Why is it valuable to read books of this nature?

Acknowledgments

My heartfelt thanks to my husband and daughter, who helped me bear the pressures of the writing life with kindness and love.

Thanks also to the many generous folks who helped in the research process and in Westerville, including:

Pam and Jim Allen of Hanby House. The gift of your help, support, and friendship are matched only by your generosity in giving over thirty years of your work to preserve the Hanbys' legacy.

Bill and Harriet Merriman of the Westerville Historical Society—many thanks for your encouragement.

Professor Margaret Koehler, mostly for friendship but also for the connection to a fabulously enjoyable creative writing class at Otterbein.

Beth Weinhardt, dedicated local archivist and historian at the Westerville library.

Michelle Fuchs, Gena Wooldridge, and your whole family for your love and hospitality.

Werner Niehaus, Steve Maurer, and the men of the Columbus Maennerchor, who made me welcome in the time-honored tradition of German hospitality.

Julie Callahan, Andy Miller, and Russ Pollitt of the Columbus Metropolitan Library for their generous willingness to go into the local history archives and look up the locations of buildings as well as other Columbus historical tidbits.

Peter Connolly-Smith, expert scholar of German American history, who helped with some of my questions about German culture. Thanks also to Mary Ann Hake for connecting me with Sharon Ozarowicz, who double-checked some language questions. Any errors in the German part of the story are strictly mine, as their help was invaluable. The editorial team also had to make some tough decisions about whether to Americanize certain conventions of the German language, as the story is German American rather than German. So if sharp-eyed German experts notice what would be any irregularities for native German conventions, know that our experts gave us plenty of accurate feedback, but we then had to use our best judgment to aim for readability.

Dr. Lynn Pearson, English architectural scholar, who kindly responded to my inquiry about her brewery architectural research by sending me helpful information.

Mark Gauen, Pastor, Westerville First Presbyterian for rummaging through old photos and providing a fantastic description of the church circa 1875.

Adam Criblez for lending me his paper on Columbus Beer Gardens and German American culture, as well as providing a few helpful bibliographical links.

Jeff Darbee, author and expert in German Village history, who gave me the benefit of his advice about the residences of German immigrants and their first- and second-generation descendants.

A tardy but sincere thanks to John Diehl of the Cincinnati

Literary Club for answering some questions about the history of his club for *Sweeter than Birdsong*, the second novel in this series.

All the people who have answered the phone at various historic Columbus buildings and let me grill them about the location of the building, whether they've ever seen antique photos, and how it looks today. You are very patient.

Sincere thanks to the publishing professionals, readers, critique partners, and writing friends who have been there for me, in some cases from the very beginning, including:

Ami McConnell and Meredith Efken, my very talented editors. Through your help, the books came together despite all the challenges and some very tight deadlines. I will always be grateful for your high level of expertise—it is a privilege and an honor to work with you.

All the other professional and expert folks at Thomas Nelson Publishing who have worked on this series, in particular Kristen Vasgaard and Becky Monds, who have put hours of labor into the cover art and copyediting, with tremendous results.

Lorena Hughes, Dave Slade, Angie Drobnic Holan, Laura Johnson, Rachel Padilla, and Barbara Leachman for your valuable feedback. The journey would not have been the same without you—I love you all!

My writer friends and encouragers, so many wonderful people that I can't name them all, but I must try to get a few in: Caroline Starr Rose, Gwen Stewart, Wendy Paine Miller, Dorothy Love, Cathy Richmond, Katie Ganshert, Jody Hedlund, Keli Gwyn, Allison Pittman, Bonnie Leon, Donna Pyle, Richard Mabry, Anne Lang Bundy . . . oh, the list goes on. Please know how much I appreciate you and how your comments have kept me going on many a tough day.

Finally, I need to thank some special people in my life:

Kathryn Pratt Russell and Josh Russell, for sending ridiculous photos and article links that made me laugh.

My parents. It's a blessing that I still have both of them with me as this third novel goes to print. I'm glad they got to see me achieve this dream, warts and all!

My agent, Rachelle Gardner, who knows everything.

My horsey friends, Lee Thomas, Sayra Siverson Salter, and the vaulting community for being a place of refuge for me and a sanity saver.

And finally, to readers, who have also kept me going when things got really tough, with e-mails, letters of encouragement, and positive reviews that made me think it was all worthwhile. I have a special place in my heart for you. Thank you.

My humble thanks go most of all to the God who created me, saved me, and came looking for me. I know you wept and laughed with me during this five-year journey. May these books share your love.

Ann dreams of a marriage proposal from her
poetic suitor, Eli—until Will Hanby shows
her that nobility is more than fine words.

BOOK ONE IN THE
SADDLER'S LEGACY

{ AVAILABLE IN PRINT AND E-BOOK }

Music offers Kate sweet refuge from her troubles . . . But real freedom is sweeter.

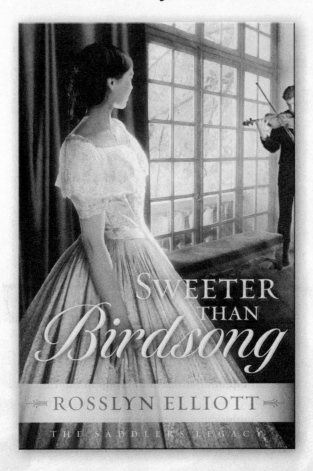

BOOK TWO IN THE
SADDLER'S LEGACY

{ AVAILABLE IN PRINT AND E-BOOK }

About the Author

Author photo by Amy Parish Photography,
New Mexico

ROSSLYN ELLIOTT HAS A B.A. FROM YALE UNIVERSITY and a Ph.D. in English from Emory University. Her first novel, *Fairer than Morning*, was awarded the *Romantic Times'* highest 4^1/2 star rating and was awarded the Laurel Award for 2011. She lives in the South, where she homeschools her daughter and works in children's ministry.

To learn more, visit Rosslyn's website:

www.RosslynElliott.com